end game

allie lasky

prologue

. . .

THE LITTLE BLUE and grey house is unassuming. My stomach swirls with dread. I double check the address. Yes, 2703, this is it. I can't believe I'm doing this. Finally, after nearly being friends for two thirds of our lifetime, we're in the same place at the same time.

When I was sixteen, I had a crush on my best friend. He was cute and charming and *so* totally not interested in me. So I got over it. Over him. I went out with other guys. I lost my virginity to a guy who didn't know my last name and who didn't want a repeat experience. Every guy I've hooked up with has been a meaningless fling.

I've never had it mean something. I want it to mean something. Barrett… he's my everything.

Knocking on the door, I'm surprised when it swings open almost immediately. I come face to face with a pretty blonde woman. She's wearing a Newton Football sweatshirt that falls to her knees, fuzzy socks, and not much else.

"You're not the pizza guy," she says.

There's a lump in my throat I can't explain. I thought I'd be okay with this, but confronted with the reality, I realize I'm totally unprepared for this next leap. It's always been the two of us, and now there are other people involved. What if he's not the same guy I knew? What if he's entirely different now? What if he doesn't want to be my friend anymore? What if coming here is a mistake?

"No, I'm not." I cross my arms over my chest, more from the cold than any defensiveness, and her eyes narrow.

"Can I help you?"

Swallowing the lump in my throat, I shake my head. "I have the wrong house. I should go."

There's a shout from inside the house that catches both of our attention.

"That's only Barrett," she says, waving her hand like she's dismissing me. Like I'm a pesky bug in her way.

Dread pools in my belly. He never mentions any girls with specifics. I know he sleeps around. It's not outside the realm of possibility that he finally found a girlfriend.

"Barrett's here?" I take in her outfit again. I know he's not number 14. Is she with one of his teammates?

"Baby, close the door. You're letting all the heat out."

"Calm your tits, Gregory," the blonde calls over her shoulder. She turns back to me. "Are you lost, honey?"

"I'm, um, I'm looking for Barrett. Barrett Zhang."

Her eyes narrow as she takes me in. The coat I got on the clearance rack at Macy's, the boots I found at Goodwill three seasons ago. She catalogs everything about me in the blink of an eye. I'm bargain basement, and he's the wealthy scion of one of the most influential families in Boston. I'm sure she's wondering how I know him—*if* I know him.

"Just a minute." She closes the door in my face.

I shove my hands into my pockets. There's a chill to the air that even three layers and a down coat can't prevent from seeping into my bones. I forgot how cold winters get here. After a lifetime of snow and sleet, the last two and a half years in sunny California have spoiled me.

The door swings open, and suddenly I'm face to face with

my best friend, all six foot five and three hundred pounds of him.

"Dee!" He calls me by my childhood nickname, tugging me into a hug. That's new. "I thought you weren't getting in until tomorrow."

"Surprise!" I manage weakly.

I wrap my arms around him. He's grown at least two inches and put on at least a dozen pounds of muscle since I've seen him last. He looks good. He's wearing gray sweatpants and a faded gray Newton Football t-shirt that stretches tightly across his broad chest and belly. His feet are covered by dingy white socks. He's never looked better.

"Come on in, you must be freezing." He pulls me into the house and closes the door behind me.

From our conversations and the recruiting video, I know all the houses in Athlete's Village are laid out the same. Six bedrooms, three bathrooms, a small kitchen, and a living room. Their main room is decked out with an enormous flat-screen TV—definitely not standard issue. On the couch and surrounding armchairs are four other guys, all equally as enormous as my best friend. His fellow defensive linemen.

"Shut up, everyone," Barrett says, and the room falls silent as all eyes turn to us. "This is Diana."

The guy on the right, with a caveman beard and a man bun, grins and checks me out. "So this is the famous Diana."

Heat rises in my cheeks. "You've talked about me?"

"Only every other sentence that comes out of his mouth is about you," Man Bun says.

"Shut up." Barrett's freckled cheeks are pink.

"We're glad to have you join us," says the bronze-skinned guy on the couch. "I'm Amir, that idiot is Greg—" He points to Man Bun. "And that's Tucker and Wes."

Wes is sitting in an armchair, reading a book. Tucker is dark-skinned with a thick beard, absorbed in his phone.

The woman from the door comes back into the room,

followed by a guy with dark hair, dark eyes, and lipstick smeared on his neck.

"Hey, I'm Sam," she says. "This is Miles. Sorry for closing the door in your face. We didn't know if you were, like, some stalker or something."

"Don't worry about it," I say with a tight-lipped smile. "Do you guys get stalkers often?"

Tucker laughs. "It's not unheard of." Somehow I think there's more to the story than that.

"So you're coming to Newton now," Greg says. He checks me out again and then glances back at the TV, where a video game is paused.

"Transferring next fall." I've just come from a tour of the soccer team's facility. It's... well, it's certainly not what I'm used to, but I'll make do. Sometimes we have to make sacrifices to achieve our goals, and my goals are worth it.

"Dee is on the soccer team," Barrett says proudly. He wraps an arm around my shoulders, and I try to ignore how good that feels. "She's freaking brilliant."

"We look forward to having you around," Tucker says, finally looking up from his phone. His eyes are a warm chocolatey brown. "You'll like Mason—that's my girlfriend, she transferred last fall. It's not a bad school to transfer into."

I force a smile. "I'm looking forward to it."

Barrett takes a seat on the couch. There's nowhere for me to sit. He tugs me down until I'm perched on his lap, my legs across his strong thighs. It feels weird, and at the same time, so right. It's been a long time since I've been able to indulge in his easy affection. His enormous hand settles on my hip like we snuggle all the time. We don't. We barely hug. It feels weird that he's being so forward, but at the same time... it feels so nice.

"What do you have planned for your long weekend?" he asks, like he probably doesn't have a full social life and academic obligations and family and—

"Not much," I tell him nervously. "Spent a few days with my parents. Signed the transfer paperwork already. Hanging out with you until I go back to LA... if you're free." I shouldn't have surprised him by showing up early. I should have told him—

"If you're here, of course I'm free," he says. "There is nothing I would rather do than hang out with you."

Wes grunts.

"Shut up," Barrett says, his cheeks going pink again. I wonder what that's about.

He tugs me towards him until I collapse against his chest. That's new, too. He's not usually so tactile. Normally, he displays his affection by pulling on my braids or buying me food. College has changed him, softened the sharp edges his parents preferred.

I breathe in his warm scent, honey and musk and something uniquely him. His strong arms wrap around me in a hug that's surprisingly fierce.

"I've missed you, Dee," he murmurs into my ear.

There's a lump in my throat. My eyes fall closed. "I missed you too, Care-Bare."

He growls deep in his chest, the sound vibrating through me where we're connected. "What did I say about calling me that?"

"Um, do it all the time?"

"Never," he says. He rests his forehead against the crown of my head and takes a deep breath. "Never call me that."

I laugh. "You'll always be my Care-Bare."

His fingertips dig into my side. "Don't make me."

Twitching away from him, I try to put some distance between us. He hauls me close. His fingertips tickle my ribs.

Greg is watching us with interest. Amir and Tucker go back to the video game. Miles is sprawled in another chair, the blonde, Sam, on his lap. She burrows into his chest, and he drops a soft kiss on the top of her head. It's sweet.

I want that. I've never had that. I've dated, I've had flings, but I've never had a guy in my life that would snuggle me and kiss me in front of all of his friends. I've never had an actual boyfriend. I've never wanted one. Now I'm wondering what else I've missed out on over the years.

Barrett tightens his arms around me. "You're not getting away from me that easily," he says lightly.

"Wasn't trying to."

We watch in comfortable silence as the guys play video games, trash-talking each other. Barrett's hand tangles in my hair, coiling the messy waves around his finger. I relax into his chest, resting my head on his shoulder. It feels so easy, so natural.

It's never been like this before. We don't do this. We don't touch. We don't cuddle. Usually, he can barely stand to hug me hello and goodbye. I don't know what's gotten into him since he went away to college, but I'm liking this side of him.

"Soon we can do this all the time," he says.

I turn to him with a question on the tip of my tongue.

"Hang out. Spend time together," he clarifies, like he's read my mind. "Video chats aren't the same as really being here in person."

"I'm looking forward to it," I tell him.

And it's only half a lie.

one

. . .

Diana

"SO THIS IS THE PLACE." My mom looks around the house with a pinched look on her face. "It's awfully small, isn't it?"

"It's student housing, it's fine," my dad says, carrying a box into the house. "Upstairs?"

I nod. "Put it on the desk."

Some of my new roommates were here when I got here. They said hi and left within five minutes of my arrival. I'm not sure what to read into that.

I never thought I'd be here. I never thought this would be how my life would turn out, giving up a full ride at one of the most expensive private schools in the country to go to my safety school an hour away from home, a second-rate program with a losing record the last three seasons.

It's for the best. I know this is what I need to do. Still, it rankles.

There's a knock on the open door.

"Hey, Dee," my best friend says, like he shows up on my doorstep all the time.

"Barrett!" I run over to him and wrap him in a hug. I'm glad to see him, but I'm more thankful for the easy safety of his presence. "I'm so glad you're here." I lower my voice: "Save me!"

He forces a smile, clapping a hand over the back of his reddening neck. "Thought I'd see if you guys need any help."

"That's so sweet," my mom says, looking between us with interest. She's never believed that he and I are just friends, encouraging me more than once to pursue him romantically. I never have, though.

"We're almost done," my dad says, coming back downstairs. He claps Barrett on the shoulder. He's always liked the football player, sometimes more than he liked me, his only child. "You're going to take good care of my baby girl?"

"Always, sir," he says seriously.

"Come on out to the car with me," Dad says. He steers him towards the front door to talk "man stuff." "How's the team shaping up?" I hear him ask as they walk outside.

My mom nudges me. "It was nice of Barrett to stop by."

"It was. He's a nice guy."

She raises her eyebrows. "And you're going to be spending a lot of time together? A lot of late nights studying?"

I roll my eyes. "We're just friends, Mama."

"I know, I know, just friends." She holds up her hands. "Things change. You'll need your friends."

Barrett and I have known each other since we were eight years old, when we met at the Chinese cultural summer camp we attended in the Adirondacks. He had a broken ankle, I had a fractured wrist, and we were both stuck on the sidelines all session long while the other kids got to run and swim and play.

We kept in touch through the years on social media and video chats, texting once we both got phones. Our friendship has only grown stronger with the distance, which is unusual as far as friendships tend to go. I have talked to him nearly every day, we texted and called each other constantly, and until the last few months, we rarely went more than 48 hours without chatting. I spent hours laying on my bed and talking to him as he lived his life and I lived mine.

With an hour and a half drive between us growing up, we saw each other as often as we could, which was definitely not as often as either of us would have liked. He made the drive out to Amherst for all of my homecoming dances and winter formals, and he came with me to my junior and senior proms. I went to all of his stuffy birthday parties and as many of his football games as I could.

And now we're finally going to the same school. We're finally going to live in the same city.

I have to admit, knowing Barrett will be here doesn't hurt. As much as I didn't want to give up USC, I know in my heart it was the right call. Having my best friend nearby makes it that much easier. I have a safety net here, however much I don't want to rely on it.

Together, Barrett and my dad carry in the last of my belongings. I have a few suitcases of clothes, some toiletries, and a box of school supplies. Tomorrow, we have plans to go get our books. Practice starts the day after.

My parents insist on taking us out to lunch. Barrett doesn't have a choice in the matter. We pile into the back of their beat up Camry. His large body fills the small space. He angles his long legs across the backseat, taking up some of my foot room. At six foot five and nearly three hundred pounds, there is a lot of him.

His hand covers mine on the armrest. "You okay?"

I force a smile. "Still processing." It hasn't hit me yet that I'm here, all that I've had to give up to get to this place. I know once it does, I'll probably have a breakdown, but until then, I'm going to put one foot in front of the other.

He swallows, his Adam's apple bobbing. "It'll be okay."

"Yeah, no, I know. I just…"

"I know."

I flip my hand over and squeeze his. "I'm glad you're here."

"Of course, Dee. Anything for you."

I'm starting over from scratch. I have a year left to finish my degrees, to wrap up my soccer career, to finally enjoy being young before real life starts. Graduation looms over me. Because I didn't play my sophomore year thanks to a broken tibia, I still retain one last year of athletic eligibility. I can keep playing. In June, I'll trade in my cleats for a grown-up job. Or maybe grad school. I don't know. That's still up in the air. So much of my life is in flux, and I don't like the uncertainty one bit. I don't thrive off chaos; I crumble in the face of it.

We end up at the pub off campus for lunch. It looks like everyone else had the same idea; the place is packed. The guys brought me here over spring break for wings and beer.

"Zhang, my man," a big, beefy guy says, clapping Barrett on the back. "This your family?"

We're not related. There's no blood between us. But because my mom, Barrett, and I are all Chinese-American, obviously we have to be family. Surely there's no other logical conclusion. We can't possibly be friends or random strangers he picked up off the side of the road.

"I didn't realize your dad is Black," the guy continues. "Small world, huh?"

Barrett forces a smile. "Dee, this is Sullivan. He's a strong safety. Sully, this is Diana. She's on the soccer team."

"Nice to meet you," he says, offering his hand. It's surprisingly smooth, no calluses. Not what I expected from a football player who works out all the time.

"You, too."

He mutters something under his breath to Barrett, who nods, his smile disappearing. It's clear to me that he doesn't actually like this dude, but just plays like they're friendly for the sake of the team. I'm familiar with that. Keep the peace; it makes everything that much easier.

"We were going to grab lunch," he says loudly.

"Don't let me keep you," Sullivan says, clapping him on the shoulder. "Diana, I'm sure I'll see you around campus. Don't be a stranger."

He gives me what I think is supposed to be a charming smile. It just makes him look constipated.

"You, too."

Mama nudges me. "Look at you, making friends."

"Just don't bring home any white boys," Dad says, frowning at Sullivan's back.

I roll my eyes. "You know that's not why I'm here."

"It's okay if you date a little. Make some new friends." Mom winks. "There's nothing wrong with fooling around a little."

"Cecilia." My dad frowns. "Let's not—"

She rolls her eyes. "I know you weren't a virgin on our wedding night, Stewart."

I clap my hands over my ears. I don't want to hear about this.

Barrett tugs on my arm, taking my hand and squeezing. That's new. Normally, I have to push him to give me a hug hello and goodbye. Since I saw him over spring break, he's suddenly cuddly and wants to hug and touch. It's not sexual —it's familiar, like coming home from a long day to find dinner is already made.

"I'll take good care of her," he tells my dad, like I'm some sort of possession. I glare at him, and he grins. "I have a good group of friends. Nobody that I'd set her up with, of course."

"Thanks," I tell him sourly.

He winks and tugs on a lock of my hair.

The host shows up to deliver us to our table. It's a small little booth in the back of the pub. I slide in, and Barrett sits beside me. He props his arm on the back of the booth behind me.

"What's good?" Dad asks.

"I've never had a bad meal here," he admits, scratching idly at his chin. He missed a spot shaving. I can see a few errant hairs on the corner of his jaw. "A few friends and I usually come here after a game. It's not a bad place to spend a Saturday night."

When the waiter comes by, we all place our orders and subsist into silence. My mom looks like she's about to burst into tears at any moment.

My dad coughs. "You can come home and visit any time you want, kiddo."

"I know, Daddy."

"Your room is always open."

"I know."

"And if you want, I can come down and get you. You don't need to take the train. I can—"

"I know. I will." I swallow and meet his eyes. "I'm going to be pretty busy with training and conditioning. I might not have a lot of free time the first few months."

We've gone over this; they don't expect me to be home all the time, and neither do I. But being an hour away is better for all of us than being clear across the country, and now they can visit, or I can go home for a weekend once soccer season is over. I know they've missed having me around the last few years, and I've missed them, too. I just wish I hadn't had to come home this way. None of us wanted this to happen.

"Don't be a stranger," Mama says. "Have a good time, but don't party too much. This year is so important."

"So no frat parties?" Barrett shoots me a sly grin. "There's a toga party tonight at the Delta house."

Dad frowns. "No."

Mama nods yes. "It's okay, Stewart. She's twenty-two years old. Let her live her life."

"I have practice the day after tomorrow. The time for parties is practically over."

"I have some friends I'll introduce her to so she has some

people in her corner," Barrett adds. His enormous hand lands on my shoulder. "Good people."

"Greg and all them?"

I remember his roommates from my brief visit over spring break. I liked them, though I'm not sure they'd say the same thing about me. Most of the trip, Barrett and I went off and did things by ourselves, only meeting them for meals.

I've always liked how we can pick up where we left off without any awkwardness. He's my best friend, my other half. Being apart was normal for us for all these years, a fact of our friendship; now we'll find out what it's like to be all up in each other's business all the time.

His eyes narrow a fraction. "Yeah."

I turn back to my parents. "See? I have friends here. You don't have to worry about me."

"You know I'm going to," Dad says. "That's my job."

"I'm fine. I'll be fine," I insist, although my eyes are welling with tears. He's acting like this is the last time I'm going to see him. He'll only be an hour away. That's nothing after the last four years.

"I've got her," Barrett says, squeezing my shoulder. "I'll always take care of her."

———

After my parents finally—*finally*—leave, Barrett helps me unpack. Basically, that means he sits on my bed, pulls stuff out of my suitcases, and hands everything to me to hang up in the tiny closet or fold into my new dresser. I have more clothes than I thought. Boston means actual seasons and weather and wearing layers. Yet another way my old life in Southern California feels a million miles away.

Barrett collapses onto my bed and tucks his arms around the pillows. "Come lay down with me."

"I have so much more to do." My floor is a tangled mess of clothes, empty suitcases, and discarded boxes.

He catches my hand and tugs. I half-stumble onto him, falling across his lap and his broad belly. He wraps his strong arms around me and hauls me next to him, his big body curling around me. He's big and strong, and I'm small and strong, and this could feel like something it's not. Instead, it feels... comforting. Natural. Almost familiar, which is crazy.

This is all new. That isn't who we are. There have always been very strict lines in our friendship. Sure, we've gone to school dances together, we've had sleepovers at each other's houses, but we aren't dating or in a relationship. We've never shared a bed. We're just friends. Best friends.

"I'm glad you're here," he says quietly. "I know it's shitty how you ended up here—"

"It's fine," I tell him.

"It's not. You don't have to pretend with me."

I sigh. "Yeah, it's shitty. It's not what I would have picked. But—"

"Yeah," he says, reaching for my hand and squeezing.

Terminal cancer. Nobody knows how long my dad has, and we all have to act like everything is fine. It's not fine. Nothing is fine.

There's a vibration against my hip. He groans and shifts, taking his phone out of his pocket.

"The guys are heading to the ASC in a bit. Do you want to see everyone?"

"I guess so. Better get it over with."

"They're looking forward to getting to know you better," he says. He thumbs out a reply and rests the phone screen side down on his broad belly. He worms his arm beneath my pillow to curl around my shoulders, so my neck is resting on his bicep. He smells good, like his soap and cologne and a scent that can only be described as *boy* that doesn't offend my nose. "But not for a little while. We have time for a power nap."

Tentatively, I roll to face him. His arm tightens around me, his hand rubbing my upper arm. His eyes are closed, a happy smile on his face.

"Rest," he says. "Stop staring at me."

"I'm not."

"You are," he says, his eyes still closed. "We have an hour until dinner."

I yawn. I guess I am kind of tired. Moving isn't for the faint of heart.

My eyes fall closed. I don't know if I actually fall asleep or if I'm just dozing, but all too soon, Barrett is shifting beneath me. Something touches my temple.

"Wake up, Dee," he murmurs quietly. He brushes some hair out of my face.

That feels nice.

"I don't wanna," I tell him, my eyes still firmly closed. I must be dreaming.

He kisses my forehead. "You've got to. It's time for dinner."

I stretch. My arm knocks against his broad chest. He huffs out a breath of laughter. I punch his shoulder, and it hurts my knuckles. Guess I'm not dreaming, then.

"Come on, sleepyhead."

"It's all your fault. I didn't want to take a nap." Struggling upright, I take in the disarray of my room and groan. "This is going to be fun to clean up later."

"I'll help you," he promises. The bed dips as he rolls to his feet. He offers me a hand and helps me up. "Tonight is just the guys. And Sam and Mason." He swallows nervously. "If you're okay with a big group thing. We can have dinner just the two of us, if you don't want to deal with my asshole friends."

"Your friends aren't assholes."

"Yeah, they kind of are."

I roll my eyes, hiding my smile. "Dinner. Feed me."

The scenery on the walk is pretty. It's a half-mile trek through Athlete's Village to the Athletic Student Center, the student union designated for student athletes. It's a glass monstrosity with study rooms, conference rooms, a banquet hall, two gyms and workout rooms, and of course, the dining hall.

I don't have a student ID card yet—that's a tomorrow project—so Barrett badges me in with a visitor pass. We grab trays and take in the cafeteria-style lines. It looks infinitely better than the dining hall at USC.

"Anything you recommend? Or don't recommend?"

He pauses, giving the question his full consideration. That's one of the things I like most about Barrett. He treats me seriously, no matter the question.

"The chicken dishes with sauce tend to be better than the plain chicken dishes," he finally says. "The Thai curries are better than the Indian curries. And the vegan options usually include nuts, so stay away from those."

I roll my eyes. "I'm not going to purposefully ingest something I'm allergic to. I presume there are signs."

"Well, tonight is cauliflower in a cashew cream sauce, so don't pick that one." He chooses two cilantro lime chicken breasts and scans it into his nutrition app.

We make our way through the cafeteria lines and fill our plates. He warns me away from the whole wheat rolls—they taste like cardboard—and points out the sandwich and salad bar, in case I don't like any of the hot entree options. Apparently, his friend Tucker is known for his affinity for peanut butter sandwiches.

His friends are already waiting at one of the tables in the back. A lesser woman would be intimidated by the sight of five enormous defensive linemen staring her down. But I've met the guys—one time, it still counts—and know they're all as cuddly as teddy bears.

Well, except for Wes. He doesn't really talk. I don't know what his deal is.

Greg stands as we approach the table. "Dee. Good to see you again."

"You, too."

I'm surprised when his soft lips brush my cheek. "We've missed you."

There's a low growling noise beside me. We both turn to see Barrett frowning, his eyes shooting daggers at his roommate. He looks like he's about to tackle him.

I clear my throat and shift closer to my best friend. "Glad to be here."

"Come, sit, sit," Greg says, all but pushing me into a chair. But I know Barrett usually takes the one on the end—he's very particular—so I slip into the seat beside his.

Wes is reading his book. He lifts his gaze briefly, makes eye contact, and returns his attention to his novel.

I recognize the rest of the guys. Miles, Amir, Tucker, and Greg are all decent dudes. Sam is sitting across from Miles, her heart in her eyes.

There's an unfamiliar girl next to Tucker. She's fairly dark-skinned, maybe black, maybe biracial. It'll be nice to have some non-white friends. Not that Barrett isn't great. We'll always have the Chinese-American connection in common. But that's just half of my heritage.

"Hi, I'm Mason," she says, leaning over Amir to shake my hand. "Welcome to Newton. I transferred in last fall."

My eyes dart back to Tucker's. This must be the girlfriend he mentioned when we met a few months ago.

"Diana."

"Nice to meet you," she says. She bites her lip as she considers me. "Biracial?"

I nod. "Black and Chinese. You?"

She laughs. "Black and Korean. We're going to be best friends."

I kind of resent the idea that we're going to be best friends because we're both biracial transfer students. I want to make friends on my own merit, not because of my racial identity.

At the same time... we *are* both biracial transfer students who are attached to the football team. We're going to interact and probably spend time together. Maybe this is her clumsy way of welcoming me to the fold. She's accepting my presence as Barrett's best friend; they all are. Nobody has questioned whether I have a right to be by his side. They just accepted it, like they accept him.

Because they're friends. Maybe one day, they can truly be my friends, too.

Barrett nudges me with his elbow. "Eat your dinner, Dee."

I make a face at him. I'm not a baby. He laughs, so all his friends do, too.

The guys talk around us. Amir goes on a rant about something that happened at practice this morning, and Greg and Sam argue about which movie to watch tonight. Barrett stays out of it, his eyes on me as I robotically eat my food. It's... fine. It certainly doesn't taste like cardboard. I'm just confused.

We fell asleep together. Sure, it was just a nap—over the blankets, fully clothed. Nothing obscene happened. But he kissed me. He *kissed* me!

And instead of focusing on that very critically important fact... all I can think about is that I kind of want him to do it again.

When we were in high school, I had a crush on Barrett. A minor crush. How could I not? He's fantastic. I wasn't, like, *in love* with him or anything. He was just my best friend, my rock, the guy who had always been there for me, and when hormones started getting involved... it was only natural to develop feelings for him. We were so close back then.

And he never showed even one iota of interest in me, so eventually I got over it. I moved on. I lived my life, I dated other boys, and never did he seem to care who I got involved with as long as it was all safe and consensual. All he's ever wanted is for me to be happy, I know that.

"Do you still want help unpacking?" Barrett asks as we linger over dinner.

I shrug. "If you want. You don't need to."

"I want to," he says. He tugs on my ponytail like he always has. "I like hanging out with you."

"I like hanging out with you, too," I admit. "And now we get to all the time."

two

. . .

Barrett

DIANA TRANSFERRING to Newton might be the worst
thing that has ever happened to me.

I want to be happy that my best friend and I are finally
going to be living in the same city, going to the same school.
For the first time, ever. Except for the fact that I'm in love with
her, and she doesn't know. Except for the fact that she is going
through what's sure to be the worst year of her life.

We sit there, eating dinner with my friends like absolutely
nothing is out of the ordinary. But this is the exact opposite of
ordinary. We fell asleep together—I *kissed* her!—and she
didn't even react.

The distance between us was always a bit of a blessing in
disguise. I could live my everyday life without being
confronted by the reality of the situation.

I can't look back and pinpoint when my feelings for her
developed. All I know is, I was going through my life on
autopilot, and then one day, my engines started revving out
of my control. I love her. I love everything about her. And she
doesn't feel the same.

Even if she did—and that's a big *if*—I know that her dad's

terminal illness weighs heavily on her. It would weigh heavily on anyone, and coupled with how close they are… Not to mention leaving her school, her teammates and friends, her coaching staff, and all the resources that a school like USC can provide… Newton is a great school, sure, but our soccer program is mediocre, our dietetics program is second-tier, and the weather sucks. Especially when compared to the Los Angeles sunshine.

"Have you met any of your teammates?" Sam asks as we linger over dessert.

"Not since the transfer interview. And that was super brief. I don't know any of them personally."

Mason winces. "Yeah, transferring last year… I had a lonely few months until I figured everything out." She and Tuck are together now, but it hasn't been all that long since they started dating again.

Diana chews on her lip. "I'm nervous," she admits.

"It's scary." My voice lowers as I meet her eyes, blocking out the rest of the world around us. "It's new, and scary, and it's overwhelming. But you can do this. You're capable of anything you set your mind to, Dee."

She gives me a nervous smile. "I'm glad you believe in me, even when I don't."

I squeeze her shoulder. "Always."

Wes grunts. I break my eyes away from hers to see the rest of the table is staring at us.

"What?"

"Nothing," Greg says, looking between me and Diana with a smirk on his face. "It's just nice seeing you two together."

"What's that supposed to mean?"

"You seem happier when she's around." He nods to Diana. "He was downright miserable to be around when you weren't here."

Dee laughs. "We've been friends forever. This is the first

time we'll get to actually spend time together in—years. We've never lived in the same place before."

Friends. My stomach clenches. We've been friends for fourteen years, since we met at that Chinese camp in the mountains. I've gone to her school dances and her soccer tournaments. She's come to my birthday parties and met my crotchety old grandmother. We're fully enmeshed in one another's lives, despite the distance that's separated us for the entirety of our friendship.

It was almost easier knowing she was on the other side of the country. There was less temptation there. There was less risk of blowing up both of our lives.

I don't want to be just friends with Diana. I don't know how to be satisfied with being just her friend anymore. And now seeing her every day... I'm sure we're going to have meals together. We're going to hang out after classes. We'll go to parties. It's not like I can avoid her indefinitely.

I don't want to avoid her. I want to spend all my time with her, even when we both have other things going on and can't spare the time. I want to love her the way she deserves to be loved.

But I don't want to sacrifice our friendship for a fling. And that's all it could be. She's not ready for the type of relationship I want with her, the forever kind of thing that doesn't end.

Because I know her. I know what we could have. Our friendship has always had this effortless ebb and flow to it. Being with her makes me happy. My day is always better when I get to talk to her. And now we actually get to spend time together in person? It's an exquisite kind of hell.

I love her, but I can't have her. I have to keep my distance. And it fucking sucks that she's finally here, finally within my reach, and still so far away.

I'm used to the situation. But that doesn't mean I have to like it.

But she came here. She made the decision to leave it all behind and come home, to come back to me.

When we make it back to her house, all the lights are still off. I guess her roommates aren't back yet. Her keycard gets her access to the house and to her bedroom, and when she flicks on the light, I'm greeted with the chaos that is moving day.

I've been on campus all summer, training for football, and I was lucky enough to stay in the same house as I was in last school year, so I didn't even have to move at the end of term. This is the second year we have the same group of guys in the house. I like them, for all their peculiarities. Miles and his quiet moods. Tucker and his peanut butter sandwiches. Wes and his book obsession. Amir and his tea. Greg and his man bun.

Diana's floor is covered in open suitcases and boxes, clothes strewn everywhere. I knew what I was getting myself into. So I crack my knuckles and plop myself down on the floor.

"I'll fold, you put away?" I ask, lifting the first t-shirt I come across.

"Um, sure."

Folding the first shirt, I pass it over to her, and I reach for the second. We make quick work of a plastic tub, and I move on to the open suitcase. Workout leggings. Okay, I can do this.

Beneath the leggings are a mess of frilly underthings. My face heats. I've given a lot of thought to what kind of underwear Diana wears over the years, but I've never seen it up close and personal.

Her eyes fall to the pile of satin and lace. "I'll take care of that," she says. She grabs the entire stack in one arm and throws it into the top drawer of her dresser.

A satin leopard print thong falls to my knee. Pinching the thin strap between my thick fingers, I lift it into the air.

"You forgot one."

Face flaming, she snatches it from my grasp and shoves the drawer closed. "I think that's enough helping," she says.

"Really?" I gave her an innocent smile. "I'm having a blast."

"I'm sure you are," she mutters.

Am I attracted to this woman? Yes. Of course I am. Do I also enjoy needling her? Yes. Of course I do. Her embarrassment over such a common article of clothing makes me smile, and when she catches sight of it, her frustration with me only grows. Discreetly, I adjust myself to hide my own growing frustration.

"I'll deal with it tomorrow," Diana decides. She tosses her phone onto the bed. "Want to watch a movie?"

"Sure."

After toeing off my shoes—my grandmother would be horrified I'm wearing them inside at all, but roommates are what they are—I gingerly take a seat on the mattress beside her. She grabs the TV remote and crawls onto the bed. She waits for me to get settled before she curls up directly next to me, her head on my chest. I slip my arm around her, and I'm gratified when she sighs and snuggles closer, turning on her favorite movie we've seen a million times.

We've been friends for fourteen years. I'm not about to throw away the best thing that's ever happened to me over a fling.

Because that's all it would be. Diana dates, but she doesn't go for relationships. She has enough on her plate between her double major and soccer. And now adding in this thing with her dad... I could never do that to her.

I pull her closer, until we're a heartbeat away from each other, and as I open my mouth to say something, anything, she nuzzles into me and sighs, fast asleep. I kiss her forehead again, and then I close my eyes, too. If I can't have her in real life, maybe I can have her in my dreams.

three

. . .

Diana

I WAKE up to the sun streaming in my window. Squinting against the glare, it takes me a minute to remember I'm in my new room at Newton. I'm not in my dorm room at USC. I'm not in my childhood bedroom. I'm getting a fresh start, a clean slate.

The house is quiet. Nobody else is up this early. For a minute, I debate rolling over and going back to sleep. No, it's no use. I'm wide awake.

My phone has a message from Barrett. I didn't hear him sneak out of bed, but I remember waking up at two o'clock in the morning to pee with him fast asleep beside me. It was so natural to come back from the bathroom to find him in my bed. I didn't think twice about crawling in beside him.

He's going for an early weightlifting session at eight—do I want to meet him for breakfast after?

I have practice at ten. The timing doesn't quite work. I roll out of bed and get dressed in plain black shorts and a nondescript black t-shirt I can wear to practice. I don't have any Newton gear yet.

The walk to the ASC is peaceful. I listen to music and chill, trying to get into the zone. I'm used to being on my own. I liked my teammates at USC, we got along great, but I doubt we'll keep in touch except on social media. I haven't heard from anyone all summer. It's like they said goodbye at the end of the season and that was that.

Badging into the dining hall, I grab a tray and start to load my plate with coffee, oatmeal, fruit, and a poached egg. I pick a small table hidden away in the corner and tuck in. I don't want to talk to anyone. I'm not here to make friends. All I want is to drink my coffee, eat my food, and slowly get ready for the day.

Nobody comes up to me. Nobody tries to talk to me. Everyone leaves me alone, which is exactly what I want, and at the same time, it feels incredibly isolating. I don't know anyone here. I don't know the social rules.

Finally, at nine-thirty, it's time to head back to the house. There are three houses for the soccer team, and I was assigned to one at random. I don't know what I'm in for. I've played on nearly a dozen teams over the last sixteen years. I've been the new girl before. There might be hazing. They might freeze me out. They might be nice to my face and talk shit about me behind my back. Or they might be perfectly lovely women. I'm far too cynical for that, though.

The group has added me to the team's social media groups, so I've become "friends" with these women I've never met. There's a group chat for the house, too, but I haven't seen any messages in that thread in the past two days despite everyone moving in this weekend.

The girls are waiting in the living room when I get back. I'm not sure who is who. Johanna Chen is the team captain, and she's the other Chinese-American girl, so she's easy enough to figure out. The other four women are Rosie, Robin, Rachel, and Rebekah—all four are tanned from a summer spent practicing in the sun, with long hair pulled back into braids. Two are blonde, two are brunette. Aside from that, they're interchangeable. They're all wearing grey t-shirts with the Newton logo and navy blue soccer shorts.

"You're late," Johanna says when I close the door behind me.

It's nine fifty. I could argue with her. It won't make us friends. After a brief detour to grab my gear bag from my room, I zip my lips and follow the girls out of the house.

Coach Aimee Larsen is a no-nonsense woman with her hair pulled back in a severe braid. Frown lines crease her face. She's skating on thin ice and we all know it. The team has had a losing record the last three seasons and, unless magic happens, her job is on the line.

We only have two weeks until our first game. Most programs would be practicing all summer. Maybe the girls practiced without me, I don't know. My transfer was effective for the fall semester—I took a class over summer session back at USC, so even if I had wanted to, I wouldn't have been allowed to come out here early. I have two weeks to learn all the plays, to learn the team and their playing style.

I'm grateful to Coach Larsen for agreeing to let me transfer. She recruited me hard when I was in high school. Newton was always my backup, my safety school. I never thought I'd have to end up here. She didn't have to agree to let me transfer. She did anyway.

There are four new freshmen and one sophomore transfer, Lauren. Coach Larsen has us stand in a circle and introduce ourselves. I don't know that I'd be able to pick out which one is which without name tags. There are so many people on the team, plus all the coaching staff and various team admins I have to remember. Everyone starts to blur together in their matching Newton apparel. The new girls and I are the only ones not wearing head to toe Newton gear.

We start with a few dynamic stretches to warm up before

they set us to running laps. Three times around the field isn't pretty for anyone. We split up by position. The eight defenders cluster around the defensive coordinator as he sets us on passing drills.

Emma and Ashton introduce themselves as the two full backs. Kristin, Jackie, and Louisa are center backs. Mischa, Terri, and Zoe are the wing backs. They're marginally warmer than Johanna was. I don't feel an overwhelming bond of sisterhood. Maybe it's too much to expect for day one. Maybe it will never develop. I only have one year left. I can get through this.

———

After practice, the team hits the showers. By unspoken agreement, we head towards the ASC. Or rather, they do, and I follow them. I stick close to Emma, who gives me a small smile before returning to her conversation with her fellow sophomores. Johanna is chatting with Rachel and Rebecca. Robin is nodding in agreement.

There are more than thirty of us. We badge into the dining hall and grab trays. Following the other girls' lead, I put food on a plate and scan it into the nutrition app. We push three tables together. I'm in the middle of the table with Jackie and Lauren, the other transfer student. It's painfully awkward. I don't know what to say, so I concentrate on stuffing my face.

A shadow falls over us. The girls fall silent. I look up to see Greg standing behind me, Wes and Amir flanking him.

"Hey, Dee," Greg says. He shifts his tray and leans down, pressing his lips to my cheek again. "How was your first practice?"

"Good. Did you guys get a good lift in?"

"What? You can't tell?" He flexes, his big arms bulging.

Some of the girls behind me giggle.

"Oh, yes, very obvious," I tell him seriously. "Where's B?"

Amir rolls his eyes. "He's on the phone with his parents. It didn't sound pretty."

I wince. Yeah, if he's talking to his parents, he's sure to be in a stellar mood.

"I'll be sure to give him some space, then."

Wes grunts.

"You're right. We should sit down," Amir says in response.

"Good to see you, Dee," Greg says. "Don't be a stranger."

"I won't." I try to go back to my lunch, only to find half the team staring at me. "What?"

"You know football players?" Jackie says.

Zoe raises her eyebrows. "You know *those* football players? Didn't you just get here, like, yesterday?"

Down the table, Johanna looks less than impressed. Rosie, Rachel, Rebecca, and Robin are whispering amongst themselves.

"I met them over spring break. My best friend is on the football team. He introduced me to his roommates when I came for my transfer interview," I explain. I have a feeling I'll have to explain this quite a bit.

"He kissed you," Lauren points out.

"It was only my cheek. Greg is a very affectionate guy." He's always giving me hugs. He does the same with Sam and Mason, Miles and Tucker's girlfriends.

Not that I'm Barrett's girlfriend. I'm simply his friend who is a girl.

Our friendship has always transcended the distance between us. In high school, he used to bribe his older brother, Dougie, to drive him out to Amherst for the weekend. Once he got his driver's license, my house was the first place he drove by himself. My parents were glad to have him. He brought a certain life and warmth back to our house.

He would come out on Friday afternoons after school, spend all day Saturday at the soccer fields cheering on my team, and then have family dinner with my parents before we went out to a house party or the movies with my school friends, who knew him nearly as well as I did. Sunday, we would have a leisurely brunch—my dad would cook, Barrett and I would clean up—and then laze around the house for a few hours before he had to head home.

His parents weren't nearly as welcoming. His house felt cold. Sterile. It was obvious his parents weren't my biggest fans. I was too loud, too black, too middle-class to fit in with these stuffy rich people. My mom is first generation whereas their family has been here since the mid 1800's. I was never good enough to associate with their precious baby boy.

To be fair, Barrett thought they were full of shit, too. He doesn't get along well with them. He always defended me against their casual slights and slightly less casual racism. We spent considerably more time at my house than at his. He willingly came with me to all of my school dances. We had a good time. He's a good dancer, didn't shy away when they played a slow song, just pulled me close and wrapped his arms around me. All of my friends thought we were dating. We weren't. We were just good friends.

Our friendship has always been purely platonic. Not once did we ever kiss or come close to it. Not once did we ever do more than hug hello and goodbye. My parents had no issues with him staying over at our house. His new touchy-feely greetings are very much out of the ordinary for us, but I'm not complaining. I'm well aware my best friend is a good-looking guy. It would be rather difficult not to notice over the years. With his hair freshly cut and a few days' worth of beard growing on his jaw... yeah, Barrett is fucking hot.

He is also so not into me, I can't even consider going there. He's going to wind up with some petite Chinese girl, someone with money and manners who knows which fork to use at dinner and can speak and write in both Mandarin and

Cantonese. Someone who will be an asset to him in his accounting career and not a hindrance.

"You're making friends fast," Zoe says, and I'm not sure I like what she's insinuating.

"They're good guys."

"Can you introduce us?" Louisa adds in.

I force out a laugh. "Yeah, I can do that."

four

· · ·

Diana

TODAY IS my last first day of school. I suppose I should feel more nervous or nostalgic. Instead I just feel kind of drained. The semester hasn't even started yet ,and I'm already exhausted. I'm taking five classes this term—three for my dietetics major, two for my psychology major. None of my teammates are psychology majors. There's a freshman that's a dietetics and nutrition major, but we've already confirmed we don't have any of the same classes.

My walk to the ASC is quiet. Johanna and I share a bathroom, but since she has a late start this morning, she's not up at the crack of dawn like me. Campus is beautiful with the early morning light filtering in through the trees.

I recognize Mason, sitting with a group of people that I'm guessing are her track teammates. She catches sight of me and waves me over.

"Hey, girl. Good morning," she chirps, sounding way too perky for this early.

"Morning."

"Sit with us," she says, pulling out the empty seat beside her. I spy four empty coffee cups on her tray—that explains it.

"I don't want to impose..."

"Not imposing," she says. "I remember what it's like being a transfer student."

"Yeah, Tucker mentioned you transferred last fall?"

"It was the best decision I've ever made," she admits, toying with the eggs on her plate. "Georgetown wasn't the right fit for me. I liked it, but I didn't love it."

"That's how I felt about USC. It was never really home."

I know that over time I'll make friends. It's kind of nice to know that Mason went through everything I'm going through now, only last year. And considering she and Tucker are together, I'm sure I'm going to be seeing a lot of her if I want to spend time with Barrett and his friends.

She introduces me to her teammates, Fred, Melissa, Mateo, and Bryce. They seem like an alright bunch. Not about to become my new BFFs or anything. We chat about majors and hometowns.

Within five minutes of conversation, I already know more about them than I do my new teammates. Fred is a dietetics major—we'll have a class together, which makes it less intimidating. Mateo and Bryce flirt with me and with each other. Melissa is perfectly nice to me.

Eventually, I'll make friends of my own. I'll find people in my classes I have things in common with. I'll meet other student athletes. I'll expand my social circle.

Or I won't.

At least I'll always have Barrett to fall back on. He has sunrise weights with the guys every morning. The football team and I are about to become very good friends. They're going to be the main bulk of my social circle until I'm feeling comfortable with the soccer girls—if that ever happens.

My first dietetics and nutrition class seems interesting enough. I get lost trying to find my second class, even though the nutrition consulting lab is only one floor above my first class. I have an hour break before my third class of the day, a psychology course in an entirely different building. I swipe my student athlete badge for a snack from the grab and go stand outside the psychology building and eat in the sunshine.

It's warm, but the heat isn't oppressive like it would be back in LA. The humidity makes my hair frizz and seize. On a good day, my hair can't decide if it's straight and wants to be wavy or if it's wavy and wants to be straight. Usually it's a tangled mess. After two decades of battling with it, I've made my peace with it.

Tucker is in my Ethical, Professional, and Legal Standards in Psychology class. I make a beeline for his side and slide into the seat beside him.

"Hey, stranger," he says, giving me a side hug.

"I am so glad to recognize someone," I admit with a laugh, and he grins.

"Stick by my side, kid. I've got your back." He pulls a plastic container out of his backpack. He has apple slices and chocolate hazelnut spread in a little compartment. He offers me the container.

"I'm good, thank you." I don't want to break out in hives —or worse, go into anaphylactic shock.

He shrugs and drags an apple slice through the chocolate. "We got a late start this morning. Didn't have time for a full breakfast. Had to run to my first class. This semester is going to be rough."

"I saw your girlfriend for breakfast."

He breaks out into a pleased grin. "She mentioned that."

"I like her."

"I do, too." He blushes. "She's good people."

From Barrett, I know their start was rocky. They dated all through high school until she dumped him the day before they left for college. He spent the next two and a half years in a depressive funk. When she transferred to Newton, they were forced to work together, and things naturally progressed from there. Barrett spent most of last semester going to her track meets with the guys, cheering on Mason and her teammates.

They also went to all of Sam's softball games last spring. I like that they all support one another. When these guys love, they love hard. Miles and Sam are cute. They clearly care a great deal for each other. It's rare to find one without the other. He's always been a quiet guy, reserved. Obviously, I didn't know either of them before they started dating, but from what Barrett's told me, he's really opened up in the last year and come into his own.

Barrett has never really talked to me about girls. I know he hooks up. He's drunk-dialed me a few different times, usually on his walk home from other girls' dorms. In all the time that I've known him, he's never had a girlfriend. I went to his homecoming dance after his football game our freshman year, and that was the end of that. He invited me to his senior prom, but I had a soccer tournament that weekend. I don't know who he took to his other formal dances. It wasn't me. His fancy prep school had formal dances every semester. He complained about them constantly. But he never mentioned who, if anyone, he went with.

For as much as he's an open book about some things, Barrett is remarkably closed off about other things. He doesn't talk about girls. He doesn't talk about his parents. He doesn't talk about his life after football, his plans after graduation.

Part of it might be the distance. The miles between us, whether we were an hour and a half away or living on opposite coasts, ever changed the fact that I can talk to him about anything.

But he won't do the same with me. I don't know how I never noticed it before.

———

My dad answers the phone on the first ring. "Hi, baby girl," he says, and I inhale sharply at the familiar comfort of his voice.

"Hi, Daddy."

"How was school?"

"Fine. How was your doctor's appointment?"

"Fine," he says immediately.

Which is how I know it was not, in fact, fine.

"What did they say?"

He sighs. "Diana…"

"You can tell me. I can take it."

"I'll be fine," he says again.

There's a lump in my throat. He won't, though. I know he won't get better. I know he won't be fine. He's not going to get better. Even with the help of all the treatments and the meds and the procedures… the clock is ticking, and none of us know how long is left on the timer.

I don't want to lose my dad. I don't want him to be in pain, I don't want him to suffer, but I don't want to exist in a world where he doesn't.

"What did you do today?"

"School stuff," I answer.

My dad laughs. "Yeah, I figured. Do you like your classes? Do you know anyone?"

"I have a class with one of Barrett's roommates, and I had breakfast with his girlfriend."

He inhales sharply. "Barrett has a girlfriend?"

"What? No." My stomach rumbles at the idea. "His roommate's girlfriend."

"Got it, got it," he says. "I was going to say…"

"Say what?"

"Nothing. So you're making friends."

"Trying to, yeah."

"And the girls in your house?"

I press my lips together. "No comment."

"That bad?"

"Remember the championship team I was on in the seventh grade? With those mean girls who made my life miserable?"

"Yeah…"

"Well, that was a cakewalk in comparison."

"Oh, honey…"

"It's fine. I'll be fine," I tell him… which is how he knows I won't be. I've never been able to hide anything from my dad, not that I've ever wanted to.

"It'll get better," he says quietly.

Is he talking about my teammate situation? Or about something else?

"I hope so," I tell him.

"It will," he says firmly. "Trust me. I'm your dad. I know everything."

five

. . .

Barrett

MY BODY IS BATTERED and bruised. All I want to do is crawl into my bed. But tonight is Monday night, the first official night of classes, and Diana and I have plans. I'm not about to cancel on her now.

We meet in the lobby of the ASC. She's wearing short denim cutoffs and a tank top, showing off her sculpted shoulders and the smooth line of her neck. I open my arms for a hug, and she steps into me without hesitation. Her cheek presses against my heart, hammering a thousand beats a minute at the scent of her perfume, lavender and sunscreen.

"Hey, you." My voice is thick with an emotion I refuse to identify. It's good to see her. It feels like more than forty-eight hours since I've seen her.

"You really missed me, huh?" She grins up at me.

"Always." I coil one of her messy waves around my finger, and her eyes crinkle with delight.

"What's with all the touching?"

"What's that supposed to mean?"

"Normally you give me lightning quick hugs. The last few times I've seen you, it's like you can't stop touching me." She looks up at me guilelessly. "I'm not complaining."

"I don't know. It just feels right."

My hands itch to touch her. I'm finally giving in to the temptation that's haunted me for the majority of the last fourteen years. Even when I thought girls were icky, I always thought she was beautiful. I've always been drawn to her like a moth to a flame. And like a flame, I've always been too worried about getting burned to consider pressing my luck.

I'm in love with my perfectly imperfect best friend, and she has no fucking clue. She's not a saint. She would rather sleep in than show up for practice, often leaving the rest of her team in the lurch. She's never been on time in her life. And she likes to eat cookie butter spread directly out of the jar, even if it's a communal container.

But I don't care. I love her anyway. In spite of her flaws. Or perhaps because of them.

"I like it," she admits, chewing on her cheek. "It's weird, it's new, but I don't hate it."

"Good. I'm glad."

Anything for an excuse to touch her. To feel her silky smooth skin. She's never going to want me the way that I want her. I will take whatever scraps of affection I can get.

There's a cough behind her. I look up to find the rest of the guys assembled in a half-circle around us. Tucker looks distinctly amused. Amir is hiding a smile. Sam is outright grinning.

Wes grunts. There's a distinct uplift to the end of it. A question.

"Let's head in," I tell them. My hand settles on her lower back, guiding her towards the entrance to the dining hall. Little sparks travel up my arm as the soft cotton of her shirt grazes my skin.

Diana grins up at me. "Such a gentleman."

I don't know how to tell her it has nothing to do with chivalry and everything to do with an itch to know her in any way that I can.

We load our plates and head towards the table that's become ours over the years. Dee takes the seat next to me, letting me sit on the end like I prefer. Across from me, Wes pulls out his book and proceeds to ignore all of us. He's not exactly what I'd call sociable. Simply being around us is enough to tire him out some days.

Mason, Sam, Greg, and Amir monopolize the conversation. It's quickly decided that we're going to head back to the house, watch tonight's episodes of Wheel of Fortune and Jeopardy!, and then we'll turn on Monday Night Football. We don't usually watch the pros in our house—after a long day at practice, the last thing we want is to devote more of our brains to football. Sometimes it's nice to have a break from it. But Greg's favored Titans are going up against Sam's Seahawks, so it's sure to be a good game, full of lots of good-natured trash talking and taunting.

Diana is quiet. She concentrates on her meal, playing with her food more than eating it. I nudge her with my elbow.

"You okay?"

She looks up, her brown eyes wide. "Yeah. I'm fine."

"How was your first day?"

She shrugs. "It was fine. Back at school. You know how it goes."

"Yeah." My accounting classes are going to be a beast. I honestly don't know if I'm going to pass my Tax Ethics course. Being on the five year plan, my advisors and I have been creative with my course assignments, trying to pick the harder classes for spring semester, when I have more time, saving the easier classes for fall term. Not that there are many easy accounting classes. Still, this close to graduation, I don't have that much flexibility in which classes are available for me to take. I've been putting off this Tax Ethics course for the last three years. It's only offered in the fall term. And it's finally my day of reckoning.

I don't like the pain in her eyes. "You sure you're okay?"

She sighs. "Just in a weird mood. Talked to my parents, and I—"

Covering her hand with mine, I squeeze, trying to reassure her. "Your dad is going to be fine."

"He might not be."

"You don't know that."

"I know. I just…" She sighs. "I'm worried."

"I know." I squeeze her hand again. "He's strong. He can make it through this."

"I really hope so."

I don't know what to say to her. The mood is subdued as she robotically eats her dinner. Tucker suggests ice cream, and she doesn't even perk up.

I can't ease this burden for her. Her father is going to get sicker and sicker. He's going to fight, but there are no guarantees. All I can do is be there for her, be a shoulder she can lean on when the going gets tough. Because it's going to get tough. There's no doubt about that.

Tugging on one of her curls, I direct her focus back to me. "You still up for tonight?"

She gives me a small smile. "Yeah. I need a distraction."

Once everyone has finished their dinner, or in Tucker's case second dessert, Wes puts away his book and we begin the walk home en masse. While we don't always eat every meal together and go home together, we try to schedule a few nights a week to hang out, all of us. We're roommates and teammates, but more than that, we're friends.

With Miles and Tucker now dating and secure in their relationships, our cohesive bond is starting to fracture. It used to be that all of us would spend our time together, day in and day out. Now they spend a significant time locked away in their rooms, having sex or otherwise occupied with their new partners.

I don't begrudge them their happiness. I'm glad they've found people that make them happy. I just wish sometimes that I could find something that makes me even remotely as happy as they have.

Miles and Sam curl up on the couch. I take my usual spot on the other end. Wes is in his favorite armchair by the window. Tucker and Mason curl up on another chair. Even though we've just finished dinner, Greg goes to make us all a few bowls of popcorn.

"Sit," I tell Diana.

She frowns. "There's no more room."

All the chairs are occupied.

I catch her hand and pull her on top of me. "Sit." She falls, her comfortable weight warming me all the way through.

"You want me to sit on your lap?" She twists sideways, her legs spread over my thighs.

"Don't make it weird." I set my hand on her hip.

Is it weird that she's sitting on my lap? No, it's not. Yes, it is. No, it really isn't. She needs support, she doesn't need me to make a pass at her. Whatever she needs, whatever it takes, I'll be there for her. Her spine is ramrod straight. I tug on her arm until she collapses against me, her head pillowed on my chest. She slings her arm around me, cuddling into me. I like that her natural reaction is to seek comfort from me, even if she's confused about my reasons.

"What's gotten into you?" she laughs.

I swallow. "I'm just really glad you're here. With me, with us. I've missed you."

Her eyes soften. "I've missed you, too."

I have to resist the urge to drop a kiss to the top of her head. She smells good, like she always does, fresh and clean and a little like *home*. I can't get enough. Closing my eyes, I have to fight back the rush of emotions threatening to overwhelm me.

I love this girl.

And she only wants to be my friend. Which—fine. I can be her friend. I can lock away my love for her and support her.

Because she needs my support. This is going to be the hardest year of her life. Between starting all over in a new school, joining a new team, and everything going on with her dad… yeah, she's going to need all the help she can get.

So I'll take a moment here and there to indulge, and then I have to go back to normal. I can be her friend.

six

. . .

Diana

THE FIRST WEEK of school falls into a routine. Wake up, have breakfast with Mason and her friends, go to class, practice, have dinner with the soccer team, where nobody talks to me or acknowledges my existence beyond "pass the salt" or "nice block." Return home. My roommates don't hang out together in the common areas. Every night, I do homework and study plays alone in my room.

Friday afternoon, we have visitors at practice. Barrett sits in the stands with Tucker and Amir as we run drill after drill. I don't have a guaranteed starting position. I'll have to earn my playing time the hard way, by putting in the work on and off the field and showing Coach Larsen that I want this.

Johanna's mouth is in a firm line as she checks out our special guests.

Barrett looks up and waves. Shaking my head, I wave back at him.

"You know him?" Her jaw is practically on the floor.

"Who?"

"You know Barrett Zhang?"

"Um, yes?"

She grabs my arm. Her nails dig half-moons into my skin. "How? You've been here for, like, a week."

"I've known him since we were eight years old."

"You have to introduce me." Johanna tugs insistently on my arm. "You *have* to."

"Okay, okay. I'll introduce you." I glance back over to Coach Larsen. "Now?"

"No. I need a shower. I need—fuck." She runs a hand over her sweaty ponytail and tugs at her sweat-soaked shirt. "I can't see him looking like this."

"What's the big deal? It's just Barrett."

"Are you kidding?"

I blink at her. "What?"

"He's fucking gorgeous," she says. "He's *Barrett Zhang*."

"Yeah, I know who he is."

"You seriously do?"

"Why is it so hard for you to believe?"

"He's, like, ten times out of your league." Her perfectly plucked eyebrows are sky high. "His family is seriously loaded. He's gorgeous. And he seems like genuinely a nice guy. How the hell do you two know each other?"

"Wow." I scoff, pulling my arm free. "Thanks."

"He's an amazing football player on top of that. He got two pick sixes last season and picked up a safety. That never happens."

Like I'm not already aware of his stats.

"Yeah, I know. He's my best friend."

"I've been trying to get to know him for, like, ever," she says. "I have such a crush on him."

I bite my lip. "Barrett doesn't really date…"

She laughs. "Clearly you don't know him as well as you think you do."

"Oh, he gets laid. He hooks up all the time," I tell her, because that I know for a fact. "But he doesn't exactly date. I'm not sure he'll give you what you're looking for."

Her smile is smug. "I don't care if I only get one night with him. I'll make it count."

Unease settles in my gut at the idea of Johanna and Barrett and their *one night* together. I don't like it. I don't want to picture them together.

I'm not sure what type of girls Barrett goes for. I don't know if he likes Asian girls or if he goes for white girls. He's never had a girlfriend that I know of, never talked about a specific girl in his life. For so long, his life has been dedicated to school, his family, and football, and not necessarily in that order of importance.

And me. He's relentlessly devoted to me, too.

I like it. He's always cared for me, he's always been there for me, even when time zones separated us. Being in his inner circle feels a bit like being let into the world's biggest secret: Barrett is amazing. It's not a hardship to be friends with him; it's a privilege. Our friendship is easily the most treasured thing in my life, even more than soccer, even more than my parents, even more than… anything. I love having him as my best friend.

Once practice is officially over, I jog over to the sidelines. He doesn't care that I'm a sweaty mess; he wraps me in an enormous hug, holding me close. I like when he hugs me. It feels almost like coming home again.

"Hey, Dee. Great practice."

"Thanks. You've got nothing better to do?"

He grins. "You know it."

"Let me go shower and change. I'll see you in ten minutes?"

Barrett nods. "I'll be here."

"Where's Mason?" I ask Tuck, who slides his phone into his pocket with guilt written all over his face.

"Still at practice. They don't allow visitors," he says with a frown.

I laugh. "Well, I'm glad you came to visit us." I raise my eyebrows at Amir. "No special lady in your life to stalk?"

It's his turn to grin. "Nah, I'm good. Not looking for anything more than one night only."

Tucker shakes his head. "You'll change your mind. Once you find that girl, it'll be over."

"Yeah, I'll take that bet," Amir retorts.

I roll my eyes. "Great. Well, I'm going to go shower. We'll walk to dinner?"

"Of course. See you, stinky." He swats me on the hip.

Laughing, I jog over to the tunnel leading to the locker room. Most of the girls are already in the showers. I waste no time in stripping down and scrubbing up, eager to get the day's sun and sweat off my skin.

Coach is waiting for us with a pile of black backpacks with the Newton logo on it.

"Gear day," she announces. "Everyone grab one on your way out."

Dressing quickly in a pair of loose denim shorts and a plain black tank top, I throw the bag over my shoulder and head back out to the stands.

Barrett grins at me as I approach. He reaches out his hand and, confused, I slap it for a low five. He laughs.

"Give me your bag," he says, taking it from my hand where I'm holding it slack. He slings it over his shoulder.

"You don't have to carry my bag," I tell him, despite the fact that I could barely manage the new backpack plus my existing gear bag.

"Shut up." He tugs on one of my braids. "Dinner, yeah?"

"I am so hungry."

He slings his arm over my shoulder, steering me in the direction of the ASC. Even though it's been less than a week, I already know this walk like the back of my hand.

Greg, Wes, Miles, and Sam are already eating by the time we arrive. They left the two seats on the end open for me and

Barrett. I take what's become my usual spot beside him and tuck into my chicken parm.

The guys are carb-loading before their game tomorrow. I'm a little grossed out by the vast amount of food on their plates.

They're big guys, all six-foot plus and close to three hundred pounds, and they're about to expend a lot of energy. Realistically, I know they need the calories. As a dietetics and nutrition major, I know that carb-loading will help them play their best tomorrow. But as a person with a small stomach, I'm a little repulsed by how big their plates are.

Barrett nudges me. "Not hungry?"

I take a bite of my chicken and renew my attention on my dinner. Practice was good, if a little long. My legs feel like jello.

From across the dining hall, I can see Johanna staring at us. She's sitting with Robin, Rosie, Rachel, and Rebecca. I don't know how to bring this up to Barrett. Does he know Johanna? It's a relatively small school. It's not that all Chinese people know each other. But she clearly knows who he is.

Do I want my best friend to date my team captain?

No, not really. I don't want Barrett to date anyone, period. He's always been all mine. I don't want to have to share him with some random girl. I don't want any other girl vying for his attention and affection, especially now that he's physically so attentive and affectionate. He's not like this with Sam or Mason. I like that it's something he reserves for me, for us.`

I don't even know what kind of girls he's interested in. He's called me on his way home from his hookups a few times, drunk and remorseful. He never sounds like he's having a good time. Casual dating isn't for everyone. I've gotten to the point where it no longer fulfills me. If I'm going to sleep with someone, I want to know them first and like them as a person, which hasn't always been the case. I don't want casual. I want something real.

At the same time, I don't know what I'm looking for in a guy. Someone who makes me feel good, I guess. Someone who understands that I don't have a lot to give. Between school, soccer, and this thing with my dad, I'm pretty tapped out emotionally. I can't add another emotional time-suck to my life.

So I guess I'm going to be celibate for a while. That doesn't scare me as much as it might have at one time.

Besides, I have Barrett. My best friend is finally in the same place as me. We can spend as much time together as we can both tolerate. Tonight he has to go to bed early in advance of the home game kicking off at one, but tomorrow night we are going to go out and party our faces off. Or whatever people at Newton do for a good time.

Despite his plate being three times as full as mine, he finishes before me. Barrett sets his hand on my shoulder.

"You okay?"

"I'm fine," I lie.

He frowns. "You don't have to lie to me."

I sigh. "Just thinking."

He tugs on one of my braids. "Don't think too hard, Dee."

Offering him a small smile, I try to concentrate on my dinner. He pushes his chair back and disappears into the cafeteria line, reappearing a few minutes later with two chocolate protein brownie sundaes. He sets one in front of me.

"Eat."

"I'm not hungry." I dig my spoon into the brownie anyway. It's rich and chocolatey. My stomach flips. He knew exactly what would turn my night around.

"Yeah, that's how I know something is wrong. So you're going to talk to me about whatever is bothering you," he says rationally.

"It's a lot of little things. Adjusting. Acclimating."

He nods. "The first week is the hardest."

"I don't miss USC. That's not it." I sigh. "It's just not what I expected."

"The team?"

"Yeah. They're… ugh."

He nudges me with his elbow. "It takes time. You'll settle in and make friends soon," he tells me.

"I hope so."

"And you have us." He gestures to the rest of the table. Tucker and Mason are sharing a sundae. Miles and Sam are holding hands across the table. Amir and Greg are focused on their own meals. Directly across from us, Wes looks up, makes eye contact, nods, and returns his attention to his book.

"I know. And I'm glad to have you guys." My heart warms at how easily his friends have welcomed me into their group. "But the girls…"

"Yeah. It isn't easy."

Barrett wraps his arm around my shoulders. I shift closer, hugging him around the middle. Everything is a little bit easier when I'm wrapped up in my best friend's arms. He chases away the bad feelings so effortlessly, I almost don't realize he's doing it until they're already gone. I kind of admire that about him.

He kisses the top of my head. "It'll get better," he says, his arm tightening around me. "It has to."

seven

. . .

Diana

THE MORNING DAWNS cold and grey. It's perfect weather for sitting outside for five hours watching a football game.

Johanna is already in the living room when I creep downstairs at eleven. "Where are you going?"

"The football game?"

Her eyes rove over my denim shorts and a Newton Soccer shirt from my new gear bag. I have the new Newton quarter-zip in my bag in case it gets chilly. I'm repping the silver, blue, and black from head to toe.

"You're going like that?" Her lip curls.

I clear my throat. "I don't have any other gear."

She nods. "Okay, then."

"Are you going to the game?" I don't know why I ask.

"Nah, I'm going to do a yoga video and get a head start on my homework," she says civilly, like she's a normal person.

"Sounds like a good day."

"I could..." She frowns. "You're going to see Barrett?"

"That's kind of the point. He's playing today. He'll be at our game on Friday."

She goes pale. "He will?" She plays with the ends of her hair.

"He's my friend. He'll be there to support me. Us. To cheer us on."

Johanna bites her lip. "Will you see him? After the game?"

"Yeah?"

"Give me five minutes," she says, hurrying into action. She leaps off the couch and disappears into her room, the door slamming shut behind her.

The sacrifices we make for friendship.

She reappears a few minutes later, now wearing short shorts and a Newton Athletics t-shirt. Her hair is pulled back into a jaunty, glossy ponytail. She's effortlessly gorgeous, and I hate that about her.

"Ready," she says, slinging her bag over her shoulder.

We've never been alone together. Since we got off to a rocky start, I've been giving her as wide a berth as possible, which is difficult considering we live in the same house, practice for the same team, and eat dinner together most nights.

I don't know what to say to her. You have the hots for my best friend, but back off, he's mine? I can't call dibs. He's a person, not a toy.

The walk to the arena is silent. Neither of us makes the first move to break the fragile peace. The parking lot is crowded with people tailgating. Bypassing all of them, we pay for our discounted tickets in the student section.

I presume Sam and Mason are here. Neither of them mentioned getting together, which—fine. They don't have to include me. I'm not Barrett's girlfriend. They have their own friends, their own lives. I don't think they're purposely excluding me. It probably didn't even occur to them that I would want to sit with either of them, the only people I know aside from the soccer team.

We pick seats right on the forty yard line, halfway back in

the student section. It's breezy. I'm glad I brought that jacket with me.

"Dee! Diana!" I turn to find Mason sitting two rows behind us with her friends. "Come sit with me!"

Without looking at my companion, I dutifully get up and move, and Johanna follows me. Mason lets out a cheer and throws her arms around me. "You made it!"

"Hey, girl," I say with an easy smile. "Thanks for finding me."

Johanna frowns.

I clear my throat. "This is Johanna. She's on the team with me."

"I'm the captain," she announces unnecessarily.

Mason's smile is tight. "How great for you."

"This is Mason. She's dating Tucker—I don't even know his last name?"

She turns around and I catch sight of the name Kingsley on her back.

"This is my first game as a WAG," she admits, like she's afraid to let us know.

Johanna blinks. "What's a WAG?"

"Wife and girlfriend," I answer. "There's a certain… status that comes with being the partner of a college football star like Tuck."

Mason gives a self-conscious laugh. "I was the high school girlfriend. Being the college girlfriend is different."

"You've got this," I tell her. "Tuck loves you."

"Oh, I know, I know," she assures me quickly. "It's just… it's weird. Everything's the same, and yet it's so different at the same time."

"I know what you mean. I haven't been to any of Barrett's college games. And now it's his senior season."

Mason's eyes are bright. "He could use someone on his side. From what King's said, his parents are…"

"Not coming," I finish tightly.

They never came to his high school games. They didn't go to Dougie's hockey games, either. The Zhang's were delightfully uninvolved in their sons' lives. It's one of the reasons Barrett and I had so many sleepovers in high school. If it wasn't academic or related to their social calendar, they didn't care. Athletics were beneath their radar.

Mason inclines her head. "Yeah, from what I've heard... yikes."

I sigh. "I've met them. They're worse."

Johanna frowns. "They can't be that bad."

"Oh, no, they are," I assure her. "How he and Dougie turned out so normal, I'll never know."

"Dougie?"

"His brother. He's at... Brown, I think? Working on his MBA." Belatedly, I realize I'm giving out all of my best friend's secrets. Secrets that aren't mine to tell. "He's a good guy. Used to pull my pigtails and then Barrett would beat up on him."

"That's sweet," Mason says, biting her lip to hide her smile. "Older or younger?"

"Barrett is two and a half years younger, but he's bigger than Dougie by at least two inches and fifty pounds. Maybe more. He played hockey."

"Hockey is a fun sport," Johanna says haltingly. Her eyes dart between us.

Melissa leans over Fred, saying something I don't make out, and Mason laughs and turns to her friends. She's not ignoring me, us; she's just being social with the group. The bleachers aren't exactly what I would call comfortable. Johanna and I sit there in silence as the guys warm up on the field and the band sets up.

Barrett looks good out there. Instantly I know which one is him, even without his name printed on the back of his jersey. It's like there's an invisible red string connecting us, like in those folk tales my grandmother used to tell. He stretches on the thirty yard line, chatting with Tucker and Wes. It's a little weird to see Wes without his ever present book.

I wonder if he'll want me to wear a Zhang jersey. I would go down to the student store and buy one tomorrow if he asked me to. I have no problem with wearing his number, supporting him. In high school, I would borrow one of his enormous Dalton Football sweatshirts to wear on Friday nights. I don't think I can ask him now. It's such a girlfriend thing to do. I don't think I realized that at the time.

He's scoping out the crowd now, a hand over his eyes. I know the moment he sees me because he jolts, and then the biggest smile I've ever seen crosses over his face. He waves.

My heart is in my throat. I don't know what's going on. I can't breathe, can't think. I wave back. What is this? It's just a wave, a simple hello from afar. I've gone to his high school games. I've been by his side for years.

But now... it's so much more than that. Why? I'm not sure. It just hits differently in a stadium of twenty-five thousand people.

Beside him, Tucker is communicating with Mason, based on the sign language he's got going on. Tucker folds his fingers into a heart and aims it up in our direction. Barrett doesn't even tease him. His attention is locked on me, on us.

I send him a thumbs up. He nods seriously, patting his chest. Over his heart.

The coach's whistle sounds, gathering his team, and he nods at me one more time before he jogs over to the defensive coordinator for a huddle.

Johanna and I sit in awkward silence. She pulls out her phone and flicks through her social media page.

I went to USC football games all the time. It was the thing to do. All the girls from the team would gather, we would tailgate for a few hours, and then, liberally sauced, we would watch the game and cheer on our fellow athletes.

It's completely different here at Newton. It feels more

important. This is Barrett's team, the guys he's spilled blood, sweat, and tears with over the last four years.

Newton wins the coin toss and defers. Once the kickoff is complete, the defense takes their positions on the field.

Barrett is a defensive end, primarily on the left side. He gets right into the thick of the scrums. I watch with bated breath as he crouches on the twenty-five yard line, fingertips of one hand on the ground. He steadies, readies, and once the ball is snapped to the opposing quarterback, he flies into action, tackling the offensive lineman and launching towards the quarterback.

The ball sails through the air, and Barrett retreats. Tucker takes out the receiver at the thirty-two yard line. Not enough yardage for a first down.

The Newton stands go wild.

It only gets better from there. Wes sacks the quarterback on second down. They convert for the first down, and Miles takes out the tight end at the fifty yard line. It's a raucous crowd enjoying the first football game of the season. The boys are playing better than ever.

There's a flag on the next play. Pass interference on Sullivan, the safety I met at the pub on move-in day. The other team gets a five yard advantage. Barrett is shaking his head, clearly pissed.

Miles says something to him, slapping him on the helmet. Barrett nods, hunkering down at the line of scrimmage. Bring it, he seems to tell the guy opposite him. He's laser focused. He manages to evade a tackle, dodge a lineman, and get to the quarterback, sacking him effortlessly. He makes it look so easy.

Johanna turns to me, giving me a high five.

"That's our boy," she yells over the roaring crowd.

Instead of feeling pride in my best friend, I feel uncomfortably territorial. He's mine. He's not hers. If I have my way, he'll never be hers.

After the game is over, a whopping 32 to 7, Mason grabs my hand and together we head to the tunnels where we can meet our athletes. Barrett already warned me it will be a madhouse, an intense crush of people trying to get a piece of them. Most people don't want to wait nearly an hour for the guys to shower, change, and exit the stadium; only the most devoted remain.

Sam is standing with a group of people decked out in Cavanaugh jerseys. Must be Miles's parents and sisters, if I'm reading the ages right.

After what feels like forever, the guys start making their way out of the tunnels. Amir comes out first, sucking on a protein shake in a clear plastic cup. On his heels are Greg and Wes with protein shakes of their own, followed quickly by Tucker. He and Mason have a heartfelt reunion, full on making out in plain view of everyone without a care in the world.

"Dee!" Barrett pushes aside another football player. Before I know it, he's scooped me up. I'm airborne, my feet dangling off the ground. He wraps me in his big strong arms and holds me close. I revel in the feeling of being in his arms. It's so easy. It feels so right.

"Hey, Care-Bear," I say.

He growls, setting me on the ground again. He presses a kiss to the top of my head and slings his arm over my shoulder, keeping me close. A glimmer of deep-rooted affection for him threatens to overwhelm me.

"Good game."

He grins. "Yeah. It was, wasn't it?" He runs a hand through his wet hair, making the short strands stand on end.

"Oh. This is Johanna," I tell him, and his eyebrows go sky high. I've told him about her—in broad strokes. I haven't told him about her little revelation last night.

"Nice to meet you," he says, offering his hand.

She takes it with an awed look on her face. "You, too."

He nudges me. "See? I told you you'd make friends."

I give him a tight-lipped smile, silently communicating that we aren't friends—not yet. He frowns at me, he doesn't get it. I guess we're not on the same level as Tucker and Mason.

"Miles, honey!" The woman in the Cavanaugh shirt is calling for his attention. Probably his mom. Red-cheeked, he ducks his head to kiss Sam before he greets his family.

The guys cluster in a semicircle around us. Amir sucks noisily on his straw. Wes's eyes are wide, his cheeks tinted a dull pink. I wonder what that's about.

Greg tugs me into a hug. "Hey, Dee. I was wondering if I was going to see you here."

"Why wouldn't I?"

He laughs. "This fool didn't scare you away?"

Barrett growls.

I grin at my best friend. "He couldn't keep me away if he tried."

Mollified, Barrett relaxes. He grabs me by the shoulder and pulls me back into his arms, into a bear hug. My sweaty back is plastered to his front as he hugs me to him and wraps his arms low around my belly, like I'll protect him from anything that comes his way.

Because I will. I'd move heaven and earth for this man. And he knows it.

"So, McRory's?" Amir says loudly, breaking apart Tucker and Mason.

She wipes at her mouth. "Works for me."

Barrett buries his face in my hair. "You good with that?"

"I'm with you," I tell him.

He clears his throat, turning to Johanna. "Would you like to join us?"

"Um, sure," she says, swallowing and tucking a strand of her hair behind her ear. "It's not an imposition?"

Amir grins at her. "The more, the merrier."

I step forward out of Barrett's arms and immediately mourn the loss of contact. I'm surprised when he takes my hand, squeezing reassuringly.

He's not usually so affectionate, especially not in front of other people. It used to be a battle to get him to hug me hello and goodbye. Now he's all over me. It's not sexual, I don't think. He just wants to touch me. I'm his security blanket. Against what, I'm not sure.

It's such an unexpected turn in our friendship, and at the same time, it feels so natural. Barrett is direct, up front. If he wanted this to be something more than it is, I feel confident he would tell me. In the last fourteen years, not once has he ever even hinted that he wanted to be more. And that's fine. My crush in high school was just that—a crush. I don't have feelings for him now.

Amir and Greg keep the conversation flowing, talking about nothing in particular as we make the mile and a half trek to the pub. I know Barrett doesn't like to dissect the game right away; he wants a little bit of time to ruminate before he tears apart his performance.

Not that there is much to tear apart. He played well. He got a sack on the quarterback in the first quarter and only went on from there. Together, the quarterback went down six times in the course of the hour. They only gave up one score. Not a bad way to start the season. So what if their offense is milquetoast at best? It's only the first game. There's plenty of time for the offense to get it together.

There's already a table waiting for us at the crowded pub. One of the benefits of hanging out with football players, I guess. Barrett takes the seat beside me, Johanna on my other side, and he props his arm on the back of my chair.

"You good, Dee?" His big hand covers my bare shoulder.

"I'm great."

He clears his throat. "I'm glad you're here."

"Yeah?"

He meets my eyes. "I wouldn't want to finish my senior season any other way."

My heart pangs at the idea of graduation. It feels so far, and at the same time, only a few short months away. I need to start thinking about what my life will look like once I'm done with school. With my dad's health issues, I should probably stick pretty close to Amherst. At the same time, I don't want to be right on top of my parents. I definitely don't want to live with them again. I might have to. I need to find a job. I need to—there's so much I have to do.

"I'm glad I get to be here for it," I tell him, and he grins at me.

"You and me, together against the rest of the world," he says.

eight

. . .

Barrett

I'M FLYING high on adrenaline and endorphins. I've just had a stellar game, eaten a fucking fantastic meal, and I have the prettiest girl on campus on my arm.

Okay. So she's not on my arm, per se. She's with me. We're going to this party together. We're going to drink and laugh and have a good time.

Diana looks drop dead gorgeous. After dinner, the guys and I dropped her and Johanna off at their house to get ready. We picked her up an hour later, once we were ready to head out. She's wearing a thin blue slip of a dress that shows off her killer legs and the gentle slope of her neck. Her shoes are thick wedge sandals that raise her about five inches off the ground. This puts the top of her head in line with my shoulders, so when she hugs me, she tucks in directly beneath my chin.

I hold her close, breathing in the comforting scent of her perfume.

"What's gotten into you?" She laughs, stepping back and hugging her arms to her chest.

Her.

Also, I went home and jacked off, and now I'm feeling

even better. After the intensity of the game, I needed that release. It didn't satisfy me, though; it gave me a desire for more.

With her. Nobody else. I don't want anyone else, so why should I bother pretending?

I open my mouth, gearing up to blurt everything out.

This is it. This is the moment. Our entire friendship is about to change. How can it not?

Instead, I hold out my hand. She stares at it for a few moments before she slides her hand into mine.

It's like coming home. Like falling into bed and finding the mattress is already warm and cozy. Like fitting the last piece of a jigsaw into place. Like my hand was meant to hold hers.

The Delta party is the place to be on a Friday night. We have a pretty decent crowd: Miles and Sam, Tucker and Mason, Greg, Amir, and Mackenzie, Miles's sister, a freshman this year. The only one who didn't want to come tonight was Wes, who mumbled something under his breath and turned back to his book. He doesn't socialize much—or at all, except under duress. He doesn't really talk to anyone that's not part of the football team. I don't begrudge him his silences; we all have our own shit to deal with.

And tonight, I have to keep my hands off of Diana. She looks good enough to eat in that silky slip of a dress. I'm so afraid that one of these days I'm going to slip up and blurt out how I feel about her. I love her. I love her so much it physically hurts. And we're just friends.

I won't be content with only one night. I don't want a casual hookup with her: I want forever. I want a lifetime with her, a real relationship. A chance at happiness. Something like what her parents have, nothing even close for the farce of a marriage my parents have.

And I know she is nowhere even close to being able to process that. Not with her dad… I don't want to set us up for failure, and if I made a move now, I would be dooming us to failure. She can't give me what I want, not at this point in our lives.

I want to pull out her hair tie and watch her messy waves fall in a riotous cloud over her shoulders. I want to pull her close and taste her eggplant painted lips. I want to map the curves of her body with my hands and then with my tongue. I want—

I want what I can't have.

The Delta house is crammed full of people. I hate the way frat houses always stink... like, who wants to smell cheap Axe body spray and secondhand smoke? To me, it smells like the place where hymens are broken and people are trash... okay, that might be a little inflammatory, but with the amount of testosterone surging through me right now, I feel like I can tackle anyone and anything.

As we make our way through the party, Diana's hand in mine grounds me, anchoring me. I lead her to the living room, where the kegs are set up.

"Want one?" I ask her, and she nods.

As a group, we make an impressive figure, all of us big and wide defensemen cutting through the crowd. People part for us, letting us through.

We assemble Sam, Mack, Mason, and Diana in a corner with Amir to watch over them. The rest of the guys and I push through the crowd to the kegs.

Sullivan, our safety, has a girl on each arm. He's whispering into one's ear as the other strokes his face, trying to get his attention. He nods to us and goes back to his girls of the evening.

People move aside to let us through. Being a football player does have its perks sometimes. We fill cups at the keg. They don't blink an eye when I fill a second cup.

There's some guy angling close to Diana when I get back. I glare at him, and he scampers away.

She pouts up to me, her hands on her hips. "I was talking to him."

"He's a waste of your time," I tell her, handing her a cup.

"You don't know that."

"I do. He's an idiot. You deserve better."

Me. Pick me. Choose me.

She takes a sip of her beer. "Thank you for deciding that on my behalf." She rolls her eyes.

"If you want to hook up, I won't stop you." I'll just wish I could. "That's not my place. You know your own mind."

She blinks up at me. "So, if I wanted to take someone home with me tonight?"

"I won't stop you. I'll just ask you if you're sure."

Her eyes are dark, lined with and shadowed, making them look bigger and bolder than usual. Her lashes are impossibly long. I like her like this, all done up, but I also like her fresh-faced and sweaty after a workout, her cheeks pink from exertion.

"And if I wanted to go home with one of your friends?"

A sick feeling punches me in the stomach. Greg has been all over her lately, hugging on her and kissing her cheek. Amir keeps smiling at her like there's a secret only the two of them share. Even Wes has glanced up from his book to check her out.

"It's not my place to object," I finally tell her.

Diana winks at me. "Don't worry, I know better than to sleep with your best friends."

I cover my heavy sigh of relief with a sip of my beer.

It's not like I've been a monk all these years. I've hooked up. I've had flings. I've always kept emotions out of it. But ever since the day Diana called me up and said she would be transferring to Newton, I've dialed it back to none. It's been a lonely six months since her visit last spring break.

Especially with Miles and Tucker settling down into relationships. For the first time, I'm well aware of what I'm missing out on. Meaningless sex doesn't satisfy my soul in the way it used to. I know what's out there now.

I know she's not perfect. Nobody is. But she's perfect for me.

I just wish she knew that.

nine

. . .

Barrett

WHAT STARTS out as a drink or two turns into five or six. Diana and I have only gone out drinking once, over spring break last year, and she was perfectly capable of holding her liquor when we went out to the pub. I didn't think twice about pouring her an extra cup or two. She knows what she can handle.

Tonight, though… tonight, she is wasted. Straight up trashed. She's stumbling, wavering on her feet. She sags against me, and I wrap my arms around her waist, helping to hold her upright. Diana giggles, burying her face in my chest.

"You're so cuddly," she exclaims, burrowing into me like she wants to wear my skin as her own. "I love how cuddly you are now."

Greg meets my eye, snickering. Asshole.

"Just for you, baby," I tell her, setting her back on her own two feet. I keep my hand on her back, holding onto her for as long as she can tolerate.

"I like this new you," she says. She walks her fingers up the center of my shirt, poking each of the buttons. "I like that you touch me."

Greg laughs outright.

"Only for you." I don't know what I'm saying. I've had a few, yeah, but I'm still mostly sober. I'm drunk on her. I need to watch out for her. One of us needs to stay in control. Tonight, that will be me.

Diana pats my cheek. "I like you."

"I like you, too, baby." So much. So, so much. Something almost like hope blooms deep within my chest. Maybe she has feelings for me. Maybe she—

"I'm really glad we're friends," she says.

And there's the crushing blow.

"Me, too," I tell her, because I am glad to have her in my life, in whatever way she'll allow. Even if it's not the way I would like.

I've loved her from afar for the last six years. I can keep on loving her from a distance for the rest of forever. I would rather have a piece of her heart than have her disappear from my life entirely. I don't think I could survive having her and then losing her in a breakup.

Tucker and Mason are hanging out with a group of her track friends. Sam and Miles are talking with a bunch of her sorority sisters. Greg and Amir disappear into the den where a group of guys are playing video games, which is where I would normally hang out. I don't want to sit around with a bunch of smelly dudes when I could be spending time with Diana. Even if she's completely sauced.

She takes my hand in hers. "Barrett."

"Yeah?"

"You're Barrett," she says, and then she giggles. She stumbles, and I catch her again. "Love you."

My heart hammers in my chest like I've just done fifty suicide sprints in full gear.

Diana groans. "I don't feel so good."

"Do you want to get out of here?"

She nods. "Can we get cheese fries?"

"Yeah, baby," I tell her, wrapping my arm around her

shoulder and steering her towards the door. "Whatever you want."

Outside, the wind rustles through the trees. Diana shivers and burrows into my chest, her arm around my waist.

I know she's drunk. I know she's not in her right mind. But a part of me really likes when she clings to me, when she trusts in me to get her where she needs to be. She knows she's safe with me. I don't take that trust lightly.

We walk through Greek Row. Well, I walk. She prances ahead of me. She doesn't know where we're going. Twice she tries to lead me up to another frat house. Calmly, I redirect her to the sidewalk. It almost feels like she's a small dog going for walkies or a toddler trying to crawl out of a stroller.

It's about a mile to the main drag of town, and another half a mile down the road to the nearest diner. As we approach the street, I take her hand in mine again and lace our fingers together. I don't want her to get too far ahead of me, not with all the cars on the road.

The diner is a greasy hole in the wall hidden between a bookstore and a coffee shop. It's dirty and grimy and perfect. Diana and I settle in a booth near the middle of the place. It's decently crowded for just past midnight on a Saturday night.

Her eyes are hazy, her mouth twisted by a lazy grin.

"I'm drunk," she says, and then she laughs.

"Yeah, you are."

"I'm sorry you had to leave the party early to take care of me."

"I'd do anything for you." I hope she can't hear the desperation in my voice.

Diana frowns, studying her hands, clasped together on the table in front of her. "I'm so glad we're friends, Bare. I don't know that I'd be able to do this without you."

"Do what?"

"This." She waves her hand. "School. Newton. My dad."

The elephant in the room. Her dad isn't going to get better; it's only downhill from here.

"Yeah. How are you doing with all of that?"

Her face crumples. "Not well."

Shit.

I slide out of the booth and onto her side. There's barely enough room for the two of us. She clings to me, her hand fisted in my shirt, her head on my chest.

"I'm really not doing well," she says to my shirt. "This fucking sucks."

"I know, honey, I know." I hold her close and stroke a hand over her hair. "I'm so sorry you have to go through all of this. I'm so sorry your dad is—"

She hiccups.

A waitress approaches, popping her gum. "What can I get ya?"

"Oh, um…" She hasn't so much as looked at a menu.

Luckily, I've been here a time or two, and I know what she likes.

"Two bacon cheeseburgers, please, with all the fixings, and two orders of cheese fries," I say. "And a chocolate milkshake."

"You got it." She pops her gum. "Anything else?"

"That'll be great, thank you."

Diana buries her face in my chest. "I don't want to face the real world. Wake me up when the food gets here."

Laughing, I tighten my arms around her and stroke over her hair again. "Sure thing."

We sit in quiet silence for a few minutes. The diner is busy with the sounds of people eating and talking, laughing. We're in a little cocoon of peace and calm in the midst of the storm.

Finally, Diana clears her throat and pulls away. "I think I'm okay now."

"You sure?"

She nods, rubbing at her eyes. "I will be."

As much as I don't want to, I know I need to pull away. I take my seat on the opposite side of the booth, folding my hands on the table.

The waitress drops off the milkshake and the extra canister with two straws. I push the glass towards her and stick my straw in the leftovers.

"For me?" She looks so surprised.

"Yeah, drunk-o, for you," I laugh. "It'll help sober you up."

Her face melts into a smile. "Thanks, Bare." She sucks on the straw and sighs happily. "Oh, that's good."

I like making her smile. I like making her happy. I'll do whatever it takes to make her feel good.

"What do you have planned for tomorrow?"

She groans. "Nothing."

"There's a pilates class at the ASC that the guys and I like to go to."

Diana grins. "You've been going to pilates without me?"

She's the reason I started going. In high school, she used to drag me to class with her every Saturday I spent at her house, and with her all the way across the country… well, it was my way of staying connected to her, to our memories.

"Sometimes we do yoga instead. It just depends on what classes are offered every weekend."

She folds her hand around her milkshake. "Who else goes with you?"

"Tucker and Mason, some of her friends, and Amir and Wes," I list. Miles hasn't yet joined us, but I don't think he's avoiding it; it's just not something he particularly cares about.

"Not Greg?"

My stomach swoops. She's mentioned my gregarious roommate more than once. He's always all over her. Does she have a thing for him?

"We're not excluding him, he just hasn't joined us," I

explain, cautiously. "He and Miles are always invited to come with."

"Good. I like Greg," she says, and my heart skips a beat.

"You like him?"

She sucks noisily on her milkshake. "Yeah. He's always gone out of his way to be nice to me. He treats me like a person, not just your friend that's hanging around."

I frown. "You're not—"

"I know I'm not," she says. "But that doesn't mean everyone treats me like—"

"Who?" I demand. "Who is treating you like you're less than?"

"Nobody."

"Diana."

"I'm talking about high school, about way back when," she says with a frown. "Your brother is a dick."

"Yeah, I know he is. He made you feel—?"

"It's fine," she says. "He can act however he wants. I know better. I know you, I know us."

"Diana…"

"Here we are." The waitress arrives at the worst possible time with our food. She sets the two groaning plates in front of each of us.

She grins at me, her eyes glassy. "How did you know exactly what I needed?"

"Contrary to popular belief, I have met you a time or two before," I tell her, and she rolls her eyes.

"You're the best, Bare," she says. A warm glow spreads through me.

"You're just saying that because I ordered you food."

"Yes."

She reaches for the bottle of ketchup, and I hand it to her. The tips of her fingertips brush mine. Sparks fly down my spine, coalescing deep in my gut.

She liberally coats her fries in ketchup like a heathen. I pick up my burger and take a hearty bite. Even though we have a little more leeway on game days, a double bacon cheeseburger is definitely not part of the diet plan. Tomorrow it's back to oatmeal, eggs, lean chicken, and protein shakes. For now, though... I take another bite.

"What do you have planned for tomorrow?"

I cringe. "Dinner with my parents."

Her face falls. "Oh. I'm sorry."

"Yeah, I'm not too thrilled, either."

As much as I'd like to invite her along for moral support, I know that it would only hurt her. My mother is cruel and my father apathetic at best and dismissive at worst, making him a real peach to be around. Neither of them are fans of Diana. They don't like that she is middle class, that she's half-Black, that she's an athlete. Hell, they don't like that my brother and I are athletes, either. They don't like much of anything.

Nothing is ever good enough for the Zhangs. Nothing pleases them. They don't care about my amazing performance on the football field or Dougie's feats on the ice. They don't even care when I get straight As in my accounting classes, because I go to a second-rate school in their eyes. Dougie went to Harvard—on a hockey scholarship, no less. He's at Brown now, working on his MBA. He got the Ivy League memo I ignored in favor of a football coach I liked and a relatively decent public accounting program.

I want to take a year or two off before I go to business school. I want to work, get my feet wet in the field. There's no doubt about it: I'm going into forensic accounting, just like everyone else in my family. I have no qualms about that.

I know it will be harder to go back to school after time away. I've heard the horror stories. But I need a break from... this. Studying all the time, trying to balance school and extracurriculars, having basically no life outside of the gym...

This is my last season of football ever. I don't think I'll join a pickup league—that's not my scene. After this year, I'm done. So I'm going to enjoy it while it lasts, savor each and every moment, and then I'm going to move on.

Diana slurps on her milkshake. My half is already long gone.

"Feeling better?" I ask her.

She lifts a shoulder. "I guess. I wasn't feeling bad."

"Just drunk."

She laughs. "Yeah. It hit me harder than I expected. I don't think I drank enough water today."

"We can fix that." I make eye contact with the waitress, who heads our way. "Can we get some more water, please?"

"Sure thing, hon." She disappears, returning with a pitcher of water. She refills both of our glasses and, after a moment, leaves the pitcher and the check with us. "Take your time, no rush."

"Thanks." I offer her a tight smile. It might be more like a grimace as I reach for my wallet. I don't care about paying the bill, that's not the issue. I'm fucking exhausted. I didn't sleep well last night, worried about the game, and then I expended a fuck ton of energy on the field. My body is battered and bruised.

Still, if my options are spending time with Diana, or going back to my empty bed alone… I know what I'm choosing—every fucking time.

———

My parents are not what I would consider warm and fuzzy people. They're more preoccupied with the family business and their reputation than in my actual life. Which usually suits me just fine.

The jitters set in once I get out of the car. My body needs to bleed off the pent-up adrenaline that built up over the course of the evening. It's late, almost eleven o'clock at night.

As I walk through Athlete's Village, my feet don't take me home. Somehow I end up standing on the soccer team's front porch, my heart in my throat. It's late, and tomorrow is their first game: all the lights are off.

Pulling my phone out of my pocket, I dial the first number that comes up on my favorites list.

Diana answers on the second ring. "Barrett? It's late."

"Did I wake you up?"

"No. I was about to turn in, though."

"Can you…" I clear my throat. "Can you come downstairs?"

Her light clicks on upstairs, casting a bright shadow over the front lawn. "You're here?"

"I just need to see you."

There's a rustling on her end. Another light clicks on inside the house—the hall light.

"I'll be right there," she promises, hanging up the call. The absence of her presence on the line hurts almost as much as the torture of the evening.

A light turns on in the living room and then Diana is opening the door. She's wearing an oversized t-shirt—one she stole from me—and a pair of short black spandex shorts, her hair tied up in protective braids. She hugs her arms over her chest.

"What happened?"

I swallow. "Dinner. With my parents."

She sighs, nodding in understanding. In three steps, I've crossed the lawn to get to her. I wrap my arms around her and hold her tightly to me. Slowly her arms come up around me, wrapping around my torso. She lets out a heavy sigh.

"It went that well?"

"Worse. They didn't so much as ask how I'm doing. They didn't make small talk. They just… didn't care. It's not like I expected any different. It's always like this. Somehow, tonight it hurts more."

Diana's arms tighten around me. "Oh, Barrett."

"I'm fine," I lie. "I'll be fine. I just—I need—" I bury my face in her hair.

I should be used to it. This isn't new to me. My brother and I were always the only kids who didn't have anyone in the stands, not even a housekeeper, because they didn't stick around long enough to care about us. My friends at least had nannies and maids who showed up in lieu of their parents, caring about them even if their parents didn't. We didn't have that. We didn't have anything.

Except money. That, we have plenty of. But money can't buy happiness, and it can't buy love.

Having Diana in my arms helps. Being able to hold her, to touch her, to see her face in person and not over a video chat… it could be worse. She could still be on the opposite side of the country. She could still be a plane ride away. Instead, she lives three blocks over and answers my call on the second ring, even when it's past her bedtime and she has her first soccer game of the season tomorrow.

"I'll be there tomorrow afternoon," I tell her now. "With bells on."

She laughs, her face pressed to my neck. Her soft breath puffs against my skin and sends tingles down my spine. "You don't have to come."

"Are you kidding? Your first game at Newton? Of course I have to be there."

"I'm just, if you have something else to do…"

Pulling back, I look her in the eye. "The only thing I have to do is be there and support you, the way you've supported me all these years." Her eyes are bright, and I have to swallow at the pent-up emotions bubbling under my skin, threatening to overwhelm me. "I will always be there for you, Dee. I'd move heaven and earth to get to you."

It's her turn to swallow. She hugs me to her this time.

"Love you, Bare," she says into my neck.

It's like a punch to the gut. She loves me. Just not in the way I'd like her to.

"Love you, too, Dee."

ten

. . .

Diana

TODAY IS THE DAY: our first game. I'm jittery with nervous anticipation. All day long, my stomach flutters with equal parts excitement and dread.

As much as I hate how much Barrett was torn up over his parents, I kind of like that he was there for me last night. I hugged away all my doubts and fears at the same time I assuaged his. He's stuck between a rock and a hard place, and it's not going to get better; if anything, it will only get worse for him as he approaches graduation and joins his father's company.

I can hardly focus in my classes. I hope Tucker took good notes today, because I don't think I retained any of the lecture.

Because of my class schedule, I don't see any of my teammates until two o'clock, when we gather in the locker room to change and get ready. Johanna is stoic and silent, a vast departure from her usual bubbly self. Rosie, Rachel, Rebecca, and Robin are similarly quiet. It's eerie. I've never been in such a quiet locker room before a game, especially before the first game of the season. They should be loud and excited, amping each other up. Not… dreading it.

I've played in big games before. Playoffs, championships.

It's different when everyone is quiet because they're focused on the important game. This is a complete lack of enthusiasm. It's like everyone has already decided that we're going to lose this game and there's no reason to get excited over it.

I can only worry about me, so I do my usual game prep. Stretching. Meditation. Visualization.

Even Coach Larsen is apathetic. Her pump up speech lacks the enthusiasm I've come to expect from coaches. She's serious, focused, but doesn't seem to care if we win or lose.

I don't get it. Why does nobody give a shit?

The crowd is decidedly lukewarm. Maybe it's the team's losing record over the last few years. Maybe it's the team itself—they recognize how unenthusiastic the players are, and are matching their lack of excitement.

The only people who seem to be having fun are the contingent of football players in the front row, right at the center of the field. Doing a quick count on a warm up lap around the field, I count six football players—Barrett, Miles, Tucker, Wes, Amir, and Greg, plus Sam and Mason. They're cheering and waving navy and silver pom-poms, having a good time.

"Go Dee!" Barrett yells. "You've got this!"

"Let's go, Newton!" chimes in Greg. He does a little shimmy in his seat, which makes me laugh.

Johanna looks over at me in disgust. "Can you please focus?"

I'm perfectly capable of multitasking. I can have a good time while I prepare for the game ahead. I can interact with our fans and still have a good game.

What I can't do is abide people treating me poorly for something I haven't done. So, ignoring the team captain, I turn and wave back to my new friends, who hoot and holler at the acknowledgement.

Yeah, my new team is fucking weird. My teammates are kind of awful. But I'm making friends, and they're pretty damn awesome.

The game starts out slowly. Although the other team is ranked low in the conference, they're at least three spots higher than us in the pre-season poll. As a transfer player, I expect to get minimal playing time as Coach cycles through the veterans.

Bea easily stops the first attempt at a goal then fumbles the rebound, and they score in the top right corner. Three minutes into the game, and we're already down a goal.

It only gets worse from there.

I'm trying my hardest, but I can't defend the entire backfield singlehandedly. Despite being the new person on the team, I play the most minutes out of the rest of the defense, almost as much as two of the left sweepers combined. The sun sets and the stadium lights come up. Half the meager crowd leaves at halftime, when the score is 0-3.

I keep expecting someone, anyone, to rally the troops. Johanna is the captain. Coach Larsen is in charge. The coaching staff is supremely qualified. So why is nobody giving a lecture or even an acknowledgement that we're playing like shit? Nobody wants to try to change things. Nobody wants to put in any more effort than they already have.

Never have I ever played on a losing team. I've lost games, yeah. I've lost in important matches. But never have I played for a team that just didn't give a fuck, and made that lack of interest known to the entire world. Why are they even on the team if they don't care? Why do we practice every day and do suicide sprints and work out all the damn time if not to put in our best efforts on the field?

———

When I finally emerge from the locker room, it's to find Barrett and his friends waiting for us. His smile is tinged with sadness as he opens his arms to me.

"Hey, Dee."

Right now, I need a hug. So I step into my best friend's arms and let him hold me for a moment.

"You played well," he says quietly, so softly only I can hear, and I can't hide my snort of derision. "You did. You were great. The rest of your team..." He chuckles, the sound laced with bitterness.

Clinging to him, I bury my face in his sternum and inhale the scent of him, honey and musk and a little bit of sweat from sitting in the heat for the last few hours.

"I don't want to go through that again," I admit, and he sighs. His hand cups the back of my head.

"I don't blame you."

"Can we just erase the last two hours?"

"I would if I could," he promises, tightening his arms around me.

At long last, I feel mostly confident enough to face the real world again. I step back and immediately mourn the loss of contact. Clearing my throat, I turn my attention to the rest of the group assembled behind him: Miles and Sam, Tucker and Mason, Wes, Amir, Greg, and Mackenzie, all wearing Newton gear and showing up for the most depressing game ever.

"Thanks for coming, guys. Wish it was a better result for you."

Sam gives me a cheery smile. "You'll get 'em next time."

"I'm sure you're hungry," Barrett says. "Do you want to go to the ASC, or do you want to go into town?"

I lift a shoulder in an apathetic shrug. "You decide. I don't have the mental energy."

He nods. "To town it is." He grabs my bag from my loose grip and throws it over his shoulder, then tosses his arm around my shoulder. "All right, guys. We're heading to Avila's. It's been decided."

Wes grunts. His light green eyes are fixated on Barrett's arm around me.

"Yes, you're all invited, too. Sorry. I thought I made that clear," he adds.

Miles gives a tight smile. "Sounds like fun."

"I could eat," Amir says.

Greg grins and scratches at his beard. "Count me in."

Wes nods and tucks his book into his backpack.

So we head into town for dinner. Barrett keeps his arm around me, steering me into unfamiliar territory. He doesn't push me to talk about the game—he knows I'm not in the mood to recap the single worst game I've ever played in, and that includes losing 0-5 in the conference finals two years ago. This was infinitely worse.

The customize your own burrito bar is bright and cheery and, at eight o'clock on a Tuesday night in the second week of classes, still fairly crowded. Barrett maneuvers into the line ahead of me. I spy him handing his credit card over to the cashier and roll my eyes. He thinks he's being stealthy, buying my dinner. If he wants to throw his money at me, I won't object: I don't have that much spare cash, and especially now, I can't ask my parents for money.

The intense demands of my soccer schedule mean I can't balance a job, school, and sports, especially not during my fifth and final year of a double major. Am I a bad person if I let my best friend—whose family is loaded—pay for me every once in a while? I wouldn't hesitate to return the favor if the situation was reversed. I'm not best friends with the guy because he has money. We're friends in spite of his family's wealth.

The guys push two tables together so the ten of us can sit together. Naturally, they all gravitate into the same positions they take in the dining hall: Wes and Mack on the end, Barrett and me next to her and Amir and Greg across from them. To Barrett's right are Tucker and Mason, and across from them are Miles and Sam, who looks content sandwiched between her boyfriend and Greg.

Mack gives me a small smile. "Thank you for inviting me. I had a lot of fun."

I raise my eyebrows. "You enjoyed the game?"

"Well, no," she laughs nervously. "But the guys made it fun. I'm just glad to be included. My new roommate is… well, I'm happy not to be in my dorm right now."

This makes me laugh. "I'm right there with you. My roommates are the worst. If you ever want to hang out, I'm game."

I don't care that she's a freshman and I'm a fifth-year senior. She's Miles's sister and, more than that, she's new to school in the same way I am, and the same way Mason was last year. Us new girls have to stick together.

And I have the benefit of my friendship with Barrett to fall back on. She doesn't. She has her brother and a bad roommate and, presumably, her teammates.

Across the table, Wes is reading his book, though I can't be the only person who notices how often his eyes travel off the page and onto the woman sitting across from him. She doesn't seem to notice, playing on her phone. With a jolt, I realize she's reading—they're both reading.

I set my hand on Barrett's leg to get his attention and his whole body goes tense. He practically jumps out of his seat. Quickly, I remove my hand. Note to self: not a good idea.

He turns to look at me. "Yeah?"

Half the table is looking at us now. "Never mind," I say, shaking my head.

"Dee."

"Tell you later." I take a giant bite out of my burrito.

He frowns, his eyes wary as he scoops a chip and guac into his mouth.

"It's not important."

"It is."

"It's really not."

"Diana."

I don't want to embarrass Mack and Wes, but I want to

squeal from how cute they are and what a good couple they would make. Except I've already been warned that Wes doesn't date, and he especially doesn't like to be touched. The grunting and monosyllables as his main form of communication are a defense mechanism—a defense against what, it hasn't been explained, and it's not my place to push.

Barrett seems to finally understand that I'm not going to tell him, at least not right now when Wes and Mack are within earshot—she's *right* next to me. He puts a handful of his chips on my plate and pushes his container of guacamole into the space between our plates.

"Thanks," I say lightly, and he quirks a smile at me.

"Anytime."

Somehow, I get the feeling he's not talking about sharing his dinner with me. It's something deeper, something I can't decipher.

"So, I kind of need this favor," I start, and then I pause for a deep breath. "It would really help me out. It would make my life so much easier."

"Done. Whatever you need," Barrett says instantly.

"You haven't even heard what I need yet."

"I'll do it," he says. "It will help you out, so I'll do it."

I just have to take my shot. I can't beat around the bush anymore.

"So you'll go on a date with my team captain?"

Barrett chokes. He erupts into a coughing fit. His face goes red as he struggles to breathe.

I pound on his back, and he twitches away from me.

"Diana."

"See, Johanna has a crush on you," I blurt.

"Johanna?" His eyebrows raise sky-high. "You mean the girl that's been making your life miserable the last two weeks?"

"Yeah?"

He swallows hard. "You want me to go on a date with Johanna?"

"She likes you. She's practically obsessed with you."

"Great. So she's a stalker."

"I wouldn't say stalker. More… fan. She knew your stats off the top of her head without having to look them up."

He makes a face.

"She's really pretty."

Here, he shoots me a deadpan 'you've got to be kidding me' look.

"And she really likes you, and it would be great for me to set the two of you up. She's totally into you."

"So you're whoring me out with a woman I've only met once, but I've heard countless of terrible stories about, and maybe I should remind you, you only met her two weeks ago."

I nod. That's about right.

Barrett lets out a bitter laugh. "Okay. Yeah. Right. Sure. Let's do this."

"You're going to do it?"

"I promised you I would do anything for you," he says lightly, but his eyes are dark and haunted.

I throw my arms around him, and he tenses in my grasp. Slowly, painfully slowly, he wraps his arms around me and holds me tight.

eleven

. . .

Barrett

JOHANNA IS… a lot. I'm not exactly sure why I'm here, except for the fact that I'm a sucker for pretty much anything my best friend asks me to do. So this girl has a crush on me. Okay. It seems pretty cruel to lead her on. I'm not about to suddenly fall head over heels for her because we go out one time for coffee.

Still, Diana asked, and it means a lot to her, so I'm doing it. This will make her life easier. Her team captain is capable of making her life a living hell. She's already been an unwelcoming bitch to her in the first two weeks of school. I'll do whatever I can to make her transition here easier.

Even if I have absolutely no interest in her.

Johanna is slightly shorter than Diana and equally fit, lithe and limber with firmly packed muscles. She has a ski-jump nose and slightly upturned monolids. Her long, dark hair falls halfway down her back in soft waves. They're not natural curls, like Diana's—she's styled her hair this way. All in all, she's pretty with nice features, and I'm sure one day she'll find a guy who appreciates her. I'm not that guy. I'll never be that guy.

Because all I can think about is how she compares to my best friend, the person who set us up.

Standing in line at the coffee shop, she rattles off her London fog latte order with ruthless efficiency, and I order a vanilla iced latte, light ice, out of habit. It's something I started drinking after Diana ordered me one, and unexpectedly I fell in love with it nearly as easily as I fell in love with her. Now it's my favorite drink, and not only because it reminds me of her.

Being the gentleman who was manipulated into this farce of a date, I wave away Johanna's attempt to pay and cover both of our drinks and a small fruit and cheese plate. If nothing else, the snack will give us something to do with our hands aside from sitting there fidgeting. Or is that just me?

"So…"

"We should sit down," she announces. She makes a beeline for a small table and chairs near the unlit fireplace in the back. Romantic and cozy. Great. I'm not sure the spindly little chair will hold my weight. It creaks out a warning as I sit down.

"So, Barrett…"

I look her in the eye. She holds the contact, confident, her spine straight and sure.

"Johanna."

She flushes pink, and her eyes dart away from mine. "It's nice to meet you. Officially, I mean."

I ignore the fact that we've met on at least three occasions now: when I dropped Diana off at her house the other night, after the football game, and at their game the other day.

"Likewise."

"You and Diana, you've known each other a long time?"

"She's my best friend," I say honestly. "We've been friends since we were eight years old. We met at summer camp and stayed in touch ever since."

She nods. "How fortunate that you are able to attend the same school."

A pang of bitterness ricochets through me. Diana was offered a full ride scholarship here five years ago. If she had taken it, she would have been here with me all this time. If she hadn't gone to USC, we wouldn't have had to spend four years in a long distance friendship.

But USC was the right choice for her at the time, and I can't begrudge her for taking a chance at what was best for her. Just because I wanted her here with me didn't mean she wanted to stay. And if she had, who's to say we would still be friends now? I like to think we would. I like to think our friendship could survive pretty much anything that gets thrown at it.

"It's pretty great to have her here," I finally say, because I still can't believe she's in town for good—or at least until graduation.

Johanna goes quiet. Things are tense between them, I know. I don't pretend to understand the politics behind it, but from what has been explained to me, Johanna is the team captain and queen bee and used to getting her way. Diana being here—also of Chinese descent, gorgeous, brilliant, and an all around awesome person—threatens her position at the top of the team's social pyramid.

Even though Diana has no interest in toppling the current hierarchy. She only wants to fit in and make friends, not waves. She's never cared about social politics. She wants to have a good time and be able to kick back with her girls, and if she isn't in the mood to spend time with them because she's doing something else, it isn't the end of the world.

Somehow I don't think Johanna is nearly as chill.

The waiter brings over our coffees—in to-go cups, thankfully—and the small fruit and cheese plate. It's not much, but it will give us something to do with our hands.

I don't know what to say. I don't know this woman very

well, and the few things I've heard about her haven't exactly been complementary. All I know is that she's interested in me. And while I'm flattered, I don't return the interest, especially after having met her again. She's pretty. I'm sure she's nice.

But she's not Diana.

I take a deep breath and meet her eyes. "I need to be honest with you. I don't want to lead you on or anything."

She looks at me sadly. "This wasn't your idea, was it?"

Slowly, I shake my head. "I'm sorry. I wish it were different."

"You really care about her."

I don't pretend to misunderstand who she's talking about. "She's my best friend."

Johanna sighs. "No. You *really* like her."

My cheeks heat. "Is it that obvious?"

"Well, you're on a date with me because of her grand idea, so…"

So, no, she has no idea. My stomach churns. I take a sip of my iced coffee, and it does little to soothe the ache deep inside of me.

"We can be friends. We should try to be friends, because of Diana."

Her laugh is bitter. "Nothing personal, but I'm not really interested in being your friend. Sure, you're a great guy, but I want more, and I have enough self respect not to go for a guy who is obviously interested in someone else."

"You don't even know me."

"You're Barrett Zhang." She blinks. "Tell me what there is to know about you."

My stomach twists. I've come across this before. She wants Barrett Zhang, scion of the Zhang family and football player and all around Good Guy, the wealthy son of a prosperous Chinese family who does good in the community. She doesn't want me, Barrett, the guy who barely has his head on straight some days and can't turn his homework in on time and sweats at the vaguest mention of spicy peppers. She doesn't want the guy who is in love with his best friend and too chicken to do anything about it.

I've dated before. I've hooked up. I've gone home with random women, or taken them back to my place for a night. I've never had a girlfriend before. It always felt like a line that shouldn't be crossed. No matter how much I might appreciate the woman in my bed for a few nights, in the back of my mind, I'm always comparing her to Diana. I've never met a woman who even comes close in comparison. There has never been anyone who succeeded in making me forget about her.

As soon as it was confirmed she was coming here, I stopped hooking up. I stopped taking women home. That seemed like a boundary I shouldn't cross. The soccer team has always been off limits on the off chance she came here. And now that she's here, I'm incredibly grateful. It would supremely suck if she had to live with and play on the same team with someone I've been with. I would never want to make her uncomfortable.

I'm not some Casanova playboy; I'm human, I'm twenty-two, and I'm fallible. When I got to college, I made the decision to live my life and not pine obnoxiously for a woman on the other side of the country who has never, not once, intimated that she wanted to be intimate with me. It's not like there was a line of people waiting to sleep with me: I'm big, I'm not white, and I was entirely inexperienced, which is not an ideal combination in attracting women, even with being a football player at an elite school.

The other players took me under their wing and taught me how to party, how to talk to women, how to be a mostly functional adult amidst all the challenges of being part of a team and not being able to play for a year as a redshirt. They kept me out of trouble when the boredom set in. The team wanted me to put on weight for a year and learn the plays, so I did. I studied. I got stronger.

Most of those guys are gone now, graduated or doing other things with their lives. One guy was drafted into the NFL late in the seventh round two years ago. He made the practice roster and was cut before the season started. I'm not sure what he's doing now.

The guys I live with now are great. We get along well. Occasionally Amir, Greg, and I will go out to a frat party on a Saturday night, but the three of us are just as happy with a quiet night in watching a movie or playing video games. It's a good fit. Until recently, Miles and Tucker were both social recluses—since they've started dating their respective girlfriends, slowly their social lives have gotten more interesting. Wes is still an antisocial recluse who barely ever looks up from his books, and I don't see that changing anytime soon.

"I'm just a regular guy," I tell her.

"Whose family is loaded," she points out. "Your parents are—"

I'm nothing like my family. Sure, we have the same name and genetics, but that's the only thing we have in common. We might as well be strangers.

I clear my throat. "I hope we can keep everything civil, at the very least."

Johanna rolls her eyes. "Yeah, sure, whatever. I'm not, like, heartbroken or anything. This was clearly a setup. I'm not going to cry myself to sleep over it."

Even though I know she's trying to cover up her own disappointment at being rejected, her casual dismissal still stings. "Right."

She shrugs. "I'm not going to waste my time."

I've never really dated. Sure, I've gone out with women. I've taken them to bed. But I've purposefully never entered into a relationship. How could I, when I compared every single woman I met to the one I can never have?

"Well, it's been swell," Johanna says bitterly. She pushes back her chair. "See you… never."

"I'll still be at all of the games," I remind her. I'm there for Diana—not for her.

She makes a face. "I'd really rather you weren't."

"That's not your call."

"You distract her," she says.

"I support her. I'm there to cheer her on."

"Is that what you're doing?" she asks. "Or are you just lying to yourself?"

twelve

. . .

Diana

SCHOOL FALLS INTO A ROUTINE—A grueling course load with afternoons dotted by soccer practice and dinners with Barrett and his friends, mandatory workouts, and silent dinners with my teammates where nobody so much as acknowledges me at the house. We have an away game at Providence, and I room with Robin who doesn't speak to me the entire time, and of course we lose, so everyone's in a stellar mood on the bus ride home.

When we get back on Saturday afternoon, it's halfway through Barrett's game at Northern Maine, which isn't televised outside of the city limits of Presque Isle, so I can't even watch him play, and that puts me in an even worse mood. He wins his game, at least.

Sam texts me after the game ends, and Sunday after lunch, we meet up at the football training center to wait for the buses to pull in. Mackenzie, Miles's sister, has joined us to make an awkward trio.

I'm not sure what to make of Sam. Though she's been friendly enough to my face, this is the first time she's reached out to me to initiate a conversation in my three weeks on campus. Then again, we don't really have anything in common outside of my friendship and her relationship with the football players.

Mason and I at least have half a dozen things in common: being biracial, transfer students, psych majors… I like her so far, we have breakfast together a few days a week, and I like Tucker after sitting beside him in class for three weeks. I'm making friends in my own right. I'm trying to make friends. I don't want Barrett to freak out and think I'm stealing all of his toys for myself.

There are about a dozen or so other people waiting for the guys, mostly women about our age, although there is an older male couple that are probably someone's parents and a few photographers who look to be from the school paper.

Barrett steps off the bus. I know the second he sees me because his face erupts into an ear to ear smile. Instead of following everyone to the underbelly of the bus for his bag, he makes his way over to me. Before I know what's happening, he tugs me forward into a sweaty hug.

"Hey!"

"Hi," he says, his face pressed into my hair. "Missed you."

My chest pangs. "Me, too."

It's funny how we survived so many years of long distance friendship so easily with regular phone calls, texting, and the occasional video chat, but now that we're getting used to spending time together every day, four days away from each other is too much. Even with texting constantly on first my road trip and then his, it's not the same as being together in person. Seeing him again, being in his presence, all of my worries and anxieties melt away. It's like a sense of calm has settled over me, soothing my ruffled feathers in one slow exhale. I can do anything as long as I have Barrett by my side.

"Yo! Zhang!" a voice calls. "Come get your shit!"

He sighs. "Be right back."

Slowly, he steps back and disentangles his limbs from

mine. Beside us, Sam and Miles are making out, his hands buried in her hair. Tucker has his hands in his pockets, looking forlorn—Mason is at track practice, so she couldn't greet him off the bus. Behind him are Wes, Amir, and Greg, who each have duffle bags thrown over their shoulders.

"How was your trip?"

"Fine," Greg says, scratching at his beard. "You should have been there."

I laugh. "I was a little busy this weekend."

He gives me a toothy grin. "Not too busy to come greet us off the bus, I notice."

Barrett jogs over to us. When he reaches our little semi-circle, he slings his arm around my shoulder. "Let's go home, yeah?"

"Movie night?" Amir says.

"How do you feel about Chinese? Or would you rather have pizza?" Barrett turns to me.

"Don't ask me. I'm not in charge here."

He laughs. "We all get a vote. This is a democracy, not an oligarchy."

Wes clears his throat. "Thai?"

Barrett shakes his head. "Diana's allergic to tree nuts. There's too much cross contamination for it to be safe for her."

"Not Thai," he says with a decisive nod. Those three words are the most I've heard Wes say in the three weeks I've been here.

"We'll decide on the walk home," Amir says. "I'm hungry, but I'm not hungry enough to decide yet."

Greg laughs. "You never want to decide. I vote Chinese."

"Pizza," Tucker says, slipping his phone into his pocket. "Mase will meet us in a little bit. She's almost done with practice."

Hand in hand, Miles and Sam lead the procession back to Athlete's Village. Barrett and I walk slowly behind them, his arm still around my shoulders like he's afraid to set me loose in case I decide to run away from him. Behind us are the rest of the guys and Mackenzie, who hasn't said a single word since her initial "Hi" half an hour ago.

"How was your weekend?" he asks, looking over at me.

I shrug. "I've had worse."

He frowns. "Dee…"

"It's fine. I'm fine," I tell him. "Just… tiring. I'm looking forward to doing nothing for a few hours."

"Maybe you need some distance from your teammates," he suggests quietly. "You're welcome to crash with us for as long as you'd like. Our couch isn't comfortable, but it's yours for the taking."

"Thanks, B." I muster up a half-smile. That's all I can manage right now. "I might have you take you up on that."

"It's yours. Always," he says seriously. "You never have to ask. You need a place to escape to, you know where to come."

My chest gets tight. "Barrett…"

"You're my best friend," he says, his voice serious, but his eyes sad. "If you need anything, you know I'm going to do everything in my power to give it to you."

Lurching to a stop, I turn to him and wrap my arms around his torso. He's sweaty and a little smelly from a five-hour bus ride with a hundred other dudes. I don't care. He folds his arms around me and holds me tight. It's clear he doesn't know what prompted this hug, but he's going with the flow, because this is what I need right now.

This man has done more for me in the last five minutes than my teammates have in the entire time I've been on campus. He's stood by me and supported me through some of the toughest years of my life, things that I look back on now and laugh, because they felt impossible back then but really weren't all that terrible. My crush deciding to ask out my best female friend. The guy I was casually seeing sleeping with someone else. Failing my geometry class in the ninth grade and nearly getting kicked off the soccer team. My dad's terminal illness.

Yeah, that one still feels pretty impossible to overcome. I don't know how to exist in a world without my dad in it. I don't want that to become my reality.

Still, I know Barrett will be there for me if I need him. He'll hold my hand during the surgeries, and he'll be at my side for the inevitable funeral. He's my rock, my constant supporter and never quitting cheerleader. He's my best friend.

Not for the first time, I wonder what he sees in me. I don't know what I can offer him in return. I don't have money, not like he does. I don't have power or influence. I don't have any friends I can hook him up with so he can get laid. I don't have anything.

All I can offer him is my unending friendship, and I have to hope that remains sufficient currency for him.

Greg clears his throat. "We've decided."

Barrett looks up at him, his brow creased. Slowly, he releases me and takes a step back. I miss the contact already.

"Chinese for dinner," he announces.

He blows out a breath. "Sounds good. I'll call in the order when we get back."

We're three blocks from the football players' house. We continue walking in quiet silence as Amir and Greg take turns flirting with Mackenzie, who stammers and blushes. There's at least a foot of distance between me and Barrett. I don't know why I'm so cognizant of it. It feels like a gulf between us.

When we get back to the house, the guys all disappear into their rooms. Sam flops onto the couch, and Mack and I take seats in the armchairs.

Now what?

Heavy footfalls in the hallway make me look up. Wes is shirtless, a towel around his big belly as he makes his way down the hall. He spies us waiting in the living room and goes pink, from his cheeks to his broad chest. He closes the bathroom door with force. A moment later, the pipes hum as the shower turns on.

I look to Sam, who has her eyes closed, and Mack, who pulls out her tablet. Right. Okay then.

My social media profile used to be active and vibrant. My former teammates haven't exactly kept in touch, and I haven't had the energy to reach out to them. The women I used to consider my sisters as recently as two months ago have practically forgotten about me in the few short weeks since I last saw them. My phone is equally silent. The only people I talk to with regularity now are my parents and Barrett.

It's isolating, not having a support network on campus like I used to. I took for granted that my team was supportive and engaged and fun to be around. I thought this new team would be the same. Instead, I have Johanna and her minions.

And, yes, I know I have Barrett and his teammates who will be there for me if I need them. I know in theory I have Sam and Mason and even Mack to rely on. But it's not the same.

The women I thought were my best friends have barely spoken to me since I left USC. Some of them have graduated and are off to bigger and better things. Some of them are still in school, about to embark on their senior seasons. Everyone is in a different place now.

It makes me think about next year. Do I want to pursue grad school? Do I want to work for a bit first? Do I want to move back home? I honestly don't know. Graduation looms over me like a rain cloud. Two more semesters and I'll have that diploma in my hand. Where do I go from here?

Footsteps on the stairs make me look up. Barrett and Greg thunder down the stairs, both freshly showered and changed. Barrett shaved, his cheeks ruddy and clear. When we make eye contact, his face flushes a deeper pink. I wonder what that's about.

"Food should be here in about ten minutes," he announces to the room at large. "Someone else gets to pick the movie."

"I'm good with whatever," Amir says, coming into the living room. His hair is wet and sticking up in every direction.

With a soft laugh, Sam gets up from her spot on the couch and moves in front of him. She puts her hand on his shoulder and pushes, and he obligingly lowers himself so she can finger comb his hair back into place. She pats his cheek lightly, and he beams at her.

Within five minutes, all the other guys have gathered in the living room. Wes makes a beeline for his armchair, his book in his hand. I don't know where to sit, where to go.

Barrett makes the decision for me. He tugs me onto the couch beside him and props his arm on the sofa behind me. At the other end is Mack, reading on her tablet. Miles and Sam sprawl on the floor in front of us with a pile of pillows—I'm not too sure I want to know what's going on beneath their blanket. Wes is in the corner with his book. Amir, Greg, and Tucker are in the other individual armchairs.

The doorbell rings, and Barrett heaves himself off the couch to pay for dinner. I know he, Greg, and Wes usually take turns buying, and the other guys contribute in other ways. They've never flaunted that they have more spending money than everyone else.

He comes back with three overloaded bags of Chinese food. They've ordered at least ten dishes plus sides of rice and noodles for everyone to share. Greg pops up and heads to the kitchen, coming back with a pile of mismatched plates. Amir disappears and returns with a handful of forks, napkins, and plastic chopsticks. Clearly, they do this often.

Miles murmurs something to Sam and then to his sister before he gets to his feet and he, too, heads to the kitchen. He comes back with three bottles of water. His eyes fall on me and silently he thrusts the bottle in my direction.

"Water?"

"Sure, thanks."

His smile is faint. His head dips, and he lumbers back to retrieve another bottle for himself.

"Ladies first," Barrett announces, blocking Greg from picking up an egg roll.

I frown.

"It's not chivalry," Tucker laughs. "If you don't eat it, the rest of us will."

Okay, that's fair. I've seen the way these guys eat on a regular day. Add in a long bus ride the day after a game? Yeah, this could get dangerous very quickly.

"All of it is safe," Barrett says. "We didn't order anything with nuts."

My stomach swoops. I know his favorite is cashew chicken with brown sauce, and he purposefully didn't order something that could send me into anaphylactic shock. Even if I were to abstain, it's still risky having it in the same room as the dishes I'm eating from. I like that he knows that. I like that I don't have to spell out how dangerous my allergies are.

Loading my plate, I take a little bit of everything. Barrett ordered large portions of nearly a dozen entrees, mostly my favorite dishes—and knowing this group, there won't be any leftovers by the time we're done. I snag a steamed dumpling and then, at the look on his face, grab a second one.

It's a free-for-all when the guys dive in. Amir bares his teeth at Greg, who rolls his eyes and takes the last egg roll. Wes hunkers down in his chair, his enormous shoulders raised as he watches the fray. Miles retakes his seat on the floor.

Barrett settles in next to me. There's a steamed dumpling on his plate, and I know for a fact he doesn't like steamed dumplings. It's something that my very Chinese mother takes personally. He credits it to eating too many growing up because it was the only thing his mother could cook from frozen without burning. He can eat other types of dumplings just fine.

Before I can question him about it, he lifts the offending dumpling with his chopsticks and places it onto my plate.

"Happy birthday," he murmurs lightly in Cantonese.

"It's not my birthday," I tell him in English, because my Cantonese is rusty as fuck. I can understand it—mostly—but I don't have an opportunity to speak it now that my grandparents have passed and my extended family lives so far away.

"It's your favorite," he says.

"Thank you."

Wes grunts and motions his hand to Amir, who passes over the remote. The resident monk turns on the TV and a superhero movie I've never seen before. Mackenzie and Wes are half reading, half watching. Tucker is on his phone. I'm pretty sure Greg is swiping left on a dating app.

Barrett tucks his arm around the back of the sofa, a few inches above my shoulders. After a few minutes, I curl into him, my head on his shoulder. His arm drops to my shoulders and squeezes lightly.

"You okay?" he murmurs quietly.

"Never better."

My belly is full, and I'm surrounded by my new friends on a quiet night in, Barrett at my side. I've found a group of people I like spending time with, a community of fellow student athletes. We cross races, genders, majors, and ages.

These people have welcomed me into their fold and into their home. Tucker is my bud; we hang out during our psychology class, and sometime this week we're going to meet up to study together. Greg flirts with me, and Amir teases me. Wes is agreeably distant. Mason and I have so much in common. Sam has been perfectly nice to me. Mack and I are both trying to find our footing here.

Slowly but surely, I'm making myself at home. I'm carving out a niche for myself, a place where I can be my authentic self.

I'm not thinking about the friends I haven't made yet. I'm not concerned about the difficulties my new team is having. I'm not worried about my dad's numerous health issues. I'm focused on the here and now, on the movie and hanging with Barrett and all the good things in my life.

There's a soft snore. Mack is passed out, her head tucked into her chin. She's curled into a little ball, clutching the throw pillow like it's a lifeline.

Wes stands up and walks in front of the couch, directly in the path of the few still watching the movie.

"Hey, down in front," Greg calls.

Wes flips him off as he pads down the hallway. His door creaks open and, a moment later, creaks closed again. He returns to the living room with a blanket in his hands. Without a word, he tucks it around the younger woman, who immediately burrows into the blanket.

"That's nice of you," Sam says, looking up at him from the floor. She curls into Miles, whose mouth is in a hard line.

He grunts and returns to his book.

Barrett tightens his grip around my shoulders. "You should stay the night," he says quietly.

It's pouring rain outside. I don't really want to walk home in this mess. Still…

"Mack is already asleep."

"So?"

"So I can't sleep on the couch if someone else already is."

He blinks at me. "So you'll stay in my bed," he says, like it won't irrevocably change our friendship.

Won't it?

Haven't we already shared a night in the same bed? Is this really that big a deal?

Yes. Yes, it is. Because even though my crush was a long

time ago, the lines are getting blurred, and I don't know how to react to this.

My blood warms at the idea, sending fire through my veins. "What?"

I'm at the stage in my cycle where everything is turning me on. I'm horny, like, all the time. I don't just want to get laid—I want the emotional intimacy, too, and I don't know how to attain that. I've relied on my vibrator quite often in the last few days. Even the innocent touch of a hand on my arm or my shoulder is enough to turn me into a panting succubus.

Sleeping beside my best friend? My very male, very *hot*, very off limits best friend?

"We're adults," he insists. "We can share a bed without making it weird."

The other night was an accident. We were watching a movie, and I crashed. He made a very nice pillow. I've never shared a bed with a man and not had it be a direct result of amorous activities. With Barrett, though… not for one moment did I think he would take advantage of me or push me into a situation I wouldn't be comfortable with. I know I'm safe with him—physically, yes, and also emotionally.

I'll always be safe with him.

"It'll be fine," he tells me confidently. "We've survived puberty, and random boners and period leaks, and all the awkwardness of being fourteen and having sleepovers. We can have a sleepover in the same bed again."

thirteen

. . .

Barrett

I'M IN HELL. Diana is in my bed, and I'm in hell. When we went to sleep, we were on opposite sides of the mattress. Now we're in the middle of the bed and spooning. Somehow in the middle of the night my arm found its way around her waist. My morning erection is nestled right up against her perfect ass. Holy fuck.

She lets out a soft moan and shifts her hips. My cock twitches against my will, and my eyes fall closed again at how perfect this feels. She moans again and shoves her ass against my crotch, rotating slowly. My hand on her hip, I grind into her. She whines. It almost seems like…

No. Wrong. This isn't supposed to happen. This isn't supposed to feel so good. Diana is my best friend, and there is a line that most certainly can not be crossed. Groping her while she sleeps is definitely against the rules.

But fuck, does it feel right to have her in my arms. It feels like this is what we were meant to be doing all these years. So I take a deep breath and enjoy the fleeting moment for what it is—all too brief. And then I have to return to real life.

Exhaling slowly, I disentangle our limbs and roll to the edge of the bed. It takes a minute for me to be able to sit upright. Everything hurts. Our game was two days ago, which means I have a few more days for the bruises to heal before going through the wringer all over again.

Shuffling to the bathroom, I lock Tucker's door—don't want Mason barging in on me again—and take care of the morning situation. After, I turn on the water and step into the shower. The tub is cluttered with Mason's hair products and soaps. I'm glad she feels at home here, I'm glad she and Tucker are in a good place, but sometimes seeing all of her stuff around all the time just makes me all the more aware of how lonely I am.

Even though I stopped sleeping around the second Diana told me she was coming here, it doesn't change the fact I want a woman. One woman only: the one who is currently fast asleep in my bed, after a perfectly platonic night between the sheets. She's all I've ever wanted. Now that she's conceivably available… I have to shoot my shot.

Don't I? I'm running out of excuses to keep my feelings to myself. I know she's stressed with the new school and the family situation, but doesn't she deserve happiness, too? Or am I just kidding myself that being with me would make her so inexplicably happy she would forget all about her dad's cancer?

At the same time, I have to concede the fact that the woman I'm in love with, the woman I've loved from a distance for so many years, is a perfectly fallible human who isn't perfect in the slightest. No matter how I feel about her, I have to admit that I don't know the reality of being with her. What would it be like? I don't want to casually date. I don't want to sleep with her and then go back to normal.

I want to be with her, with everything that entails. I want a loving, committed relationship, like what Miles and Sam have, like what Tucker and Mason share. I want what her parents have.

It's not purely sexual, this attraction I have. It's not purely romantic, this pull towards her. I care about her as a person and as a potential partner. She's my best friend, and at the end of the day, I want to preserve our friendship as much as I can. I don't know what I would do without her in my life. I don't know that I would survive it.

When I think about the type of woman I want to marry one day far, far into the future, there's only one person who comes to mind. When I think about the way I want to raise my eventual, theoretical children, there's only one partner I want to do it with. Diana is my end game. Whether we make this happen now, in six months, or in twenty years, I know it's going to be her. I only hope she and I can figure this out before we unhappily marry other people and get divorced. I only hope she and I can figure this out so her father can see his daughter happy.

I like to think she would be happy with me. So what if I've never been anyone's boyfriend before. Seeing the changes my friends have gone through in the last year… it's essentially what I've already been doing, just with sex and intimacy thrown in. I'm the first person Diana turns to when she's upset and needs to vent or be cheered up. She comes to me with her good news, even before she tells her parents. She relies on me for advice and support, judgment-free. She's that person for me, too.

Who knows what will happen after graduation? I'm pretty sure I want to take a few years off before I pursue my MBA, which means I have to stay local in Boston, within easy commuting distance of my family's forensic accounting company in the financial district. I'm not sure what she's doing next year, if grad school is on the horizon or if she's going to take some time off to be with her dad.

I'm going to do everything in my power to be there for her. I'm going to give her everything I can.

By the time I'm done with my shower, the water's gone cool. Wrapping a towel around my waist, I head back to my room. Diana is sitting up in my bed, the blankets pooled around her waist. She's fully dressed in leggings and one of my t-shirts, her hair mussed. She's absolutely gorgeous.

I like seeing her in my shirt. I like seeing her in my bed.

"Good morning." Crossing the room, I grab clothes from my dresser. How am I going to maneuver into my shorts with her here—without flashing her?

"Morning." Her cheeks go pink as her eyes scrub over my form. My cock gives a twitch behind my towel at the intensity in her eyes. She clears her throat and looks away.

"Did I wake you?"

Diana shakes her head. "It was time for me to wake up."

She scoots out of the bed and pulls the blankets over the mattress.

"I'll take care of it," I tell her.

Her eyes dart to mine and then to my chest and belly again.

I'm a big guy, six foot five and right around three hundred pounds. Solid. Strong. I have to be in order to succeed on the football field. Everything about me is big, from my hands to my arms to my chest to my belly. I'm strong as fuck. But I'm also big.

Does she care? She's never brought a guy home before, so I don't know what she's into. Does she go for the jocks with the perfect washboard abs? Does she like white guys, black guys, anything but Chinese guys? Will I ever be enough to measure up to her expectations?

Without a word, she ducks into the bathroom. Tucker's mom is a dentist, so we always have extra toothbrushes on hand. I kind of want her to keep one here, along with all of her regular overnight gear. She should have her sleep bonnet and fuzzy socks here.

But no pajamas. I can't lie, I like the sight of her in my shirt too much. It might be the only way I get to see her wearing my clothes.

Because we're going to do this again. I like having her in my bed, even if nothing is happening. Sleeping beside her, our limbs tangled together… yeah, that's got to happen again.

When she comes out of the bathroom, her hair is fixed, and her face washed. She's not squinting anymore, so she must have put her contacts back in. She toys with the hem of my shirt. It looks more like a tent on her.

"So…"

"So?" I towel off my hair.

"What happens now?"

I check the bedside clock. "Now, we go to breakfast, and then we go to class."

Her eyes go wide. "Shit. We have to go to class today."

Luckily, I know her schedule nearly as well as I know mine. We have an hour and a half before her first class of the day, and two and a half hours until mine starts. She has a full day of school, study group, and practice ahead of her. So do I.

Not for the first time, I wish we were in the same major, or at least in the same classes. Dietetics and accounting don't call for classes that overlap, and it's more important that we set ourselves up for future success than take a class together because I can't stand to be away from her. A few semesters ago, she took statistics, and we studied together over the phone as much as we could. It wasn't nearly as much as I would have liked.

I clear my throat. "I have clean shirts if you want to borrow one."

"Oh. Um…"

"No pressure."

She digs through her bag, coming up with a clean pair of leggings and a new sports bra, but no shirt. "Um, yes, please."

With a wave, I usher her to my dresser, where my shirts are neatly folded and organized.

"These are the smaller ones," I say, pointing to the Newton

Football shirts I got my freshman year, when I was about forty pounds lighter. They're only an extra large instead of an extra-extra-extra large.

She pulls out a navy blue shirt and holds it up to her chest. It stretches down her thighs, the sleeves nearly to her elbows.

"I'm going to look like I'm wearing my boyfriend's shirt," she complains.

"Is it really that big a deal?"

She makes a face. "Only when I'm not actually seeing anyone, and everyone starts gossiping behind my back."

I don't pretend to know the first thing about female social politics. I keep to myself, stick with my guys. Nobody gives me a hard time for getting laid or for abstaining. Nobody gives a shit, period.

"I can see if Sam has an extra outfit…"

Diana shakes her head. "No. I'll be fine. It's fine."

She ducks back into the bathroom, emerging a few minutes later in the fresh clothes. My cock twitches at the sight of her wearing another of my shirts. She looks absolutely gorgeous, her wavy hair loose and free, her face devoid of makeup.

"Let's grab something to eat," I suggest. If she really hates the outfit, she has enough time to head back to her house and change… but that will cut into our limited time together, so I don't want to suggest it.

As we head down the stairs, I see Mack has vacated the couch, the blankets left by Wes neatly folded on the coffee table. His door is open—he's not home, either. Tucker is probably still asleep, and if the sounds coming from Miles's room are any indication, he and Sam are getting busy, so now wouldn't be a good time to interrupt anyway.

"Maybe you should leave a few outfits here," I suggest casually.

Diana looks at me, confusion creasing her forehead.

"In case you want to stay over again. Keep some stuff here. I'll clear out a drawer for you in my dresser."

"You don't have to do that."

"I want to." I open the front door for her to pass through. "Mason keeps a bunch of her hair products in our shower. If you wanted to, you could leave some things, too."

"That's different," she says.

"How?"

"Mason and Tucker are dating."

"So?"

"So we're not."

Yeah, she doesn't need to remind me of that.

"You're my best friend. I want you to feel comfortable. And if that means keeping a spare set of contacts and a sleep bonnet and a pair of jeans at my place, I'm more than fine with that," I tell her. "It's not an imposition, not in the slightest."

She purses her lips. "I'll think about it."

Which means no.

fourteen

. . .

Diana

EVERYONE'S EYES are on me. Everyone is watching as I strip off Barrett's shirt and toss it onto the locker room bench to change into my practice clothes.

"Who did you hook up with?" Louisa, a full back, leans across her locker to stare at me.

"I didn't."

"So whose shirt is that?"

"A friend's."

"I don't see any hickies," Mischa says.

Terri's eyes go wide.

"Really. We had a slumber party," I insist.

Zoe laughs. "You mean a naked slumber party."

"No, we were fully dressed."

Rachel and Rebecca make eye contact, not bothering to hide their smirks.

It's almost like hooking up with some guy would increase my social currency with these girls. They're more interested in me now than they've been since I've met them.

"Trust me, if I hooked up with someone last night, I would be in a much better mood."

And not nearly so confused.

I'm not the type of girl guys want to be with long term. I'm not the type of girl guys want to bring home. I'm not the type of girl who gets a happy-ever-after. I want to go on a date, a real, proper date. I want to be wined and dined and courted. I want to be cherished. I want what I can't have. College guys? All they're interested in is getting laid.

Barrett hasn't mentioned any women. He hasn't gone out with anyone to my knowledge since I've been here. I feel bad for holding him back, and at the same time, I'm glad I don't have to share him. He's mine.

So if I happen to have a sex dream about my best friend the night I sleep beside him in his bed… totally not a big deal. It's not the first time. It probably won't be the last. If I happen to come alive at the feeling of his thick dick pressing into me and imagining he was *pressing into me*…

"A few of us are going out to McRory's tonight," Emma says. She's my partner on the defensive side more often than not. We don't talk much off the field. "You want to come?"

Are they only being nice to me because they think I hooked up with someone last night? Maybe. Am I going to look a gift horse in the mouth? Hell to the no.

"Sure, I'm down," I say casually.

Fully dressed, we head to the gym for weights. Today is lower body, so squats galore. I like squats. I would much rather work out lower body than upper body. Our workout is written on the whiteboard. Our practice facility is connected to the indoor tennis court and the natatorium, so we share the weights room with them. Only a few sports are lucky enough to have their own personal weight rooms, like football.

There are a few straggling swimmers finishing up their cardio. One tennis player, so identified by the Newton Tennis on her shirt, is doing bicep curls. For the most part, we work out as a team during the season—once the season has ended, as long as we log our assigned workouts, they don't care when we do them so long as we do them.

Emma nods at me. "Partners?"

"Sure."

I can spot her if she wants. Normally I get someone who clearly doesn't want to help me spot. It would be dangerous to try to lift two hundred pounds over my head without someone there to help me if I need to bail.

Lifting weights is—well, it's not exactly easy, but it's something I'm capable of. I can lift, I can bench, I can squat. I'm strong, both physically and mentally. I've been working out for a long time. This is something I am capable of, no matter what team is on my jersey or if I've made friends yet.

Emma and I cycle through the rotations Coach has set up. They're all exercises I've done before. None of this is new, even if the sequences are different and the weights are heavier. A squat is a squat is a squat.

We don't chitchat. She has on her giant headphones and chomps on her gum, bobbing her head to whatever song is playing.

I don't know much about her. She's a junior, originally from Colorado, and is allergic to nuts, same as I am—we get special allergen stickers on our sandwiches when we have travel games. I know nothing of substance about her as a person. She's a decent defensive player. I don't hate playing alongside her.

There isn't any room for me at Johanna's table in the social hierarchy. I'm not a yes girl, that's not me. The other defensive players haven't exactly been welcoming. Lukewarm, perhaps. I don't hold it against them. It's hard to let someone new into the fold, I get that. Still, I think maybe this could be my ticket into the cool kids' club. Wearing a guy's shirt to practice? Fuck, I could steal half of Barrett's closet and he wouldn't notice—he'd probably give them to me if I told them what I wanted them for.

I want friends. My own friends, not just his. I want to prove I belong here, that I deserve to be here. I'm more than just Barrett's friend; I'm my own person, and I have contributions to make.

———

McRory's pub is a casual, laid back bar that serves amazing food. Barrett has brought me here a few times. Somehow, it is both the definition of a raucous college bar and a laid-back local pub at the same time. The staff know their regulars and treat all of the college kids as if they are regulars, too.

There are eight of us out tonight—Mischa is a freshman and underage, so while she can get in, she can't drink, and it's not fun to be surrounded by people drinking when forced to abstain.

"Fuck, girl, I wish you were in our house," Emma says.

This makes me raise my eyebrows. She's been perfunctorily kind, but she hasn't gone out of her way to engage with me off the field.

"Defense should stick together," Ashton chimes in.

Quickly I do the math. There are eight of us. There are six bedrooms in each house in Athlete's Village. That means one of them isn't in the defense house.

"I'm in with the goaltenders and two forwards, we're all sophomores and juniors," Terri says. "Robin was in an overflow house last year—she was with me and some people from other teams—but she wanted to bunk in with the seniors this year."

I wonder why. She doesn't go out of her way to engage with Johanna or her minions. She doesn't really talk to me. She keeps to herself.

Maybe she's just an introvert. Maybe she's shy. Maybe she hates us. I won't know unless I ask her directly, and I'm not sure I want to open that door.

The waitress delivers our drinks and I take a sip of my

vodka soda. I'm not trying to get drunk, I only want to have a good time.

The girls talk about people I don't know and events I wasn't invited to, maybe because they were before my tenure here. I don't think they're purposefully trying to exclude me, not like Johanna and Rachel, Rebecca, and Robin have.

"We should make this a regular thing," Emma says out of the blue. She tips her head in my direction. "You should come out with us more often."

"I don't think I can go out drinking every Monday night," I admit. I'm already a little worried about what tomorrow will bring.

She laughs. "We can go out on other nights, too."

I want to ask why this is the first time they're really talking to me outside of practice. We've played in two games and had one overnight road trip. Nobody talked to me then outside of the bare minimum. At meals, I sat with Johanna and her minions as they ignored me, and during our free time, not one person suggested doing something together.

I know I could be the bigger person and initiate. I could invite them to go for a run or grab coffee or whatever. But I'm new: I don't know the social hierarchy yet, except that Johanna is clearly the Queen Bee, and anyone who defies her is scum on the bottom of her shoe.

"So this is just for defense? None of the forwards?"

Kristin rolls her eyes. "Johanna is such a bitch."

This makes me raise my eyebrows.

"Oh, I'm sorry. You've been here three weeks and you hadn't noticed?"

I bite my lip. "Well…"

Jackie and Louisa laugh.

"Yeah, you'll fit in just fine," Zoe says.

"Oh, look, my glass is empty," Emma says.

Kristin laughs. "You just want to talk to that cute guy at the bar. I saw you checking him out."

Emma shrugs, ambivalent. "So kill me. He's hot and I haven't gotten laid in, like, forever."

Scoping out the bar situation, I look for the guy they're talking about. There's a collection of football players Barrett introduced me to at the frat party. He doesn't usually hang around with the offensive guys. I recognize Sullivan holding court in the center of the group.

"You don't mean Sullivan, right? The guy in the middle?"

Emma's eyes go wide. "You know him?"

"He's a safety," I tell her. And not a very good one. Barrett doesn't think too highly of him. "I can introduce you two."

"You are, like, my new best friend," Emma declares. She takes down her ponytail and reties it again. "Okay, I'm ready."

I knock back the rest of my drink. It's mostly ice at this point.

"Let's do this."

There's no point in being subtle. These guys probably wouldn't recognize subtlety unless it hit them over the head.

Sullivan goes quiet as we approach. His eyes go wide.

"Diana! You're Barrett's girl."

"Friend," I correct. "We're friends."

Some of the football players laugh. Sully turns to them with a glare and they go silent.

"Who's your friend?" He isn't subtle about checking her out.

"This is Emma. She's on the soccer team with me." I look him up and down. "She could probably teach you a thing or two about defense."

One of the guys snickers.

If Sullivan is anything like Barrett, he can't resist a challenge. This will egg him on. I'm not trying to neg him or insult him: I'm trying to instigate a little healthy competition.

I drift down the bar, keeping a subtle eye on Emma and Sully. There's a cluster of hipsters in flannel shirts drinking cheap beer. I can't decide if they're trying to be on the periphery of the football guys or if they hate sharing the bar with them.

The guy on the end gives me a nod. "Hey."

"Hi?"

"That was stealthy." He moves closer. "What's your name?"

My eyes flick over him again. He's thin and wiry, with dark hair that falls nearly to his shoulders and thick eyebrows. His cheeks are covered in a healthy dose of scruff, hiding his features. My stomach churns.

"I'm Diana."

"Trey," he says, holding out his hand. I glance down at it. After a moment, I take it for a shake. His grip is limp and too tight at the same time.

"Nice to meet you."

He clears his throat. "Can I buy you a drink?"

"Oh, I'm with some friends." Looking over my shoulder, I confirm my suspicions: the entire table is watching me. I waggle my fingers at them in a sarcastic wave, and Louisa bursts out laughing.

"It's not forever," Trey tells me. "It's a drink."

Why not? It's not like I have anyone else interested in pursuing me.

"Sure."

"What are you drinking? Margarita? Blended or on the rocks?"

"Vodka soda."

He frowns. "You don't want, like, a daiquiri or a piña colada or something?"

"Nope. I'm drinking vodka sodas tonight."

Tequila is not my friend, and those fruity drinks only serve as a surefire indicator I'll wake up the next morning with a hangover. I've got class tomorrow: I can't afford to miss a single session.

Trey waves at the bartender. "A vodka soda and a Miller Lite," he orders before the bartender can say anything.

She glances at me, maybe to check if I'm okay. I nod, and she relaxes.

"Coming right up," the bartender says with a clearly fake smile.

I like her. I want to be her friend, too.

My phone buzzes in my pocket, and I know without checking that it's probably Barrett. Despite my text that I would see him tomorrow, he's probably wanting to know why I skipped out on having dinner with him. It's for the best possible reason: I'm making friends!

I know he'll be happy for me. He can't enjoy being my only friend on campus. He's probably as desperate for me to expand my social network as I am.

"So, Diedre, what's your major?"

I don't correct him on the error of my name. It's loud in here; I probably just heard him wrong, or he didn't hear me.

"I'm doing a double major, dietetics and psychology."

At USC, the dietetics major required enough courses that amounted to a minor in psychology here, so it made sense to do the full double major when I transferred over. I want to be a registered dietician and that involves a fair amount of counseling people on nutrition. Besides, psychology is interesting. The human mind is insane.

Trey grins. "I'm a psych major, too."

My stomach swoops, like I missed a step coming down the stairs. "Really?"

He nods. "I'm a senior."

"Me, too."

There's no career in professional soccer for me. Maybe one day I can work with the national team in a nutrition counseling position, but that's a long time down the road. Right now I have to focus on putting one foot in front of the other: graduating, then finding a job, maybe grad school.

Emma and Sullivan have hit it off, wandering away from his crowd of hangers-on to talk at a quiet table in the corner.

"Maybe I can call you sometime," Trey says. "Can I get your number?"

Exhaling slowly, I look him over again. He's cute. He smells nice. He's reasonably charming. I'd love an orgasm that originates from an actual dick and not a silicone vibrator, a hard body pressing up against me in all the best ways. I've missed sex. It's been a lonely few months. Waking up wanting this morning, I'm only more aware of what I can't have.

Trey's not my forever, but he might be fun for a few nights.

"Sure."

When he pulls out his phone, I rattle off my phone number. My phone buzzes with a text—he must have messaged me his number.

"I should get back to my friends," I say after an awkward pause. "I'll see you around."

He grins at me, his eyes flicking over my body again. "Yeah, for sure."

fifteen

. . .

Diana

IT'S BEEN FIVE DAYS. Trey hasn't texted me since I responded to his first "hey" message at the bar. I'm trying not to think about it.

Barrett is acting weird, too, ever since our impromptu sleepover. I've been hanging around with the defensive girls at dinner—breakfast is usually grabbed on the run to class and lunch is on my own, since my schedule doesn't align with Johanna and the minions, nor with Barrett's—and I've barely seen him all week aside from in passing. I haven't even told him about Trey… not that there's anything to tell. I met a guy, I gave him my number, and he hasn't used it.

On Saturdays, I have to be on my own. Barrett is busy all morning prepping for his games. I don't want to distract him. I hit the gym for a quick run on the treadmill and take myself to breakfast at the ASC.

Mason and Sam are eating with a bunch of their respective teammates. I've never seen the two friend groups interact before, softball players mixing with track and field. Awkwardly, I head over in their direction.

"You exist!" Mason crows. She jumps out of her seat and

throws her arms around me. "We haven't seen you in forever and a half!"

She practically pushes me into a chair.

"It's been a little busy lately."

"It's that third week. It gets me every semester," Sam says. "Right when you think you can handle it—bam! Your world blows up."

"Tell me about it." I tuck into my breakfast.

The girls introduce me around the table. Tamar and Aleesha are Sam's teammates, and I've already met Fred, Bryce, and Mateo a few times in passing. Fred is in one of my dietetics classes and now that I'm putting a face to the name, Tamar is almost definitely in my new nutrition counseling study group. Huh. What a small world.

"The game starts at four, so we're going to start tailgating around noon," Sam says. "My sorority has a tent where you can come hang out."

"Thank you. That would be… thanks."

She shoots me a smile. "Any time. You're one of us now."

"It's nice to be part of the group."

"The only thing better than going to the game would be if the guys could hang out with us," Mason says. "But that would kind of defeat the purpose. Even when they're not playing in a specific game, they're down on the field with the rest of the team."

"I like watching them play," I admit. "I grew up going to as many of Barrett's games as I could. It's definitely easier now that he's playing on Saturdays instead of Friday nights." And being in the same time zone doesn't hurt. "My parents are going to try to come in for a few of his games."

"That'll be nice, having some family there," Sam says. "I know they're not—you're not—"

"No, we're not related," I say dryly.

"He's mentioned he considers your parents part of his

family. He really likes them," she tries to backpedal. "And since his parents are kind of… well…"

"Not supportive," Mason says delicately.

"Yeah. That. Since his folks refuse to show up to his games, it's nice that your parents will. He deserves to have people showing up for him," Sam says. "I worry about him and Wes. They don't have anyone local. Amir at least had his brother." At my confusion, she explains: "he went to Northeastern. Graduated last year. Local makes a big difference when the rest of your family is back home in Wisconsin."

That's for sure. When I was across the country at USC, my parents were only able to come out to visit once a year, and I couldn't come home for every school holiday or long weekend like I can now. Between the distance and the time zones, it was difficult to arrange a time for us to chat regularly that didn't interact with my school schedule, practice times, and their everyday life of work and dinner.

After a leisurely brunch, we head down en masse towards the football field and the party in the parking lot. Tailgating is one of my favorite parts of the football game experience, hanging with friends and my family as we get ready for the fun to begin. The only downside is that Barrett can't join us, too busy preparing for the game he's about to participate in. And I would never want to distract him.

We're in the student section, right on the thirty yard line, about halfway up the field. The stands are decently packed. I'm in between Sam and her teammates, and Mason and her group of friends, in the middle and, because of it, part of neither group's conversation. They're both wearing sweatshirts that were probably pilfered from their boyfriends' closets, both of them nearly swimming in the extra-extra-extra large hoodies with the guys' names and numbers on the back. It makes me feel self-conscious about the old Dalton Football sweatshirt I swiped from Barrett's closet back at the end of high school. It has his name and number on it. I like that I'm carrying a piece of him with me no matter where I go.

Trapped in the middle of the two friend groups, I feel both part of the group and isolated at the same time. I don't know Tamar, even though we're apparently in the same study group, and I've only met Mason's friends in passing. I haven't established myself here yet, the way she has. If I didn't know, I would never guess she transferred in last fall; she fits in with them like she's been here since day one.

Mack appears at the end of our row, wearing a Newton Football t-shirt and carrying a book. "Hey."

"Hey girl!" Sam grins at her. "Come sit by me." The tall freshman squeezes down the row until she slips in between us.

"It's okay if I…?" Mack clutches her book to her chest. It has a bubblegum pink cover and a cartoonish caricature of a couple arguing on it.

"Of course! The more, the merrier," Sam says. "You don't want to sit with your parents?"

"They're running late. Coming from Ashley's cheer competition this morning," Mack says. "They thought they would be done an hour earlier."

"Got it." Sam wraps her arm around her boyfriend's sister. "Well, you're always welcome to hang with us. You're one of us now."

The game is… well, it's nowhere near as fun as last time. Providence College is big and strong, coming out of the gate with an axe to grind. Barrett and the guys are doing their best, but they're fighting for every yard. The end of the first quarter is almost a relief; they're down a touchdown, but there is plenty of time to make it up. At half time, the Wolfpack are tied even through sheer grit and determination; by the end of the third quarter, they're down two scores, and as the sun goes down, the situation is starting to get bleak.

The final score has Providence up 48 to 17. The crowd has

grown silent, the mood sour. Nobody likes to lose, and to lose in such a devastating fashion… Nobody is happy.

After the game is over, we meet the guys in the tunnels beneath the stadium. It's not a quick change: by the time we file out of the packed stadium, the guys have enough time for a post-game debrief, a shower and change, and to grab a quick protein shake from their training staff.

The girls are subdued as we wait for the guys. The friends have gone on ahead to the bar, leaving just the girlfriends and family members waiting. Mack has her head down, absorbed in her book; she read whenever the offense was on the field, only really paying attention when her brother, part of the defensive squad, was actively playing.

Amir comes out first, talking on his cell phone in a language I can't understand. Wes and Greg are behind him—Greg greets all of us with kisses to our cheek, ever the flirt, before he falls quiet beside us. Wes makes eye contact and nods before returning his attention to his shoes, his cheeks pink.

The other three guys come out together, talking quietly.

Barrett's skin is flushed with exertion. He crosses the space between us and scoops me into a hug, holding me airborne.

"Hey!"

He laughs and holds me impossibly closer. My boobs are mashed into his chest. His lips brush against my forehead in a soft kiss.

It's my turn to laugh, a little bewildered. "What has gotten into you?"

"I'm really glad you're here," he says quietly.

"Of course I'm here. I told you, I wouldn't miss your game."

"No. Here. At Newton," he says. He swallows and raises his eyes to meet mine. I'm still hovering in midair. "I'm sorry about what brought you here, but if you have to be close to home, I'm glad it's here with me."

Inexplicably, tears spring to my eyes. I tighten my grip around him and bury my face into his neck. It's too much. It's just too much.

"Barrett…"

"I know," he murmurs. Slowly, he sets me back onto the ground. "I know, Dee."

I sniffle. I don't want to cry, not now. Not over this.

He releases me and ducks his head, rummaging through his backpack. He withdraws a sweatshirt and wraps it around my shoulders without a word.

"You're shivering," he says. He ducks down and slides the tab into the zipper, drawing it up to my chest. The sweatshirt falls nearly to my knees. It smells like him, honey and musk. Instantly, I feel ten times more cozy. It's like being wrapped up in his enormous hug. I love it.

He slides his arm around my shoulder, tucking me into his side. "So, what now?"

Miles and Sam are making out. Tucker and Mason are clearly having a moment, staring deep into one another's eyes. Amir has hung up his phone, having a quiet conversation with Greg and Wes, who grunts occasionally as they chat.

I curl into Barrett and soak up some of his warmth. "You hungry?"

He laughs. "Uh, yeah."

"So let's go get you something to eat."

"Because it's that simple."

It's my turn to laugh. "It is. Either you go out with the group or just the two of us. I'm sure there will be a party tonight we'll all end up going to. We'll feed you, we'll change clothes, and then we'll get drunk."

His mouth curves into a panty-melting smirk. "Drunk cheese fries at midnight again?"

My stomach twists. "Okay, so I'll only have a few. It's your turn to get drunk tonight. But I'm not carrying you up the stairs if you wimp out on me."

He laughs. "Yeah, okay. I'll try to keep it under control."

———

Without much deliberation, dinner is at McRory's pub, the guys' favorite hangout. Miles, Sam, and Mackenzie have split off to eat dinner with their sister and parents. Mason and I are clustered in with Barrett, Tucker, Amir, Wes, and a group of the younger defensive core, all vying for the guys' attention by being as outrageous as possible. They seem to think flirting with Mason and I is a good idea. Oh, are they wrong…

Tucker looks to be about ten seconds away from punching out this loudmouth freshman who keeps hitting on his woman. Mason isn't fazed, ignoring him and not feeding into it in the slightest.

Me? I'm focused on Barrett, who's quiet and withdrawn. That's not like him. Yeah, he doesn't like losing, but he normally doesn't take it as personally as he seems to be tonight.

I set my hand on his arm. "Do you want to talk about it?"

He stares at me. Cupping his hand around his ear, he leans close. "What was that?"

"Do you want to talk?"

He frowns. "About what?"

Moving closer to him, I set my hand on his shoulder for balance as I speak into his ear. "Whatever has you so down tonight," I say.

"I'm fine."

"Bullshit."

Barrett laughs. "I will be after a few drinks."

I purse my lips at him. He dips his fingers in my cheeks and pushes my mouth up in a facsimile of a smile.

"Relax, Dee. I just need to burn off tonight. It was…" He sighs. "Everything hurts. I want to curl up in my bed and sleep for a week."

"Do you not want to go out tonight? We don't have to party if you—"

He shakes his head. "No, I'm good. I want to."

"You sure?"

"Yeah. I'll drink a few beers and everything will feel better." He squeezes my upper arm. "You good?"

"Why wouldn't I be?"

"You're quiet tonight."

It's my turn to laugh. "I talked a bunch during the game. I'm all talked out."

He slides his arm around my shoulders and draws me to him in a side hug. "I'm glad you're here with me."

"There isn't anywhere else I'd rather be."

Barrett steals a French fry off my plate. I push the plate towards him and he takes another, still hugging me. He brings the fry to my mouth, like he's about to feed me, then yanks it away and eats it himself. Jerk. I pinch his side, and he twitches. More than he should.

"You okay?"

"Bruise," he says quietly, not trying to catch the attention of the other guys, who are ignoring us.

"Where are you not bruised?" It's a serious question. I'm not being petulant; I'm genuinely concerned.

"I'll be fine."

I roll my eyes. Not what I asked.

"You don't have to worry about me," he says.

"Evidently I do."

Barrett sighs. "My whole body is one giant collection of bruises. I'm fine. I'll be fine. I'll go home, sleep like twelve hours, and then get a massage tomorrow."

I purse my lips.

"Tomorrow is recovery day. I'll rest. Tonight we're going

out."

"Yeah we are," one of the sophomores across the table chimes in. I turn to glare at him, and the tough guy shrinks back. "Sorry, I'll stop eavesdropping."

Yeah, that's probably a good idea.

We get our checks, and without a word, Barrett plucks mine from my hands.

"Hey!"

"I've got you," he says, pulling out his wallet.

"But—"

"You'll get the next one," he says, like there will be a next time. This isn't the first time he's pulled this stunt.

"Thanks, B," I say, because that's all I can really say. I don't like being dependent on my best friend's charitable nature to be able to afford a decent college experience. I order the cheapest things on the menu, I eat at the dining hall for most of my meals, I don't spend frivolously. I can't afford to.

He opens his mouth, like he wants to say something, before he sighs and shakes his head.

"We're going to head back to the house," he says to Tucker, who nods.

Mason lights up. "We'll go with you."

The five freshmen and sophomores perk up, clearly fishing for an invitation.

"We'll meet you at the Delta party in about an hour," Barrett says, handing his card over to the waiter.

The walk to the guys' house is slow and unhurried. Tucker and Mason are holding hands. They look cute, as they usually do, completely wrapped up in one another. They're so clearly in love with each other, my teeth hurt from looking at them.

Tonight I don't feel like changing my clothes. My jeans, stolen Dalton sweater, and Barrett's Newton sweatshirt are all the effort I want to put into tonight. I'm not looking to hook up with anyone. I'm going to go home and sleep in my own bed all by myself. The only thing I do is take my hair out of its ponytail and pull it back into a fresh one.

Still, I'll put on a pretty smile and hang out with Barrett and his friends for a few more hours. I'm not ready to go back to the soccer house and deal with Johanna and the minions. I would be fine hanging out at Barrett's place and watching a movie or playing cards. But he wants to go out, so we're going to go out.

The Delta house is packed by the time we arrive. The place already reeks of a thoroughly unpleasant aroma that permeates through the house. Sam and Miles are with a cluster of women I recognize as her sorority sisters, mainly by the Greek letters on their shirts and the fact that I don't recognize them as her softball teammates. Miles is talking with another dude, probably one of the sisters' boyfriends. He looks thoroughly uncomfortable.

Amir and Greg push through the crowd to the keg and we follow in their wake. People move out of the way for the big guys in a way they wouldn't if it were me and Mason on our own. Greg chats with the fraternity brother manning the keg as Amir pours me a cup, then hands one to Barrett behind me. Duly armed, we are ready to party… whatever that means.

The beer is lukewarm and a little flat. I take a bigger sip and make a face.

Barrett laughs. "Not your flavor?"

I shake my head.

"I'll get you a vodka soda," he says. My stomach warms at the idea that he knows my drink order by heart—he knows what I like, and he has no qualms about obtaining it for me.

"I can get it."

"We'll go together," he says. He holds out his hand and I take it. He squeezes my hand and pulls me through the crowd as we head toward the kitchen. He nods to the guys in the kitchen before he starts to make me a drink. He passes it over and I take a sip. "Better?"

"So much."

He quirks his mouth upwards in a grin. "Yeah?"

"Oh, shut up."

Barrett laughs outright. "You love me."

"You make good drinks."

He takes the flat beer from my hand and takes a sip. He makes a face and then takes a longer drink. "You're right. This is kind of gross." He drinks some more, full on chugging now. In about thirty seconds, he's downed the entire cup of mostly foam, very little beer. He tosses the empty cup into the nearby trash can and picks up his original cup, which looks to be about the same.

"Ready?"

"Freddy," I say, and he grins.

He reaches out and grabs my hand again. This time he leads me in the direction of the game room, where most of the football players are gathered. There are about fifteen dudes spread out, playing video games, and a cluster of women in the corner jostling for attention and being ignored.

Barrett only has to look at a freshman for the guy to get up and move to the floor. He takes the guy's seat and I settle on the couch beside him, sipping my drink. Greg and Amir are on the other side of the room with Sullivan and another guy I've seen around campus whose name I don't know.

I'm not in the mood to dance. I'm not in the mood to talk. All I want to do is hang out with Barrett and just... be. The guys trash talk each other and play their games. It all goes over my head. I'm included, I'm part of it, but they leave me alone.

My phone buzzes with a text. It's Trey. My stomach flips as I open the screen to reveal the message.

Hey. What you up to?

Seriously? These thirsty white boys think they're so hot.

Still, I'm a little bored. I don't have anything else to do. So I text him back. It's not like my best friend is paying me any attention. He's drinking his beer and staring off into the distance, looking like he'd rather be anywhere else.

At a party.

I leave out the fact that Trey's not invited, and that this probably isn't his scene. Hipster psychology boys probably wouldn't be caught dead at a frat party, and if they were, they would probably spend the entire time denigrating it.

Why am I even remotely interested in this dude? He hit on me at the bar, he bought me a drink, and then he didn't text me back for almost a week. He's clearly looking for someone to warm his bed tonight and is hedging his bet. So why can't I stop thinking about him? Am I so desperate for friends, for companionship, that I'm going to take the first hand that's offered to me?

My phone buzzes in my hand, and I have to resist the urge to check it.

Yes. I'm also lonely, desperate, and a little horny. So if I hook up with this guy, if I sleep with him once or twice and then don't see him again... yeah, I'm okay with that. He's not my forever. But he could be fun for a few nights.

I take a sip of my drink. Barrett glances down at me and smiles.

"Everything okay?"

Pressing my lips together, I nod. We've never really talked about dating or hooking up or anything. He's called me a few times after he's hooked up with some random girl, when he's drunk and lonely and regretting it. I've texted him from my conquests' bed looking for an excuse to leave. I've never had a real boyfriend, and as far as I know, he's never had a girl-friend. He sleeps around. He goes out. But he doesn't play for keeps. He's never been interested in that.

Barrett and I... we're closer than we've ever been, but now that we're together all the time, I'm noticing the distance between us. The chasm between who he is with me and who he is with everyone else. I can't figure out which one is the real version of him.

Any other night, I might suggest he go out into the main room and chat up some girl. There have got to be tons of women who are ready and willing to go home with a gorgeous, hotshot football player, even if they've lost today's game. And Barrett is a genuinely good guy, charming and attractive and fun to be around. I'm sure he's got moves.

Still, tonight… I don't want to share him. He's mine, all mine. I don't want to give him up.

Setting my hand on his arm, I catch his attention. "Do you want to dance?"

Barrett makes a face. "You want to dance."

"We don't have to," I tell him quickly. "I thought it might be fun."

"Dee, everything hurts so bad, I just want to go home and lay down," he says. "I don't even want to jack off, I'm so tired. So, no, I don't want to dance. I don't want to do anything."

My phone buzzes again. Trey. I turn the screen off and tuck the phone into my pocket.

"Do you want cheese fries?" I ask instead.

Barrett smiles softly. "Yeah. Let's go get you some cheese fries."

sixteen

. . .

Barrett

THERE'S a body in the bed beside mine. The faint rattle of lungs breathing tells me the person is alive. The petite frame and generous curves tell me the person sharing my bed is female. The long, dark hair and bronze skin tells me what I was afraid of: once again, Diana is in my bed.

My head pounds and my mouth is as dry as the Sahara. I roll away from her and she sighs, burrowing into the blankets. It takes considerable effort to sit up, and even more to swing my feet down to the floor. Standing up is near impossible.

I definitely drank too much last night. My body is sore and tender after the punishment I took in yesterday's game. Hobbling to the bathroom, I lift my shirt and survey the mess of bruises on my belly, chest, and sides. There's a knot between my shoulder blades that tangles as I lift my arms in a stretch. My knee is swollen, my thigh scratched from a particularly brutal fall late in the third quarter.

Everything hurts. This is nothing new. I've been playing football since I was nine years old. It's my fourth year playing with fully grown men at the collegiate level. I know what I'm in for: a world of hurt. And a sense of accomplishment. A feeling of pride. Camaraderie with the guys on the field with me, battling it out.

This is my last season of football. After thirteen years, it's almost time to be done. As much as it abuses me, as painful as it is, I still love the sport. I still have it in me to get through this season. Next summer, when I'm not preparing for the upcoming season for the first time in my life, I'm sure I'm going to miss it.

Football has been part of my life nearly as long as Diana has, but if I had to decide between one or the other, I know what I would choose in a heartbeat. She's my everything, my best friend. One day, I hope we're more than friends. For now, I'm content to have her in my life in any way I can, no matter how much it tortures me.

By the time I make it out of the shower, she's awake and on her phone. Diana scrubs a hand over her face and groans.

"What's wrong?" My morning voice is scratchy and rough.

She sighs. "I didn't think I drank that much…"

My stomach sinks. "What happened?" She only had two drinks, and then we went for cheese fries and burgers again. I thought she was mostly sober by the time we crashed into my bed at three o'clock.

"I texted this dude."

There's an itch beneath my clavicle that I can't quite scratch, a burning sensation spreading through my chest. "Oh?"

"He didn't text back," she says. She sounds… disappointed?

"How'd you meet?" I ask ever so casually, digging in my dresser for a pair of boxer shorts.

"At the pub the other night."

The night she went out with her soccer teammates? The night she cancelled on me and then didn't answer my texts while she was being chatted up by some dude?

We aren't dating. We aren't in a relationship. There is no reason for me to be upset over the fact that she was flirting with some guy at the bar… except for the fact that I wish that guy was me.

I clear my throat. "What does your day look like?"

Diana runs her hands through her hair, detangling the waves. "Laundry, lunch, a little bit of homework before the team meeting, then we get on the bus for the airport at three."

"I'm sorry you're missing the pilates class."

She gives me a half-smile. "I'll be there next week."

"Yeah, but I won't."

Her smile drops. "Oh, yeah."

This is how the season goes. I have a game, then she has one; mine is home, hers is away. She comes back Tuesday night and then has a home game on Thursday; I leave Friday morning for my away game. If we play our cards right, I might be able to see her on Wednesday for a bit, in between my study group for forensic accounting, the team film review, and her psychology department dinner. Or maybe Thursday after her game we can meet up for a late dinner or something.

The only saving grace is that we're finally physically in the same place. We aren't playing phone tag from opposite sides of the country; now, we have the same home base. Plus, my season ends at the end of the semester; this will end in a few short months.

Tightening my grip on my towel, I attempt to maneuver into my shorts, and succeed in nearly flashing my best friend. Diana swallows loudly, so loud I can hear it from across the room.

"I'll be right back," she announces loudly, and escapes into the bathroom.

Quickly, I pull on clothes and run my towel over my hair. When I hear the shower turn on, I select one of my smallest t-shirts for her to change into, should she decide to need it. It'll still be almost a dress on her.

When she emerges from the bathroom with my spare towel wrapped around her torso, her hair wet and loose around her shoulders, my pulse ricochets up three beats. Her pretty purple toes flex into the carpet. My stomach twists.

"I'll let you get changed," I announce. "I'll be downstairs."

Taking the stairs two at a time, I arrive on the ground floor to find Mack folding the blanket that covered her last night. She looks up and smiles shyly at me.

"Thanks for letting me stay here last night," she says.

"Any time." I can't speak for all of my roommates, but I totally don't mind if she crashes on our couch—especially if it means Diana has to bunk in with me.

Mack is family. She's Miles's sister, she's a freshman, and she's a fellow athlete. From the little I've overheard from Miles, her roommate is a raging bitch, so if she wants to hang out here, I'm not going to complain. She's quiet. She doesn't bring guys back to crash on the couch with her. She hangs out, she reads, and she gives Miles shit, which is something he needs sometimes. Yeah, it could be a lot worse.

"Did you have fun last night?"

She makes a face. "I don't think I like parties very much."

"Why? What happened?"

"There's too many people," she says, and I laugh. "I don't know what to do with my hands. I don't like beer very much. I can't relax."

"It takes some getting used to," I admit. "The party scene isn't for everyone. There's no shame if it's not your cup of tea. Wes doesn't party, either, and Tucker will go out, but he doesn't drink. You have to find what you're comfortable with."

"Yeah, maybe."

"You're only eighteen. You have plenty of time to decide what you do and don't like. There's no need to force yourself to be someone that you're not," I remind her. "Don't put yourself in a box for the sake of everyone around you. Be who you want to be, whatever you are or aren't interested in. Own that."

Mack nods her head, biting her lip. "I'll think about it."

There are footsteps on the stairs and then Diana appears at the landing. My heart skips a beat. She's wearing the shirt I left for her with my hoodie from yesterday over it, her wet hair tied back in a braid. She looks absolutely fucking gorgeous.

"We're going to grab something to eat," I announce to the room at large. I look at Mack, who is standing awkwardly at the end of the couch. "Would you like to join us?"

She swallows. "You want me to come with you guys?"

"The two prettiest girls on campus on my arm on Sunday morning? Hell, yeah," I say with an exaggerated wink, and like I expect, Mack goes pink.

Diana laughs. "You're incorrigible."

"You love me."

"Eh, maybe," she says, and I can't help the flutter in my stomach at the concession that maybe, possibly…

"C'mon," I say, pulling on a hoodie. "It's time for breakfast."

Mack lays the blankets on the couch and picks up her backpack and jacket. Together the three of us make our way out of the house and through Athlete's Village towards the ASC. At midmorning, the dining hall is decently populated. There is a table full of freshmen football players at the back of the room. I nod to them as we pass by. A few of the guys look surprised to see me with two pretty girls, especially this early in the day and with Diana clearly in my shirt.

Wes is already sitting at our usual table at the back of the room, two tables over from the freshmen. He looks up from his book with surprise written on his face.

"Good morning," Mack chirps, much too happily.

He grunts, and she slides into the seat across from him as Diana takes the seat beside her.

I still can't believe we get to do this, that we can hang out basically whenever we want, schedules permitting. Our friendship has always been from a distance, coordinated through visits and summer camp and a lot of late night phone calls because of the time difference. It was worth staying up late to talk to her.

Diana has settled in well with my friend group, too. She gets along with Sam and Mack, who's recently started hanging out with us, and she and Mason have seemed to really click. She has no difficulty keeping up with the guys. She's charmed Tucker and Amir, and she flirts with Greg, who isn't shy about flirting back. I don't think anything is happening there. She's never shown any interest in any football players before, not at USC and not in high school. Even when my high school's quarterback would flirt with her at the parties after our games, she never paid him any attention.

I don't know what kind of guys she's interested in. She's never posted pictures with any guys on social media. She goes out—she's called me before or after a date, wanting to talk everything over, and sometimes she's texted me from the bed of some dude who disappointed her—but she doesn't date, not really. As far as I know, she's never had a boyfriend. As far as I know, she's never wanted one.

If nothing ever happens between us, if we stay friends for the rest of our lives... I won't be happy, exactly, but I can be content. If she decides she wants to go out with someone else... that's going to sting. I don't like that she was texting some dude last night. Not because I'm being possessive over her. More because it stings that I'm right in front of her and she doesn't see me.

At the same time, I don't want to sacrifice the amazing friendship we've had for the last fourteen years over something fleeting. I don't want a fling: I want to be with her, to love her and honor her for the rest of our lives... which I realize is a strange reaction to a woman I'm not dating. Diana and I are friends, first and foremost, and I won't do anything to jeopardize that.

———

When I was in high school, Diana introduced me to the torture that is pilates class. It's a low impact fitness class that blends the stretching of yoga with high repetition counts and core stabilization. It's great. I love it. It's a brilliant way to recover after a tough football game when I'm not ready to lift hundreds of pounds of weights or grind my joints into dust doing cardio.

Mason is a fan of pilates, too, and because of her influence, Tucker, Amir, and Wes started going to class on Sunday afternoons, too. Before long, we recruited Greg and Miles to join our fun, and now our group of six guys will huff and puff and sweat our way through the hour of intense core work.

Diana is on the way to the airport for her game against West Virginia, otherwise she would probably be with us. She's a big fan of both yoga and pilates classes as a low-impact workout in between heavy lifting sessions and on the field drills. I can't do hot yoga, though—I don't want to do anything in hundred degree heat, much less exercise. There's a reason I picked a school in New England instead of going to Texas or Arizona to play football.

Okay, so there are lots of reasons. I'm from here. I didn't want to go far. And I wanted a decent accounting program. After all, that's why I'm here: to get an education. Football comes second to that—according to my parents, at least.

Flat on my back, my legs in the tabletop position, I breathe and let the instructor flow through the variations of core exercises. It doesn't matter how many weights I lift, how much core strength I have, or how often I do this: every time is hard, like I've never done this before.

Wes and Amir are on my left, Greg and Tucker on my

right. Miles is on the other side of them, with Sam and two of her teammates. Slowly but surely, we have indoctrinated every one of our friends into our cult of attending pilates class every Sunday.

But Diana's not here. She should be here.

She's where she's supposed to be, with her team on their way to a soccer game. It's not fair of me to wish she were here with me instead. My football career isn't more important than her soccer career. It's because of football and soccer that we're here, that we have the privilege of competing for our teams and our school.

It's nice to spend some time with the guys. Miles has Sam now, and Tucker and Mason are attached at the hip. We had a lot of fun during the summer, the six of us thrown into our house for the second year in a row while we battled out two a day practices and summer training.

Mason stayed on campus, training with the track team, so she's been around a good deal lately. Sam went home to Mississippi for the break. Now that she's back, now that school is in session again, we're back to the Saturday night routine of fraternity parties and sorority events after football games. Mason's track parties are legendary, too—I've snuck into a few of those over the last year, and let's just say, those kids know how to party.

Sundays, though, are reserved for the guys. We start with recovery brunch, get massages or help with stretching from the team staff, and meet up for pilates class at four every week. After class, we'll grab dinner and then head back to the house to watch a movie. Since Wes would rather stay home, it's our little way of enjoying the time with our core group. We might crack open a few beers, or something stronger if the movie calls for it, and then we spend a few hours on the couch hanging out and maybe playing a few video games.

This year is our final year together. More than half of us are graduating this spring; Amir and Greg still have another year of eligibility left, so they might stick around for one more season… and maybe a few semesters, depending on the progress they make in their degrees. Greg is probably headed to the NFL, following in his father's footsteps. Amir has talked briefly about going back to Wisconsin, but the more he talks about grad school, the more it seems like that's the last thing he wants to do.

I'm not afraid of going to graduate school, of getting an MBA or whatever degree my father decides is necessary. What I want—a break between now and then—may or may not be feasible. It's not a hardship to agree to work for his company; it's what I've been groomed to do my entire life.

Diana has said a few times she might want to do grad school, but she's nowhere close to applying and pursuing it. Wherever she decides to live after graduation, I'll do everything I can to ensure we can stay together as much as possible. We can rent an apartment in whatever part of town she wants. I'll make the commute work.

Hell, if she wants to move back to Amherst, I'm sure there's a way I can manage to work partially remote and commute the rest of the time. As much as my parents don't like Diana, they understand familial piety. Her dad is sick. She wants to be close to him. That's something to celebrate.

No matter what happens, I want to be with her. Wherever she is, I'll find a way to make it happen—for my sake, as well as hers.

seventeen

· · ·

Diana

JOHANNA IS PISSED that I'm hanging out with Emma and the rest of the defense instead of kowtowing at her feet. I can see it on her face, in the set of her jaw and the way she crosses her arms over her chest and can't look at me. Somehow I can't bring myself to care. I know that she's going to make my life difficult in a myriad of ways, but right now, it all feels like a little too much drama.

I don't care that my roommate and captain is upset. I don't care that my living situation is sure to get awkward. I've spent too many years tiptoeing the line to give a shit. After almost a month on campus, I'm finally starting to make friends. Emma invited me to sit next to her on the bus, I sat beside Zoe on the plane, and then Mischa, the freshman, on the bus to our hotel.

So what if I got a slow start in winning over my team-mates? So what if I was distracted by Johanna and her minions in the first few weeks? We're putting the pieces together now. I don't care that we live in different houses; we're all part of the same team, and that's what matters.

This trip, I'm assigned to room with Kristin, who is… fine.

She's personable enough, and she's never been overtly mean to me. She likes to keep the hotel room cold, like I do, and she turns in early, but she claims not to be distracted by lights or noises, so she doesn't care if I stay up and watch TV or something.

I'm wired. I can't sleep. I have the weirdest itch to call Barrett, but I'm not sure what to say. I'm sorry I fell asleep in your bed last night? I don't regret it. Normally I never sleep well when there's a partner in my bed, but with Barrett, I feel more well rested than I have in… days. Weeks.

Maybe because he's a partner in the most pure sense, a compatriot in sleeping. He holds me, but he doesn't smother me. He lets me cuddle. I've never felt comfortable cuddling with any of the past partners who have shared my bed.

Even though Barrett and I have never done anything remotely like this before, it's not weird. Instead it feels oddly right. Comforting without being comfortable.

I roll over in my starchy hotel room bed and stare blankly at my phone. I have this inexplicable urge to talk to him. I'm not sure why. This morning, we were together, and it wasn't nearly this awkward. It wasn't awkward at all, except when he started flirting with Mack. I wasn't a fan of that. She's too young for him. Then again, I don't think he has any interest in her; he's said twice that he considers her like a kid sister.

The idea of Barrett dating sets my teeth on edge. I'm not entirely sure why. He's entitled to be happy. He's allowed to go out with women. He's single and it doesn't look like that's going to change anytime soon. Why shouldn't he date? Why shouldn't he hook up? So it didn't work out with Johanna; there are plenty of other women out there who would be interested in him. He's gorgeous, he's actually a decent guy, he's smart, and his family is loaded.

It's not like he would ever date me; that's simply out of the question. His parents would never approve, and there is absolutely no way I would ever pass their intense scrutiny.

They barely like that we're friends; they definitely would not appreciate us turning into more. No, we're not going to happen. He deserves a chance to be happy.

I'm broadening my social horizons; it's only natural for him to do so, too. He hasn't mentioned anyone in awhile. As far as I can tell, he hasn't hooked up with anyone since the start of the semester. He's probably overdue to get laid.

A chill runs up my spine. I don't like the idea of Barrett going out and getting laid, either. I'm not territorial. I just don't like it. He's mine.

I recognize that it's not healthy to feel so strongly about a man I have no real ties to. We're friends. That's all we've ever been, and that's all we'll ever be. We work so well as friends, I wouldn't ever want to jeopardize what we have.

Even though I have Barrett, even though the girls and I are finally starting to get along, I'm still lonely. I'm surrounded by people, most of whom I would consider my friends now, and I've never felt so alone. Even when I first got to USC as a freshman, knowing nobody, it didn't feel like this.

I can't depend on Barrett and his friends for all of my social interaction. No matter how much I like them, I need to branch out and make my own support system. Though there are a few girls from past teams that I keep up with, by and by, I've let most of them fall by the wayside over the last few years.

When I'm done with school, when I'm on my own, I won't have anyone to rely on. At the end of the day, it's just me, myself, and I. If I want to have friends later on, I have to start the process of finding them now. I can't count on them still being here next year.

My finger hovers over Barrett's contact before I sigh and close my phone screen. It's late. I don't want to bother him.

The phone buzzes and lights up with a text from the very guy I want to talk to.

Ate a peanut butter sandwich and rocky road ice cream for dinner tonight, Barrett tells me.

And you don't even need an epi-pen, I fire back.

He replies in half a second. *You know I'd never do it if you were here.*

I do. And I appreciate that, more than I can ever tell him. He takes my allergies as seriously as I do. Nobody, not even my parents, cares as much as he does.

How was it?

Meh. I don't miss it as much as I thought I would, he writes. A pause. *I would rather have you here.*

I'd rather be there, too.

We'll go to dinner when you get back.

I have a psych mixer thing tomorrow.

Drinks? After?

You'll meet me at the bar at 9?

He doesn't like to go out drinking on weeknights. Weekends, sure, he's down to party. Barrett cares enough about his grades that he doesn't drink during the week—or the night before a game, unlike some of the football players I knew back at USC, who got drunk at every available opportunity.

I like that Barrett is so committed to school. Yeah, he might have a job post graduation because of nepotism, but he's putting in the work now to be qualified and worthy for more than just his last name.

He knows what he wants. The only question is what order he will accomplish it. Does he get his MBA now or in five years? Does he start out in actual accounting or are they going to funnel him directly into the corporate executive pipeline?

Me, the future is still up in the air. I don't know if graduate school is in the cards for me, at least right now. I don't want to move far away. Now that I'm back, I want to stay in New England. I need to be within easy commuting distance of Amherst. I don't want to be more than an hour or so away should anything happen. At the same time, I don't see a reason to sacrifice my future or my wants and needs forever just because of my dad's diagnosis. He wouldn't be happy if I put my entire life on hold for him.

I've spent the last however many years working to be the best soccer player and balance school at the same time. Now, soccer is almost over, and the end of school is drawing ever closer. I don't know what happens next year. Do I go off to grad school? Do I get a job somewhere? An internship? I honestly have no clue. There's no road map, no other person making this decision for me.

When it comes to a career, I want to do something with nutrition and dietetics. I want to help people. What that looks like, I'm not certain.

So much is undecided. It sets my teeth on edge. I don't know what city I'll be living in, if I'll be in grad school, if I'll have a job. I know nothing. All I know is that Barrett will still be my best friend, and will still do everything in his power to make me happy. Because that's what he's done all along. I don't foresee that changing anytime soon. I hope.

———

I'm not exactly sure what I expected of a psychology department mixer held at a local bar. Maybe for it to not be a stuffy, pretentious event? Yeah, right.

Ostensibly, the meet and greet is supposed to be an informational meeting for people who are interested in going to grad school next year or the year after. Somehow, I have a feeling a good percentage of the people here are more interested in the three free drink tickets passed out when we walked in.

Tucker and Mason were already here when I arrived, talking with a woman I vaguely recognize as being in one of my classes.

"Diana! Hey!" Mason says, giving me a hug. "Good to see you. How was your game?"

Well, even though we didn't win, the team gelled a whole lot better, so I'd consider that a win.

"Not bad. Did I miss anything while I was gone?"

Tucker laughs. "Only Barrett looking sad and despondent without you."

"Oh no. What happened?"

"He missed you," he says, like he can't believe how thick I am.

"I missed him, too," I admit, and he grins.

"Oh, have you met Dvora?" Mason says. "She's in our study group for abnormal psych."

She gestures to the woman beside her. She's about my age, about my height, with fair skin and dark hair in a perfect curly high ponytail. My hair has never not once looked as good as hers does right now. Her tortoiseshell glasses and funky oversized blazer pair perfectly with her hot pink miniskirt and fishnet tights. She's effortlessly stylish and immediately I hate her and want to be her at the same time.

"Nice to meet you, I'm Diana."

"Dvora," she says. "I think we're in the same ethics class?"

"I thought I recognized you," I say with a half laugh. "I transferred in this semester, so I'm still meeting everyone."

She smiles. "And you want to go to grad school?"

"Considering it. I'm a double major, also studying dietetics, and I'm not sure what direction I want to go in yet. Keeping my options open," I explain. "And you?"

"I want to go into research," Dvora says, definitive and sure. I like that. "My minor is in statistics."

"Good luck," Mason says. "I nearly failed stats both times I took it. Miles—my friend—he had to tutor me. In the end, I still ask him for help with my homework whenever we have to compile statistics."

"Barrett and I used to study together back when I was still

at USC. We would screen share and he would walk me through my homework," I admit. "I'm so glad my best friend is a math whiz."

Tucker shrugs. "They never offered to help me with my homework."

Mason flips her hair over her shoulder. "You're not as pretty as I am."

"You've got that right." He ducks down and presses a kiss to her temple. "I'm glad my buddies were able to help you succeed. We need to take advantage of every opportunity that comes our way."

There are eyes on me. The guy from the other night—Trey—is leaning against the bar. His eyes scrub over me again. I raise eyebrows at him and slowly his mouth spreads into a grin.

"You know that guy?" Tucker asks, nodding in his direction. His lip curls in distaste.

I shrug. "I gave him my number last week and he never called me."

"Oh." It's clear he's not sure what to make of this. "Want me to go beat him up?"

"Nah, I think I'm good," I tell him, patting his massive shoulder. "I appreciate the sentiment, though, big guy."

He frowns. "You don't get to call me that."

"I don't?"

"That's Mase's name for me," he says, a little petulantly, and I laugh.

"Okay. I'll come up with some other nickname for you," I promise, and he cracks a grin.

Mason and Dvora are talking. At the sound of her name, she popped her head up, smiled in our direction, and returned to her conversation.

"So, do you like the dude?"

I shrug. "I mean, we talked at the bar for a few minutes. He bought me a drink."

"And then he didn't have the balls to call you?" He shakes his head in mock disappointment.

"He texted looking for a hookup."

His eyes go wide. "And you turned him down."

Biting my lip, I look away. "I might have been a touch inebriated at the time."

"Shit. Does Barrett know?"

"Know what?"

"That you've got the hots for some wimpy hipster dude?"

I roll my eyes. "Okay, so he's not an athlete, but that doesn't mean he's a wimp."

Tucker coughs "Bullshit" into his fist.

"He seemed nice enough."

"Yeah, and then he texted you trying to get into your pants, so clearly he's a stellar dude."

Mason looks over at this. "What's going on?"

"Your boyfriend wants to be my overprotective big brother, despite the fact that there is absolutely no reason for him to be."

Tucker frowns. "That's not very fair."

"Barrett doesn't care who I hook up with. So why does it bother you?"

"I just want this guy to respect you. Drunk texting you for a hookup doesn't sound like he would treat you the way you deserve to be treated."

Mason laughs bitterly. "Oh, Tuck, I love you."

Even Dvora, who I've never talked to, is shaking her head. "What planet are you from? Have you never gone on a date?"

"I've only ever dated one woman," he says, and Mason smirks proudly. "I don't play the dating game."

"You also had my twin brother ask me out for you because you didn't have the balls to do it yourself," she reminds him. She wraps her arm around his. "Luckily, I thought you were the cutest boy in school, or it might not have worked out."

He leans down and bestows a gentle kiss on her lips.

"You're my Princess. I'd like to see some other guy try to break us apart again."

She smiles and fists her hand in his jacket, pulling him closer.

I turn to Dvora. "They could do this all night."

She laughs. "Shall we hit the bar, then? You can flirt with your dude and I can get a much needed drink."

"I think I like you," I announce, and she grins.

She leads the way to the bar, landing conveniently close to where Trey and his buddies are hanging out. She angles her body closer and makes eyes at his friend. I follow behind her, accidentally on purpose crowding Trey's stool as we wait for the bartender to have a free moment.

"Hey," Trey says. "Dana, right?"

"Diana."

"How's it going?"

"Oh, you know," I say with an ambiguous shrug.

His eyes scrape over me again. I'm wearing jeans, a plain black v-neck, and a light jacket—nothing fancy, certainly not as dressed up as Dvora, but comfortably stylish all the same.

Trey hums. "So you're interested in grad school?"

"Interested in keeping my options open. Not trying to limit myself yet."

We make eye contact. My stomach swoops. A familiar buzzing pulses through my veins.

"I can get with that," he says with a confident grin. "Can I get you a drink? Vodka soda, right?"

He remembers!

"That would be great." I try to hand over one of my drink tickets and he waves it away.

"I've got it," he says.

"Like you've got my number?"

"Oh, ho," says one of the guys behind him.

"Yeah, I've got your number," Trey says, puffed up with bravado. "Maybe this time I'll use it."

"See that you do."

The bartender comes over and Dvora places her drink order. Trey leans over the bar and asks for a vodka soda and a Bud Light.

"You here with anyone?" Trey asks.

"Some friends." I glance over my shoulder. Tucker and Mason are blatantly watching me. When we make eye contact, Tucker lifts his chin and looks away. Mason laughs and waggles her fingers at me.

"Your friends?" He nods towards Tucker.

"That's Tuck. He's on the football team."

"Oh."

He sizes him up. Tucker is a big dude. To look at him, you wouldn't expect the big guy is one of the softest, most cuddly guys in the world. He has a heart of gold. He's big, physically imposing, and Black, which leads to some stereotypes that couldn't be further from the truth. Tuck wouldn't hurt a fly, and especially not me.

"I think we've had a class together," Trey says noncommittally.

"He's a psych major."

"Cool."

The bartender pushes our drinks towards us. Since it looks like he's not going to, I reach into my wallet and pull out a few bucks to shove in the glass stuffed with far too few bills. I don't care that it's a "free" drink from a drink ticket—she's working hard, she deserves to be paid a fair wage.

I take a sip from my drink. It's well made for cheap well vodka, I have no complaints. Taking a second sip, I survey the crowd.

"Are these events always this popular?"

Trey gives me a sideways grin. "Usually, yeah. Psych is one of the biggest departments at the graduate and doctoral level."

"I wouldn't know. I just transferred in."

He does a double take. "Oh? From where?"

"USC."

"Cool. How was South Carolina?"

I laugh. "No, the University of Southern California. I was on the soccer team."

He looks me over again. "Really?"

"I transferred in, so now I'm on the Newton team."

Trey gives an awkward chuckle. "I didn't even realize Newton had a soccer team. I'm not really into sports ball."

Okay, strike one. How can he not like sports?

Strike two. He calls it sports ball?!

"Soccer is a huge part of my life."

"Maybe I'll check out a game one of these days," he says.

I don't want to lie and say it's a good team to watch. Frankly, we suck. But we could use the support of the student body, our friends and peers. Even if we don't play well, it would be nice to have fans in the stands.

It's clear some of the girls have given up. Others are trying hard, just can't put everything together: they're good in practice, and then fall to pieces during actual games. There's a distinct lack of communication between forwards and defense; it's like Johanna and her minions exist in an entirely different realm than the rest of us.

"Maybe you should," I tell him, and he gives me another one of those sideways grins that makes my stomach swirl. I can't tell if it's attraction or indigestion.

Mason catches my eye in the crowd. She's reserved me a seat near the front, and it's quickly filling up.

"I'll see you around."

Trey grins at me. "You, too."

Making my way through the crowd, I slip into the chair Mason has saved for me. She squeezes my arm and goes back to her conversation with Dvora. My phone buzzes in my back pocket and I pull it out, fully expecting it to be a message from Barrett or my parents.

It's not. It's Trey.

Great running into you again, he wrote. *We should go out sometime.*

My stomach swoops. Looking over my shoulder, I meet his eyes and smile. He inclines his head briefly.

My phone buzzes again. *It's a date.*

eighteen

. . .

Barrett

I'M USED to being on the road. This is nothing new. When I
first got to college, the sheer amount of travel required was
surprising, even though it shouldn't have been. On average,
we travel a larger distance than we did back in high school.
Now, we drive or fly the day before the game, so we have
time to rest and get settled in before the preparations begin
for the game itself. Roughly one in every two games is on the
road: sometimes it's three at home in a row, and sometimes
it's every other game traveling. We don't get to pick the
schedule; we have to accept what's given to us, or we don't
have to play on the team anymore.

There's a familiarity to away games. Typically, I room with
Tucker, who is probably my best friend on campus after
Diana. Now that he's dating Mason, he's only slightly more
annoying; now he's constantly talking to her instead of
constantly absorbed in his phone and her social media
profiles, and if he's not talking to her, he's talking to me about
her. I get it. She's the love of his life. He's over the moon that
they're back together. I don't need to hear about it every day,
at home and away.

I wonder what Diana is up to. She got back to campus this

morning from her away game at Amherst College. Her parents came to the game and took her and some friends out to dinner. Not Johanna and her minions—other girls, ones I haven't really met yet. I'm glad she's settling in and making friends. I'm glad she gets to spend time with her family.

Between my flight to Philadelphia and her road trip home, we've been missing each other all day. She gets carsick if she's looking at screens in the car, so she isn't a fan of texting or reading while she's on the bus. Most of the time, she tries to catch a nap or hang out with her teammates on the trips to and from games. It's one of the few times we get to bond with one another, when we're trapped in a tin can for hours on end.

Tucker is in his bed, texting with Mason. Normally they have an hour long phone call where they talk sweet nothings into one another's ears, but tonight her brother is in town for a game against the New England football team on Sunday, so they both have reasons to stick to keeping it PG-13.

He's not a bad roommate, all things considered. We live together and share a bathroom on a day to day basis, so we're familiar with one another's daily habits. He likes a freezing cold shower in the morning and then a long, steaming hot shower about an hour before bed. He likes to keep the room at a cool seventy degrees when we're sleeping, which I'm all aboard for. He doesn't snore too loudly. He doesn't masturbate while I'm in our shared hotel room. All in all, not a bad guy to share a room with. I've certainly had worse roommates over the years.

My phone vibrates with a text, and Tucker shoots me a smirk.

"Little lady checking up on you?"

Ha. I wish.

Instead it's my brother. He's in town for a wedding. Do I have any time to meet up?

Dougie is a former college athlete, so he knows I don't

have a lot of free time during road trips. He also respects that I take football seriously, even more seriously than he treated hockey, and I have commitments. Still… my brother and I barely ever see each other. We're not really friends, not yet. Maybe in a few years we can be, when we're equals and both working in our family's forensic accounting firm.

As I'm about to reply yes, I can meet for breakfast, a video chat from Diana pops up on my screen. I don't care that it's rude to take a phone call with someone else in the room. I accept the call.

"Hey." I sit up in bed and tuck my hand behind my head. It's a good angle for me. It makes my biceps look huge. I'm all for it.

In the next bed over, Tucker snorts.

"Hey." My best friend grins at me, her eyes crinkling. "Long time no see."

We've been missing each other all week. In theory, I get to go home and see her again. In reality, I get home on Sunday afternoon and she leaves on Tuesday for another away game, this time against Montana, so she won't be back until Friday. Then Saturday, I have another game, which is technically an away game, but since it's against Boston College, there's no real travel involved. Hell, my parents live closer to Boston College than they do to Newton.

Not like they're going to show up. My parents haven't been to one of my college football games. They went to a single game in high school, *one*, and that was only because it was my senior homecoming and I was getting an award. I doubt they're going to come to homecoming this year. They've never come to Parents' Weekend. Somehow I don't think they're going to come to Senior Night, either.

My freshman year, Dougie came to Parents' Weekend, even though he obviously isn't my parent. We went to the pub and he bought me dinner, then he sat me down to tell me he was proud of me, but he probably wouldn't make it to too many more of my games. Back then, it was competing with his hockey schedule; later, he was too busy at Brown to make the trip into the city any more than absolutely necessary. Okay, so maybe he isn't as much of an asshole as I like to pretend.

I get it. My parents aren't exactly great to be around. He has to put himself first. That means not kowtowing to my parents' intense demands and absurd expectations. If he hadn't been so serious about hockey, I never would have pursued football. It's because he led the way that I felt confident enough to follow in his footsteps… at least, in my own way.

"Miss you," I admit now to Diana, who smiles wistfully.

"We'll figure it out one of these days," she says.

I sigh. There's a lot I hope we can figure out.

"Dougie texted me. He's in town," I blurt.

Her eyes go wide. "Are you going to see him?"

"I don't know."

"You should. Absolutely. Do it," she insists.

"Easy there, cujo."

Diana laughs. "Your brother is cool."

"He's a dick."

"Yeah, but he's still cool," she says. "Let him take you to brunch or something. Wait. Why is he even in Philly?"

"He has a wedding. One of his prep school friends."

She rolls her eyes. "I swear, that boy has a bigger social life than the two of us combined."

It's my turn to laugh. "That's not hard."

"True."

My brother is a social animal. He loves meeting people and making connections. He excels at small talk. Me? No, thanks. I went to etiquette classes because my parents required it, and I went to a few social events as required, but for the most part, if it wasn't about football or Diana, I wasn't interested. I never have been. That's why Dougie excels at the social interaction side of business school, and why he'll have a job in our family's business doing something to build relationships, and my job will be running numbers. I like numbers. They don't lie, except when we get artistic.

"I can't even imagine getting married," Diana says.

I sit up a little straighter. "You can't?"

"I mean, not right now." She bites her lip and looks away for a moment before her eyes find mine again. "I kind of need to be in a relationship before I can get married, and it doesn't look like that's happening anytime soon, so..."

"I didn't realize you'd thought about it."

"My dad..." She sniffs and clears her throat. "He's the one that's supposed to walk me down the aisle. And there's the father daughter dance. What will I do if he's not here?"

Her eyes well with tears.

"Dee..."

"It's all hypothetical. I've never even had a boyfriend," she admits.

I'll be your boyfriend, I want to tell her. I would marry her in a heartbeat. I want forever with her.

But I can't tell her that.

"Do you want one?"

Pick me! Choose me!

In the next bed over, Tucker snorts again, and I shoot him an irritated glare.

"Kind of," Diana says for the first time ever. "I met this guy and we've been texting. We're supposed to go bowling tomorrow night."

My stomach clenches. My whole world tilts fourteen degrees to the left.

"Who?"

"Um, I met him at the pub a few weeks ago."

"The guy who wouldn't text you back?"

She blushes. "Yeah. I ran into him again and... well, he's cute and he seems nice, so..."

"I hope it works out," I lie.

I don't want it to work out. I want her to be happy—I just want her to be happy with me.

"Thanks, B." She gives me a shy smile. "What about you?"

"What about me?"

"Any girls on the horizon for you?"

I laugh. "No, I think I'm good for now."

"Guys?" She raises her brows pointedly. "I totally won't judge."

"Diana, I'm not interested in men. I like women. I just don't want to date anyone right now," I tell her.

"Oh."

"What's with this sudden interest in my sex life?" Maybe if I downgrade it to the transactional physicality of it, she won't realize all I want is her.

She goes pink. "Well, we've spent the last few weekends together."

"So?"

"So if you wanted to, you know… go out and get laid…" She bites her lip. "I just don't want to stand in your way."

"I'll take that under advisement," I tell her seriously.

"I don't want to be a burden."

Rolling my eyes, I scoff. "First of all, you're not, but I think you should trust that I would tell you if you were."

"I do," she says quietly. "I do trust you."

"So believe me that I would tell you if I needed space, to get laid or otherwise," I tell her.

Her eyes rove over my face. "Okay."

"Okay?"

She nods. "Okay."

Tucker's phone rings with a video chat.

"Listen, babe, I've got to go. I'll talk to you later," I say as he answers Mason's call.

She gives me a small smile. "Goodnight."

When we hang up, I exhale slowly. My chest feels tight and itchy. I don't like this. Sinking down in the bed and rolling over, I text my brother back. *Breakfast works great. See you tomorrow.*

———

"You sick fuck," Dougie shouts as he enters the hotel lobby. "How dare you?"

Everyone in the packed lobby turns to look in his direction. The fucker thrives off the attention.

Rolling my eyes, I stand and walk towards him. My brother pulls me into a perfunctory hug and claps my back. Everyone is watching us.

"Damn it, when did you get taller?" he whines.

He's three years older than me, but I'm three inches taller and close to a hundred pounds heavier, most of that muscle now that he's not working out five hours a day anymore. He also still can't grow a full beard, whereas mine comes in fully in about four and a half days.

Even though we're not exceptionally close, I have to admit it's kind of nice to see my brother. With him being off at Brown and me being busy with school and football, we don't cross paths often. For now, neither of us are being manipulated into attending the dozen or so charity events my parents attend every month, but as soon as we both graduate in the spring, that will start up again. Dougie is a classic extrovert, he thrives on being around people, whereas I prefer to keep my cards closer to my chest.

I didn't fit in with the other rich kids at my fancy prep school—I was too Asian, even though my family has been here for three generations. I didn't fit in with the other Asian kids at my school—I was too much of a jock. And I didn't fit in with the other football players—I was too much of a nerd, too interested in math and accounting to socialize the way they did. My brother defied the molds, whereas I disappeared into them.

Dougie heads in the direction of the hotel's restaurant and I lumber after him. Technically we're supposed to be having breakfast in the team room, but if we want to spring for the expensive restaurant, they can't stop us. Most of the guys on the team don't have the kind of spending money we do, nor do they have the desire to venture out of the team's block of rooms. And Dougie can't visit the team sponsored rooms if he's not actually part of the team.

"I didn't realize you were in town this weekend," I comment idly as we take our seats at an out of the way table.

"Sean and Soo-jin are getting married," he says.

I'm not familiar with Soo-jin. Sean was on the club hockey teams my brother played with all through middle school. He's a normal upper middle class white guy. He got a partial scholarship to Notre Dame, busted his knee his freshman year, and was never able to play again. Last I heard, he had dropped out of Notre Dame and transferred to UMass so he could be close to home again.

I didn't realize they kept in touch all this time, enough to be invited to his wedding. I don't speak to the majority of the guys I've played with over the years. The only real friendship of mine that's lasted is the one I share with Diana. It's the only one I've ever put real effort into.

"Glad you were able to make it out for it."

Dougie shrugs. "They seem happy. I had the weekend free. I didn't have a good enough reason not to come."

"It's nice that you've been able to stay friends all these years."

"He's a good dude," my brother says.

I'm not the guy that has a bunch of friends; that's never been me. For the most part, I keep to myself and I keep my social circle small. When I meet someone I want to keep in my life, I keep them close.

"So, Mom called me the other day," Dougie says, and it's my turn to roll my eyes.

"Oh no. What did I do wrong now?"

"Are you really shacking up with Diana?"

"Shacking up?"

"Yeah. Are you finally sleeping with her?"

My face heats. Yeah, we've slept together, emphasis on *slept*. It's certainly nothing I'd write home to my mom about. For one, she's never liked my best friend. On top of that, she's never shown an interest in whoever I go out with, except to confirm they're Chinese... which, usually, they were. If I'm not careful, she'll start the old ladies matchmaking for me like they do for my brother and all my cousins.

Dougie laughs. "So you finally—"

"No, we're not... we aren't..." I sigh. "She's interested in some dude."

"Shit. Sorry, dude," my brother says with a sympathetic frown. "There are other fish in the sea."

"Yeah. I guess. Did I tell you she set me up with her team captain?"

He nearly drops his coffee cup. "Um, what?"

"Yeah. She thought it would be good for me to date her captain, who pretty much hates her for no real reason. That went well," I comment blandly, and Dougie snorts.

"I can tell."

"Maybe I should just let Mom and the aunties do the matchmaking thing. It has to be better than this."

"If you want a wife, yeah, do it," my brother says. "If you're not ready for marriage, hold off as long as you can."

"Like you are?"

He shrugs. "I told them I want two years after I start working to find someone on my own. I need to get through school first. She recognizes that it's my priority for right now. I can't afford to be distracted."

"And they're okay with that?"

"I'll find the proper little Chinese girl and marry her," he says easily. "She'll have a good family and good breeding and a trust fund and whatever the hell else they require. As long as we get along decently, I'm down. What she or I do outside the covenants of marriage is nobody's business but hers and mine."

"So you've put thought into this." I've heard rumors of other people having these types of arrangements, you do yours and I'll do mine, and as long as there are no children stemming from these... extracurricular activities, everything is fine and dandy.

"Look, marriage is a business transaction," Dougie says. "Mom and Dad want grandchildren. Ideally, I'd find a lesbian everyone approves of and we'll conceive through IVF and neither of us have to get our hands dirty. If we have to do it the hard way... well, I'm sure I'll figure out a way to make it as non-invasive as possible."

When I think about the future, my future, I don't want a loveless marriage. I don't want to be as miserable as Dougie makes it sound. He might treat this as a business transaction, he might want an obedient little wife, but I want someone that I love and trust by my side. I want Diana.

But she doesn't want me. She wants this generic hipster boy who can't possibly treat her well enough. She deserves to be treated like a princess, celebrated and cherished. She deserves the world.

How long do I wait? Do I put myself in misery forever? I want her, I love her, but I respect that she's her own person. She doesn't have to return my feelings.

"Have you talked to her about it?" he asks.

"Who?"

"Diana."

"Why would I talk to her about marriage and grandchildren?"

Dougie rolls his eyes. "Okay, whatever. You can be in denial all you'd like."

"I'm not in denial."

"So you admit you have feelings for her?"

I blink. "You know?"

"Damn it, B, I'm pretty sure everyone knows except her," he says, shaking his head. "If you want to pursue her, do it. If you don't, give yourself the freedom to move on. You owe it to yourself."

Blowing out a breath, I take a sip of my coffee and let the anxiety swirl around me.

"You don't have to make any decisions now," Dougie cautions me. "Get through school first. Hold off the old biddies at least until you're done with your MBA."

"I… I don't know if I'm going to go for it, at least not right away," I admit.

He raises his brows. "And you've said this to Dad?"

"Well… no."

"Good luck," he laughs.

"I want to work. I want to see what I like before I go to business school. I don't know who I am yet, not really."

"Do we ever?"

"Yeah, some people do."

"And you think working will magically grant you some sort of enlightenment?"

I sigh. "No. But it would at least give me some space. I've spent so much time invested in school, invested in football. I need to see who I am and who I want to be when I'm not distracted by all of… this."

"Okay, yeah, I get that," Dougie says. "I still don't think Dad will go for it."

"I only want a year or two, enough to learn the company a little bit. I don't know that I want to go into management, and it'll get awfully crowded with the three of us, Uncle James, and Nate at the top."

"You want to be a number cruncher?"

"I want to learn everything there is about the business, and that involves, yeah, crunching some numbers."

My brother shakes his head. "Okay, man. You do you. If you need it, I can be there when you tell Dad."

"Really?"

Never in a million years did I think he would volunteer to be part of what's sure to be the most painful conversation in the history of the world. Maybe because it will make him look good in comparison. Yeah, that sounds like him.

"Any idea when you're going to tell him?"

"I'm more focused on avoiding as many family dinners as possible," I admit. "They're more draining than a football game, and doing them back to back..."

He winces. "Yeah. At least you're not living at home."

"Oh, no. I couldn't survive that."

"No idea how we survived for so long in that house," he laughs. "They should have just shipped us off to boarding school the minute we turned eleven."

I roll my eyes. Both of us requested to go to a boarding school more than once over the years. Our parents never gave in. It would be unseemly to send off their kids, they decided, despite the fact that most of our peers from our exclusive, upper-crust elementary school ended up at boarding school for either middle school or high school.

I'm sure that deep, deep, deep, deep down inside, my parents love us... when they don't think of us as pawns or extensions of themselves. They're just... difficult sometimes. Okay, most of the time.

It's a fact that we're both going to join the family business; the only question is when. It's what we've been raised for, groomed for. I don't have any complaints about going into forensic accounting, and it might be nice to work alongside my father, my uncle, and my cousin Nate. Our company is truly a family business, where all of the family members contribute. Even my mother worked there for a few years when we were younger in the Legal department before she decided she preferred Family Law to corporate. She does often contract the company's services on behalf of her clients, though…

There was never an option for us to go into law or any other field. It's always been clear that the plan was for us to study Accounting, take the CPA exam, and then get an MBA. It's the same path Dad and my uncle James took, and the same path as our cousin Nate took. It's the same path that Dougie is on now, and the same one I'll likely be on.

I'm not complaining about the plan. I'll get my MBA. I just want a breather first. Is that so wrong?

nineteen

. . .

Diana

TREY and I meet at Pinzer's, the local bowling alley, shortly before seven on Saturday night. He's wearing dark jeans and a yellow and green flannel shirt, his beard freshly trimmed and neatened. He looks good. My stomach flips in nervous anticipation.

I haven't been on a date in six months, since before my dad was diagnosed, and the last time I got laid was a few days after that whole mess happened. I'm way overdue. Tonight I'm freshly washed and prepped everywhere that matters, just in case. My hair looks amazing, if I do say so myself, and my sweater dress and ankle booties are rocking the fall vibes.

Johanna gave me the side eye when I walked out of the house. I wouldn't put it past her to try to lock me out of the house tonight for daring to go out without her permission, if it wouldn't get her kicked off the team and stripped of her captaincy. I don't have the mental energy to worry about her. She's exhausting enough on a good day.

Trey greets me outside of the bowling alley. He walks towards me and reaches out for me, his hands grasping mine. He ducks down and offers me a chaste kiss on the cheek. It feels... kind of nice. I'm used to sketchy college boys who don't know how to treat a woman like a lady. So what if he texted me last week looking for a hookup? He's out on a date with me now.

And it's not like I expect this to be much more than a night or two of fun. He's cute and hopefully we can have a good time together. He's not my forever.

"You look great," he says right off the bat.

"Wow. Thank you."

"You ready to head inside?"

"Um, sure."

Pinzer's is everything I would expect of a sleazy, run down bowling alley in a college town. The faded fluorescent lighting turns everything a mellow yellow color. The smell of disinfectant, smelly feet, and cigarette smoke hits me like a tidal wave when I walk through the door. That's something I haven't missed about being back home. People here smoke more than they do in California. I've gotten used to everywhere I go being smoke free. My allergies are none too happy with me for being back in the land of cigarette smoke everywhere.

"Hey, Donovan," Trey says to the guy manning the front desk. "Two, please."

"I take it you come here a lot."

He shrugs. "Often enough."

Donovan asks me for my shoe size and then hands over a pair of used bowling shoes for me to wear. He doesn't have to ask Trey—he already knows which shoes to grab. He rings us up. Trey pulls a wrinkled twenty dollar bill out of his pocket and hands it over.

"Thank you," I tell him, because my mama raised me to have manners. I don't expect him to pay for me, but he's the one who initiated this date: by the common principles of dating, the person who invites is the person who pays. I'll offer to buy us drinks or something once we get settled.

He gives me that sideways smile of his.

We're assigned to lane twelve, right in the middle of the bowling alley. The lanes on either side of us are occupied, one by a trio of senior citizens drinking beer and cussing each other out, and the other by a group of what look to be preteens or early teenagers. The bowling alley attracts an eclectic crowd in our sleepy little college town.

"So, you come here often?" I ask Trey, who's tying his bowling shoes.

He shrugs. "What is often?"

Considering I've never been here, and I can count on one hand the number of times I've gone bowling in the last decade, I'm going to bet we have different definitions of the frequency of "often."

With soccer and now a double major, I don't have a lot of free time for hobbies. Add my dad's terminal illness on top of that… Most of my limited time without responsibilities is spent vegging on the couch or laying in my bed, recovering from the stress that has taken over my life. Sometimes Barrett joins me, and we can sit in silence for a few hours and just… be. Sometimes I'm by myself. It's exhausting being around people and being "on" all the time. Sometimes I just need a break from it all.

As much as I want to go home for a quick visit, the timing hasn't worked out. I've had games every weekend since school started, including Parents' Weekend, when my parents are coming down for a visit anyway. My first chance to go home will be for Thanksgiving. For the first time in the last four years, we don't have to spend the holiday in a hotel room eating dry room-service turkey and stuffing. I haven't been able to come home for the holiday since I went away to school—my soccer schedule didn't allow for it. Now, it's only an hour drive instead of a full day of air travel each way. I can take the train or my parents can drive down and pick me up. I'm close by.

I don't know how many more Thanksgivings I'll have with my dad; how many more holidays he'll be around for. Nobody knows, not even him. The not knowing is the worst part of all this.

Spinning on my heel, I blink back the tears welling in my eyes and walk off in search of the perfect bowling ball. If I take a few moments to regroup, that's okay, too.

Trey has already found his ball by the time I make it back. He's rolled up the sleeves of his flannel, showing off his forearms. I am a sucker for strong forearms. Biceps, too. I'm crazy about arms. Thick legs, strong legs. That ridge of muscle above the glutes and below the hips that gets shown off in tight football pants. The only thing that doesn't really get me going is abs. They're just… whatever.

I've never gone out with a non-athlete before. Most of the guys I hung around with at USC were on the men's soccer team or the lacrosse team, and the football guys were always down to party. Once I had a very, very short dalliance with a baseball player, until it turned out he was only playing me.

Even now, outside of Dvora—who I am determined to befriend, whether she knows it or not—I don't spend time with anyone who isn't an athlete. My day is occupied by practice and team activities in between our games. We eat almost all of our meals in the student athlete dining hall or manage a quick snack from the grab and go stations around campus.

It's never been an issue before. I like sports, even the more obscure ones like badminton and table tennis, and I like to cheer on other athletes as they compete. I'm a huge football fan—Barrett wouldn't have it any other way—and because of his brother I follow both college and professional hockey. After a girl from my hometown made it to the Olympic Trials, I've started becoming a fan of elite gymnastics, and now that I'm at a school with a top-rated gymnastics program, I know I'm going to be going to their meets once the season starts.

My roommate freshman year was on the tennis team, and I used to live next door to two wrestlers, so I've always made sure to dedicate time to seeing them compete, too.

For Trey to not only disregard athletics but to call it sports ball... well, I'm hoping that doesn't cast a shadow on the remainder of our time together. Just a fling, after all.

He's entered both of our names into the computer at the center of the lane. He's spelled my name wrong—he's written it down as Delia, which is so wrong, my stomach twists. Does he have me confused with some other woman?

I turn around to tell Barrett and come face to face with the realization that he's not here. He has a football game tonight. I'm on a date with a guy who isn't him. It feels like a betrayal of our friendship to be out with another guy.

Never have I wanted him to be here more. I want him beside me as we take in Trey's antics and laugh. I want to curl up beside him and rest my head on his shoulder while his heavy arm wraps around me and holds me close. I want...

This is getting dangerously close to the line I will never cross. Barrett is my best friend. He's the other half of my soul. But he's not my boyfriend. We're friends, and that's the end of the story.

When I was sixteen, I came close to blurting out how I felt about him at least a dozen times. I wanted to be with him. Neither of us had ever really dated anyone. He'd told me about this cheerleader at school who once gave him a handjob over his pants under the bleachers, and I'd admitted to playing spin the bottle a few times at birthday parties and, once, Seven Minutes In Heaven with a guy who tried to shove his tongue down my throat. We don't talk about sex or relationships. We don't talk about dating.

As far as I'm aware, he hasn't gone out or hooked up with anyone since school started. Then again, neither have I, so maybe it's not that weird.

Tonight might be the night. I glance over at Trey, who's

taking his turn at the head of the lane. His leg is angled backwards, his toe pointed, his arm outstretched as he releases. The ball tilts off center and he shakes his head.

There has been a distinct lack of flirting going on tonight. It almost doesn't even feel like we're on a date. We aren't talking or touching or generally looking at one another. I go up, I bowl my turn, and I come back, and Trey is focused on taking his turn. I expected there to be witty banter. When I'm with Barrett, neither of us ever shuts up.

I cannot keep comparing this dude to my best friend. No. That's not an option. Barrett and I are friends and nothing more, and that's how it's going to be. It's not like I want to date him. I just want him here with me all the time and want to talk to him and occasionally I want to kiss him and—

Fuck.

Blowing out a breath, I tuck my hair behind my ears and straighten my shoulders. I'm out on a date with a cute guy. He might not be an athlete, but he's a psychology major like me, so theoretically we're going to have a few things in common. He was at the grad school mixer. I can bring that up!

He's taking his turn now. No, I can't bring it up—he's busy bowling and paying virtually no attention to me.

"I could use a beer," I announce. "Do you want a drink?"

He glances at me over his shoulder. "But we're bowling."

"We're allowed to drink while we're bowling," I point out.

He frowns.

"Never mind. Forget it."

Trey sets the ball down in the return carousel. "No, we can —let's get you a drink."

That sits uncomfortably on my shoulders, like it's my fault we're putting the game on pause.

"You take your turn," I tell him instead. "I'll go grab a pitcher. I'll be right back."

Truth be told, I could use some space. This is all just... a lot. I haven't been on a date in a long time. I've almost forgotten how to do this.

The bar is empty for eight o'clock on a Saturday night. The pimply-faced bartender looks to be even younger than me. I go right up to the bar and survey the offerings on tap.

"Hey," the bartender says, giving me a careful once over.

"Hi. Can I get a pitcher of Blue Moon and two cups?" I hand over my ID and a twenty dollar bill.

With an aggrieved sigh, the bartender lumbers slowly to the back counter and grabs a pitcher. Like he's fighting through molasses, he makes his way towards the taps.

I'm at the point that I might seriously pay him money to take longer, because that means it's that much longer before I have to go back. Maybe that's a sign I should just end the evening now. I can go back to my house and crawl into my bed. Or maybe I'll find a party and—

No. Just because this date is not what I was expecting doesn't mean I'm going to duck out early. A little beer will make the bowling a little more palatable, and maybe it will make Trey a little more personable.

I can do this. I am a strong, confident, capable woman. I can do anything I set my mind to. I can make it through an hour or two with a nice guy. So what if we're not destined to be together forever? It doesn't have to be love at first sight. It doesn't even have to be lust at first sight. I like him well enough. That's enough for now.

With the pitcher and two cups in hand, I make my way back to the lane. Trey has taken his turn and is sitting in the hard plastic chair, absorbed in his phone. I catch a glimpse of the screen: from the millisecond I was able to see, it sure looked like a dating app.

So maybe this date isn't going the way either of us antici-pated. I don't know what to say. There's a distinct lack of flirting going on, from both of our sides.

He looks up as I approach and gives me that sideways

smile of his that never fails to make my stomach lurch unpleasantly. It doesn't feel like attraction this time; it's more like indigestion, and that should be telling enough.

"Thanks for getting the beer," he says. He reaches for a cup, and I fill it for him before handing it over.

I offer a pleasant smile. "You got the lanes. It's only fair I contribute, too."

Barrett never lets me split things with him, which irks me like none other. I know he has money, I know he likes to spend his parents' money on me, but it makes me feel like I can't be his equal in that respect. And I'm not. He is going through college debt-free, and not because of a football scholarship—he earned his starting place on the team fair and square, but he insisted the scholarship money be used for another player who needed it more. He has a multimillion dollar trust fund that becomes his to use freely at twenty-five. My parents are comfortable, but my only inheritance is the proceeds from their life insurance—something I hope I never have to claim, though I'm sure I'll have to sooner than any of us would like.

Barrett has never treated me differently for not having access to the same kind of resources he does. He's always the first to grab his wallet, whether it's just the two of us or we're in a larger group, and he never complains or expects me to pay him back. I try not to take advantage of his generosity, and I always offer to pay my own way. I would never just assume that it's his responsibility to pay. That's not fair to him. He's not my personal piggy bank.

He lets me pay him back in other ways. He stayed at my parents' house at least once a month all through high school. I took him to parties and introduced him to my friends until they became his friends too, knowing how difficult a time he found making friends at his hoity-toity prep school. He's my equal, my peer, no matter how much money is in his bank account. I don't think either of us realized how much he craved normalcy until my family offered it to him. He was able to see firsthand how other families treat one another, and it only reinforced how terribly awful his parents are. Family loyalty and obligation only go so far.

Trey takes a sip from his beer and gestures towards the head of the lane. "It's your turn."

Right. Setting down the pitcher, I dust off my sticky hands and pick up the sparkly black ball that's become mine. On my first throw, I manage a measly two pins. On the second try, I knock down seven more, leaving one lonely pin standing to be cleared away. Not bad. Certainly not my worst effort.

There's no flirty banter as I make my way back to the firm plastic seats. Trey cracks his knuckles and heads to the ball carousel. With a few moments of reprieve, I pull out my phone and check the score. Newton is up by three points over Temple. Not nearly enough of a cushion to make me feel comfortable.

Barrett seemed a little off last night. A little sad. I don't like that. I know something is bothering him, but he won't tell me what it is. And us missing each other… we've barely seen each other, even though now we're living in the same city and going to the same school. I miss the bastard.

I don't really want to be on this date with Trey right now. I would much rather be at home by myself or out somewhere with Barrett. I'm not feeling this.

So I drink some beer, and when it's my turn, I bowl a decent frame, and then I drink some more beer. There's an end in sight. When the game is over, we'll go our separate ways, and I'll never have to see him again. Aside from in class, of course. I take another healthy sip of my beer. There's no escaping this awkwardness.

twenty

. . .

Diana

BECAUSE I HAVE a game this afternoon, I don't have a chance to meet up with Sam and Mason to watch the football buses pull back into school. I'm so focused on my preparations for the game that I almost don't recognize the behemoth of a man standing outside the locker rooms.

"Did you forget about me already?" the giant says, and I shriek as I see him for the first time.

Barrett laughs.

"Don't scare me like that." I swat at him with the cleats in my hand, and he chuckles, shaking his head.

"Sorry, Dee."

"You're the worst."

"You love me." He tugs on my braid, and my stomach flips.

"Yeah, I kind of have to. I'm stuck with you."

He frowns.

I'm just teasing. It's supposed to be a funny-haha type of comment. I don't mean anything by it.

"I do love hanging out with you," I tell him gently. "You're my best friend."

Barrett shakes his head and clears his throat. "Yeah, if you say so."

"How was your trip?"

"Good. We got in early," he says.

I check my watch. I wasn't expecting him for another two hours, at least part way through my game.

He tucks his hands into his pockets. "Well. I'll let you get to it. I'm sure you're busy with your game. You should prepare."

"Yeah. I've got—" I let out a shaky breath. "I'm glad you're back."

His smile is half-hearted. "Yeah. Me too."

"What's wrong?"

"Nothing," he lies.

"Barrett."

He sighs. "We'll talk about it later."

"That means something is bothering you."

"I don't want you to worry about it, not with your game. It's not my place to distract you."

"Fuck the game."

His eyes go wide. "Diana."

"Seriously. I don't care. You're upset. You can tell me what's going on."

"I had breakfast yesterday with Dougie," he says with a shrug. "Just… family shit."

I reach out and squeeze his arm. "I'm sorry."

"Yeah, me too." His smile doesn't reach my eyes. "But my family will still suck a bag of dicks after your game, so don't you think about it now. I'm sure we'll talk it to death later."

I frown.

"It's fine. I'm fine," he says. I roll my eyes. "Okay, so it's totally not fine, but it's not like the next three hours is going to change anything, so I'm going to pretend they don't exist for now and deal with it that way."

"We're going out tonight," I inform him.

Barrett raises his eyebrows. "Okay."

"We're going to eat fried food and drink and we're going to talk until you feel better."

"I don't know if that's possible," he says with a dark chuckle I'm not a fan of.

"Then we'll drink until you feel numb."

"It's a date," he says.

My traitorous heart thumps loudly in my chest, so loud I swear he can hear it.

"I should get ready for my game," I finally tell him.

He blinks. "Right. Duh. Your game. Good luck, Dee. You're going to do awesome."

I offer him a winning smile. "Of course I will."

Shaking his head, he laughs. "Never change, babe."

Rolling my eyes, I pat him on the chest and turn on my heel, heading for the locker room. Inside, most of my teammates are in the midst of getting changed. Terri and Zoe enter behind me, heading towards their lockers.

Johanna looks up from her locker and narrows her eyes at me. "You're late."

"I know."

"Where were you?"

"I got held up." I can't tell her I was with Barrett—I'm not exactly sure what went down between them, just that it didn't go well, and neither of them are talking.

She scoffs in derision and, on cue, her minions roll their eyes and scoff, too.

Heading to my locker, I lock eyes with Emma, who rolls her eyes—this time at the theatrics, not at my being five minutes late to an *optional* pre-game warm-up. Technically, it is only recommended that we warm up together as a team before the game—they can't force us to do it together. I like to prep with a quick yoga session and a sedate jog earlier in the day, before the more earnest warm-up and stretching session immediately before we play.

The dissent in the ranks has only grown more pronounced since I've befriended Emma and the defensive squad. Before Johanna could claim that it was only a few of the underclassmen who weren't cooperating; now it's more than half of the team that's visibly fed up with her bullshit.

Coach Larsen is in her office, in theory, keeping an eye on things. In practice, she's checked out. We haven't won a game all season, after three consecutive losing seasons. She's holding onto her job by a thread. It wouldn't surprise me if she doesn't last the remainder of the season.

When we take the field for warm ups, there are only a handful of people in the stands: Barrett, his teammates, and a few scattered friends and family members. Less than a dozen people in total. He cheers and waves, and Johanna rolls her eyes again. I'm so done with her. If I never saw her again, it wouldn't break my heart. But not only is she my team captain, she's one of my roommates; like it or not, I'm stuck with her, at least until the end of the year.

The game itself is brutal. Bea melts down and trips over her own two feet on what should be an easy goal kick and instead turns into a three on one charge to overpower her and land a shot right in the uppermost left corner, her well documented weak side.

It's 0-1 with five minutes gone, and it only gets worse from there.

Emma and I stick it out as best we can. I get subbed halfway through the first half, and as I stand on the sidelines and drink my water, I realize something. This isn't fun anymore. I'm not enjoying this. I still love soccer, don't get me wrong. But playing for this team, playing for this school, playing with these women… I don't love it. Maybe we got off to a bad start. Maybe we started on the wrong foot. It's not getting better. I like Emma and Terri and Zoe and all the girls. On my best days, I can only tolerate Johanna and the minions.

We don't gel, though. We get along off the field, but when

we're in the middle of a game, it's like we lose all capability of communicating. We stop being strong, confident, capable women and instead turn into a lackluster team that can't get our shit together.

It's almost a relief when the game is over. It shouldn't be that way. I used to love soccer with all my heart. Now it's like a lukewarm fondness, more for nostalgia's sake than any actual emotions left over.

"C'mon," I say to Emma, throwing my arm around her shoulder. "We're going out tonight."

"We are?" We don't normally go out, especially after such a horrific loss.

"I need pizza. Like, in an IV," I tell her, and she laughs.

"Yeah, okay."

Because we're still in the locker room, and technically the coaching staff could overhear us, I leave out the part about us going drinking—that part is implied.

"My friend is going to meet up with us. He might bring some guys, too." I look out at the rest of my team. I get a weird thrill of being the person with all the friends, all the connections. This hasn't happened before.

"Are they hot?" asks Zoe.

"Are they single?" asks Terri.

I laugh. "Two are single, one is basically a monk, and the other guys are in relationships." I conveniently leave Barrett off the list. Let them think he's off limits. "But they know people. How's Sully?"

Emma blushes and looks away. "He was okay."

"Just okay?"

She shrugs. "Not a disappointment, but there won't be a repeat. He made damn sure of that."

Ouch.

"Sorry, girl."

She clears her throat and lifts her chin. "It doesn't matter. I just won't sleep with any more football players."

"You're okay to hang out with them?"

"I mean, yeah, I guess so. They're not going to hit on me?"

I pause. "Amir probably won't, he knows when to keep it in his pants. Greg, on the other hand, is a total slut. I don't think he knows how not to be. He hits on me all the time, even though Barrett and I are—"

Johanna looks over with interest.

"Best friends," I finish lamely. "So by the transitive property of the bro code, he shouldn't be flirting with me."

Louisa frowns. "Is he gross?"

"No, he's a total sweetheart. Just… slutty. Doesn't know when to turn it off." I should probably give them fair warning. "I don't care if you sleep with him, but you have to know that he is not the kind of guy who will call you after or want to hang out. He doesn't go out with the same woman twice. That's just the way he operates."

Emma sighs. "I think I'm done with football players."

"Guys are gross," says Zoe.

"If only they didn't have dicks. I'd love it if I could just get a dick on demand without having to deal with the guy attached to it," Terri says.

"That's called a vibrator," Emma says. "They're infinitely better."

———

Barrett is waiting for me outside the locker room, flanked by Amir and Greg. Tucker and Mason are a few feet away, holding hands, and Miles has his arm around Sam's shoulders. Even Wes and Mackenzie have shown up—him clutching his book like it's a lifeline, her looking like she'd rather be anywhere else. I don't take it personally; I know it's how she feels about nearly all social situations, and she showed up in spite of it.

"Hey. Good game," Barrett says. He steps forward and

wraps his arm around me in a sideways hug. "You played well."

I laugh, because we lost 0-3—though he is right, I did play pretty damn well.

"Thanks."

He's gone home since I saw him before the game—he's freshly shaved and wearing a different outfit, dark jeans and a button-down shirt beneath an army green bomber jacket I told him I liked on him last week. I like that he remembered.

Or maybe he didn't, and I'm reading too much into it. He has two light fall jackets. He can't wear them both all of the time.

"Pizza time?" I look up at him and he grins at me, his eyes crinkling.

"You got it. You guys coming with?" He addresses this to the semi-circle of women behind me.

"Sure, thanks," says Emma, clearly the spokeswoman for the group.

"I need breadsticks, like, stat," I tell him.

Barrett laughs and takes my backpack from my slack grip, tossing it over his shoulder. I know better than to fight him on this front.

"Your wish is my command, m'lady."

Snorting out a laugh, I push past him with my shoulder and head off in the direction of town. I haven't been to the pizza place before, only ordered in, but I've walked past it nestled beside the all-night diner and the cute brunch place.

My best friend falls into step beside me. His arm slings around my shoulder again as he forces my pace to slow.

"Don't leave the rest of us behind, Dee."

We pause as the group catches up to us. We've amassed quite the crowd: six big football players, five soccer players, plus three more athletes. We're a group of people who are elite at what we do, all different shapes and sizes and colors, each of us a little different from the next.

The pizza place is hopping for a Sunday night. It's a casual eatery that smells like red sauce and warmth. I rub my hands together to ward off the chill. I've forgotten just how cold fall can be. In the southern California sunshine, summer lasts past Thanksgiving, and there's a singular week of fall at the end of November before the brutality of winter begins.

It's way too early for snow—it's not forecast for the next two weeks, which is as far out as I like to rely on meteorologists—but it isn't out of the realm of possibility for it to fall before Halloween, coming up in three weekends. I don't miss snow as much as I thought I would. Now it's just a hassle, a reality of life to deal with. I especially don't like playing soccer in the snow. The cold has a way of permeating everything, settling in my bones.

Barrett guides me towards a table at the back of the restaurant. The big group gets split amongst three tables, all in the same vicinity: me and Barrett at a small table for two, next to Emma, Terri, Zoe, and Louisa with Amir and Greg, and Miles, Sam, Tucker, Mason, Wes, and Mackenzie in front of us.

This way I'm with all of my friends, but there's still a little privacy for us to have a serious talk about whatever went down with his parents. I like his thoughtfulness in orchestrating this.

A harried waitress makes her way over to us. Barrett orders three pitchers of beer and an emergency breadsticks order while we peruse the rest of the menu. This isn't the type of place that would offer a Thai chicken pizza (no peanuts) or a black bean tostada pizza, my two personal favorites. All of these pizzas are slathered with a healthy dose of their homemade red sauce and a heart attack inducing amount of cheese.

"What do you say we get two and split?" Barrett suggests. "I can't decide what I want."

I grin at him. "Neither can I. You get to choose."

He laughs, and sure enough, when the waitress comes back with the beer, he places an order for a pepperoni and black olive pizza and a sausage and mushroom pie. As an afterthought, I tack on a side salad for us to split. I haven't eaten enough vegetables today, and if he's been on the road, he probably hasn't, either.

With the menus returned to the waitress, he has no choice but to meet my gaze.

"Are we going to talk about it?"

He sighs. "Do we have to?"

"If you really don't want to…"

"No, I just…" He pinches the bridge of his nose. "It's not going to get any better. You know? It can only get worse."

"What part?"

"I need to tell them I'm not applying to any MBA programs." He folds his hands in front of him. "I'm not opposed to doing an MBA. I'll do it, I don't care. I just need some time off first."

"That's reasonable."

"I'm not even saying I don't want to work for my dad. I do. I want to work there," he says.

"I believe you."

"I just… I can't do three more years of school, not right now." Barrett blows out a breath. "It's too much Between school and football and y—"

"And what?"

He swallows. "And you."

"Me?" What impact do I have on his decision not to go to business school?

"If your dad gets worse… I want to be there for you." He meets my eyes. "However you need me, I want to be there with you."

My stomach drops. "That could be years from now." I don't want it to happen anytime soon.

"I know," he says quietly.

"Barrett—"

"You're not going to convince me out of it," he says stubbornly. "There are a lot of reasons. This is the least I can do."

"I'm not going to fight with you," I tell him quietly. "If you want to… be there…" I sniff. I can't even think the words, much less say them. And for him to offer this, to put his life on hold—for me? I just… I can't.

He nods seriously. "I like your dad. He's a nice guy. He's gone out of his way to treat me well. He doesn't deserve what's happening to him."

"No, he doesn't."

Reaching across the table, he takes hold of my hand, and I squeeze his thick fingers for dear life. "There are a half dozen business schools my parents would accept in Massachusetts. It doesn't have to be Harvard or bust. I'm not opposed to moving to Amherst."

"You're not moving to Amherst."

"Are you?"

"I don't know," I admit. "It's still up in the air."

"Then it's in the cards for me, too."

"You're not going to drive two and a half hours each way with no traffic from Amherst to the financial district. That's insane."

"I can come out to you every weekend, or work out a way to work from home, or whatever I need to do," he says.

"I might not even move back home."

He's surprised at this. "You're not?"

"My dad doesn't want me to put grad school on hold. I'm staying local to New England, but I'm looking at grad schools in the region. I like this program at UMass Lowell, and it would let me go home on the weekends. The one at UNH might be a little farther, I wouldn't be able to go home as frequently. And Northeastern is, like, my dream school, but I can't afford it without a serious scholarship, and I don't want to take out any more student loans than I have to."

"That's fair," he says seriously.

"So don't go making any plans based on me. I don't know where I'm going to be next year."

He squeezes my hand. "Wherever you are, that's where I'll be."

I roll my eyes. "Get real. You can't—"

"I've spent the last four years without you. Now that I have you back in my life, I'm not letting you go again so easily," Barrett says.

Although I'm gratified to hear that I mean as much to him as he means to me, I don't know what his intentions are here. What exactly does he think is going to happen?

"But—"

"We'll get an apartment together somewhere," he says. "I'll have a car, so I can drive you home on the weekends, and we can—"

"Hold up. Wait a minute."

He pauses.

I shake my head, a little stunned. "You're making all these plans. Have you ever stopped to consider maybe I should be privy to these plans?"

Barrett laughs at himself. "That's what I'm doing now. I'm telling you. So you have time to decide if it's something you want or not. If you're in grad school, I can cover the rent, and then—"

"I'm not going to freeload off of you."

"It's not freeloading if I'm offering."

"Yeah, it still is."

"Dee…"

I lay my cards on the table. "I'm not opposed to living together. We can get an apartment together, fine. That sounds like fun. But I'm going to pay my fair share, and we'll have to find somewhere that fits my budget, not yours."

His parents will probably want to buy a place for him to live soon enough so he's not renting indefinitely. My parents definitely can't help contribute in the same way. My dad had to cash in his retirement fund to pay for all of his treatments —it's not like he'll be around to use it later, he might as well spend it now. I can pay for utilities, or food, or something. We'll come up with an equitable trade. It's always bothered me, but he's never cared how much money my parents do or don't have in comparison to his wealthy family. He likes my parents.

"So it's a plan?" Barrett gives me a hopeful smile.

I let out a heavy breath. "Yeah. Let's do it. Let's be roommates."

His smile stretches from ear to ear. "You won't regret this, babe. We're going to have so much fun."

twenty-one

. . .

Barrett

THE MORNING OF THE PARENTS' Day football game dawns dreary and cold. We're fully into fall and heading straight into winter, and I am nowhere near ready for the six (or ten) months of intense cold about to come our way. I go about my preparations for the game the same way I always do: a hearty breakfast, a stretching session, a quick massage from the team's trainers, a slow walk on the treadmill, and a protein and carb packed lunch in the team room of the football facility.

I don't have my phone on me. I can't allow for any distractions this close to game time.

I wonder what Diana is up to. I think she was planning to take a hot yoga class this morning before she meets up with her parents for the game. Knowing her, she'll skip lunch to load up on all the snacks at the arena. She loves a soft pretzel, and has told me more than once the only reason she comes to my games is to get at the fresh pretzels. I know she's joking: she also likes the hot dogs and the nachos she usually splits with her dad, and the ice cream sundae she splits with her mom.

The game goes as well as can be expected. I manage two

sacks in the first half and a truly epic hit in the third quarter that takes down two guys at once. There are thousands of people here, but I swear I can hear Diana cheering and calling my name when I bring down the quarterback for the third time on a desperate drive at the start of the fourth quarter. My chest puffs out and my shoulders raise at the idea that my girl is cheering for me.

After the game, I shower with the guys and clean up before heading to the tunnels to meet the families. On a normal day, they have to meet us outside. Because it's Parents' Weekend, we're allowed to bring out families back to see our sweaty, smelly locker room if they so choose.

Diana and her parents are clustered with Sam, Mason, and Mackenzie and the Cavanaugh and Kingsley families. My heart nearly stops at the sight of her wearing my jersey.

Striding forward, I push past Miles and Tucker and wrap my arms around my best friend, lifting her into the air.

Diana squeals. "Barrett!"

Closing my eyes, I hold her to me tightly. I bury my face in her hair.

"Put me down!"

Gently I set her feet back on the ground, but I don't end the hug. I'm not ready to let her go yet.

"You're here." My voice comes out rough as sandpaper. I clear my throat.

"There's nowhere else I'd rather be," she says. She tries to wiggle free.

With a sigh, I indulge in one last inhale and release her.

"Good game, son," Stewart says. He claps me on the back.

My chest warms with affection for the man who's welcomed me into his house and into his family.

"Thank you."

Cecilia gives me a hug, too, though hers is a little less intense than her daughter's. "I'm so glad we were able to come see you play again."

"Me, too." I hug her tightly and then release her on a sigh.

Feeling blindly behind me, I grab for Diana and wrap my arm around her shoulders, tucking her in close to my side. Her arm slides around my hips, and I take a moment to marvel at the fact that this gorgeous woman allows me to manhandle her anyway I choose.

"Dinner?" Stewart suggests.

Miles catches my eye. He's standing with his family and Sam, and behind him are Amir and Wes, whose families couldn't make it out. Greg's dad is off to the side on his cell phone, talking to someone that isn't his son.

"I think some of my friends are getting together with their families," I say lightly, and his face falls. "Would you be okay if we all went together as a group? The team booked up the steakhouse, so all we have to do is show up and we can get a table."

Stewart's face clears. "That sounds great."

He's a football fan, and more than that, he's a fan of mine. He's always cheered for whatever team I'm playing on, even when I was a scrawny freshman in high school. For him to get to hang out and rub elbows with some of the other football players…

I turn to Cecilia. "Is that okay with you? Sharing us?"

She beams at me and pats my unshaven cheek. "Of course, honey."

Diana releases me, and I take the opportunity to grab her hand in mine. I can feel her twitch. Even with all of my growing affection and the increase in physical contact, holding hands is new. It's a distantly couple-ish behavior. That's a boundary we've never crossed.

Still, I can't resist touching her, even in a way as innocent as this. I want to keep her close to me all the time.

The walk to the parking lot is treacherous. There are crowds everywhere, families of the team and families of the students who attended the game. People push in around us, and I'm even more thankful for Diana's hand in mine, keeping us tethered together in the intense crush.

"This is insane," she says.

"I know."

"I've never seen it this packed," she says, and I laugh.

"Baby, you haven't seen nothing."

I've been slipping "babe" and "baby" in here and there the last week or two. If she's noticed, she hasn't mentioned it. It's as natural to me as breathing. Not that I don't want to use her name; I do. But I also like the idea of a special pet name for her, beyond just the simple nickname of Dee.

When we reach the car, Stewart clicks it open, and I grab the door handle, ushering her inside. She smiles prettily up at me as she ducks down and into the car.

My entire body aches, and I lumber slowly to the opposite side, sliding in beside her. There's not a lot of legroom in the backseat of the sedan, so I angle my body towards her just so that I will fit and not because I can't get enough of her.

The steakhouse is packed, too. I show my student athlete ID card, and we're quickly ushered to a back room with a bunch of other tables full of football players and their families. Miles and his family are at a long banquet table with Tucker, his brother the professional NBA player, and their moms. I nod at the guys as we're shown to a table a few feet from where Wes, Amir, and Greg are with Greg's dad, who doesn't look pleased to be there.

Pulling out a chair for Diana, I help her into it and take the seat beside her. I might set my arm on the back of her chair. Just casually.

I could seriously down a steak right now. Maybe two. I worked up quite the appetite on the field, and because it's a special day, I'm more inclined to go for something indulgent than I typically would post-game. Normally it's all about recovery meals and refueling with clean calories, minimal oil and butter and lots of protein and healthy fats. I certainly don't eat like this every day.

Tonight? I want a steak. And maybe for dessert, I'll spread Diana's legs and go to town on her—

Oooookay. That's enough of that.

Shifting in my seat, I pick up my menu and peruse it to give myself a break from the surge of testosterone coursing through my veins like wildfire. I'm jittery and already at half mast, my blood burning with excess adrenaline. I played a fucking awesome game today, I'm about to eat a delicious meal, and I have my best friend beside me. Things could be worse—a lot worse.

"So what did you think?" I ask Stewart. "Was it as good as watching on TV?"

He grins. "Even better. You played phenomenally, son."

I try to hide how much my chest puffs up at his easy praise. "Thanks. But—"

"No buts about it. You played great," he insists. "We should have been coming to your games all this time, all these years. We'll do better."

"You don't—"

"Your next two games are away, but we'll be back for your next home game," Stewart promises.

Diana is surprised. "You will?"

"We might get there a little late," Cecilia concedes. "You have a game that afternoon, too. If you want to join us, you're more than welcome to."

My best friend looks a little baffled. "Yeah? You're going to my soccer game and my best friend's game? Of course I want to be there with you guys."

"Great," Stewart says with a smile. "It's a plan, then."

My body warms at the idea of having my surrogate family in the stands for my future game. I don't care that they're Diana's parents; they've taken me in and welcomed me so thoroughly over the years, I can't imagine my life without them in it.

They support me in a way my parents never have. Sure, I have plenty of money at my disposal. I can pay for dinner tonight, even though I know Stewart will object, and I can override him easily enough on that front. But my biological family has never cared about me enough to care about *me*, the person, as anything other than the second son and continuation of the Zhang name.

Cecilia and Stewart are interested in me, the person. They ask how my classes are going and if I survived my forensic accounting midterm, which I had mentioned to Diana last week I was stressing over. They ask about my plans for Thanksgiving—probably going home with Miles and his family again, because my parents are usually celebrating the weekend with their friends in Aspen, and I have a game that Saturday. Cecilia invites me to come home with Diana to their house, which I will have to strongly consider over the next few weeks.

As much as I want to be with my best friend all the fucking time, I also know this could be her last Thanksgiving with her father. Everything they do together could be their last. They don't know how long he has: terminal could mean six months, or it could mean six years. I don't want to intrude on their precious family time. Wes's family is proof enough that life is fleeting: you never know how much time you have with someone until it's over.

twenty-two

· · ·

Diana

BARRETT IS BEING ABNORMALLY touchy-feely today. He held my hand earlier while we were walking, and now his arm is around my chair, and he called me baby, and twice now he's brushed some hair behind my ear. It should feel weird and clingy and annoying... but it doesn't. Because this is Barrett, and I know he loves me in his own way.

I'm chalking most of this newfound cuddliness to the testosterone that must be firing on all cylinders in his brain. There's no way he would ever put the moves on me—especially not in a restaurant, with my *parents* watching!

This must all be in my head.

It's probably because I haven't gotten laid in so long, and that date with Trey was a total bust. He didn't try to kiss me at the end of the night, and when I sent him a "that was fun!" text a few days later, he never responded.

Maybe it's for the best. Maybe I'm not cut out for dating.

Tonight, when we go out to a party—because I don't care what Barrett says, after his incredible game today, we aren't staying in tonight—I can find some girl for him to hook up with and he can help wingman me a fellow to warm my bed.

My stomach churns. It must have been the nachos I had at the game.

"You okay?" Barrett glances down at me.

"I'm fine."

"You're quiet."

"Just hungry."

His eyes search mine for an answer he won't find.

"If you say so."

As much as I hate it, I kind of like that he's perceptive enough to know it's not the full truth, and also that he knows when to let sleeping dogs lie. I'm not going to talk to him about any digestive distress, imminent or otherwise.

He bends down and presses a kiss to the top of my head, which is so unexpected in a moment when we aren't alone, I jerk back.

"What was that?"

He blushes—hard. He goes from a low-key flush to full beet red in the span of twelve seconds.

"I—I don't know."

"Barrett."

"It just felt right," he says, clearly uncomfortable. He clears his throat. "Can we just pretend it never happened?"

I eye him warily. He's sweating now, his face so red it looks like he's just stepped off the football field.

Sighing, I straighten my shoulders. "What never happened?"

He lets out a breath of relief. "Exactly."

My dad snorts, and I remember that we have an audience.

"Are you looking forward to the game tomorrow?" I ask my parents. "It's been awhile since the three of you were all at a game together."

"Yeah, it'll be fun," Barrett agrees readily.

My dad laughs. "We're talking about the Newton soccer team, right?"

I roll my eyes. "We're not that bad."

"Yeah, you kind of are," my mom says. "Some games are harder to watch than others."

Compared to some other teams I've been on over the years… okay, so maybe we haven't won a single game all season. Maybe morale is hanging on by a splintering string. But they don't have to call us out for it.

We make it through dinner all right. Barrett keeps his hands to himself, and I mostly focus on my steak and baked potato. The food is good. My parents maintain the conversation, chatting about our family and neighbors and asking Barrett about school. It feels so natural to have him here with us; I almost can't imagine spending time with my parents *without* him here. Not for the first time, I'm incredibly grateful I decided to transfer home for this year. I didn't realize how much I needed to be here until I got back, and now that I'm here, I can't imagine being anywhere else.

After dinner, we linger over drinks and dessert until the waiter starts pointedly clearing all of the tables around us. Barrett and I walk my parents back to their car before we start the walk into Athlete's Village.

I'm kind of surprised when he wraps his arm around my shoulders again, hugging me against his side.

"Thanks for tonight, Dee," he says.

"For what?"

"For sharing your family. For letting me hang out with you guys."

"Of course."

He clears his throat. "So. Tomorrow. Your game."

"Yeah?"

"Then dinner with your parents again?"

"If you want to."

"I do."

"Then yeah, we'll do it."

"Great."

I poke him in his side and he twitches.

"What about tonight?"

"What about it?" He tightens his grip on my shoulders.

"What party are we hitting up?"

"Actually, I'm kind of beat," he says.

"Really?"

"Yeah. Would you mind…"

"What?"

"Maybe we can just put on a movie and chill?"

My eyes go wide. "You want to Netflix and chill?"

That's distinctly… couple-y. We've watched movies together, we've hung out. Coming from having dinner together with my parents, it feels different. Weighty.

He laughs, a little awkward. "In the most literal sense of the phrase. We'll watch something and hang out and just… relax."

"You don't want to drink and get laid?"

Barrett shakes his head. "My whole body hurts. I'm exhausted. Tomorrow night we can party after your game, but for tonight, I want to hang out with you—just you. No crowds, no loud music, no craziness. I have some vodka if you really want to drink. I just… I'm in the mood for something low-key tonight."

There's a lump in my throat. "Yeah. That's okay with me."

He gives me a winning smile, and my stomach flips. "Great."

By the time we get back to his house, Wes is already installed in his usual armchair with his book, and Mack has taken over the couch with her tablet. She looks up and smiles nervously at us when we come in.

"Fuck, it's getting cold out there, isn't it?" Barrett says as he hangs up his coat.

She nods. "Winter starts earlier and earlier every year."

"Fuck global warming," Wes says, turning a page in his book.

It's the most I've heard him say in the last few weeks.

Only two other times has he spoken since I've met him. He's not dumb. He's just shy.

"We're going to watch a movie," I tell them. "Do you guys want to join?"

Wes looks up and meets my eyes. His eyes are a clear green, intent on mine, as he studies the offer for any hidden agenda.

"Thanks, but not tonight," he says, a little gruffly.

"Maybe next time," Mack says. "I just got to a really good place in my book. I wouldn't pay attention."

"Next time, then," I agree.

Even though we haven't spent a lot of time together one on one, I like her. She's friendly and personable in a crowd, but she's happy enough falling back and hiding in the shadows. It's not anything sinister; she's just not fond of being the center of attention.

We head up the stairs. Barrett tugs at his tie as he lumbers slowly behind me. Once we're in his room, he strips off his jacket and pulls his tie all the way off. I'm wearing leggings and an oversized Zhang jersey, so I'm already comfortable. He rolls up his shirtsleeves and takes off his belt. He collapses onto his bed with a sigh.

"Don't you want to change?"

His eyes snap up to mine. "Huh?"

"Put on sweats or something. You don't have to hang out in your dress clothes."

"In a minute." He pats the space beside him. "Come lay here with me."

Tentatively I take a seat on the side of the bed. Barrett wraps his arm around my waist and tugs me into the depression beside him.

I laugh. "Can I at least take off my shoes?"

"Yeah. I guess so."

He releases me, and I roll over until I can sit up. Unzipping my boots, I kick them off and retake my spot next to him.

Barrett slides his arm beneath my neck. Curling into him, I rest my head on his bicep and breathe. What are we doing? Are we really just going to lay here and stare at the ceiling?

After a few minutes, he sighs, and starts to sit up.

"Be right back," he mumbles. He digs in his dresser drawer, coming up with a pair of sweatpants, and disappears into the attached bathroom.

I scrub a hand over my face. What are we doing? I'm out of my comfort zone here.

When Barrett opens the bathroom door a few moments later, he's changed into a Newton football t-shirt and sweatpants, and traded his daytime contacts for his thin black-framed glasses. Now he looks like my best friend, the man I want to see.

"What do you want to watch?"

"I don't really care."

He laughs. "Okay, so then I'll pick."

Climbing onto his bed, he slips his legs beneath the covers and picks up the remote to start scrolling through the movie catalog. I veto his first seven suggestions before he lands on something I can reasonably tolerate, an action movie featuring a Korean-American actress in the lead role. The reviews are mostly focused on her "unparalleled sensuality" and not on her actual acting abilities.

The movie is… not terrible. After the first five minutes, I slide under the covers, too, and Barrett curls his arm around me. Slowly, slowly, slowly I shift closer, until my cheek is resting on his chest. His propensity for cuddling is new, but I can't deny how much I like it. It's like having all the good parts of a boyfriend—someone to cuddle with, someone to watch movies and do things with, someone to come to my games and hang out with my parents—without the benefit of sex. If he told me now to drop trou… well, it would irrevocably change our friendship. But I can't say I wouldn't at least be tempted.

The last time I had a crush on my best friend, I was a sixteen year old kid. Before that, I was a child, navigating crushes and puberty for the first time. Over the years, we've done pretty much everything together. But we've never crossed that line.

Now I'm starting to wonder what would happen if we did. Would it be awkward? Would it be as comfortably familiar as our friendship? Does he even want the same things I'm wanting?

———

I wake up disoriented, which is never good. I'm not in my bedroom at my parents' house or at the soccer house. It takes me a moment to realize I'm in Barrett's room, and the heavy arm around my waist must be his. Next to me, his body is thick and warm, lulling me back to sleep. It's only the urgency of my bladder that keeps me awake.

Sliding slowly out of bed, I make my way to the attached bathroom and take care of essential business. It's later than I expected. I slept so soundly, I was able to sleep in an extra hour and a half past my regular wake up time. I guess my body needed the rest, even if I wasn't consciously aware of it.

Barrett wakes up as I'm pulling on my second boot.

"Come back to bed," he says, his face creased with pillow-case lines.

"I've got to go."

"Noooooo."

"I have to get ready for my game."

He flops back against the pillows with a sigh. "If you have to."

A grown man pouting shouldn't be so adorable, but some-how, because it's him, it is. It tugs on my heartstrings and my stomach flips. For half a second, I debate crawling into the bed with him, until the reality of our situation hits me again.

We're friends. We've been sleeping together, but only to sleep. Climbing into bed with him now in the bright light of day is a whole other thing.

"I'll see you in a few hours," I remind him.

He grabs my hand as I'm walking by his side of the bed. With a sharp tug, he pulls me onto the bed and wraps his arms around me.

"Good morning, Dee," he says, burying his face in my rat's nest masquerading as hair.

"Morning, Bare. How did you sleep?"

He must be sore. He played phenomenally, but there were a few tackles in the second quarter that looked like they hurt. He's probably bruised black and blue from head to toe.

He groans. "Great. You?"

"You're not the worst guy to have ever shared a bed with," I tease, and he releases me so fast I almost have whiplash. I clear my throat. "Thanks for letting me crash here."

"Of course. You're always welcome here," he says, side-stepping the not funny joke entirely.

"Thanks." I struggle to get up off the bed. "I'll see you later," I promise.

"Count on it." He sinks back against his pillows again.

"Go back to sleep."

"No, I'm up. I need to get up." Barrett makes no move to actually get out of bed, though.

"Okay. Cool. Well, I'll see you in a few hours."

Mack is still asleep on the couch when I make my way downstairs. Quietly I sneak out of the house and into Athlete's Village. There's almost nobody out and about at eight o'clock on Sunday morning.

Jogging through the streets, I head back to the soccer

house, where Johanna is sitting bleary-eyed at the kitchen table with a cup of coffee.

"Where have you been?"

"Out."

"You need to tell us when you're not coming home," she says petulantly.

"I wasn't planning on not coming home. It got late quicker than I expected."

She looks me up and down. "You were with Barrett Zhang?"

"Yeah."

She looks away and presses her lips together.

Okay, now I have to know what went down with the two of them.

"How was coffee with him a few weeks ago? You never said."

Johanna snorts. "Yeah, I'm sure."

"What's that supposed to mean?"

"Why don't you ask him?"

I blink. "Okay. Sure. I will."

The last time I brought it up, Barrett changed the subject and then pretended I hadn't said anything. Neither of them seemed pissed or hostile. I just chalked it up to personality differences and forgot about it.

"Will it be an issue?"

"Why should it?" she says.

"I don't know. He's coming to our game today."

"Well, good for him," she mutters into her coffee.

"You'll be civil?"

Johanna rolls her eyes.

It's too early for this shit. Leaving her to wallow in coffee, I trudge up the stairs to my room. Taking a quick shower, I scrub off yesterday's grime and detangle my hair before pulling it back into a no-nonsense braid. By the time I'm dressed and ready to go, Rosie is poking her head out from her room.

"The coast is clear?" she whispers.

"What do you mean?"

"Johanna went on a rampage last night," she reveals. "She threw the biggest queen bitch fit I've ever seen."

"Shit. I'm sorry."

Rosie waves it off. "Not your fault."

Except actually, I think my being out with Barrett might have been part of it...

She disappears into her bathroom, and I head into my room. While she's in the shower, I pick up any visible mess— my shoes go in the rack in my closet, my dirty clothes in the hamper, my vibrator back in the bedside drawer, my books into my backpack or in a neat pile on my desk.

By the time I'm done, the front door is slamming. Johanna and the minions must have left without me. I'm not surprised they didn't wait. That would require them to show a modicum of emotion they're unable to understand. Camaraderie as a concept shouldn't be foreign to them, except that they're incapable of expressing it.

It's fucking exhausting. I don't like losing. Nobody does. But I especially don't like losing every. single. game. It's demoralizing and almost makes me regret transferring in. Almost. Because Barrett is here, and there's the proximity to my parents, and my new friends... yeah, it's not all bad. It could be a lot worse. But it could also be a lot better.

twenty-three

. . .

Barrett

AFTER DIANA'S GAME—HER team loses, 1-2, so not as miserably as what's become usual—it's time for us to go to dinner. Amir and Wes joined us for the game but bow out of any extended family time, which I totally understand. If Stewart and Cecilia weren't Stewart and Cecilia, I wouldn't want to hang out with my friend's parents, either.

Leading them down to the locker room, I show Diana's parents where we're going to meet her. She's one of the last people to leave the locker room, and when she emerges, she's bundled up in a coat and scarf like it's full winter and not early fall.

"Hey, baby," I say as she joins us. She gives each of her parents a hug before she turns to me. I wrap her up in my arms and debate never letting her go.

"Hey, Care-Bare."

With a teasing growl, I tug gently on her braid. "What did I say about calling me that?"

She smiles prettily up at me and for a brief moment I nearly lose my mind and kiss her. I want to so fucking bad. I'm this close to throwing caution to the wind. Her snappy retort pushes me away, though.

"Um, do it all the time?"

"Never," I tell her. "Never call me that."

She purses her lips at me and, I swear to Christ, my heart nearly beats through my chest to get to her. "Hm, I don't remember that."

There's a click behind us, and I turn to see Cecilia stowing her cell phone in her purse.

"Did you just take our picture?" Diana demands.

"It was a good photo op," she says, a little defensively.

"I want to see it," I tell her.

"I'll send it to you. To both of you," Cecilia promises.

"Thanks," I say with a levity I don't exactly feel. Stewart is grinning, too.

I'm glad her parents seem to like the idea of the two of us together as much as I do. It's nice that we have their support. Between the flirting last night, their politely inquisitive questions during the game, and now this... yeah, I think they'd be okay with us becoming an "us."

The most important thing is making sure we're okay. I don't want to lose Diana, and I especially don't want to lose her parents. They're my family now, too. I almost want them to be my parents, too. They've been there for me so many times. I don't know where I'd be without them.

"Dinner?" Stewart suggests. "What are we in the mood for?"

"How authentic is the Chinese place in town?" Cecilia asks.

"The people who run it are of Chinese descent and none of the cooks speak English."

"Sounds perfect," Cecilia says.

Being of Chinese descent, I have very little tolerance for American style Chinese cooking. I want the legit stuff, the kind of things the maids used to make for me and Dougie growing up, the kinds of things my parents wouldn't dare to serve their guests.

Cecilia is the same way. Her aunt and uncle ran a Chinese restaurant where she grew up in Wisconsin, and she spent quite a bit of time in the shop with her grandmother and cousins. She's taught me and Diana some of the classic techniques they used, handing down a piece of our history and our heritage.

Diana wasn't really interested in the cooking side of things, she just wanted to eat. Because Cecilia isn't actually my mother, I was able to appreciate her spending time with us that much more. It's something that my mother or my grandmother have never shown an interest in, and especially never cared about doing with me.

Roughly I know the story of how my family came here from China. In broad terms I know of the struggles they've faced, though I've learned more from history books than family stories. But I don't really know my family's story. I know my maternal grandfather made a fortune, lost it, and made a second fortune in lumber. I know my paternal grandfather was one of the first Chinese-American students to graduate with his CPA *and* his MBA from Harvard in a time when managing even one was unheard of. I know he basically wrote the book on forensic accounting in the pre-computers world, and was one of the early adopters of computers in banking.

But I don't know anything about the Chinese experience. I know my personal experience, being Chinese American and an athlete in a high-intensity prep school where neither of those were expected or typical. Growing up, my classmates were the children of Senators and elite finance and high-powered tech conglomerate CEOs. I went to birthday parties with kids whose parents bought them a literal stable full of ponies for their sixth birthday—and a Jaguar for their sixteenth.

But lavish presents aren't the same as lavished love, and when I see Diana and her parents, I know she's never wanted for love and affection from either of her parents. They care about her deeply and aren't afraid of showing it. From the easy way they tease her on the way to the car and the way they dissect her game (that they watched! in person!) without criticism of that goal in the second half she definitely should have caught, they aren't shy about showing how much their daughter means to them.

The drive to Double Chins is quick and easy, unlike the drive to the steakhouse last night. There are considerably fewer people in the streets. Women's soccer isn't as much of a crowd-pleaser as men's football, and especially not with the team's continued losing streak. Also, as the weekend winds down, parents are starting to hit the road—Stewart and Cecilia are going back to Amherst after dinner, I already know.

This place is the epitome of family style. When I come here with the guys, we get nine or ten dishes and split them amongst the six of us, so everyone gets a little bit of everything. That's the best way to feed a crowd of always-hungry athletes.

Because it's only five o'clock, the place isn't packed yet, which means we have our choice of tables. The host seats us at a table in the very center of the room and leaves us to peruse the giant menus.

"So, what's good here?" Stewart asks.

"I've never had a bad meal here."

He grins at me. "So, I'm thinking cashew chicken, Kung pao beef, and a coconut curry."

Diana groans. "That joke stopped being funny, like, twenty years ago."

"Oh? You don't want to eat with us?"

She rolls her eyes. We all know he would never deliberately order something she is allergic to. Her entire family is extremely conscious of her allergies and what isn't safe—

whereas my mother continuously offers me peaches, even though she knows I'm mildly allergic to them.

When the waiter comes over, a young guy of East Asian descent who speaks with a Southern drawl, Cecilia is in charge of ordering for the group. She gets enough food to feed us three times over. Then again, considering how much I am capable of eating and the game Diana just played in… maybe it's barely enough.

Conversation is as easy as it was last night, as easy as it was during the game. Stewart and Cecilia are good people, and more than that, they're good parents. They actually care about us and ask questions because they care about the answers. They want to know how we're actually doing, and not just the trite responses about school being busy and midterms being overwhelming.

Our food gets delivered and we dig into the plethora of dishes covering the table. Diana pauses halfway through scooping gai-lan in oyster sauce onto her plate.

"What's wrong?"

"Nothing. I just… I thought…" She sighs. "Never mind."

"Dee."

"I thought I saw this guy."

My heart starts to pound. "This guy?"

"We went out once. It wasn't great," she says. The first glimmer of information about how her date was.

"I'm sorry to hear that," I tell her—which isn't a lie.

"So yeah, I'm not really in the mood to see him."

Stewart cranes his neck to look, totally obvious. "That white boy?"

Okay, now I have to look, too. I try to be a lot more casual about it, though.

By the host's stand is a weedy, stringy looking white guy with long, unwashed hair and a patchy beard. He's wearing a flannel and dark jeans with holes in the knees. I don't know if the unkempt look is what he's going for, or if his student housing lacks the amenities of a shower. With him are a middle-aged bottle blonde woman wearing pearls—fake pearls, I can tell from here—and a sweater set, and a tall, balding man in a boxy brown suit.

The guy goes still when his eyes land on Diana. I can practically see his heart in his eyes. It's not hard; she's fucking amazing. She's a bonafide catch. He could do a whole hell of a lot worse than Diana Whitehall.

Not that I want him to catch her.

He mutters something to the people with him before he's striding over. Diana shrinks in on herself, which makes my blood boil. This asshole is making her feel insecure? I'm going to kill him. I'm going to rip his face off and tear him limb from limb.

"Easy there," Stewart mutters to me, and I release the death grip I have on my flimsy plastic chopsticks.

The guy approaches. "Hey, Diana," he says, giving her a smarmy grin.

"Trey. Hi."

"How've you been?"

"I'm great." She has absolutely no inflection in her voice, so he can't tell if she's telling the truth or being sarcastic.

She doesn't ask about him.

Cecilia opens her mouth and Stewart stops her with a quick look.

"I had a great time the other night," Trey says.

I stifle a snort, and Stewart cuts his glare to me.

Trey's eyes narrow as he takes me in. "Who're you?"

"Barrett's my best friend," Diana says. "Are those your parents?"

He glances over his shoulder with a grimace. "Yeah. We're… well. It's Parents' Weekend."

"Yeah. That's why I'm with my parents now, too."

For the first time, he acknowledges that Stewart and Cecilia are with us.

"Nice to meet you, Mr. and Mrs…" He looks back at Diana.

"Whitehall," Stewart supplies tersely. "So you're the asshole that's trying to date my daughter."

Diana rolls her eyes. "Okay, Daddy, that's enough."

"No. I want to know all about him."

"You really don't need to do that," she says. "Not on my account."

Trey's face falls. "What does that mean?"

She scoffs. "Come on."

"No. Tell me."

"You didn't actually have a good time the other night?"

He flushes. "I did."

"You must have been on a different date than I was on," she says bitterly.

I cover her hand with mine, and she turns to me, a soft smile curving her lips.

Trey clears his throat. "I was coming over here to ask if you wanted to go out again."

"Seriously?"

"Maybe we can get coffee sometime," he says. "Tuesday, after our abnormal psych class."

"I don't think that's a great idea," she says slowly.

My heart skips a beat.

"Come on. Have coffee with me. It'll be great."

"Diana," Cecilia says softly. "Give the white boy a chance."

If this dude minds being called a white boy, he doesn't show it.

"Fine," Diana sighs, sounding less than thrilled. "Coffee. Tuesday."

Trey's grin makes my stomach ache. "Great. It's a date."

twenty-four

. . .

Diana

I CAN'T CONCENTRATE on my abnormal psychology professor's lecture. All I can think about is the fact that in a few short minutes, Trey and I will be going on another date. And why? I'm not sure. It's clearly not love at first sight. Maybe he had a better time than I did, but that's not saying much.

A shadow falls over my desk. It's Trey, wearing another stupid flannel. "You ready for this?"

Well, I was, but I didn't exactly want the rest of the class to know we were going out. Now they're going to gossip about it. I hate being the center of attention, especially about something that is nobody's fucking business.

"Sure." I give Trey a fake smile. He isn't perceptive enough to know that it's fake, which kind of irritates me. Barrett knows my fake smile from my real smile. He knows when I'm being sarcastic and self-deprecating or actually looking for pity.

The walk to the nearest coffee shop is silent. Neither of us are talking, and I'm not in a hurry to start a conversation.

When we reach the Freudian Sip, Trey opens the door and ushers me inside. Okay, he gets points for that. We order our drinks and each pay for our own. I'm not trying to take anything from him, especially not something that would lead him to believe there's going to be a third chance for him to shoot his shot.

"I didn't realize your dad is Black," he says.

I give him a tight smile. "Yep."

"So you're half-Black."

"Yeah."

"And half…"

"Chinese."

"Oh. That's cool."

"Yep."

"I've never known anyone that was half-Chinese," he says.

"Well, now you've met me. Hi. I'm not a circus animal."

He flushes. "That's not what I meant."

"I'm sure."

"Where is your family from?"

"Amherst."

"Cool. Cool. I'm from Shelburne." He names a town about half an hour northwest of where I grew up.

"Practically neighbors, then."

"Yeah. We might have gone to some of the same parties," he says.

"I doubt it. I spent a lot of time in Winchester."

"Oh? That's kind of out of the way."

"It's where Barrett grew up. He spent a lot of time with me in Amherst, but during football season, I would visit him in Winchester."

Trey clears his throat. "Yeah. What's his deal?"

"Who? Barrett?"

"Yeah."

"He's my best friend."

"But you just transferred in a few weeks ago. How do you have a best friend already?"

I roll my eyes. "We've been friends for fourteen years."

"Oh."

"I was recruited by Newton back in high school, but I chose to go to USC. He came here. We've kept in touch, and now that we're here together, it's better than ever."

And it is. Barrett and I see each other nearly every day, whether it's for breakfast with his roommates or lunch between classes or dinner after practice. We'll hang out and watch Wheel of Fortune and Jeopardy! with Wes and the guys. On the weekends we've both been home, we've gone out to parties and drank and danced together.

And now we're starting to sleep together, too. I thought it would be weird. I thought it would be awkward. But aside from that very first day when I freaked out after having a sex dream about my best friend, it hasn't been. I have adapted to this, too, as I've adapted to everything else that's come my way.

"This really isn't working out, is it?" Trey says.

"What do you mean?" So maybe it isn't just me.

"Neither of us are into this the way we should be."

I let out a sigh of relief—and maybe that should tell me.

"It's not you, it's me," I tell him, and he laughs a little sadly.

"No, it's me."

"It's both of us," I offer, and he cracks a smile. "I'm sorry. I—"

"There's nothing to apologize for. Sometimes it just doesn't work out. Nobody is at fault."

Still, I feel like part of this is my fault. I haven't exactly been enthusiastic about him. I'm holding him at arm's length, both now and during the bowling adventure.

"You should give your friend a shot."

I blink at him. "What?"

"Your friend. Barney."

"Barrett?"

"Yeah, him," Trey says, curling his lip in distaste. He clears his throat. "He has feelings for you."

"What? No."

He shakes his head, like I'm the world's biggest idiot. "Yeah, he does."

"We're just friends."

"Well, he wants to be more."

I stare at him, disbelieving. There's a reason we've never crossed that strict line. No matter how much I've wanted it in the past, the fact that he's shown absolutely no interest in me means that I will never pursue this.

"Just think about it. And when you two get together, don't invite me to the wedding."

Snorting out a laugh, I agree to that. "Yeah, because there won't be a wedding."

He rolls his eyes. "If you say so."

Parting amicably, I take my coffee and start the leisurely walk back to my house in Athlete's Village. I have an hour before I have to be at the fields for practice, so I indulge in a few moments of peace and quiet being the only person in my house. I didn't think it would get to me, but living with five other women—five women who don't particularly like me—is starting to wear on me. I spend as little time as possible in my house, mostly hanging out with Barrett at his place. It's not sustainable. One of these days, he's going to get tired of me and tell me to go home.

Daylight's savings time has come and gone, so it's dark when I emerge from practice, sweaty and tired. I should really take a shower here in the locker room, but I'm not in the mood.

To my surprise, when I emerge from the locker room, Barrett is waiting for me. He shoves his phone into his pocket and starts towards me.

"Hey. Were we meeting up today?"

"No plans. I was in the neighborhood," he lies, because

the football complex is on the complete opposite side of the athletic center. It's a good seven minutes' walk. "I thought maybe you wanted to grab dinner?"

"Yeah. Don't we grab dinner almost every night?"

"We do," he acknowledges, and doesn't say anything else.

"So… why is this night different from all other nights?"

"I thought we could go somewhere just the two of us," Barrett says.

Oh.

"Sure."

"There's a dining hall on main campus that's supposed to have really good lasagna. You in?"

"Are there breadsticks involved?"

"You know, I think so," he says slowly, a grin spreading over his face.

"Then yeah, count me in."

He slings his arm around my shoulder, ignoring the fact that I'm hot and sweaty. I probably smell disgusting after a three hour practice.

"How was your date?" he says, oh so casual.

I snort. "Is that why you want to go to dinner? So you can scope out the situation?"

He's quiet for a moment.

"I care about you, Dee," he finally says. "I want to know about your life, even the parts you think I'm not interested in. I want to know everything."

"Well, it was a bust," I tell him. "Like the first date. There's no spark, no chemistry. I thought I was interested in him, but I think really I was just bored."

He winces. "That's not fun."

"Yeah. So rather than string either of us along, we went our separate ways. I'm not about to cry into a milkshake over it. I'm just going to move on."

"That's good. Healthy."

I don't know about that.

The dining hall looks the same as any of the other establishments on campus. We swipe our student ID cards for entry and peruse the offerings. He's right. The lasagna does look amazing, and there are piles of soft, pillowy breadsticks alongside it. I fill my plate with lasagna and the simple Caesar salad and follow Barrett to a small table for two tucked away in the corner.

It's an oddly intimate tableau for what should be a simple, friendly dinner. Like the night when we got pizza with my teammates and his friends, he went out of his way to get us a table alone so we could talk.

Now I don't know what to say.

"I leave on Thursday for U-Conn," Barrett starts, cutting into his lasagna. "You'll be in North Carolina, right?"

"South Carolina. Patterson University," I explain.

"Mason's brother went there."

"Oh. Cool." I've never met Micah, but I've heard plenty of stories about him. He seems like a cool dude.

"He was drafted into the NFL, so he bounced a year early, or I'd suggest you hit him up." He makes a face. "Maybe not. He's kind of a slut."

"Is that something you want to do?"

"What, be a slut? Or go into the NFL?" When I nod, Barrett laughs. "That's not in the cards for me."

"Why not?"

"Well, first of all, I already have a job waiting for me after graduation," he points out. "Beyond that, I'm not nearly good enough."

"You're not a bad football player."

"No, I'm decent," he acknowledges, which is an understatement. "I'm just nowhere near the level I would need to be in order to make it to the NFL. Plus I don't want to put my body through that level of abuse. I've been battered and bruised enough in the last decade."

"Okay, that's a fair point," I concede.

"Even if I was interested in having that fight with my parents—and I'm not—I don't think I would be able to make it. I'm good at this level. Comfortable. At the end of the season, I'll retire gracefully, and I'll be okay."

"You're not going to miss it?"

"Oh, I am," he assures me. "I miss it already. All good things come and go in life, and the time for football in mine is ending. I'll still watch Newton and Patriots games. My cousin Nate's boyfriend has season tickets to the Pats, so I'll try to go with him. And I'll… move on. Like you're moving on with this dude."

I roll my eyes. "There's nothing to move on from."

"He sure seemed interested the other night."

"Well, he wasn't interested today, and neither was I. It's over before it can even start," I tell him sternly. "Neither of us are invested in it. It's best that it ends now, before either of us get attached."

"So I need to find you another guy?" Barrett says, with a funny look on his face like he doesn't like that idea.

"I don't need a boyfriend. I just want to get laid."

He turns away, an expression on his face like he's sucked on a slice of lime after a too quick tequila shot. "You sure you don't want a boyfriend?"

"I said need, you say want. Do I want one? Yeah, kind of," I admit. "But I'm not in the right headspace for a real relationship, so I'm fine with a fling or a one night sort of thing. Ideally I'd find some guy who was interested in a friends-with-benefits type of situation."

I don't know how much more I can put myself on the line. It's practically glowing and neon, begging him to fuck me.

Instead, Barrett coughs and shoves an enormous piece of lasagna into his mouth. I guess he's not volunteering for the job. Damn. I almost thought he'd be interested in it, the way he's been all over me and kissing me the last few weeks.

"What? Am I supposed to pretend I don't like sex?"

His cheeks go pink.

"Barrett, I'm twenty-two years old. I've had sex before. I like sex."

"Stop saying sex," he hisses.

"I didn't take you for a prude."

He glances around us. Nobody is paying us any attention. "I'm not a prude."

"Sex. Sex. Sex."

He's beet red now. Perspiration dots his temples. "Diana."

"What?"

"Can we not?"

"Oh, so are you saying you don't like sex?"

He swallows. "I do."

"So why is it a secret? We both like having sex."

He's sweating in earnest now. I had no idea this topic would incite this kind of reaction in him. Why is he so repressed? He's been able to talk about hooking up before. Hell, he told me about his first handjob. So why does this freak him out so much?

"I like sex," he says quietly. "I wasn't aware our friendship covered that boundary."

"Well, why not? You've bought me tampons. I've felt your boner. We—"

"Diana."

"What?"

"When did you—?" He shakes his head. "I don't want to know."

"We've slept in the same bed together," I remind him. "You were grinding into me in your sleep and then you grabbed my boob. Then you started snoring."

"Sorry," he mutters, not meeting my eyes.

"I'm not complaining. It felt nice. You were asleep."

"Still. It's not right."

I roll my eyes. "Okay, if you say so."

"I do."

"So anyway," I say loudly, a little more loudly than I intended, and his eyes go wide. "This weekend is out, so next weekend I'm going to go to a frat party and get drunk and find some guy to take me home," I declare.

Sex is nothing more than a distraction, a pleasant way to spend my time. It doesn't have to mean anything. It drives me out of my head, forces me to think about the here and now, and not what's coming down the pipeline.

Barrett shoves a breadstick into his mouth.

"I'd go out to a bar or something this week, but I have a dietetics paper that is kicking my ass, and I don't like to hook up during the week."

"That's a good rationale," he says slowly. "Next weekend is Halloween. There will be tons of parties."

I beam at him. "See? Teamwork makes the dream work. Team Let's Get Diana Laid."

He coughs. "I'm not on this team."

"You're not?"

"I'll be the hulking bodyguard who beats up anyone who doesn't treat you right," he announces.

"I don't need a bodyguard. I need a wingman."

"Fine. Then I'll be your wingman," he says, wincing like there's a bitter taste in his mouth. "Although for the record, I am thoroughly against this plan."

"Why? Am I not entitled to a night or two of good sex?"

"You are," he concedes.

"So…"

Barrett shoves a giant piece of lasagna into his mouth and doesn't answer me.

twenty-five

. . .

Barrett

"I NEED HELP," I announce to Tucker and Miles at breakfast. The rest of the guys haven't joined us yet, still finishing their showers and eventually getting food. Miles has an early class, and Tuck is always one of the first guys showered and dressed after weights, so it's not surprising that they're the only ones ready to eat.

"With…?" Miles looks up from his bacon with a frown.

"Diana wants to get laid."

"So sleep with her," Tucker says, like it's that easy.

I cut my eyes to him. "I don't want to just sleep with her. I want—"

"You want more," Miles finishes for me.

"Yeah."

"Does she?"

I sigh. "Not with me."

Playing back the conversation last night, I almost convinced myself she was dropping a hint when she mentioned finding a friend with benefits.

But I don't want to sleep with her and discard her after. I don't want to pretend I'm not absolutely in love with her. I care about her as a person and as a friend. I want an actual relationship with her, and as she reminded me last night, she's not in the right headspace for that.

So I'm stuck between a rock and a hard place with no end in sight. Hence, asking my friends who are in stable, committed relationships how to fix this.

"You need to find someone else," Tucker announces.

"I don't want someone else. I want her."

"Well, she doesn't want you."

I flinch.

"What are you going to do, mope around for two and a half years and hope she changes her mind?"

"Well, it worked for you," I remind him.

Tucker's laugh is bitter. "Yeah, I guess so. But I wouldn't recommend it. Pining after someone who isn't interested is the worst feeling in the world."

"Yeah, tell me about it."

Miles shakes his head. "I wouldn't be so sure she doesn't have feelings for you."

"I am."

"No, seriously. She's always around," he points out.

"So? Mack hangs around us all the time, but she's not in love with Wes or Amir or Greg," I rationalize.

Miles winces at the mention of his younger sister. "That's different."

"How?"

"You and Diana are friends, best friends. Mack is a freshman. She's still finding her friend group."

"She has no friends," Tucker corrects. "She hangs out with us and with Wes, and that's basically it."

"So you've noticed that, too?" I roll my eyes. "Diana thinks Mack and Wes would be a good couple."

Miles grimaces. "She's too young, and he doesn't date. And even if she wasn't and he did, she knows better than to go out with my teammates. That's off limits."

"And Diana is off limits for me," I finish. "She's my best

friend. I don't want to lose her over a failed romantic experiment. So my options are stand by while someone else swoops in and steals her heart, or—"

"Or you move on," Tucker says.

"How did that work for you?"

"It didn't," he says flatly. "I tried getting with someone else, but it only made me feel worse about myself. So I didn't date, didn't hook up, and if we hadn't gotten back together, I still would be alone and celibate."

"And you're okay with that?"

He shrugs. "I didn't want anyone else. I wasn't going to pretend otherwise. She's it for me. She always has been."

Miles looks to me. "Is Diana it for you?"

I've been in love with this woman since we were fourteen. I've wanted to take our friendship to the next level for close to a decade, even before either of us were ready for that. She's the only person I want to hang out with, in a romantic setting or a purely platonic situation. When I think about my future, all I can see is her. I want to spend the rest of my life making her happy. I want to raise kids with her. I want *her*.

I let out a heavy exhale. "I think so, yeah."

"My advice? Figure out for damn sure," Tucker says. "If she's it, and you let her pass you by, then you're going to spend the rest of your life wondering what could have been."

"There's that saying, if you love her, let her go," Miles offers. "It's bullshit. If you love her, stand up and tell her. Don't hide it. That shit deserves to be said out loud. and she deserves to hear you say it."

"And if she laughs in my face?"

He pins me with a stare. "Do you really want to be friends with someone who would laugh in your face?"

Well, no. Not really. And I don't think she would actually *laugh*. Maybe giggle nervously because she doesn't know how to react.

"Incoming," Tucker mutters, and turns around in his seat.

He greets Sam, Mason, and Diana with a bright smile. "Good morning, ladies. Good morning, Princess."

"Hey," Diana says. She nods at him before she slides into the seat next to me. "This seat taken?"

"Only by you." For now and for forever.

I'm glad she's making friends, and I'm doubly glad she gets along with my friends and their girlfriends. Miles, Tucker, Wes, Amir, and Greg have become like brothers to me, and Sam and Mason are like my kid sisters. We're all one giant family, infinitely more supportive and loving than my actual family.

Diana tucks into her breakfast. She looks gorgeous today, with her wavy hair pulled back from her face in two thick braids and shimmery pink shadow on her eyelids. Her eyeliner is particularly sharp. She loves a good cat eye, or so she's told me half a dozen times in the last six weeks. Her dark green sweater nearly swallows her whole, and her dark brown boots go all the way up to her knee, emphasizing her long, muscular legs.

Fuck.

"The lasagna was good last night," she says casually. "Do they serve it often?"

"Every Tuesday."

She gives me a crooked smile. "We'll have to go back there next week."

"It's a date," I say, super casually, and her eyes widen. No. Oh, no. She's not into it. She's horrified by the idea of a date with me. "I mean, not a—not a date. I just meant… It's a plan."

Her smile now is a little forced. "Yeah. It's a plan."

Tucker coughs. I glare at him and he narrows his eyes at me. Miles shoves a piece of bacon into his mouth.

The last time I used that phrase—*it's a date*—she didn't blink twice. Now she's freaking the fuck out. It doesn't give me a lot of confidence in her supposed feelings for me.

It's a welcome distraction when Wes, Amir, and Greg join us and the attention shifts off of me and my humiliation. Diana is quiet beside me, focusing on her oatmeal. I'm almost afraid to talk to her for risk of everything blowing up further.

"I should get to class," she finally says.

"I'll walk you," I offer.

"Don't be silly. Your first class is on the complete opposite side of campus from the dietetics building."

Which… is true. I just want to spend some time with her, hopefully without all of my idiot roommates listening in.

"Well, another time, then," I tell her, and her smile is tentative.

"Yeah. Another time."

She practically bolts across the dining hall, eager to get away from me.

"Dude, you are so fucked," Amir says.

"How do you mean?" He's not wrong.

Wes rolls his eyes. "Does she know you're in love with her?"

I sigh. "So it's that obvious?"

Greg laughs. "Yeah, man, it's pretty fucking obvious. I think the only person who doesn't know is her."

———

When we board the bus for our trip to U-Conn, it's been two days since I've seen Diana in person. She leaves in about two hours for her trip to South Carolina, so I know she's still local and in town. She's just avoiding me.

As I settle into my seat, I pull out my phone and send her a quick text. *Have a safe flight, Dee. I'll see you when we both get back.*

Her read receipts are on. She's seen the message. She doesn't reply.

I don't know where to go from here.

Miles is across the aisle from me, texting with Sam. Tucker is messaging Mason. Even Amir is texting with the new field hockey girl he met last weekend at the No Parents Party, and Greg is absorbed in his phone, too. Only Wes isn't on his phone—he has a book to distract him.

As much as I want a relationship, I want Diana more. My best friend is my favorite person in the world, and I want to celebrate that. I want to take our friendship further than it is now. I want to build a future with her that is more than pure friendship: I want to build a life with her.

And she doesn't feel the same. She's looking for a one night stand or a friend with benefits. I'm not built for that, not with her. With other women, yeah, I've managed that in the past. But Diana is different. She means more to me than a meaningless fling I'm never going to see again. I'm going to see her again, and I'm going to want to have her again and again.

I don't want just one night: I want forever with her.

She's not interested in me. I have to accept that. I don't know how to deal with this ache inside of me. I've made some subtle moves to hint at wanting more and she's been oblivious or ignored all of them.

It's a terrible feeling to be in love with someone who will never return those feelings. It's even worse when that person is your best friend.

She means more to me than Dougie or the guys or even my parents. She's the one who's been there for me for the last fourteen years, since we were innocent kids trying to figure our lives out. Now, we're twenty-two and about to take the world by storm, and I'm still trying to figure my life out.

There's no way I can move on from her. There's no way I'm ever going to want anyone else. So I'm going to have to find ways to get her to see the virtue in a relationship with me —while acknowledging this could be the most emotionally trying year of her life. Between our impending graduation, her dad's impending deterioration, and all of the impending change… yeah, it's a lot to deal with.

Throwing a wrench into our friendship is just another challenge for her. Living together, being roommates… I don't see how this possibly works. She wants a one night stand, and I want forever with her. There's no magic way this works out for both of us to get what we want.

The bus lurches and we're on our way to Connecticut. The travel weekend has a rhythm to it: pack up, bus ride, arrive; team dinner, review plays, get a good night's rest; wake up early, breakfast, stretch, treatment, lunch, prepare for the game; play the actual game; and then we shower, change, shove all the food in sight into our face holes, and then prepare to return home, either that day or the next day depending on how late our game is scheduled to run.

It's over almost as soon as it begins, and at the same time, it feels like it lasts forever.

These are the days I'm going to look back on fondly, the defining moments of my college experience. While my future career might involve travel, it won't be with all of my brothers en route to a physical contest. While I might spend time with friends, it won't be with the men who have become my family over the years.

When we pull into the hotel, the guys push and shove to be the first off the bus. Once we're all free and clear and breathing fresh air again, we grab bags from beneath the bus and start organizing all of the luggage, leaving the equipment stowed.

The room assignments tell me I'm bunking with Miles tonight. He's a good roommate. Quiet. Keeps to himself. Aside from his nightly phone call with Sam—which I generally pretend not to overhear, locking myself in the bathroom or taking a walk through the hotel hallways for half an hour —he doesn't brag and throw it in my face that he has a steady girlfriend who loves him and I have my right hand and a best friend who won't give me the time of day.

Team dinner is a loud, raucous affair. I sit with my roommates, same as usual. We generally keep to ourselves. The quarterbacks are assholes and the running backs think they're hot shit. The wide receivers and tight ends are party animals. Offense in general is full of douchebags.

The defensive squadron is tight-knit. I can tolerate Sullivan and the group of freshmen minions he's corrupted well enough. The cornerbacks and safeties are loud and brash. They think they're the most popular guys on the team, when the truth is, nobody knows who any of us are. It's something our group of reclusive defensive linemen actually enjoy about our position. When we're hunkered down on the line and getting ready for the snap, nobody knows who we are: we're just a mass of navy blue, black, and silver uniforms, each of us indistinguishable from the next.

After dinner, we have the opportunity to hang out in the team room and watch a movie, or gather in one of the left tackle's rooms to play video games. Normally I'm all about that. Tonight, though, I opt out.

I want to call Diana. I want to talk to her, to clear the air. I'm not so sure that's a good idea. I'm about ten seconds away from blurting out my feelings for her in the most obnoxious and tone-deaf manner possible. It's bursting up inside of me. For so long, I've had to keep my feelings hidden. For so long, I've had to pretend like everything is fine. It's not fine.

twenty-six

* * *

Diana

BARRETT HAS BEEN MORE clingy than usual, and I don't think I'm the only one that's noticed. Emma referred to him as my boyfriend—as in, what is your boyfriend up to this weekend while we're on the road—and Sam keeps giving me mysterious smiles whenever I run into her on campus. He's definitely more tactile lately, and twice he's referred to our normal plans together as dates. The first time, it didn't bother me. The second time… yeah, something is definitely up there.

What I can't decide is if it bothers me. Does he actually think we're dating? No, we'd probably have to talk about it, and from his reaction when I subtly hinted I wanted to be friends with benefits… yeah, no. It's clear he has no intention whatsoever on going down that road.

Is it just because we're finally in the same place at the same time? Physically, at least. We're not separated by half a state or an entire country between us anymore. Now we're three blocks from one another and we can see each other pretty much as often as we want to, schedules permitting. We spend time together after our games and in the evenings and on the weekends, we've gone to two parties and we've hung out in his room. We spend plenty of quality time together.

Lately there's been something different between us, and I can't quite put my finger on it. Is it because we have slept together in the same bed? What am I supposed to do, insist on taking the occupied couch or sleep on the floor? We're grown adults; we should be able to handle sleeping in the same bed for some platonic cuddling. Is it because I had that sex dream about him? I don't think he even noticed I was on the brink of coming with him in the bed beside me.

Whatever it is, Barrett is acting more... proprietary isn't the right word. He's definitely more protective, making sure I'm eating and happy and warm, lending me his sweatshirt or grabbing a snack from the dining hall to meet me between classes. He's been putting his arm around me more and more, occasionally even holding my hand. All of this coming from a guy who could barely stand to touch me the last time I saw him before we went away to college... he couldn't even give me a hug goodbye before I left for USC.

And now he's all over me. It should be weird. It is a little weird. But it's also strangely comforting. I know he's not trying to grope me or take advantage of me. It's almost like he's decided we should be a couple and, instead of asking me for my opinion, has simply started to go for it.

Because if he asked me... I'm not sure what I'd say. I like Barrett. He's my best friend. I've definitely had a crush on him in the past, and I've had more than one sex dream about him over the years.

But date him? Do I want to date my best friend? If it all blows up, I'd be losing both my boyfriend and the person who makes my whole world make sense, and I don't know that I'd be able to handle that.

Does that make me selfish? I love Barrett, I love spending time with him and I love what we share. I don't want that to change. Just because he's seemingly decided he wants more from me doesn't mean I want it, too. And I don't know that I'm capable of giving him what he wants.

My nerves are already fraying at the seams. Between dealing with Johanna and her bullshit, trying to navigate school and applying to grad schools within a reasonable geographical area, and my dad's terminal illness... I don't think I have the emotional bandwidth to start any sort of romantic relationship. And I can't ask anyone else to shoulder the work on my behalf.

I've never had a real relationship, but I know it takes work and dedication on both parties' behalf, and I don't know that I have the time or mental energy to spare right now. Sam and Mason have made that clear. My mom has made that clear. Relationships take work, and if I can't put in the work now, I don't know that I'm ready for one.

And then there's the fact that this is Barrett. He's been my best friend since we were eight years old. Barrett was right when he talked about how our friendship has survived so many trials and tribulations over the years: puberty, period stains on white shorts, cracking voices, buying tampons, inappropriately timed boners, and more. First crushes and first kisses and first everything.

For years I've tried to deny that I'm attracted to my best friend. He's gorgeous. I've always known that. He's a genuinely good person, he's fun to be around, and he makes me laugh. And then add in the sex dreams I've had about him, and the time he grabbed my boob in his sleep... Yeah, it's not hard to put it all together. My best friend is hot. And when he's wearing those tight football pants, the stretchy white fabric accentuating everything about him... yeah, that's not half bad to look at, either.

But even if I'm reading all of his signals right... do I want to date him? I honestly don't know. His family hates me. Sure, Dougie and I get along fine, but I know how important his parents' opinion is to him. We come from two very different worlds, and I definitely don't fit into his pretty, perfect life. His mom probably wants him to get with someone who's marriage material, and that's definitely not me. His dad probably wants him to get with someone who has a trust fund, and that's definitely not me.

What we have is good. We're in a good place right now. For the first time, we're living in the same place, and now we're making plans to live together after graduation. If I get into Northeastern, my holy grail grad school, it will all work out. He'll be a quick train ride from the South End to the Financial District, where his family's business is located. I can take an easy train back to Amherst to visit my family—or, if I agree to his asinine plan, he can drive me home.

Of course, this is all predicated on me both getting into Northeastern's exclusive Applied Nutrition program *and* receiving a substantial financial aid package from them.

So I'm not going to count my chickens before they hatch. I have a few other schools on my short list, and if I don't get into any of them, I can take a year off and volunteer and retake my GRE and strengthen my application. Sure, Northeastern is basically my dream school and the best option for me, but it's not the be all end all program. I have options.

When it comes to Barrett, though… I'm not so sure I have options. I love him—as a friend. Is he hot as fuck? Do I want to sleep with him? Yeah, I think so. But do I want to take that step? I honestly don't know. I'm not even sure if I'm reading all the signals right.

————

My bus pulls into campus late Sunday afternoon. My whole body aches with the kind of bone weary exhaustion that comes from a healthy dose of exercise. I left everything on the field this morning. We didn't win, but it wasn't for lack of trying on my part. The lone goal scored today happened while I was sitting on the sidelines, and a small part of me thinks that if I was on the field instead of Terri, I might have been able to stop it.

Despite the pouring rain, Barrett is waiting for me. My heart warms with deep-rooted affection for him. His own bus pulled in only a bit ago—he has his duffel bag with him, sitting in a puddle not covered by his umbrella. He stands apart from the crowd of boyfriends and girlfriends who have come to greet us. There are usually five or six people who come to meet their partners off the bus, but he always stands off to the side, not part of the group.

Emma shoots me a knowing look. "He's back."

I don't bother to hide my smile. "Is he?"

"So when are you two going to make it official?"

"What do you mean?"

She rolls her eyes. "He's clearly in love with you."

"He's my best friend."

"Yeah, and he's in love with you, too. He's been here to meet every single bus, and he comes to all of our home games," she points out.

"So?"

"So you need to make it official and take him off the market, before someone else tries to snatch him up." She looks pointedly over at Johanna, whose mouth is downturned in a frown. "You know there are other people out there who would beat you up to get a chance with him."

"Yeah."

For all my waffling about, I don't want anyone else to have him, either. I want him all to myself. I just don't know what that means for us.

When we step off the bus, Barrett grins at me. He steps forward and holds the umbrella up to provide me cover.

"Hey. How was your flight?"

"Not bad. Your trip?"

He gives me a crooked smile. "Not bad."

We stare at each other for a moment before a shout behind

me catches my attention. I step forward, so I'm fully covered by the umbrella, and then I wrap my arms around his neck in a quick hug.

"What do you have planned for tonight?" he asks casually.

"Um, nothing much. You?" It's a Sunday night. I need to get ready for the week ahead, get a good night's sleep.

"There's a party at the gymnastics house. Greg is seeing one of the girls this week. You in?"

I can't tell if this is another one of his "dates" or if he's truly asking me as a friend.

Either way: yeah, I'm in.

"Sure. I need to head home first and shower."

He laughs. "Like the rain isn't enough?"

"I should probably wash my hair if we're going out."

"Fair." He knows how much I hate washing my hair—if I am choosing to wash it, that must mean it *really* needs to be washed. "Pick you up at your place at nine?"

"I'll be ready," I promise.

He shoots me a grin that reverberates right through me. "It's a plan."

I'm almost disappointed he didn't call it a date, which is absolutely ridiculous. We're not dating. We're not together. We're friends, best friends. That's all we've ever been, and all we'll ever be.

I don't have an umbrella, and I wasn't expecting rain, so I flip up my hood on my sweatshirt (definitely not waterproof) and leave the safe space he's created for us. I grab my overnight bag from beneath the bus and sling it over my shoulder.

Suddenly, the rain stops.

No, it doesn't. There's an umbrella over me—Barrett is exposed now, getting caught in the downpour. He's sacrificing himself to keep me moderately dry.

"What are you doing?"

"You need it more than I do," he says, which is blatantly false.

"Barrett."

He tugs my hand, until I'm forced to stand beside him under the cover of the umbrella.

"There. Now we're both good," he says.

I roll my eyes. "What, are you going to walk me home now?"

"If I need to."

"You don't." I clear my throat. "I appreciate the offer, though. I'll see you in a few hours."

Barrett leans down and presses a soft kiss to my cheek. "It's a plan."

Taking a deep breath, I step backwards, out of the cover of the umbrella, and pull my hood up again. I turn on my heel and start off in the direction of the soccer house. We could totally walk home together. My house is only a few blocks away from his. I could be mostly dry right now.

But right now, I need a few moments to myself. I need to get my head on straight. I'm getting all sorts of mixed signals from him, and I don't know what kind of answer I can give if he asks the question I'm afraid he's going to ask.

Johanna's beat me home, so I have to wait for her to finish her shower before I can take mine. Washing my hair takes for-ev-er. I hate it. I hate it so much. It's a necessary evil, though, and if we're going out, I want to look my best. For who, I'm not sure. Maybe for me. Maybe for whoever I hook up with tonight. I want to get laid. I want a night off, a night for myself.

When I get out of the shower, I'm surprised to find seven missed calls from my mom. We just talked this afternoon before I boarded my flight home. I click on her contact and the line rings. She answers almost immediately.

"Hi? Mom? You called me, like, fifty times."

"Diana." My mom's voice is ragged. My panic sensors kick into overdrive.

"What's wrong?"

"Your dad…"

I swallow a lump in my throat. "What happened?"

"He was in a car accident. He broke his leg and maybe some ribs. He might have a concussion." Mom sighs heavily. "Because of the blood thinners he's on, surgery is risky."

"Okay. I'll come up. I'll find a train tonight and—"

"No. Don't come."

"Mommy." My voice cracks. I can't believe she's pushing me away. I can't believe she doesn't want me there.

"I just mean…" She sighs again. "They're monitoring him overnight. Nothing will be decided tonight."

"I can still come up, be there for you."

"They're only letting one person in to see him at a time. Visitor's hours are over in twenty minutes. Come tomorrow."

"O-okay. I can do that. I can…" My voice trails off. I feel very young when I ask: "Is he going to be okay?"

"I don't want to lie to you," my mom says. "Try not to worry tonight. Go out with your friends. Take the edge off. Tomorrow, you can take a train up here. I'll have Aunt Jo pick you up."

"Mommy." My voice cracks on the second syllable.

"I know, baby, I know."

"How are you holding up? Did you find him? How long was he—"

"We'll talk about it tomorrow." She sounds weary, exhausted. "I should go. I want to see him before visitor hours are over."

"Okay. I'll talk to you later. I'll send you and Aunt Jo my train info."

Mom sighs. "Thanks, baby girl."

twenty-seven

. . .

Diana

I TURN up on Barrett's doorstep like a woman possessed. Tears stream down my face. I'm sure I look like a hot mess right now. I don't care.

Wes answers the door and blinks at me. With a questioning grunt, he beckons me inside and holds out his hand. It takes me a second to realize he's trying to take my damp raincoat.

"Thanks, Wes."

"You okay?"

I take a deep breath. "No. Not really."

He frowns.

"Is Barrett here?"

He nods, lifting his chin towards the stairs. Slowly I trudge up the quick flight of stairs, making my way to my best friend's room. I knock on the door.

"Yeah?"

"It's me."

"Dee?" He wrenches open the door, his face going slack as he takes me in. He's shirtless, his big hairy belly on display, wearing only a pair of dark jeans and socks. I can see the waistband of his boxer shorts above the line of his jeans. "What's wrong?"

Let's get to the more important question here. "Do you still have that vodka?"

"Come on in." He holds the door open to me. As he passes his bed, he pulls a t-shirt off the bedspread and shrugs it over his head en route to the mini bar set up in the corner. He retrieves a bottle of vodka and two shot glasses. "Do you want to talk about it?"

"Talk about what?"

He steps closer to me, until he's close enough that he can run his thumb beneath my eye. He comes away with a mess of tears, mascara, and concealer. "Whatever has you crying."

"Vodka first."

He pours each of us a shot. I take mine and clink the glass against his before I down it. When I see he hasn't taken his, I take it out of his hand and down the second shot. I don't even need a chaser.

"Shit. It's bad, isn't it?"

"My dad..." I can't say the words.

Barrett pulls me into a hug. His strong arms wrap around me and envelop me in his warm and familiar scent. His breath ruffles against my freshly washed hair. "What happened?"

I screw my eyes shut and bury my face in his neck. "He's in the hospital."

He pulls back. "What? How? We just saw him last weekend. He was doing so well. Has the cancer spread?"

"It's not—not that," I assure him quickly, because I know he cares for my father. "He was in a car wreck. Broke his leg and did something to his ribs and might have a concussion."

"Shit. I'm so sorry." He maneuvers me until I'm sitting on his bed with him perched beside me. He takes my hands in his. "What can I do?"

"Distract me."

I was supposed to go out and get laid tonight. Drink some tequila, flirt with a pretty boy, and get out of my head—and that was before this recent development. I don't think that's going to happen now. I'm too keyed up. My dad isn't allowed to have his phone on him, no screens after a concussion, and I can't even tell him how much he means to me.

"Okay. I can do that." He sighs. "Are you going home? Can I pay for your cab?"

"My mom doesn't want me to come home, not tonight." I try hard not to let the bitterness reflect in my voice. "She says tomorrow will be better."

"Okay. So tomorrow morning, I'll put you in a car and it will take you straight to the hospital. You shouldn't have to worry about the train schedules."

I swallow. "Thank you." I don't have it in me to protest my friend's extravagant generosity. He's helping in the only way he knows how.

The vodka is starting to hit my system. In this light, staring down at me and holding my hands, Barrett looks even more gorgeous than usual. It takes nearly everything in me not to lean forward and kiss him. I didn't eat nearly enough at dinner tonight. My timing was all messed up, coming from the airport and eating on the go. A soft pretzel and an apple, while delicious, are not nearly enough sustenance for the alcohol I need to consume tonight.

"I need food," I announce.

Barrett nods. "Okay. Let's feed you."

He stands and pulls me to my feet. When I rise, he wraps his arms around me again, pressing my face into his neck.

It's pouring rain, and almost nine o'clock. We're not going to the dining hall tonight. We'll have to make do with whatever meager offerings his fridge has—the fridge he shares with five other guys, and is nearly always empty. My stomach swoops, and it has nothing to do with hunger. No, this is a different kind of appetite speaking up. He smells good.

I'm feeling impulsive and itchy inside my own skin. Normally, I'd go home and *take care of the situation* with the help of my vibrator, but tonight… I don't want to be alone. I don't trust myself to be alone. Knowing the headspace I'm in, I'll probably end up at a frat party and let some guy I don't know take advantage of me just to get me out of my head, and it will only leave me feeling worse in the aftermath.

No. I'll hang out with Barrett, I'll snuggle with him and let him comfort me, and I'll get through this terrible night without resorting to fulfilling my baser urges.

My best friend tightens his arms around me. "It'll be okay, Dee."

"You don't know that."

"I don't," he admits. "But I have faith, and that will have to be enough to get us through."

"I don't know what I'd do without you."

"Hopefully you never have to find out." He gives me a lopsided smile. "Come on. Let's get you something to eat, and then you can drink your way through the liquor cabinet."

He takes me by the hand and pulls me out of his room. As we reach the top of the stairs, he releases me to put his hand on the banister, guiding himself down. Wes is back in his chair, reading his book. It's a Sunday night in the middle of term. If the other guys are home, they're otherwise occupied, which works out just fine for me. We don't always have to do everything as one enormous group.

"We don't have a lot of food in the house," Barrett warns me. "Do you want a banana?"

Ordinarily? Yeah. It's another thing entirely to eat a banana while staring my (very hot, very male) best friend in the eye. All I want is a distraction. All I want is to not hurt.

"We have… hot dogs, shaved turkey, eggplant parm, and string cheese," he announces, staring into the fridge. "Or popsicles."

I blink at him. "That's..." Very phallic. Or is that just where my mind is going?

He tugs on his jeans. "I think Greg did it on purpose."

"Cheese stick, please."

He passes one to me and takes one for himself. He peels strips from the mozzarella, eating the little strands individually. I chomp off the head of the cheese stick.

Barrett swallows. "You animal."

"I'm hungry."

"I could make you a hot dog."

"I'm not hungry for food."

He raises his eyebrows. "Oh?"

It's bubbling up inside of me. We've never taken this step before. We've never really even acknowledged that it could potentially one day maybe exist. And now here I am, about to throw a wrench in our beautiful, perfect friendship.

I sigh. "You're going to say no."

"Why am I going to say no?"

"Because I know you."

"So then maybe you shouldn't ask." His Adam's apple bobs in his throat. "What do you want to ask me?"

"I need you," I tell him.

"You have me, Dee. Forever."

A thrill runs through me. This is so deliciously forbidden, so deliciously against the rules of our friendship. Still, I have to push. I have to try.

"Can I suck your dick?"

He drops his cheese stick. "Jesus!"

"Please. I need... I need a distraction. And it would get me out of my head." I'm almost begging now.

In the other room, Wes snaps his book shut. It takes him two tries to heave himself out of his chair, and then he speed-walks to his room and slams the door.

We're alone now.

"I need something that will force me to get out of my

brain," I try to explain. "I don't want to get drunk because then I'll have a hangover, and I'm not trying to have a hangover while I visit my dad in the fucking ICU. I want to have one more drink, maybe two, and then I want someone to shove their dick so far down my throat I can't breathe or hurt or think. Ideally, your dick."

I trust him. He's not going to take advantage of me. If anything, I'm the one taking advantage. He's not going to abuse me or mistreat me. If anything, our friendship might get a little awkward once I've sucked his cock.

We can handle awkward. What I can't handle is being in my own skin right now.

Barrett's face is beet red. "Jesus, Diana."

But I notice he adjusts himself in his jeans.

"Please. It wouldn't—it doesn't have to change anything."

He pushes past me, out of the kitchen and up the stairs. I give him a three second head start before I follow him up the stairs and into his room. He locks the door behind me with a *click* that sounds ominous in the quiet room.

"This would change everything," he says quietly.

"It doesn't have to."

His eyes rise to meet mine. "You seriously want to… to suck me off?"

I nod. "I need to focus on something other than how much my heart hurts. Please. It can be as messy as you want, you can pull on my hair. You can even come in my mouth. I… please."

"Jesus." He looks away, his face red, but I notice an impressive bulge beginning to form in the crotch of his jeans. I can't look away. I'm staring openly at his dick now. "This doesn't feel right."

"Why not?"

"Because."

"That's not a reason."

"We've never crossed this line before," he says slowly. "There's always been—"

"It's just a blowjob. It doesn't have to change anything."

Barrett swallows again. Taking a deep breath, he unbuttons his jeans and undoes the fly. The zipper is loud in the silent room, the only sound except the thundering pound of my heart. He shoves his jeans and shorts down his legs. His cock bobs up against his belly, rigid and red.

"You're hard."

He lets out a bitter chuckle. "Yeah, well, we've been talking about blowjobs. It's not… difficult."

I look up at him. "Can I touch you?"

He jerks his head in a semblance of a nod. He almost looks angry—at me? At himself? I'm not sure even he knows.

Crossing the room to him, I press lightly on his chest, until he gets the picture and sits on the edge of his bed. I kneel between his spread legs, staring at his cock. It's gorgeous, hard as steel and soft as velvet, the swollen mushroom head an angry red. I wrap my hand around the shaft, and he exhales slowly. I run my thumb along the prominent vein beneath the tip.

"Can I taste you?"

He lets out a ragged sigh. His eyes on mine, he nods slowly, and I maintain eye contact as I lean forward and swipe my tongue over the head, lapping up the bead of pre-come dancing on the tip.

"Jesus, Diana," he says, this time almost like a prayer. He swallows loudly. "Do that again."

So I do.

Tightening my grip on him, I start to stroke as I suck the head into my mouth, learning his body. If the sounds he's making are any indication, he likes when I rub the tip along the inside of my cheek, and he likes when I cup his balls in my hand.

Holy shit. I have Barrett's cock in my mouth, and I'm touching his balls. Holy fucking shit.

Leaning forward, I take more of him into my mouth, sucking harder now. He spreads his knees a little wider, letting me get closer as I stroke the parts of him that don't fit into my mouth. He tastes a little bit salty and a little bit sweet and a little bit perfect.

I release him, and he lets out a disappointed moan. Making eye contact again, I take his hands and place them on the back of my head. He gets the hint, threading his fingers through my hair and grabbing hold of my ponytail with the other hand. He tugs ever so gently, and I swallow around his length, breathing hard, as a lightning bolt of lust courses through me.

"Holy fuck," he breathes. "You like this?"

I nod.

He pulls on my head, gently, gently, forcing me to take more of him into my mouth. It's not a hardship—I'm genuinely wanting more, more, more. The taste of him is thick in my mouth, his pre-come coating the back of my throat. I swallow again, and he sighs. His pelvis tilts up, pushing more of him into me, and I lower my head and take as much as I can.

Barrett holds my head in place as I lick and suck, and when I swallow around him, he starts to fuck into my mouth, slowly rocking deeper, deeper, deeper. I'm surrounded by the heady scent of him, the familiar musk and honey sweetening the deal.

"Fuck, Dee. I'm… holy fuck," he breathes. His fingers tighten in my hair and I suck, hard, around his length. He moans. "Baby, this feels so good. You're doing so good."

The praise makes me glow, and I renew my attention with vigor.

"I can't believe you want to do this, that you want to…"

He groans, thrusting up into my mouth. "So good. So perfect. It's like you were made to suck dick. My dick. Only suck mine."

A little thrill runs through me at the idea that I might get to do this again. I don't want this to be a one time only type of thing. He tastes too good, and he fits so perfectly in my hand, I can't imagine this could be my only opportunity to touch him, to taste him.

Licking down his shaft, I shift so his length falls across my face. He's thick and heavy, and the tip leaves a sticky trail of pre-come across the bridge of my nose. He sighs, and I suck on the sensitive vein beneath the head.

"Fuck, Dee. I could come just from that."

I return my attention to his length, stroking over him as I devote myself to all of his sensitive spots. I learn his body, what makes him sigh and what makes him moan, and when I lick over the tip again, he tightens his hands in my hair and pushes himself past my lips.

"Please, baby. I'm so close. Please let me..." He lifts his hips, fucking into my mouth.

Relaxing my throat, I let him take control as he takes what he needs—what I need. A few quick strokes and then he groans, my mouth flooding with his hot, sticky, salty come. I take it all. He works himself inside my mouth until he's done and then I pull back ever so slightly.

Meeting his eyes, I swallow, and he lets out a feeble moan.

"Fuck, baby, you're going to kill me."

"Good?"

"Holy fuck, good," Barrett says. He's red and sweaty, breathless, his belly heaving as he works to get air into his lungs.

I don't know what to do now. His spent cock rests against the inside of his thigh. Even deflating as it is now, it's a pretty cock.

"Take your pants off."

From my knees, I rock back on my heels and stare up at him. "What?"

"Take your pants off," he repeats. "It's my turn now."

twenty-eight

· · ·

Barrett

"THAT'S NOT what this is about," she says, a little nervously.

"I want to taste you."

From between my spread knees, she stares up at me. "Barrett…"

"Baby, I want you to relax and get out of your head. An orgasm will help you. Right?"

She nods, hesitant.

"So let me help you out the same way you helped me. I want to bring you pleasure." I soften my voice to conceal how much I want this. Need this.

She doesn't look convinced. "You want to…?"

"I'm all about equality," I tell her with what I hope is a confident grin. In reality, I'm freaking the fuck out. I came this fucking close to telling her I loved her. I was half a second from blurting it out. So burying my face in her pussy? Yeah, let me tell her I love her in another way, the only way she'll accept it from me.

Diana rises slowly to her feet. I offer her a hand, and she takes it, her calloused palm sticky from touching me. She stands nervously in front of me.

"Now what?"

It's my turn to stand. Tucking myself away, I do up the front of my jeans and then set my hands on her hips.

"Now, it's my turn." My eyes dip to the front of her jeans. "May I?"

She undoes the button, and I pull down the zipper over her mound, my thumb stroking her over the denim. She shudders, and I move my hands to her hips, working the thick material down and over her ass. When the waistband is lowered enough, I cup her thick ass in my hands, massaging gently.

"This okay?"

She nods, holding her breath. "Y-yeah."

"You're good?"

"I'm good." She still sounds a little shaky.

I caress the thin line of her thong to where it disappears between her ass cheeks. "You'd tell me if you weren't?"

Her eyes flash. "I'm not some innocent virgin, B. I'd tell you if I wasn't having a good time. Get on with it."

Laughing, I step back and pull the denim down over her legs, helping her step out of it. She's wearing soft pink cotton panties. Sweet, innocent.

Urging her backwards, she climbs onto my bed and falls back against the pillows, her dark hair a perfect halo surrounding her.

"You're gorgeous," I tell her, as my finger dances along the waistband of her panties.

"I'm still clothed," she reminds me, and I smile, because she is so perfect and mouthy and just—I fucking love her.

Ducking my head, I press a soft, lingering kiss over the top of her mound before I move towards the inside of her thigh. Nuzzling softly, I run my finger over her center, above her underwear. She twitches.

Slowly, slowly, slowly, I peel her panties down, revealing her to me. She's pretty and pink and perfect, covered in a few days' growth of stubble. I like that she's not perfectly groomed. I like that I'm the only one who gets to see her like this. I press a soft kiss to the hood of her clit as I strip away her underwear, flinging it aside.

Diana sighs, spreading her legs for me, and I maneuver my way until I'm propped up on my belly, her legs draped over my shoulders. My hands on her hips, I lower my head and taste her.

Taking my time, I explore her, licking and nuzzling and sucking. I spread her lower lips and draw the bud of her clit into my mouth, sucking firmly. She lets out a soft sigh, her hands threading through my hair. She directs me down a little and over to the left, and as I find that spot, she tilts her hips into my face and grinds onto me, searching for more.

When I ghost my finger along the seam between her legs, she makes a needy sound deep in her throat. She's hot and wet, and when I circle my finger over her entrance, she tightens her grip in my hair.

"Touch me," she demands, a bit breathlessly. I'm all too happy to oblige her.

Slowly, I work my finger inside of her. She's tight, so tight it nearly makes me dizzy. But this isn't about me. I scrape my teeth over the bud of her clit, and she twitches, pulling on my hair. Licking and sucking, I give her the pressure she wants as I move my finger, learning her silky velvet walls.

"Inside," she says.

I slip a second finger inside of her, rotating and scissoring. She gasps.

"Inside," she says again. "I want you inside of me."

Hold up. Wait a second.

"Dee…" I look up at her, a question on my face.

She rises onto her elbows. "I need you inside of me."

That's not what this is about. We agreed to oral. We agreed to a blowjob. We did not agree to full on intercourse.

Sex with Dee? Yeah, my cock jerks to life at the idea. It

would be great. It would be fantastic. Explosive. It's every-thing I've ever wanted.

No. What I want with her is a life together, a future. Many evenings of this, not just one.

"I'm sober. I'm consenting. I want sex," Diana says firmly. "If you're not interested, I understand."

"I'm not *not* interested," I admit. I press a kiss to her inner thigh. "It's a big step."

"You're eating me out. Your fingers are inside of me right this very second," she reminds me, as if I'm not intimately aware. She clenches around my fingers, and my cock twitches at the idea of being inside of her. "It's not that big a step."

We'll have to agree to disagree there.

I work my fingers in and out of her. I find that spot inside of her that makes her go crazy, and when she gasps and sinks back against the pillows, I lower my head again and suck at her in earnest.

Diana rides my hand, rides my face, until her entire body tenses and then she releases. The moan is ripped from her throat as she clenches around my fingers, drenching my hand. I don't let up until she releases my hair and twitches her hips away.

I meet her eyes. "You sure about this?"

She's breathing hard, her skin flushed and dewy. "I've never wanted anything more."

"On your hands and knees," I tell her, giving her a light swat on the ass.

She scrambles to comply, rolling over and propping herself up. Reaching for my bedside drawer, I pull out a condom and a bottle of lube. She's wet, practically dripping, but a little extra lubrication never hurt anyone.

With her on her hands and knees in front of me, I slip two fingers inside her again, and she groans, her head hanging down between her shoulders.

"Fuck, Barrett," she says, her walls clenching around me.

That's what this is. It's fucking. It's sex. We are certainly not *making love*. This is needy and brutal. Almost transactional. We both helped each other get off. Now we're getting off a second time.

Together.

Withdrawing my fingers from inside of her, I draw them up between the split of her legs. She moans, spreading her knees farther and pushing back her shoulders, putting herself on display for me. I rub my well-lubricated finger over her crack but don't explore any further.

"Not this time," she says, a little out of breath.

Am I supposed to infer that there will be another time? Am I supposed to infer that she's okay with the idea of anal? My cock jerks, and I feel dizzy all over again.

A quick stroke and then I'm ready for the condom. I roll it down my length and give the base a healthy squeeze. I can do this. It's totally not a big deal. It's only sex with my best friend in the world and the woman I've been in love with for the better part of fourteen years.

Notching my cock against her entrance, I check one more time.

"You good?"

"I'm golden," she says. "Fuck me."

Pushing in, I'm blinded by the tight, wet heat surrounding me. It's almost too much. She tilts her hips back, taking more of me into her, and involuntarily my hips jerk forward into her.

"Wait a second," she says, and I freeze with my cock halfway inside of her. She scoots up the bed, until my dick comes out, and I fall back on my haunches.

"What's wrong?"

She moves about six inches up the bed and grabs hold of my headboard. She turns back over her shoulder to glance at me. "Nothing's wrong. I just need something to hold on to."

I move closer to her, notching myself at her entrance again. "You good?" My voice comes out hoarse.

"Fuck me," she says.

And so I do.

She's tight, impossibly tight, and hot and wet and silky and perfect. Clutching the headboard, she clenches around me and sticks her ass into the air. My hands land on her hips as I pull her onto me, then work her body forward, so she's the one doing the fucking.

"Harder."

She's bossy, and I fucking love her for it. I fold myself over her back and fuck into her roughly, my hands tightening on her hips.

With one hand, she releases the headboard to slide between her legs, and I remove her hand and put it firmly back on the bed.

"Did I say you could touch yourself?"

She shudders out a breath. "N-no."

"Mine. You're mine." She clenches around me, and I see stars.

She wants to be fucked out of her head, taken and used. She's not some fragile flower; she's strong and capable, and right now, she needs some extra support to stand tall. I'll take the brunt of this, take the emotions and worry out of her head so all she can focus on is feeling good again. She needs to let go.

Ducking my head, I press a kiss against her shoulder blade, a gentle caress, before I move my free hand to her breast. Rolling her nipple between my fingers, I pinch at the beaded bud, and a fresh gush of wetness engulfs my cock.

"Do that again," she says.

"What's the magic word?"

"Please," she says, and I do it again. "Please." Diana moans, her head hanging between her shoulder blades. She clenches at me and works her hips, taking as much of me as she can. "Fuck, Barrett." She's panting now. "Holy f-f-f—"

Releasing her breast, I slide my fingers to where we're connected so intimately, gathering our combined wetness and lubrication. I rub at her clit until she starts to clench around me, and I move my hand away.

"Barrett—please…"

"Please what?" I don't recognize the gravel in my voice. I don't think I've ever sounded this hoarse in my life.

"Please let me come."

Instead I brush my fingers along her lower lip, until she sucks them into her mouth. She sucks eagerly, taking in the taste of her and me and probably a little bit of latex and lube. She doesn't seem to care. She sucks greedily.

My thumb works between us, pressing against her ass, and she swallows thickly around me, thrusting her hips back for more. She wants this, she wants me, she wants to be surrounded by me. I'm not kidding myself; I'm just a guy with a dick to her, anonymous and faceless. It's about getting off, getting out of her head. I move my free hand to her clit. I know what she likes now, what she wants, what she needs. And I give it to her, letting her take what she is so desperate for she's actually begging.

Diana comes with a shout, her walls tightening around me so tight I almost black out. She gasps, breathing hard, and I remove my fingers from her mouth to grasp her hips again.

"You good?"

"So good." She sounds tired, a little shaky. "So fucking good."

Widening my stance, I fold myself over her and fuck into her harder, more forcefully now. She's happy, sated, but she's still a willing participant as she rides my cock like a fucking champ.

It takes one, two, three, four strokes before my balls start to draw up and I come like a freight train. My hands tighten on her hips as I spill into her, into the condom.

Holy fuck.

Diana collapses onto the bed beside me, breathing hard. Her legs splay out, boneless.

"Fuck, Barrett," she says.

"Yeah?" I can hardly look at her. I'm too afraid to see what's written on her face. I went too far. I was too rough. She wasn't into it as much as I was. It was—

"Yeah," she says. She lets out a heavy breath. "Fuck."

I roll over, preparing to get out of the bed.

"Where you going?"

"I'll be right back," I promise. In the bathroom, I deal with the spent condom and wash my hands. I stare at myself in the mirror and try to tamp down the urge to throw up. We just had sex. We just had amazing, explosive, definitely not vanilla sex.

Holy fucking shit.

When I return with a warm washcloth, Diana's eyes soften. Slowly I help her clean up, pressing a soft kiss to the front of her hip as I do.

She sighs, running her hands through my hair. "That feels nice."

"Yeah?"

She nods, biting her lip.

"Say it," I tell her.

"What?"

"Say whatever you want to say."

She sighs. "Come lay down next to me."

Scrambling up the bed, I move to lay beside her, and I'm surprised when she scoots closer and rests her head on my chest, her arm slung low around my waist.

"We just had sex," she says out loud.

"We did," I agree carefully. Where is she going with this?

Diana picks up her head and looks at me. "Does this change anything for you?"

I don't have to think. I already know. "No. Nothing has changed."

I'm still irrevocably in love with her, and all it was to her was a way to pass the time.

twenty-nine

· · ·

Diana

THE CAR RIDE to Amherst is silent except for the hum of the car's engine and the smacking of the cab driver's gum. I crawled out of Barrett's bed early this morning, around maybe five or six o'clock, and returned to my house to pack a quick bag. I don't know how long I'm going to be home. I don't know how long my dad will be in the ICU. His immune system is already so weak from all the treatments, and all I hear about hospitals is people picking up infections and illnesses that they didn't have when they went in. And then the rehab facility… There's a lot I don't know.

What I do know is that I'm scared. Terrified, really. My dad is hurt, and he's sick, and I don't know that he's ever going to get better. This isn't the end—at least, it shouldn't be the end, it's "only" a broken hip—but the very real truth is that the end could be sooner than any of us anticipated.

He's terminal. He's not going to get better. Whether he has a few months or a few years, we still don't know. We won't know until after the fact, until everything is over. I have to treat each and every moment like it might be the last one I get with him—because it might be.

I'm not ready for my dad to die.

I don't know if I'll ever be ready. But sooner or later, whether I want to or not, it's a reality I'm going to have to face. He's sick. He's in pain. I don't want to curse him to a half-life of pain and suffering. I just want my daddy back—my strong, capable dad who used to throw me over his shoulders and play keep away with me in the yard for hours and go on hundred mile bike rides just for the hell of it.

The chemo takes a lot out of him. The biweekly blood draws and intensive drug regimen probably don't help. He's sick. He's dying. All they can do is make him comfortable. He's not going to get better, not really.

And now he's hurt.

I'm a ball of anxiety on the entire two hour car ride. I stare at the window without seeing the scenery. I don't want to be doing this. I want to be having a good time with my friends, going to class, going to practice, living my life… not visiting my father in the ICU, not knowing if he's going to walk again, not knowing if he's going to walk me down the aisle at my entirely hypothetical wedding, not knowing what the rest of his life will look like.

My mom meets me in the hospital lobby and gives me the biggest, tightest hug I've ever gotten in my life.

"Hi, baby girl."

"How… how is he?"

"He's doing good," Mom says. "They're doing rounds in an hour or so, and then hopefully he can be released from the ICU and admitted to a regular room."

I let out a sigh of relief. "That sounds good."

"Come on. Do you want to see him?"

Slowly, shyly, I nod. She takes my hand and leads me towards the bank of elevators. The ICU is on the fifth floor.

"It'll be okay. It's just bumps and bruises," she says, punching the button for the floor.

"A broken leg isn't—"

"No, but it could be worse," she rationalizes. "He's waiting for you."

"And the concussion? Any update?"

"He does have one, so he's staying off screens, but other than that he looks good," she says. "He's bored. The nurses keep coming in and checking on him every fifteen minutes. He wants to go home."

"Is he… does he have pain?"

"They're keeping him well medicated."

So yes—he's in pain. Between the broken leg, the bruised rib, and on top of that, the terminal cancer… my heart aches.

The elevator releases us, and my mom directs me down a hall to a set of rooms near the bathroom. There's a desk outside of the two rooms, where a nurse wearing scrubs is typing on a computer.

A rapid beeping comes from a monitor on the left and she springs into action, bolting into the room.

"That's Frank," Mom says. "He keeps taking off his heart monitors."

I let out a quiet sigh of relief that my dad isn't the one setting off the alarms. If he felt better, he would probably try, he would think it's funny.

Mom pulls aside a curtain and—there he is.

My daddy looks different. He's sleeping, snoring, with a trail of drool coming out of his mouth. His left knee is wrapped and elevated and there's some sort of contraption around his right leg.

There's a chair in the corner. Mom settles into it and pulls out her book.

"You're reading? How can you be reading at a time like this?"

"He's sleeping. I was here last night and as soon as visitor's hours opened this morning. It's a long day. It will… It's going to be awhile."

Standing at the foot of the bed, I stare at the man in the

hospital bed. He looks like my father, and he snores like my father, but the man I know is not this bed-bound creature in front of me. I don't recognize him. My dad barely takes sick days, and he never catches colds. He's never ill. And now he's hurt and sick.

"Sit down, baby girl," Mom says. "It'll be awhile."

Collapsing into the chair beside her, I rest my head on her shoulder and stare unblinkingly at the bed. I don't know what to think, what to feel. I don't know how to process this.

As a psychology major, I can recognize that I might be helped by a little bit of talk therapy. Tucker and Mason are both in therapy and have both said it's helped them. Maybe I should try that. Maybe then I won't try to cope with terrifying situations by having sex with my best friend.

I have no idea what came over me last night. I was scared, and I was horny, and I was anxious. It felt good to get off, especially with an actual person that isn't my vibrator. Two orgasms helped keep some of the anxiety and helplessness at bay overnight. I couldn't do anything last night. I might not be able to do anything now. I'm here, I'm present, and sometimes, that's all we can do.

I hope Barrett and I are okay. I pretty much begged him to let me suck his dick—and he let me, which might be the most crazy part of all of it. He's the one who insisted on returning the favor… which, yeah, I do appreciate. He gave as much as he let me take.

I'm the one who insisted on taking it a step further. I'm the one who begged him to go inside of me. I'm the one who got on my hands and knees for him to fuck me. He didn't protest, yeah, but he didn't seem all that enthusiastic.

Until he slid inside of me. Until he fucked me. It's sex, instinct probably took over for him. There was a naked, wanting, willing woman in his bed. He probably didn't stop to think about what would happen to our friendship if we went through with it. I know I didn't.

Is it bad that I kind of want to fuck him again?

It feels wrong to dissect the amazing sex I had last night while my dad is lying hurt in a hospital bed, but if the alternative is coming to terms with the reality that my dad is lying hurt in a hospital bed…

I've always used sex as a distraction. It helps me escape when the everyday monotony of my completely normal, everyday life gets too much to bear. Although typically, I pick a guy I won't have to see again or talk to after the fact. We can go our separate ways and that's that.

As much as I want to talk to Barrett, my best friend, I don't know that I'm ready to talk to Barrett, the guy I slept with last night. The guy whose dick I sucked. The guy who went down on me. The guy who fucked me, but didn't kiss me the entire time. I've never had sex with someone I've never kissed… until now.

I know Barrett. He's been my best friend for fourteen years. And now I know him intimately, in a way I never expected. I know what his dick tastes like. I know what his orgasm face looks like. I know how it feels to have his dick inside of me, fucking me, pulsing as he came inside of me.

Mostly I know that I want to do it again. Not the fear, not the anxiety—I want the comfort and familiarity of the best person I've ever known, as I've embarked on a journey there is no coming back from. We can't ever be "just friends" again.

———

After rounds, my dad is released to a general admission room to await his surgery this afternoon. He's awake sporadically during the day. The pain meds make him sleepy and a little out of it, so he's not up for chatting. He dozes. My mom reads her book. I stare unseeingly at my phone screen.

By lunchtime, I need a break. I haven't eaten anything all day

—there was no way I could eat this morning, I was too amped up. Now I can't sit here, sitting still and doing nothing. I take a trip to the hospital cafeteria and scarf down a truly disgusting turkey sandwich. I didn't realize they could make something so simple taste so bad. It's only two slices of damp and somehow stale bread, a single slice of Swiss cheese, and a few pieces of turkey, and somehow it's the most vile thing I've ever eaten.

I bring a sandwich back for my mom. She hasn't moved. She's still reading, though she's switched from her tablet, charging in the corner, to a paperback book. She has a soft canvas bag beside her laden with books, water bottles, and snacks.

Dad is awake now, inclined slightly in the bed.

"Hey, baby girl," he says when I walk back into his room. "I missed you."

"I'm right here, Daddy." I take his hand in mine, careful of the IV. "How was your nap?"

"Oh, I've had better," he says.

I force a laugh. "I suppose so."

"They're going to take me back for surgery in a bit," he says. "Listen, your mom—she's doing the best she can. We all are. We're all doing the best we can."

"I know."

"The life insurance paperwork is—"

"No, stop," I tell him. "I don't need to know."

"Yeah, you do," Dad says gently. "The life insurance paperwork is in the safe. There's a policy that goes to you, and another to your mother. I want you to use it for something good. Buy a house. Don't use it for school. It's once in a lifetime money. I can't give you much, but I can give you this."

"You're going to be alright."

"Surgery is always risky, and we never know what will happen," he tells me. "All of our assets are set up to go to your mother, and when she passes, they'll go to you, so don't expect any big inheritance next week."

"I'm not. I don't. That's not—"

"I know, baby girl. I know." He squeezes my hand. "There's a spreadsheet on my laptop with all of the usernames and passwords for my accounts. The credit card is due in a few days. Your mom knows which checking account the payment will come from. She might need help logging in and making the actual payment. I submitted the mortgage payment a few days ago, and all of the other bills should be up to date."

"Okay," I sniff, holding back tears. "I can help her with that."

"I'm going to be out of it for a while. She called my office and hers, and you should call your coach. I'll be in the hospital for a few more days, and then they'll release me to a rehab center for awhile. I don't know how long you can stay away from school…"

"I'll take care of it."

He swallows. "Thank you for coming home. I'm glad you're here. I wish it were under better circumstances, but I am glad to see you."

I force out a laugh. "Yeah, me too. What happened?"

"I don't remember." He lets out a grunt of frustration. "I wasn't trying to injure myself."

"I know. I know."

Around two o'clock, they take my dad over to pre-op. I hold his hand for a few moments and tell him how much I love him.

And then we wait.

Mom reads her book. I drink a bottle of water and stare at the wall behind where his hospital bed was. After awhile, I pull out my phone and text Coach Larsen, giving her a brief overview of what happened and that I'll be away for a few days, maybe longer.

Athletic department rules state that if I miss practice, it's up to the coach's discretion if I play in the next game, and if I miss several practices in a row, she's entirely within her rights to bench me until further notice. I can't worry about that, though. The school can't pull away my athletic scholarship if I miss a few games. My professors should all understand, too, once I explain the circumstances. It's a legitimate family emergency. I'm sure I can get a note from the doctors if they really push.

As an afterthought, I send a group message to the defensive squad, giving them a broad strokes overview of what happened and that I'll be away until further notice, and then I send another message to Johanna and the minions. I don't expect them to respond, but at least this way they can't say they didn't know why I'm not coming home for a few days.

Barrett's texted and called. I don't know what to say to him, so I say nothing at all.

A little past four, a doctor comes out to give us a status update. My dad's surgery went well. He's in recovery now, and in a little while he can be released back to his room. The scary part is over.

When they wheel him back in, he's out of it, still high from the anesthesia and the pain medicine. My mom kisses his cheek and speaks to him quietly, so quiet that I can't even hear her, and I don't think he can, either.

And then we wait.

The nurses come in and check on him. I stare unseeingly at the wall. The day passes on and on and on.

I want to go home. To school, to my parents' house, I don't care. I don't want to go home without my dad. And he's not ready to go home.

thirty

. . .

Barrett

IT'S BEEN a week since Diana and I had sex. Aside from a quick "got to the hospital" text on Monday morning, I haven't heard from her since then. It's been radio silence. She's been posting pictures of her dad on social media, old photos from when she was growing up. Nothing recent. I texted Stewart and asked how he was doing, but there hasn't been any reply. I don't want to bother Cecilia, but I'm half a minute from reaching out to her, too.

I've texted Diana, too, and I've called her twice. She hasn't answered. By Wednesday, I got the hint and stopped reaching out. When she's ready, she'll pick up her phone. When she's ready, she'll talk to me.

Because we need to talk. We had sex, spectacular, earth-shattering sex. What started out as an innocent blowjob—if blowjobs can be innocent—turned into full intercourse, and from her reaction, I thought she was having a good time. She's the one who escalated the situation from me going down on her to me being inside her. She's the one who wanted more.

Okay, maybe I wanted more, too.

My world moves on without her in it. I go to class, go to

practice, go to meals with the guys. Sam keeps eyeing me as if she's expecting me to fall apart and break down at any moment. She's not that far off. Stewart means a lot to me. He's been more of a father figure to me than my own dad the last few years.

But what has me on tenterhooks is Diana and her lack of response. I'd like to know that she's okay. I'd like to know that we didn't irrevocably destroy our friendship. I'd like to know that it will all turn out okay.

Stewart is dying, but he's not, like, *actively* dying right this minute. He broke his hip. After his surgery—which, yes, might be risky because of his compromised immune system— he'll go to a rehab facility and get stronger. It's not the end for him, not yet.

Wes has been giving me a wider berth lately. As far as I know, he's the only one who has even an inkling that something went down between Diana and me. It's not like we were fucking on the living room sofa; we went up to my room, and we were relatively quiet, respectful of my roommates. I think most of them were home. Nobody has said anything.

I wasn't awake when Diana slipped out of my bed. I don't know what time it was. All I know is that we went to sleep with her head on my chest, my arm around her, and when I woke up, she was gone. I sent her some money to cover her cab fare and—

Shit.

What if she thinks I was paying her for the sex?? What if she thinks I'm trying to bribe her? She probably thinks I'm scum, that's why she's not talking to me. I'm the kind of guy that—

No.

Diana knows me. She knows I offered to pay for her cab ride. We discussed it. I didn't want her to have to worry about train schedules and finding a ride from the station. I just wanted her to get home, to get to the hospital. She knows I love her and respect her. She knows I would never purposefully do anything to hurt her.

All I can do is love her from afar. All I can do is support her from afar. She won't let me in—she might not be able to let me in, not after the events of Sunday night. When she's ready, when she's able, I'll be there for her in whatever way she needs me. Until then… I just have to wait.

So I go to classes, and I go to practice, and I live my life. My dad calls me on Thursday morning. I ignore his call. That afternoon, we board the bus for our trip to Virginia Tech. Friday, during film review, my mother calls me. I ignore her call.

I am a dutiful son. I obey my parents. I treat them kindly.

But right now, I can't talk to my perfectly healthy, perfectly dismissive parents. Not when Stewart is in the hospital. Not when I don't know how he's doing. Not when so much is in flux.

I do check their voicemails, though. I'm not a monster. My dad's was an incoherent rambling about finding the trail, most likely a pocket dial. He doesn't call me all that often to begin with. My mom's message reminded me that there's a family dinner coming up next weekend and attendance is compulsory.

Dougie texts me, too, which is only slightly unusual. My brother and I aren't close, which is more a function of our equally busy schedules, and not because we don't genuinely get along. He's fine. I'm fine. We're just busy with school and, for me, practice and travel for games.

He'll be at dinner, though. So will our cousins. It'll be nice to see them. They're all older than me by a few years, so we're not buddy-buddy. I'm hoping that as we get older, we can be closer. Kyla is married now, and Nate has a steady, long-term boyfriend, so they're starting to settle down and think about futures and babies. Vince is kind of a dick. Hannah is great, she's a fashion designer, so she's busy shuttling between Boston and New York. Everyone else is in the area.

And soon, I will be, too. Soon I'll be living in the city and working with Dad, Uncle James, and Nate, and living my grown-up life.

The only question is, what will the rest of my life look like? Will Diana feature in it? I hope so, but after the last week, I'm not so sure she wants to be. I know she's going through a lot. I know our… escapades last weekend probably didn't help the situation.

So much is in flux. There's so much up in the air, so much I don't know. All I know is that I have to live relatively close to the Financial District, in order to make the commute to the office not suck too badly. Other than that… I know nothing.

And it's fucking terrifying.

thirty-one

. . .

Diana

THE HOSPITAL RELEASED my dad to a rehab facility after three days in the hospital. He'll be there for a week or so before they let him go home. Because my parents' house has stairs and his bedroom is upstairs, he has to relearn how to walk up the stairs before he's ready to be set free.

The rehab facility smells sterile. It smells like old people, too, and antiseptic and sadness. His roommate is a crusty old broad named Marjorie who farts a lot and generally seems displeased with the world. She's been here for a week already.

Dad loves her.

The physical therapist comes by a few times a day, practicing mobility and stretching. He has to relearn how to stand and how to walk. He's weak, and even with the help of a walker, he's unsteady on his feet.

I have never felt so helpless in my life. I don't like this feeling. There's nothing I can do. By Wednesday, he's recovered enough to do slow, slow laps around the halls, and I join him to get some movement in. We walk to the cafeteria and drink watery coffee and eat stale pastries. We walk through the garden and sit outside in the chilly sunshine. We walk as much as we possibly can, which is not a lot at all. He gets tired easily.

He asks about school, about soccer, about Barrett. There isn't much to tell him; we talk all the time, so he's already up to date on most of the extracurriculars going on in my life, and I'm not about to tell him about what transpired between Barrett and me on Sunday. We reminisce about my childhood, about fun family vacations to Mexico and China and South Africa, and silly memories like when I helped him build a jungle gym in our backyard when I was six years old or when he would ride his bike around the block towing me in a buggy when I was three.

We talk about his family. I'm not close to his parents—my mother's family is more tight-knit in the same small Wisconsin town, whereas my dad's side of the family all live across the country in Scottsdale, Reno, and Tahoe, with a few adult cousins scattered elsewhere. I heard one cousin lives in New Zealand now. I'm not sure; we don't keep in touch.

He tells me about his family's Coming to America story. It's something I've heard a dozen times and never gets old. My great-grandparents left everything behind in South Africa to come here, only to get trapped in North Carolina by the arcane Jim Crow laws. They were able to build a life for themselves in a small town in the mountains, and then fifteen years later, a devastating forest fire took out their homestead and left them with nothing once more. It's such a dramatic story, it deserves its own book.

He tells me about how his parents, my grandparents, met way back when. He tells me about his first date with my mother. He tells me about when he first decided he wanted to marry her, and how he was so nervous to propose, she thought he was trying to break up with her. He tells me how she first told him she was pregnant with me. They weren't trying, but they weren't *not* trying, either.

We're both all too aware that time is running out. Nobody

knows how much time he has left. It could be weeks, it could be months, it could be years. Time is fickle that way. Nothing is guaranteed.

Mostly we just spend time together, not necessarily talking, just enjoying our time together. My mom is there too, reading, puttering around. She brings a pile of blankets down to my dad's favorite armchair, so he can set up a home base downstairs, and she makes his favorite meals because his stomach is still a little upset. He's eating a lot of red jello and chocolate pudding, too, which is something he's never enjoyed until he had it in the hospital after surgery and it was the best thing he'd ever eaten.

———

While my mom makes her signature banana bread (chocolate chips, no walnuts) just for me, I sit at the kitchen island and watch her work. Her classic version includes the walnuts that could kill me, so she takes the time to make me a special batch even though it goes against her very being to omit what she sees as a vital ingredient.

I don't actually like banana bread. I don't like bananas, either. But this is what she's known for. So I'll take a few loaves of it back to school, and I'll give it to Barrett and the boys. I know B loves it. I don't understand it. Bananas are gross. I like making Barrett happy, though.

I'm avoiding my dad. He's taking a nap, which is fine. But I'm avoiding him. I don't like seeing him like this, weak and in pain. I only want to remember the good, not the bad. I want to remember my dad as a strong, capable man, not the version of him he is now.

But this is who he is. It would be a disservice to who he is at his core to block this time out. A person is allowed to be weak. They're allowed to be fallible. They're allowed to be failed by their own bodies. They're allowed to be human.

There is a hard road ahead. My dad is not going to get better, not really, and we're all going to have to stand by and watch. We're powerless to help him. He's taking meds, he's doing procedures, he's doing everything he needs to in order to keep going on.

But eventually, it won't be enough. The clock is ticking. His goal isn't to live forever—it's to live as long as he comfortably can. And that terrifies me.

thirty-two

. . .

Barrett

THE GUYS and I are watching our Sunday night Jeopardy! and Wheel of Fortune marathon when the doorbell rings. Amir is on the end of the couch, so he gets up to answer the door. I shift in the armchair and scroll through my phone again. It's been a week. I still haven't heard from her. I want to, I want her to reach out, but I know I can't make the first move. Not this time.

"I need to see Barrett," Diana says.

Amir glances at me. "It's Sunday."

"Please," she says, and I swallow at the neediness in her voice. "He's here. I know he's here."

Amir lets her in, shutting the door behind her, and Wes pauses the TV in the middle of a Wheel spin.

"We need to talk," she says, lifting her chin. I start up the stairs to my room and she follows me. I try not to remember the last time she was in my room.

"What are you doing here? Not that I don't want you here," I'm quick to reassure her. "I wasn't expecting you."

"We need to talk."

"Agreed."

She takes a deep breath, clasping her hands over her stomach. She looks decidedly green around the gills.

"Barrett…"

"Holy fuck. Are you pregnant?"

"What?"

"Because we can totally make this work," I tell her quickly. "We'll get married and—"

"No, I'm not pregnant," she says. "Why would you…"

"You're holding your stomach."

She cracks her knuckles and releases her arms. "No, I'm not… you would marry me?"

"In a heartbeat. If you were pregnant, if you wanted to have a baby… yeah, I'd do it."

"You want a baby?"

"Well, I mean, I'd like to graduate college first." I let out an awkward chuckle. "There are a few other goals I'd like to achieve before that happens. But if you were… it wouldn't be the end of the world. We could make it work."

"We used a condom," she reminds me.

"I know."

"And I have an IUD."

"I know."

"It's only been a week."

"I know."

"I'm not pregnant," she says again.

Is it weird that I'm a little disappointed?

"So, why are you here?"

She swallows again. "I miss you."

"I miss you, too."

"I needed to see you."

It's my turn to swallow. "I needed to see you, too."

"Can we…" She takes a deep breath. "Can we pretend like last weekend never happened? Just for a minute?"

If that's what she needs?

"Yeah, of course."

"Good." She sighs, her face creasing. "My dad is home. He survived."

"So he's out of the hospital?"

"Out of the hospital, had surgery, recovering nicely," she summarizes. "It was… I never want to do that again."

"Dee…"

"I just…" She chews her lip. "I need a hug. I needed to see you, and I needed a hug."

I take a step towards her, and when she doesn't flinch, I pull her into my chest and wrap my arms around her. She takes a deep, shuddering breath, and then she sags against me, her forehead pressed to my neck. She isn't ready for a relationship. She doesn't have any more to give.

"It wasn't fun," she says quietly. "It was absolutely terrifying."

"I know, baby." I run a hand over the back of her head. "I'm sorry you had to go through that."

"And it's only going to get worse." She hiccups into my neck. "He might get better in the short term, but long term…" She sighs.

"What can I do for you?"

"Just hold me."

I tighten my hold on her. I can do that. I can do that from now until eternity.

In reality, eternity is about four minutes, and then she sighs and steps back. I release her and take a half-step backwards myself.

"Do you want to talk about it?" I broach hesitantly.

"What's the point?" she says bitterly.

"Dee…"

"We had sex," she says flatly. "It's not that big a deal."

"Except clearly it is."

"It's whatever," she says, and I flinch at the reminder that to her, it was nothing. "It's not going to change us. Right?"

"Right," I lie. "It was…"

Because it's already changed me.

Amazing. Earth-shattering. Life-changing. Spectacular.

"It was a mistake," she finally says. "A lapse in judgment."

"Is that what it was?"

"I was hurt. I thought it would help me manage the pain."

"And did it?"

She considers. "It felt good."

"Yeah, it did," I agree quietly.

"But it can't happen again."

"Okay."

"It was one time," she says.

"Okay."

"And we won't talk about it anymore."

"Okay."

"Can I stay the night?" she asks.

"Okay." I'd do anything she asks. This? It's not a hardship, not in the slightest.

thirty-three

. . .

Diana

BARRETT IS IN MY BED. Or rather, I'm in his bed.

How did this happen again?

Except we were both worn out last night. Neither of us wanted to discuss the things we very much need to discuss. Okay, so maybe he wanted to talk. I wasn't ready. I'm still not ready. I still don't know how I feel. I had sex with my best friend, and it… wasn't bad. It was great. It was fucking spectacular. It was exactly what I needed.

But we crossed that invisible line.

Barrett sighs in his sleep and pulls me into his chest. His belly is pressed against my back, and I'm pretty damn sure I can feel his dick, too, pressed up against my ass. It should be weird. It should make me uncomfortable. Instead, I feel… oddly warm and cozy. Like I want to do this again every night. Do I like him in that way? Am I still attracted to him?

It would be so easy to fall into a relationship with Barrett. We're already best friends, so adding sex to our friendship wouldn't be that huge a change compared to what we already are. We spend all of our free time together, often to the detriment of our studies. We go to dinner, just the two of us or with a group of our friends. We go out to bars and parties, and we have fun when there's no alcohol involved. We just click.

He's the person that makes my world make sense. He's the person I want to spend all my time with. And, yeah, he's gorgeous. That's not exactly a secret. But that high school crush is long gone.

I think.

Do I want to date him? I honestly don't know. I don't know that now is the right time for us. So much is in flux. Graduation, grad school, maybe living together, my dad...

I can't lose Barrett, not at a time like this. I need him as a friend more than I want a relationship, even if that relationship is with him. I don't know that I would be able to survive without him. If something were to happen to us, if we stopped being friends... I don't think I could take it.

He's the most important person in my life. He always has been, even when we were separated by the entire country between us. He makes my world make sense. A world without Barrett in it is unfathomable.

I'm pretty sure he's angling for more. The sex was pretty damn fantastic. He holds my hand all the time, and he's started calling me "baby." I can't deny it feels nice. I enjoy it. If I let myself indulge in the fantasy, it almost feels real. But when I hinted at a friends with benefits situation, he was not enthusiastic about the possibility of more.

So it will be up to me to draw a line in the sand, to enforce the boundaries of our friendship. I was the one who muddied the waters; it's up to me to put things right again.

Barrett wakes up maybe fifteen minutes after I do. He sighs and tightens his grip on me before it suddenly slackens —like he's suddenly realized exactly who he's been clutching in his sleep.

"Dee?" His voice is thick and gravelly.

"Yeah?"

He lets out a sigh of... relief? I'm not sure.

"Good morning."

I roll over, putting some distance between us, until I'm nearly at the far edge of the bed and facing him. "Good morning."

"How'd you sleep?" His eyes are still mostly closed.

"Good." Great. Fantastic. "You?"

He sighs. "Good. I didn't mean to fall asleep. I'm sorry."

"Nothing to apologize for. I asked you to let me stay."

"Yeah. I guess you did." He rolls onto his back. "Ugh. I don't want to get up."

"I'm not kicking you out. It's your bed."

He's quiet for a moment.

"Thank you," I tell him. "For last night."

Barrett sits up. He scrubs a hand over his face. "Yeah. We should talk about it, shouldn't we?"

"It was a blip. It was one night," I rationalize. I sit up and cross my legs. We're both on the far edges of the bed, most of the mattress between us. It's like neither of us is ready to be physically close again, despite how pressed up against each other we were while we were asleep.

"Agreed," he says carefully.

"It won't happen again."

"I have feelings for someone," he blurts.

I swallow. "You do?"

My pulse hammers at a thousand beats per minute. He has feelings for someone else, and he let me suck him off? It was just sex, I remind myself. He has feelings for someone else and—why is he not pursuing her? I hate her. I want him to be happy. That's all I've ever wanted.

"Yeah." He blushes. "But she's made it clear she's totally not into me, so I just have to live with it."

"Barrett..."

"So what happened between us can't happen again. Not when I have feelings for... her."

I feel very small. "Do I know her?"

He clears his throat. "Yeah. You've met."

"And you're not going to tell me who she is?"

"Nope. Not when she's made it clear… yeah, that's not going to happen."

My stomach aches. I don't like the feelings I get when I picture Barrett with some other woman. I'm not a jealous, insecure person. He deserves to be happy.

But why has he never mentioned her? We've been by each other's side since the semester started, and not once has he gone out with anyone or even chatted up a girl at a party. I thought he was this confident, self-assured guy. Has my vision of him been tainted by time? Or am I imagining a perfect, idealized version of my best friend? Who is he, really?

For so long, it's just been me and Barrett. I've always been the most important woman in his life. We've gone on sporadic dates with other people, but neither of us have ever had a full-fledged relationship that I know of. If he's had a girlfriend, he's kept it a secret.

And now he has feelings for some other woman, someone who isn't me.

I know he's had sex before. He's called me after, drunk and regretful, and rambled about how it wasn't right. The other night definitely wasn't his first time, not the way he fucked me. He's still looking for the right one. Or maybe he's found her.

Who the fuck is this woman that won't give him the time of day? I want to slap her upside the head. Barrett is amazing. He's a fucking catch. He's the perfect candidate to be a boyfriend.

"How did you meet?" I ask quietly.

"I've known her for a while. It's a small school." he says.

"Is she an athlete?"

"Yeah."

"Is she Chinese?"

He rubs the back of his neck. "Yeah."

My stomach sinks. His parents will be happy, at least.

"Is it… it's not Johanna, is it?"

His face screws up. "No. Fuck no."

"Because she…"

"She's not even close to being on my radar," he says firmly. "I've liked this woman for a while. At one point, I thought something might happen, but she doesn't want what I want, so I've stopped pursuing her."

"There's someone else. You'll find—"

"I'm not interested in anyone else. I'm interested in her."

I swallow. "She sounds… perfect."

"She's not perfect, not even close," he says with half a laugh. "But she would be perfect for me, and I would be perfect for her, if only she would agree to go out with me."

"And she won't?"

"We want different things," he says. He scrubs a hand over his face. "I don't want to talk about this."

"Okay." I won't push him, not on this. "You and me, we're still good?"

"We're golden, Dee," he says. "We're great."

———

Tucker and I meet outside the psychology building at nine. He opens his arms, and wordlessly I step into his hug. I need this easy comfort from him, the simple reassurance that I didn't singlehandedly wreck all of my friendships in one fell swoop.

"How you doing, girl?" he asks quietly.

"Oh, I'm great."

He laughs. "Yeah, I can tell."

"Thank you for letting me borrow your notes."

"Any time. Hope they make sense," he says.

They'll have to do. I was able to text at least one person in each of my classes for help with notes, and none of my professors quibbled over me missing a week of class. The word "ICU" really brought them around quickly. There was a quiz in my dietetics class that I can make up, and I was able to submit my nutrition paper via email, so I shouldn't be too far behind… hopefully. I have a metric fuck-ton of reading to do this week on top of practice every afternoon and two home games back to back.

Tucker pats me on the back. "How is he?"

"He's… fine."

He rolls his eyes, and I roll mine, too.

"My dad's in a rehab facility for a few more days, learning how to walk again."

"That's not who I'm talking about."

"Huh?"

He gives me a smug look. "Barrett didn't come back downstairs last night. Wasn't he with you?"

My face heats. "Yeah. How did you know…?"

"So?" He raises his eyebrows suggestively.

"We had a slumber party."

"I remember when Mason and I used to have slumber parties, back before we got together," he says with a fond smile. They were high school sweethearts… until college started and she blew up their relationship, and they only recently got back together last semester after she transferred to Newton and tried to win him back. "We would all be in one bed, the two of us and her twin brother and sometimes my big brother. I would always try to spoon with her, even when I was nine years old. I was in love with her before I even knew it."

"And now you know you're in love with her. She knows it, too."

"Yeah. And we still have slumber parties," he says with a smirk. "Only this time we're both naked, and our brothers aren't in the bed with us."

I roll my eyes. "You're so pleased. I get it. You get laid regularly. You have a steady girlfriend. Big deal."

"Yeah, it is a big deal," Tucker says. "You weren't here, so you don't know how hard it was when we first got together. It wasn't all sunshine and roses. It was work. It's still work sometimes."

We've never talked this much, especially not about something so unrelated to school. Still, this is a different side of Tucker I've never seen before. I like that he's opening up, that he's letting me in.

I feel very small when I ask: "Do you regret it? Going from friends to more?"

"No. Fuck no. Not in the slightest," he says firmly. "Even though we were best friends growing up, we were always meant to be more. Once we're done with grad school, we're going to get married. I don't have to put a ring on her finger yet to know we're going to spend the rest of our lives together."

"Wow. I want that."

"You want to get married?" He raises his eyebrows.

"No. I want that person."

"What about Barrett?"

"What about him?"

"Well, you guys are best friends. Have you ever thought about turning it into more?"

I blow out a breath. "He has feelings for someone."

"Bullshit."

"He told me this morning, he's crazy about her and has been for a while. She's an athlete and full Chinese and perfect for him. So even if I were interested, and I'm not sure if I am or not, he's not available. Not for me."

I blow out a breath. I don't know how I feel, I just know that I don't like feeling limited or boxed into a corner. His parents have always hated me, so even if he magically did have feelings for me... it would be just another fight with them. I don't want to cause a rift between him and his family. I know how much they mean to him.

Tucker frowns. "I'm sorry, girl."

"Yeah, me too."

I don't think I realized how much I wanted something to happen with Barrett until he took that option off the table. Because even if I'm not ready for a relationship, I'm not opposed to… activities with him, in bed and out of it. He's not interested in being my "friend with benefits" or anything in that vein. He just wants to be my friend.

I want to be his friend, too. I really do. I just want… more. Life is fleeting. We don't know how long we have. If Barrett makes the pain go away…

Tucker and I head into the psychology building and make our way towards our class. Dvora is sitting at the front of the room, and I smile and nod at her as Tuck and I take our usual seats on the opposite side of the room. We've been texting a little, and she sent me some notes for one of our other classes. It helped. It all helps. We might be competing for the same small openings in graduate school, but for now, we're all a community.

We make it through class without incident. The professor lectures, and we take notes, and then there's an open discussion over the assigned reading. I'm behind, so I haven't read it yet, and I don't really contribute anything of substance. It's on my mile long to-do list.

After class, Dvora approaches us. "How are you doing?"

"I'm good," I tell her.

"We missed you at the psych mixer last week," she says.

"Next time. I wanted to be here. I just… couldn't."

"No, you're right, I totally get it," she's quick to reassure me. "Your dad is more important than a mixer. How's he doing?"

"He's getting better."

It's easier if I don't mention his terminal cancer. He

doesn't want to be seen as someone who's sick. He just… exists.

Dvora gives me a small smile. "Good. I'm glad."

Yeah, me too.

"Are you going to the study group this afternoon?"

"What time?" It's the first I've heard about it.

"We meet in the psych library at three," she says.

I can make it work. I should be done with practice by two, maybe half past. Plenty of time to grab a shower and a snack and make it over there.

"I'll be there," I tell her, and she grins.

"Great," Tuck says, jumping into the conversation. "It's a good group."

I can't help but feel a little hurt that we're seven weeks into the semester and I'm only now finding out about a study group. Tucker and I have been studying on our own. He's never mentioned anything about having other study buddies.

I can't rely on Barrett and my teammates to be my only friends. I have to build a support network for myself the old fashioned way, through sheer grit and determination. Transferring to Newton as a fifth year senior, I don't have the luxury of years of bonding time tying us together. I barely talk to my old friends from USC. They're great, we keep in touch on social media more than anything else, but we didn't form the kinds of lasting bonds that I'm so desperate to find. It's time for me to put in the hard work, and hope that it pays off in the end.

thirty-four

. . .

Diana

MY NEW STUDY group is a good mix of people. It's a small group. Everyone clearly already knows each other. Still, I'm glad they're including me, allowing me to be part of their established group. After our study session, we agree to grab some lunch at the diner in town. It almost feels like having friends. Are they my friends? Why is this so hard?

Curtis is a lanky redhead with skin so pale it almost physically hurts to look at him. He's wearing a button-up shirt with the sleeves rolled up and dark brown khakis. He looks like he should be a middle manager at some corporate behemoth. Mandy is so bubbly and friendly, I want to think she was a cheerleader in high school. If she wasn't, she missed her calling. Her manicure is perfect and her eyebrow game is on point; she's wearing a full face of makeup and lash extensions to go with her torn jeans and oversized sweatshirt. Dvora went for fashion over comfort today. She's wearing a soft looking dark green sweater dress, mustard yellow tights, and brown booties. It shouldn't work together, but she manages to pull it off.

Me? I'm wearing leggings and a wrinkled t-shirt, a Newton soccer sweatshirt tied around my waist.

"Have you read the latest Sybil Hedgewick book?" Mandy asks suddenly in a lull in the conversation.

"Never heard of her," Curtis says.

"It's a romance novel," Dvora explains. "I'm on the wait-list at the library. I can't wait."

"It's so good," Mandy says.

"Is that the one about the blue aliens, or the dinosaurs shifters?" I ask. "I've read both series, but I'm a few books behind."

"Mason likes those books," Tuck says casually. "I couldn't get into them."

"You don't like dinosaur porn?" Dvora laughs.

"I prefer humanoid porn," he says with absolutely no shame whatsoever, because it's absolutely not a shameful topic. "But no, it was more the concept of the dinosaur shifters. Like, how does that even work? Dinosaurs lay eggs. How would they mate with humans?"

"Oh, I could tell you stories," Mandy says. "There are forty-seven books in the series explaining how it works."

"I'm only in the thirties," I admit. "I got burned out."

"Book thirty-six picks up the steam a bit," Dvora says. "By the time you get to thirty-nine and forty, it's like you're right back at the beginning again."

"I'll have to give it a try. Now I know what audiobook I'll be listening to during my run this afternoon." I make a mental note to borrow the book on my tablet before I head to the gym in a few hours.

Curtis shakes his head. "You're going for a run?"

"And pilates class."

"But you're, like, skinny."

"I'm a soccer player. We have to stay in shape," I explain. "We work out seven days a week, upwards of twenty hours a week, and that's before we include games and travel time. It's a big commitment. It takes its toll."

"I'm almost looking forward to football being done," Tuck

admits. "Sure, I'll miss it, but next year in grad school I won't have anything to distract me from school."

"Except for Mason," Dvora cuts in, and he laughs.

"Yeah, except for her. We're committed to going to the same school next year. We've spent so much time apart," he says. "I don't want to be apart from her any more than I absolutely have to be."

"Aww." Mandy swoons. "You guys are, like, couple goals. You're so great together."

He gives her a tight smile. "Takes a lot of work. It's not easy, but it's worth it."

"Whatever happened with your guy from the party?" Dvora asks me.

It takes me a second to realize she's talking about Trey. I've already forgotten all about him.

"Fizzled out," I say lightly.

"Aw, that's too bad." She frowns. "He was cute."

I shrug. "It wasn't meant to be."

"Yeah, I know how that goes." Dvora sighs. "On to the next one, I guess."

"I'm not in any hurry to date right now."

"Oh?" Curtis looks interested now.

"With my dad being sick, it's like the last thing on my mind. I don't have the mental bandwidth."

"I get that," Mandy says. "When my parents were getting divorced, I couldn't stomach the idea of dating anyone. Now that everything is finalized, it's like I can breathe and be myself again."

"Right. I just need some time. I would hate to jump into something for the wrong reasons."

Again my mind drifts to Barrett and the new changes in our friendship. It's not just since we had sex; since I moved to Newton, there's been a new layer of tension there.

Am I reading too much into this? Am I manifesting something where nothing exists? We've been friends for fourteen years. We've been through those awkward pre-teen years and even more painful teenage years.

There are no other guys on my radar. The blip with Trey was just that—a blip. It didn't go anywhere, and looking back, I'm kind of glad for that. It wasn't right. There was no spark, no fire. I was more interested in the glimmer of excitement of something new than actually interested in him. It wasn't fair to him.

And it's not fair to Barrett if the same thing is happening now. We've been friends for so long. He deserves to be with someone that will love and cherish him, and I don't know that that's me. It's not that I don't love him. I do. He's amazing. He's my best friend.

With school and my dad and soccer and graduation and applying to grad school… I don't know that I have the mental energy to devote to anything else. I can barely find the time to do my laundry every week. I'm definitely slacking in every conceivable area in which I can, and not by choice. Something has to give, and I'm worried one day soon, it will be me.

"I think I need to go to the bookstore," Dvora announces as the waitress drops off the check. "I have an urgent need to check out the Annabelle Phelps backstock."

"Do you want company? I have to pick up a new book anyway," I say, a little self-conscious. Maybe she wasn't issuing an invitation. Maybe she needs a little time to herself.

"That would be great," Dvora says with a smile. "Your job is to make sure I don't buy more than five books. My wallet can't handle much more than that."

I laugh. "Deal."

After the check is dealt with, we say goodbye and head towards the bookshop. Dvora is so effortlessly chic and fashionable, I feel a little like a slob standing next to her. What does she see in me? I'm a wreck, a mess, and she's so effortlessly put together. It's only natural to feel insecure. That's like my default setting these days. I'm all too aware of my clearance rack shoes and school-issued clothes.

"What genres are you into?" she asks as we enter the small, cramped shop. I see Wes tucked away in the crime fiction section.

"Mainly romance. I like happy ever afters," I explain.

"Me too! Twins!" Dvora is excited now. "Any particular sub genre? Contemporary, historical, paranormal…?"

"Contemporary. I love best friends to lovers, and I like books with athletes." I clear my throat. "I like reading about strong, confident friendships that can't be wrecked by a couple getting together or breaking up. The side characters are sometimes my favorite part, the way they interact with and support the main characters."

"Okay, seriously, I think we were destined to be best friends," Dvora says.

I grin. "I think I'm okay with that."

We peruse the stacks, exclaiming over new books and reading the synopsis aloud to one another. I find a couple of books that look interesting. She has seven already in her basket.

I lose track of how long we browse. Maybe five seconds, maybe two hours. It hardly feels like time is passing, we're having so much fun. At the end, Dvora has eleven books picked out, and I have a respectable six to take home with me.

"You want to grab some coffee?" she asks.

Keep this afternoon going? Sure. Why not?

"I'm in," I tell her, and she grins.

"Perfect. I know just the place."

thirty-five

. . .

Barrett

THE PHARMACY IS PACKED. The line to pick up prescriptions is nearly fifteen people deep, and I'm not thrilled about needing to wait. All I want to do is go home and curl up in my bed and sleep the day away. Instead I get ten thousand phone calls from the pharmacy yelling at me for not picking up my anti-depressants on time. I have enough to get me through the next few days; they give me a ninety days' supply. And, worst case scenario, I skip a dose. Big deal. My mental health won't tank if I skip one little pill. The incessant automated phone calls got to me, though, and so now I'm here in town on my only truly free day off for the next three weeks.

There are already three people in line behind me, so I can't back out now. I do a double take when I recognize Johanna Chen standing behind me, her eyes on her phone.

"Johanna. Hey."

She doesn't look up, like I'm not even there. Is she that pissed with me for turning her down that she won't even look at me?

"How's your weekend going?"

She scoffs.

"You really won't talk to me?"

"What's the point?" she mutters.

"You don't like making awkward small talk in the pharmacy line?"

"No, not really."

But she locks her phone screen and shoves her phone into her back pocket, looking up at me guilelessly.

"You guys leave tomorrow for your road trip? Virginia, right?"

She nods. "And then we have a home game later this week."

"How's the record?"

She looks pained. They still haven't won a game, a fact I am all too aware of. Diana is stressing it. She thinks Coach Larsen is going to get fired any day now, and she wouldn't be that far off. I'm surprised she hasn't been canned already, halfway through the season and not winning a single game, except for the fact that women's soccer is hardly scrutinized by the athletic department.

We shift forward half a foot.

"What else is new?"

She rolls her eyes.

"It's so weird that this is our senior season. I don't know what we're going to do next year without sports dictating so much of our lives," I admit. "I've been playing football for so long."

"I've been playing soccer for seventeen years," she says evenly. "I'm not ready for it to be over."

I offer her a smile. "At least there are rec leagues. You can still play."

Johanna shrugs. "Yeah, maybe."

We shift forward.

"What's your plan for next year?"

She sighs. "Apply like crazy for a job, so I don't have to move back home and live with my parents."

"You don't want to stay with your family?"

My family is not the typical Chinese-American family, in that they would rather not live with their offspring. In our culture, young adults usually stay with their family until they're ready to get married. My parents don't want us living at home—they barely wanted us living there when we were children. They're already talking to my cousin's boyfriend, a realtor, about finding an apartment for me for next summer. He pulled me aside and asked me what I was really looking for, and he added my few requests into the properties my parents have him searching for.

I don't have a lot of needs. I'm looking for a two bedroom, decent square footage, relatively modern and updated, and at least one assigned parking spot. That's it, that's my list. So much of where I live will depend on Diana next year. If we really are going to be roommates, if she gets into grad school... so much is up in the air.

The pharmacy opens up another register. The line is moving quicker now. It's almost my turn. By the time the pharmacy tech pulls my prescription down, Johanna already has hers in her hand. We exit the pharmacy at the same time.

"Well, it was good seeing you," she lies.

"Do you want to grab some coffee?" I'm not sure where the idea comes from. We're not friends; we're hardly acquaintances. We don't exactly like each other. And then there's the fact that the last time we had coffee together...

"I think we'd better not," she says.

"Why not?"

"We're not friends, Barrett," she reminds me.

"So?"

"So people who aren't friends don't grab coffee."

"We can change that."

"Why would you want to?"

I shrug. "I'm having a good time talking to you. More than

I expected. And I don't have anything else going on this afternoon."

To my surprise, she isn't offended by my comments—if anything, I think she respects me more for admitting it.

"Lead the way," she says.

The coffee shop is crowded with the weekend hubbub of life in a small college town. We order our drinks and find a table in the center of the shop, one of the only free tables at this time of day.

Johanna crosses her arms over her chest. "You wanted to talk? So talk."

"How have you been?" I venture neutrally.

She rolls her eyes. "You don't care."

Not really. She has a chip on her shoulder now and she's been a total bitch to Diana. I have no reason to be nice to her.

I don't deny the point. Instead, I take a sip of my drink and fold my hands on the table.

"I need your help," I admit.

She scoffs. "Let me guess. This is about your little friend."

"Yes, actually."

Johanna rolls her eyes again. "I don't know why you think I'm the person to help you."

"You're teammates. Roommates," I remind her. "You're both Chinese. You know of my family. That's not nothing."

"Fine. Whatever."

"You called that I had feelings for her within, like, five seconds of us meeting."

She looks uncomfortable. "So?"

"So. Maybe you have some ideas. How can I get her to see me as more than a friend?"

"I don't see why you're asking me. I barely even know her."

"You have more in common than you think you do."

Knowing them both—Diana so well, and Johanna so superficially—I know that they're both athletes, both fierce competitors, both seniors, both Chinese-American, both hard workers, both deeply connected with their families, and both intense about school. Where Johanna is more social and connected to her team, Diana is finding it harder to settle in and make friends, and where Diana is effortlessly outgoing with new people, it's harder for Johanna to let people into her circle.

She has her minions, but I don't know that Johanna actually has any real friends. She never seems particularly happy when she's with the girls from the team, and I've never seen her with anyone outside of the athletic department.

Maybe that's because I mainly see her after their team loses a game or when Diana is getting more attention than her in the dining hall. She doesn't seem to have a good relationship with her defensive core, which is a failing as a captain. I don't know that she cares. She's never particularly opened up to me before—and why should she? As she said, we're not friends. We're hardly even acquaintances.

"Now's your chance." Johanna nods at the door.

Diana is with another woman, the two of them laughing at some joke only they are privy to. She's made a friend! I'm glad she's making friends. She needs them.

Every fiber of my being aches to call out to her, to beckon her over. Something pins me to my seat. I watch from a distance as she and the woman stand in the line five people deep before they're able to order, and then they wait at the end of the coffee bar for their drinks. When they receive their to-go cups, Diana doctors her drink with a splash of milk and some sugar. As she stirs, she looks up.

And then our eyes meet.

And then her face falls.

And then before I even know what's happened, I feel dread start to settle in my veins.

"Go get 'er, big guy," Johanna says, taking a nonchalant sip of her coffee.

My palms start to sweat. My stomach lurches. I should—I should go talk to her. Before she gets the wrong idea. Before she gets upset. Before she…

I rub my hands on my jeans. I can do this. It's Diana. She's my best friend. Of course she isn't going to jump to conclusions and assume the worst.

Who am I kidding? Diana always assumes the worst. She is the queen of jumping to conclusions.

She says something to the woman beside her, who looks over in our direction. Her dark eyes narrow, and she replies, not looking pleased.

I'm not all that pleased myself, now that I think about it.

Whatever the woman says, Diana lifts her chin and throws her shoulders back, a telltale sign that she's pretending to be confident when instead she wants to run away. I hate that I made her feel that way. She weaves her way through the tables, making her way over to us.

"Hey, B," Diana says, her voice uneven. "Johanna."

"Hey, Dee." I take in her comfy outfit, leggings and a Newton soccer sweatshirt. "You look great."

She rolls her eyes. "We had a study group."

"And then hit up the bookstore?" I nod to the bag in her hand from the book shop a few doors down. The flimsy paper bag looks like it's about to explode.

Diana shuffles her feet. "Yeah, maybe."

"I'm going to the bathroom," Johanna announces loudly. She scrapes back her chair and walks away without a backward glance. I track her through the small coffee shop as she settles in a far corner with her coffee and her phone.

"So. You and Johanna," Diana says neutrally, following my line of sight.

"We're just having coffee."

"Yeah. Because the last time you two had coffee—"

"That was then. This is now."

Before it was a date. Now it's… I don't know what it

is. But it's certainly not a date. We're both well aware of that. I wouldn't be asking her about another woman if this was a date. I wouldn't be leading her on if this was a date.

It's not a date.

Not when the only person I want to go on a date with is standing right in front of me, looking like her world doesn't make sense anymore.

"You said you don't have feelings for her," Diana says, almost accusing me of lying.

I push back my chair and stand. "I don't."

"And yet you're here. Together."

"We were in line at the pharmacy and ended up here. Nothing nefarious is going on."

She narrows her eyes. "I didn't say there was."

"No, you were just thinking it," I point out. I know her.

"Barrett."

"What?"

"Is it…" She swallows. "Is it Johanna?"

"Is who?"

"The girl you have feelings for."

"No."

"You're sure?"

"One thousand percent sure," I tell her.

"But she's pretty and she's an athlete and she's Chinese. She ticks all your boxes," she says.

"Yeah, she's all of that," I agree.

"So? What's the problem? How many female athletes are there of Chinese descent in our small school?"

"Enough."

Diana scoffs. "Barrett. Are you seriously not going to tell me who she is?"

"Nope."

"But I've met her."

"Oh, you know her."

She frowns. "I don't know any other female athletes of Chinese descent."

"You do. You know her."

Open your eyes. I'm standing right here in front of you. Is it really that unfathomable that it's her? Am I so far off her radar that it's not even a possibility?

"I'm racking my brain, but I can't think of who she is," she says.

I take a sip of my drink. It's lukewarm now.

"She must be pretty amazing," Diana says, a bit sadly, "for you to want to keep this such a big secret."

"It's not that it's a secret so much as I'm just obnoxiously pining for someone who doesn't want me back," I admit. "If she felt the same way, I'd tell you in a heartbeat. But I know her. She doesn't want a relationship. She doesn't even want to date me. If anything, she only likes the idea of me, and she'd get bored within a few weeks." I swallow my fears, and then I add, "she has enough going on right now to worry about managing my feelings."

"But you have feelings for her."

"I do."

"You want to be with her."

"I do."

"So why aren't you?"

"Because you're not interested," I say evenly. My heart hammers in my chest like I've just done five solid minutes of suicide sprints. My palms start to sweat.

"She might be," Diana says.

I wait.

Her face creases. "She might be."

"She's not."

"But she…" She swallows. "You said 'you're not interested.' Not 'she's not interested.'"

"Yeah."

"But then…"

I wait.

Diana swallows. "Barrett."

"Yeah?"

"I'm confused."

"What are you confused about?"

"I'm pretty sure you're insinuating something that I don't think…"

"Yeah?"

She meets my eyes. "Tell me. What's her name?"

My heart thumps loudly in my chest, so loud I swear she can hear it. "I think you know her name," I tell her quietly.

"I need to hear it."

Does she? Do I need this? I can't keep hiding, running away. She's going to badger me until I give in and tell her. I'm making too much of a production over something that was supposed to help me push her away, and only seems to have brought her closer.

I love her, but she's my best friend, and that's the most important thing to me. I don't want to get hurt, but I would never want to hurt her, either.

Aren't I allowed to be happy? Would it really be that bad?

"Diana Marie Whitehall."

She flinches and takes a step back. "I don't understand."

"What is there to understand?"

"Barrett…"

"I'm crazy about you, Diana, and you're not interested in me. You don't want to be with me. So I'm not going to put you in an awkward position where you feel like you have to say or do something you're not comfortable with in order to make me feel better. That's not what this is about."

"What is this about?"

"I love you," I tell her. "I've loved you every day since I was fourteen years old, and I'm going to keep on loving you for the rest of my life, regardless of how you feel about me.

You're not going to change my mind. But I'm not going to pressure you into anything."

She swallows. Hesitation is written across her face.

"This is why I didn't want to tell you. Because you aren't ready to process how I feel about you," I admit. "Nothing about our friendship has to change. We can still—"

"Everything has changed, Barrett," she says quietly. "Everything is different now."

thirty-six

· · ·

Diana

BARRETT HAS FEELINGS FOR ME.

What.

The.

Fuck.

I'm the mystery girl that Barrett's been talking about nonstop for the last few weeks. The girl he's been "obnoxiously pining" for. The girl he thinks isn't interested in him.

"I don't think I can do this," I admit quietly, and his face falls.

"Okay."

"I need some space."

"Okay."

I love you, I want to say.

Because I do love him. Maybe not in the way he wants me to, but I do, in my own way.

I swallow. "Since... since you were fourteen?"

Slowly, he nods. "You're upset. I should have told you. Or maybe I shouldn't have. I don't know."

"I had feelings for you back then," I admit quietly. "When we were fifteen, sixteen... I would have given everything to hear you say it back then."

"And now?"

I sigh. "And now, knowing the depth of your feelings..." I scrub a hand over my forehead. "I don't have the emotional energy to devote to a relationship, and if something were to happen between you and me—"

"Which I'm not pressuring you for," he adds quickly. "I shouldn't have blurted it out like that. That's not fair. That's on me."

"I wouldn't want to casually date you," I tell him. "It would be serious."

"Agreed," he says nervously. "I've slept around. I've been with enough women to know what I do and don't want. And what I don't want is meaningless sex with someone whose last name I don't even know. I want something real, something meaningful."

"I don't know that I can deal with serious right now. My dad..."

"I know."

"He likes you."

He smiles, for the first time in what feels like forever. "I know."

"He wants us to get together."

"He does?"

I nod. "He likes you," I say again.

His smile fades. "I want to be your friend. It's important to me that we are friends."

"Agreed." I mimic him.

"I would never do anything to hurt you," he says quietly.

"I know."

"But if you don't feel the same way... if you're not interested in the things I want..."

I sigh. "I just don't think I have the capacity right now. And you deserve someone who would devote their time to you."

"I don't want you to devote time," he says. "I want you to feel the same way about me."

"I haven't given it much thought," I admit. "You were always so…"

"So what?"

"Off limits."

I laugh, a little self-consciously. We're standing in the middle of the coffee shop. Awkwardly I gesture to the table, and I sink into the seat that Johanna vacated. Barrett sits, too, and wraps his hands around his mug of coffee.

"You're my best friend. I always thought…" I sigh, shaking my head. "When we were in high school, I had the biggest crush on you. I thought something might happen. But you never said anything…"

"I was scared," he says. "I didn't want to lose you."

"And now?"

He chuckles, a little sadly. "I'm fucking terrified. But I can't keep living with the fear. I love you. That's not about to change any time soon, even if you don't feel the same way about me."

I chew my lip. Barrett is hot. He's gorgeous. And he's fun and he's funny and he makes me laugh. He knows all the right things to say to get me out of my head or cheer me up if I'm in a foul mood, and he knows when to give me space and when I need to not be alone. He knows *me*.

He's in love with me.

And I…

It would be so easy to fall for him. I'm halfway there, if I admit it to myself. I adore him, and I'm attracted to him, and I enjoy being around him. I feel bereft when he's not beside me.

But dating? A relationship?

That's… a lot.

Is it, though? Isn't it literally the same thing we're already doing, plus the sex which we both enjoyed? My parents have a great relationship—we wouldn't end up like his, because we're starting out with feelings being involved.

I wasn't abused. I wasn't the product of divorce. I wasn't traumatized. I had a freaking idyllic childhood. There's no reason to be afraid.

But taking that step now…

"I don't want us to fall into something because it's easy. If we were to date, I would want it to be real," I tell him. "I want to do it for the right reasons."

"Agreed."

I swallow. "And right now…"

He sighs. "Yeah. It's not the right time."

"When we were fifteen or sixteen wasn't the right time, either. Looking back, I don't think it would have worked out," I admit. "We would have gotten way too serious, way too fast, and I would have given up USC to stay here with you. And there's no guarantee we would have stayed together all these years. So many high school relationships don't last."

"I know."

"A lot of college relationships don't last."

"I know." Barrett takes a deep breath. "Which is why I'm not pressuring you into anything you aren't ready for."

I wish I didn't know. I wish I hadn't pressed him. I don't want to know. I don't want to carry the weight of this decision on my shoulders. He likes me. He loves me. He wants a relationship with me.

And I… am struggling. I don't know how to deal with this. There isn't a book on how to navigate romantic feelings for best friends. Maybe I should ask Wes. I'm sure he would know. He may not have any practical experience, but I'm sure he's read enough about it.

"Is there a… trial period?"

He quirks a small smile. "Like a thirty day free trial?"

"Yeah. Can we… is there a way we… try?"

"That's dating."

"I know."

"You want to date me?"

"I don't not want to date you."

He frowns.

"I don't know what I want."

"Okay."

I take a deep breath. "That's a lie," I admit. "I know what I want. What I don't know is if I'm capable of what I want."

He swallows. "And what is it that you want?"

"I want to love, and to be loved in return."

"I would. I do. I—"

"But I don't know that I have the capability to give you what you deserve."

"Oh."

"So as much as I want to… I don't want to hurt you more."

Barrett licks his lips. "I don't want either of us to get hurt."

"Me, either."

"So where does that leave us?"

"I don't know," I admit. "I just don't know."

———

My walk home is quiet. I'm absorbed in my thoughts. I need some time to process everything. Barrett likes me. Barrett loves me. Barrett has feelings for me. By the time I get back to the soccer house, I have no idea how I feel anymore. I'm just a little bit numb, and it has nothing to do with the cold weather and the chill in the air.

Is this why he's always holding my hand and kissing my cheek? Is this why he's suddenly so eager to share a bed for slumber parties? Is this the only reason why he's friends with me?

No. I can't think like that. I can't psychoanalyze every

single action and interaction with my best friend cf fourteen years. I have to trust that Barrett's intentions are pure and rooted in friendship, even if he harbors desires for me.

My roommates are all downstairs when I get in, which is not unusual. It's not out of the ordinary for Johanna and the minions to monopolize the TV, but typically Coach Larsen doesn't make house calls.

"Good, you're here," Coach says as I hang my coat up on the rack behind the door. "We can get started."

I check my watch. Did I forget a team meeting? I don't think so. It's only my roommates here; we're missing Emma and the rest of the defensive core.

"I've been hearing a lot of negativity from this group," Coach says. "Frankly, the situation is becoming toxic. This has gone on long enough. It's well past time to move past whatever bullshit is standing in our way. We are all adults here. We're all on the same team. It's time to act like it."

Chancing a glance at Rosie, I see she's just as confused as I am. She shrugs and settles into the armchair, crossing her legs. I perch on the edge of the other chair.

"We get along great," Johanna lies. She's sitting in the center of the couch with Rachel and Robin on one side and Rebekah on the other.

"I don't have any issues with Johanna or the—the rest of the girls," I say honestly. I have to stop myself before I call them her minions to their face.

For a blip of a second, I nearly lost my shit when I saw her and Barrett having coffee together. Once she left and he confessed his feelings... I'm still not sure why they were together, but I trust him when he says he doesn't have feelings for her.

Because he has feelings for me. What the actual fuck?

Coach Larsen doesn't look impressed. "You need to trust one another. You need to be a team."

I look to Johanna now. I thought we were a team. In real

life, I trust them about as far as I can throw them, but on the field, I trust that they can do their job and I can do mine. Our goaltending needs work and our forwards are mediocre at best; our defense has been generating most of our offense, working overtime and pulling double shifts in order to cover the back half of the field.

Off the field… yeah, things could be better. They are hardly my favorite people in the world. I wouldn't choose to put them on my team. But they're on my team, like it or not, so I have to live with them for now.

Coach Larsen launches into a lecture, two months too late, and I sit there and let the words wash over me. I'm doing my best. I'm putting in the effort. The team didn't fall apart because I transferred here; they were already splintering. Right? Or am I the problem?

thirty-seven

· · ·

Diana

I'M NOT OKAY.

I'm numb the entire weekend of Thanksgiving. I don't know what to think, how to process this. I can't even celebrate my dad coming home from the rehab facility.

All I can think about is Barrett.

My best friend.

The person who makes my world make sense.

The man who is in love with me.

Nothing makes sense anymore.

Why am I so cut off from my feelings? Why does none of this make sense? It shouldn't be this difficult.

Wednesday night, my dad comes home from the rehab facility. With the help of his crutches, he can slowly navigate through the house, and the banister on the stairs means he can get up to his bedroom on the second floor, so there's no reason he has to be away from home for the holiday.

My mom cooks the turkey on Thursday, and we have dinner, just the three of us. In high school, we used to travel back to Wisconsin to see her family for the weekend, and once I got to college, they would come out to visit me in LA at USC or wherever my team was playing.

I kind of like that it's just the three of us. I don't know how many more of these holidays we're going to have. None of us know, not for certain. It could be six months. It could be six years.

On Friday afternoon, we watch the Newton game as a family. My school is only a quick two hour drive away. We could go in person. Except right after my dad's surgery, when he's still learning how to navigate the stairs in our house with his walker, is probably not the best time to go sit in the snow for four hours and watch a football game. So we watch on TV and cheer for the home team.

It's humbling seeing my strong, capable father hobble around on a walker. He's regaining strength every day, relearning how to walk and sit and stand, but it will be a slow recovery. We don't know how much time he has. We have to enjoy the limited time we have left.

At halftime, Newton is down one score. Dad puts the talking heads on the intermission show on mute and turns to me.

"What's wrong, baby girl?"

"Nothing's wrong."

"You've been quiet all weekend," he says. "You can talk to me. Tell me what's bothering you."

My dad has always been there for me. He's quiet and strong and capable. So what if we've never talked about this kind of stuff before? So what if this is unchartered territory for us? We've been able to talk about everything else in my life; we should be able to talk about this, too.

"Barrett has feelings for me," I blurt.

My dad barks out a laugh. "Finally."

"What's that supposed to mean?"

"We've all known it for years. It's about time he's finally told you."

"Wait. You knew?" My whole world starts to spin.

He shakes his head. "He really isn't good at being subtle, baby girl. We all know. It's as clear as day."

I swallow. "I had no idea."

"He didn't want you to know, not until you were both ready."

I don't know if I'm ready now.

"Well, have you given it much thought?" Dad asks, after I've had a few moments to sit with this latest revelation.

I give him a mulish look. "It's practically all I've been thinking about since he told me."

"And...?"

"And... I don't know."

Dad rolls his eyes. "What is there to debate? He's a great guy. He loves you."

"I know. He's my best friend."

"So? What's the problem?"

"I don't want to lose him." My throat feels tight and itchy. "If he were to walk out of my life... I don't know that I could take it."

"Why would he walk out of your life?"

"What if we break up?" I swallow thickly. "What if it doesn't work out?"

"I have faith that the two of you could find a way to stay friends," Dad says. "You've made it through all these years. You can make it through a break up, too." He pauses. "Not that I think you would break up any time soon. I think you could make it work."

"I've never been in a relationship before. I've dated, yeah, but not... not like this." That's the closest I can come to talking to my father about my romantic life. "And I don't think he has, either."

"So you'll learn together. There's no need to hurry this along. Take it slowly. Don't rush into anything you're not comfortable with."

This is Barrett we're talking about: my best friend, the guy who makes my whole world make sense. He would never do anything to purposefully hurt me. He likes me. He loves me. He wants what's best for me.

"Thanks, Daddy."

He smiles fondly at me. "Any time, baby girl."

He turns the volume back up on the TV as the halftime comes to close and the game resumes. The boys are down a score… and then it gets worse. The quarterback throws an interception on third down, giving the other team another chance deep in the zone.

The defensive core is trying their hardest. They want to win, I can see it written on their faces, but sometimes wanting it isn't enough. Sometimes nothing we do is enough.

"Hey, Diana," Dad says as the game turns from third to fourth quarter.

"Yeah?"

"Don't feel like you have to rush into anything because of me."

"What do you mean?"

"I don't want you to do something you're not ready for, because you think our time is running out."

"Daddy…"

"I'm going to die," he says firmly, though his voice is shaking. "I'm going to die soon. Don't get engaged, don't get married, don't have babies just because you think that will make me happy. You deserve to have your own timeline."

"I'm not ready for… for marriage and babies and…" I wave my hand in the air to encompass everything else.

When I went to Barrett's house, for half a minute, he thought I was pregnant. He offered to marry me right off the bat. He had no qualms about that, even before I knew how he felt about me. Now…

"I know. But don't rush through your life in order to get to the good parts. You're in the good parts now, baby girl," he says. "Everything will happen in its own time. If Barrett isn't the one, okay, you'll find the right one. Don't settle for someone or something you're not ready for."

"I'm not. I won't."

"Okay, good." He reaches over and squeezes my hand. "You deserve the sun and moon and the stars, Diana. I can't give them to you. But I hope one day you find someone that can. If Barrett is that guy, if he's not... I think you owe it to yourself to give him a chance."

I swallow. "I'm going to," I decide. "I don't know how, but I'm going to."

It's snowing, a light dusting that turns the whole world murky grey. In the sanctity of Athlete's Village, untouched by cars, the roads are a pristine white. I sit outside of Barrett's house in my clearance rack boots and hand-me-down coat and wait. And wait. And wait.

My phone is in my pocket. I'm sure I could solve this with a text message or a phone call. That feels like cheating. I could hurry this along by clearly communicating that I want to talk to him. I'm scared. I'm shaking in my boots, and it has nothing to do with the cold weather whipping through me. I don't want everything to change.

Everything has already changed.

There are people walking through Athlete's Village, students coming home from weekends away or traveling for games. Every time I see someone on the horizon, I immediately think it's him. It's never him.

Tucker, Miles, and Amir make their way down the street. They look at me oddly as they climb the porch stairs.

"He's not here," Tuck says.

"I know."

"He won't be here for awhile. He went to his parents for dinner."

Oh. I didn't know that.

Tucker's smile is pitying. "Does he know you're waiting for him?"

"Nope."

I don't want them to tell him I'm here, but I can't stop them if they wanted to reach out to their roommate and tell him.

Miles sighs. "He misses you."

Offering them a tight smile, I huddle in my coat. "I miss him, too."

"Come inside," Amir says gently. "You can wait for him inside as easily as out here."

It feels wrong. It feels like cheating. But I follow them inside the house.

Automatically I trudge up the stairs to Barrett's room. Depositing my weekend bag at the side of the bed, I toe off my shoes and shed my coat. His room is as neat as a pin, like it always is. He needs order and organization in the same way other people need air, and I... am not that way. I'm messy. Everything about me and my life is messy. My feelings are messy.

Does he really want a part of this?

Curling up on his bed, I spread his blanket over me and take a deep breath. It smells like him, like home.

I don't know what happens, because the next thing I know, the bed is moving. I lift my head to find Barrett laying beside me. I don't know what time it is. He's wearing sweatpants and a t-shirt, and I know that's not what he wore to dinner with his parents.

"Go back to sleep, baby," he says. "We can talk later."

"We should... we should talk now." I yawn. I can hardly keep my eyes open.

Barrett shifts on the bed and slings his arm around my waist. His feet tangle with mine.

"Later," he says. He presses a kiss to the top of my head. "You're here. We can figure the rest out later."

When I wake up some time later, Barrett is nowhere to be found. The bed is warm beside me. I can hear the shower running in the attached bathroom, so I know he hasn't gone too far. Rolling over, I stretch my arms above my head. It's six o'clock in the morning, way too early to be awake.

The shower turns off, and I can hear the curtain being pulled aside. The walls are really, really thin. I know we tried to be quiet that night we had sex, but now I'm wondering if everyone already knew. Could they hear us?

I'm not embarrassed or ashamed at the idea of his friends knowing we had sex. There's nothing shameful or embarrassing about having sex with Barrett. What I'm not so crazy about is knowing that everyone knows all about my business. I don't even know what is going on with Barrett and me; for everyone else to be privy to the sensitive details...

The bathroom door opens and Barrett steps out, running a towel over his head. He's wearing jeans and a fresh t-shirt, the long sleeves pushed up his strong forearms.

"You're awake." He blinks. "Did I wake you up?"

Struggling to sit up, I pull the blankets up around my waist. "Nope. It was time for me to wake up."

"Oh." He moves to his dresser and pulls out a pair of white socks.

"I've been thinking a lot about what you said," I admit.

"Oh?" He looks at me over his shoulder. Whatever he sees on my face, he turns around and perches at the end of the bed.

"You love me. You have feelings for me," I state.

"Yes," he says, agreeing readily.

"You want more than friendship."

"Yeah."

"So… what does that mean?"

"Well, it could be a lot like our current friendship," Barrett says slowly. "I could hold your hand."

"You already do that a lot."

He blushes. "Yeah, I know."

"And what else?"

"There could be kissing."

I swallow. "We've had sex, but we haven't kissed. Didn't we do this backwards?"

Barrett sighs. "You were hurting. You wanted a distraction. Sex with you, yeah, it was amazing, but I knew it was to get you out of your head. I was just a warm body for you."

I open my mouth to object. I can't. He's right.

"I knew what it was. I went into it willingly," he tells me. "But kissing you… when I kiss you, I want you to know how I feel about you. That's why I didn't even try."

"But if we were… more than friends?"

"Oh, I would kiss the hell out of you," he says readily. "We would cuddle."

"Like we did last night?"

"Yeah, and almost every night it's feasible." He shrugs. "Sometimes we have conflicting schedules or need some space or alone time. We could have weeknight sleepovers in addition to after a party or a game."

"So…"

"So basically we take our existing friendship and ramp it up a notch," he says. "I could call you baby and you wouldn't freak out."

"I like when you call me baby," I admit.

"And we're already going on dates, we just aren't calling them that," he points out. "Spending time together just the two of us, going to dinner, going to a party, and then going home together at the end of the night."

He's right about that. We've practically already been dating without the label for the last few months.

"And sex?"

Barrett swallows. "When you're ready, when *we're* ready, we can have sex. We don't need to rush if we're not at that point yet. We have forever to get there."

"Get where?"

"If you're not attracted to me…"

I scoff. "B, I asked to suck your dick."

"Yeah, I know, but…"

He's not getting it.

"I wouldn't have asked if I didn't want to," I tell him flatly.

"You wanted to?" He looks confused.

"You're gorgeous. You're hot as hell. Yeah, I'm attracted to you. I have been since I was sixteen."

He blinks. "You—?"

"Yeah. I wouldn't be ready to say those three words yet, but I definitely like you as more than a friend. That's not in question," I tell him. "What I don't know is if I can handle a relationship. I've never had a boyfriend before. I don't know how to balance school and soccer and you and everything."

"The same way you balance everything right now," he says.

"I don't know how to do this."

"You don't want a relationship?" He looks like his world is falling to pieces.

"I don't know what I want. What I want is you," I admit. "And you want a relationship, so, yeah, I'll try."

"I want to love you," Barrett says. "Whatever that looks like for us, that's what's important. I want to love you."

"I want that, too."

He reaches across the bed and takes my hand. "We don't have to overthink this. We can play it by ear." He squeezes my hand. "When I thought you were pregnant…"

"I'm not," I assure him quickly. "I got my period a week later."

"I trust you," he says. "But when I thought you were... I offered to marry you, yeah, but I *wanted* to marry you. I want to spend the rest of my life with you. And I understand if you're not there yet. There's a lot of road to navigate between now and then. I just want you to know where my head is. This isn't some casual, superficial fling. This is the real thing for me."

I swallow. "Your parents..."

"They will have to deal," he says firmly. "I'm in love with you and that's not about to change because of family duty. They don't get to control my life."

"No, but they control your trust fund."

"Okay, so worst case scenario, we wait until I turn twenty-five to get married," he says, like it's that simple. "That's only three years, and we'll need most of that time to be ready."

I blink at him.

"I've put thought into this," he reminds me. "It's been on my mind, in one way or another, since we were fourteen. I'm not afraid of a future with you. If we wait to take that step, I want it to be because *we* want to wait, not because of money."

"Twenty-five million dollars is nothing to walk away from."

He shrugs. "I don't think they'll disinherit me, but I'm willing to take that chance. You're worth it to me."

"Barrett. That's insane." Does he realize how insane that is? No, he doesn't, or he wouldn't be nearly so callous about it.

"I'm a good son. I've never done anything to make them unhappy. If they're not happy with my being with you, I would cut them out of my life with no reservations," he says. "Money isn't everything. I will have a good job after graduation, more than enough to support the two of us, and it doesn't matter whether I stay with the family company or if I join another firm. This is worth it. *You* are worth it."

Tears well in my eyes.

Barrett squeezes my hand. "I'm not crying over it, so you shouldn't, either."

I swallow. "This is all just… a lot."

"If you need time, you can have all the time you need," he says softly. "I'm ready. I can wait for you to be ready, too."

thirty-eight

. . .

Barrett

"I NEED TO TAKE A SHOWER," Diana announces.

"Okay." Is she asking permission? She doesn't need to ask to use my shower.

"Do you…" She swallows and meets my gaze head on. "Would you like to watch?"

Yes. Hell yes. A million times yes.

Still, I have to be cautious here. Maybe I'm misunderstanding her… "You want me to watch you take a shower?"

"Well, I would offer for you to join me, but you just got out of one yourself," she reasons. "We have to get comfortable being naked with each other."

"Okay, I follow you so far…"

"So if you wanted to stand there while I was in the shower, we could talk and we could… figure this out."

What is there to figure out? I love her, she likes me, and we're going to try for a relationship.

She springs out of bed. "Oh! I forgot."

"Hm?"

Pulling her weekend bag onto the bed, she digs inside. When she finds what she's looking for, she takes a deep breath and lifts her eyes to mine once more.

"You said I could keep some things here."

"Yeah, of course. You should feel comfortable here," I tell her readily.

From her bag she pulls a pair of jeans and a set of leggings, a black lace bra, a handful of underwear—I don't look too closely at the mess of cotton and satin and lace—and a sleep scarf.

"I'm already comfortable here, because you're here," she says. "I'm not afraid of taking things to the next level with you. We're mature adults. We can handle our friendship growing and transitioning."

"What's with the pile of underwear?" I count at least five pairs of satiny, silky underthings. Some are boy-short style, some are thong style, some I can't identify.

She pins me with a flat look. "I'm still missing my favorite panties, the ones I was wearing that night. I'm hoping if I have a few days' worth here, I can get my favorite pair back."

"I don't know what you're talking about."

"I'm not some conquest. You don't get to keep a souvenir like the letters we used to get at summer camp," she says. "I'm here to stay. You can see my underwear any time. I'll show you right now if you want. I only want my favorite panties back."

I frown. "Of course you're not—it's not a souvenir. It's a memento."

"It's underwear," she tells me flatly. "My underwear. I'm not saying you can never see them again. I just want them back."

With a sigh, I stand and move to my desk, pulling out the second drawer. From within I pull out the soft pink panties and pass them over.

"What else is in that drawer?" Diana asks.

"Not much," I lie.

She rolls her eyes. "You know I can tell when you're lying?"

"I have no idea what you're talking about."

She laughs outright. "Show me. Please?"

Clearing my throat, I open the drawer again and withdraw my special Diana box.

"It's all the things that remind me of you, going back years."

She lifts the lid. Slowly she pulls out the contents, looking them over one by one. A squishy yellow hair tie she wore around her wrist to my freshman homecoming game. A keychain she got me from her trip to Green Bay in middle school. A letter she wrote me while at soccer camp the summer before eleventh grade. The friendship bracelet I made during our second summer at Chinese camp when we were nine years old—it was on her wrist for four years straight.

She gasps, holding up the frayed thread bracelet. "I thought I lost this!"

"It fell off your wrist. I was going to try to fix it for you, but I couldn't figure out the clasp. I didn't steal it," I assure her quickly.

"I believe you," she assures me. "I can't believe you kept it all this time."

"I'm not, like, some creepy stalker. I don't have a shrine to you."

"I wouldn't care if you did," she says. She reconsiders. "Well, maybe. I don't think so."

"You're my best friend. I kept things that reminded me of you, of how I felt about you."

Ticket stubs from a concert we went to the week after I got my driver's license. The invitation to her Sweet Sixteen party. A postcard she sent when her soccer team traveled to England for a tournament. Tickets for my high school football games, where she sat in the stands by herself for four hours and cheered me on, rain or shine. Little things I kept over the years that reminded me of her, of us.

"Barrett..." She looks up at me, her thumb rubbing the fraying braided bracelet.

"Yeah?"

"I really like you," she admits.

I swallow. "I really like you, too."

She frowns. "You're awfully far away."

"I am?" I'm only at the edge of the bed.

Diana nods. "I think you should come closer."

Grinning, I stand and circle the bed until I'm standing in front of her. She scrambles up onto her knees. She threads her arms around my neck.

"I really like you," she whispers again.

"Good."

And then I kiss her. It's our first kiss, so I want it to be—

It's slow and unhurried. Light, gentle kisses, as we learn each other all over again. I cup the back of her head, my fingers tangling in her wild mess of waves, and she sighs, leaning into me. She opens her mouth for me, and as much as I want to devour her, as much as I want to explore, I know now isn't the time. She tastes like honey and sweetness and a little bit sour from morning breath. She's perfect.

She's absolutely perfect.

It's like a puzzle piece inside of me is sliding into place, making my heart whole once more. I don't know how long I've been going around with a piece of me missing. She's had it all this time; she's been the answer all along.

My life isn't magically going to be better because we're dating now. I won't be a better, more complete person because I have a girlfriend. What I'm going to have is a friend, a partner, an equal. She's the person that makes my world make sense. She always has been. Whether we're friends or more, and I sincerely hope we stay more, she's always been my favorite person in the world.

That's not to say she's perfect. She's not. I'm not. But we

can still be good for one another, perfect for one another, even with all of our perfect imperfections.

Her hands start to roam, moving over my shoulders and down my arms, touching, exploring. I catch her hand before it can move too far south.

"We don't have time," I tell her, and then I steal another kiss. She pouts against my lips.

"We have plenty of time."

"Not if we want to do this properly. We need to go on a date first."

Diana laughs. "Haven't we already been dating for the last fourteen years?"

"Tonight. We'll go to dinner, just the two of us. We can go to that French restaurant in town, order wine and sit in the candlelight and just be with one another," I suggest.

"You've put thought into this."

Not really.

"If we could have the perfect first date…"

She looks up at me, chewing her lip.

"I would take you to the Emerald Necklace, and we would tour through Boston and see all of the sights," I start. "Stop for lunch in Chinatown, then window shop on Boylston Street, and if you saw something you liked, I would get it for you—not to show off how much money I have, but because I want to shower you with presents pretty much all the time. We would go to a sports game, either baseball or football or hockey or basketball depending on the season, and afterwards go for ice cream at this place in Cambridge. Then we would work our way home, wherever home is, and I would have a second dessert."

She raises her eyebrows. "Oh?"

"I would spread your legs and feast on your pussy, and I would show you just how much you mean to me. Once you come, we would cuddle until you fell asleep with your head on my chest, and—"

"You wouldn't get yours?"

I shake my head. "Not on our first date. On our second, yeah, it's fair game, but that first date is about showing you how much you mean to me."

Diana covers my heart with her hand. "You already have."

———

After class, practice, and the general commotion of the day is over, I shower and shave and head over to the soccer house to intercept Diana. She had a meeting with her advisor today, working out her schedule for next semester, so I know she's super stressed and in need of a nice night out.

The door is opened by one of the minions. I'm not sure her name—she's never actually been introduced to me, and I don't actually care all that much. I'm glad she and Diana are on slightly better terms now, but she's still a shapeless, nameless non-entity to me.

"Is Diana here?"

She rolls her eyes. "She'll be down in a minute." And then she shuts the door in my face.

Okay, then. I guess some relationships haven't been miraculously repaired overnight.

Three and a half minutes later, the door swings open to reveal my best friend—my *girlfriend*.

"Hey, baby," I say, and her grin lights up her entire face.

"Hey."

Feeling like a bumbling giant, I thrust a bouquet of sunflowers at her. "For you."

They're her favorite flowers, the ones I'd bring her after every soccer game and for her school dances.

Her face melts. "Thanks, B."

I duck down and press a soft kiss to her cheek. Her hand fists in my coat and pulls me towards her for a real kiss. Mindful of the night ahead, I keep it short and sweet.

"Hi," she says.

"I missed you," I admit.

"We had lunch together six hours ago."

"And that was five hours and fifty-eight minutes too long."

Diana sighs. "What am I going to do with you?"

"Love me?"

She smiles. "Yeah, I think I can do that."

I nod towards the flowers. "You should put those in water."

"Come on in, then. It'll take me a minute." She pushes the door open and steps aside to let me in.

Johanna and the minions are sitting on the couch, watching a reality TV show. I nod towards the soccer players, who don't pay me any attention.

Diana fills a cup with water and sets the flowers in the middle of the kitchen table. I kind of like that she's sharing them with her roommates. If flowers make her happy, I'll buy her flowers every week. What's most important to me is making her happy, and I'll do anything I can to make her smile.

She turns to me. "Ready?"

"I've been ready since I was fourteen," I say, and I'm rewarded with a giggle and a smile.

"Yeah, yeah, yeah," Diana says, pulling on her coat. "Just because it didn't happen until sixteen for me…"

I hold my hand out for her. "Baby, I'd wait forever for you."

She takes my hand. "Well, now you don't have to wait anymore."

None of her roommates comment on our departure. She closes the door behind her and then tugs on my hand until we're face to face. Diana kisses me again, more thoroughly this time.

"So what's the plan?"

"Well, I don't think we're going to make it into the city for the most epic first date ever," I say slowly. "So how about we try that over winter break?"

"I'm down."

"Tonight, I thought we could do dinner and maybe a movie?" I suggest. "We can talk and snuggle a little. Then I'll have my second dessert and—"

She stops in the middle of the sidewalk. "Second dessert? You were serious about that?"

"Baby, I want to taste you pretty much all the time. Now that I've had a taste, I don't think I'll be able to live without the flavor of you on my tongue."

She blushes. "Barrett…"

"If you don't want to, I won't push you, but I'd like to make you come—preferably more than once. We can take this as slow as you want. We don't have to rush."

"I want to feel you inside of me," she says. She takes a deep breath and then meets my eyes, lifting her chin. "I want you to hold me in your arms and love me. We can do rough, we can do dirty, but I want tonight to be about us and our feelings for one another."

"I can do that. We can do that," I tell her.

"Good," she says, regaining some of her spark. "It's a date, then."

It's my turn to grin. "Fuck yeah, it's a date."

We continue our walk through Athlete's Village and through town until we get to the little French restaurant tucked away in a far corner of the main strip of town. It's not a popular place for the college students, frequented more by professors and parents. Part of that is due to the menu, and part of that is due to the cost. I have the luxury of a functionally unlimited black American Express card.

The scene is perfect: dim lighting, candles, wine, checkered red tablecloths. When I give my name, the host whisks us away to a quiet table in the corner, away from everyone else.

I help Diana into her seat and then take mine across from her. She reaches across the table, and I take her hand in mine.

"I love you," I tell her quietly, and she smiles.

"I know," she says, and I laugh. "I care about you a lot."

"I know," I say, and it's her turn to laugh.

"So what now?"

"So now we be ourselves," I say. "Us being in a relationship doesn't take anything away from our friendship. You're still my best friend. But now we get to kiss and hold hands and…"

"And?" She raises her eyebrows suggestively.

"Yeah. And. It adds to our friendship, it doesn't subtract anything."

"I think… I was comparing every guy I met to you, and nobody ever measured up." She blushes. "It was wrong to do that, when you and I were just friends, but…"

"The reason I never dated was because I knew you were the one I wanted, and even though I tried to convince myself it could work with someone else, in my heart I knew there was no comparison."

"Barrett…" She squeezes my hand.

"I don't regret it. It was the right course for me."

Diana frowns. "You've hooked up before. You've called me when you're leaving some girl's place and you're drunk and…"

It's my turn to blush. "Yeah. I've… fooled around. But it never meant anything. You were on the opposite side of the country, and I had no reason to believe that would change anytime soon. There was nothing to indicate that this could ever happen. So I lived my life. My previous partners knew and accepted that it would never go beyond one or two nights."

"That's kind of how it was for me," she says. "I never tried to make it anything more than what it was. I always knew it would never work out."

There's a lump in my throat. "I'm glad we're trying now."

"Me, too."

Our quiet moment is interrupted by the waiter, who delivers the bottle of wine. He pours us each a glass. As much as I'm not a fan of wine, it feels appropriate for the moment, more so than ordering a beer. Romantic lighting, candles, soft violin music, fancy French food… it's all part of the first date experience. We're grown ups now, or as close to it as we can be at the moment, and she deserves a grown up date.

There will be other nights where we go to a frat party and stumble into the diner, drunk, in search of cheese fries. We'll grab a burrito and curl up on the couch, watching movie musicals. We'll go to dim sum and talk and laugh and eat until we've had our fill. We'll live our lives.

Tonight, though… tonight is for us, to celebrate us.

We talk all through dinner, catching up on our day. Conversation flows freely. She tells me about her academic advisor appointment. She's going to be able to graduate this spring, even if it involves taking a class over winter intersession. As much as I'm disappointed we won't be able to spend winter break together, I'm more pleased that we can graduate together, that we can go through that process together.

Northeastern is still her top choice grad school—she submitted the application over Thanksgiving break—but she's keeping her options open. If she has to move to Amherst or Lowell or New Hampshire, she wants us to try long distance for the two years of the program. I'm fine with that. My job after graduation won't easily allow me to work from home, so I'm going to have to stay close to the city. I like that at worst she'll be within easy driving distance, and at best she'll be right next to me.

We talk about… everything. Marriage. She's fine waiting until we're twenty-five, even though she disagrees with the reasons I want to wait. I know it will devastate her if her father isn't there when the time comes, but there's no reason we need to rush this step, either. She wants kids—a whole house full of kids, she was lonely growing up an only child, so she wants a large family. I'm on board with that… provided we wait until we're both out of school first.

"This shouldn't be this easy," Diana says over dessert.

"What do you mean?"

"We agree on… everything."

"We don't agree on everything," I contradict. "We're compatible in the things that are important to us, and the things we aren't, we can figure out a compromise."

"Oh yeah? Like what?"

"Like… my parents. Like what to do on a Saturday night. Like where we want to live after graduation," I explain. "Do I enjoy watching movie musicals? Not particularly. But you do, so I'm happy to watch them with you. Do you like going to basketball games? Not particularly. So I'll take my brother, or you can hang out in the suite during the game, and we can meet up afterwards."

"You'd be okay with that?"

"We don't have to be attached at the hip just because we're a couple. Sure, I want to spend all my time with you. But we both have our own lives. We can't lose sight of who we are individually for who we are as a couple."

Diana pouts. "I like who we are as a couple."

"I do, too." Leaning across the table, I take her hand in mine and kiss her knuckles. "Think of it as friends with benefits with feelings," I say.

She laughs. "Friends with benefits with feelings?"

"It can be casual, it can be serious, or it can be anything in between. My feelings aren't going to magically go away just because we have a fight or hit a rough patch. I know you, and you know me, and we've been through enough over the years that I think we can get through pretty much anything."

Including her dad…

"I think we can, too." Her smile turns a little sad. "My dad doesn't want me to marry you or have kids with you right away."

"Neither do I," I tell her honestly.

She blinks. "But…"

"We have our own timeline. There's no need to press fast forward on our life together. I don't care if it takes us a year or five years or ten. What's important to me is having you in my life. The rest? We can figure it out later. For now, it's about us."

thirty-nine

. . .

Diana

"THIS HAS BEEN THE PERFECT EVENING," I say as we walk back to Athlete's Village hand in hand.

"You're perfect," Barrett says immediately, and I laugh and curl closer to his body.

"You just want to get laid," I tease, and he stops in the middle of the road.

"You're perfect," he says again, meeting my eyes. "I would never lie to you or manipulate you to get you into my bed. I love you just the way you are, perfect imperfections and all."

My heart twists. I care for him so fucking much. I squeeze his hand, and he pulls me into a hug in the middle of the street.

"You're amazing, Dee," he says quietly into my ear.

I sniff. "You're really good for my ego."

He laughs and drops a kiss to the top of my head. "I can be really good for other parts of you, too."

It's my turn to laugh. "I know you said you wanted second dessert…"

"Yeah?"

"Do I get a taste, too?"

"You can have as much as you want," he says.

"In that case…" I release his hug and take his hand again. "I want the whole thing."

"Tonight?"

"Yeah. We've spent basically the last fourteen years dating each other. I think it's high time we consummate this thing."

Barrett laughs. "I'm down with that."

We continue on our journey back to his place. If I had a more amicable relationship with my roommates, I might consider bringing him back to mine, but we aren't there yet. Besides, I like his house and I like his roommates. They're a good group of guys. Sam and Mason are awesome. Mack is great. They're my friends now, too.

Everyone is clustered around the living room when we enter the house. Wes is in his armchair and Mack is sitting on the floor near him, both of them reading their books instead of paying attention to the superhero movie on the screen. Miles and Sam are cuddling on the couch, and Tucker and Mason are canoodling on the armchair. Amir and Jill, his new girlfriend, are curled up on the floor in front of everyone. Even Greg has a date, a leggy brunette I've never seen him with before.

"Hey, B," Sam says as we walk in. "You want to watch with us? We can make room."

"We're good," he says. "Thanks, though. Maybe next time."

Miles's eyes narrow as he takes in our clasped hands. "Are you…?"

"Good night!" I chirp, way too enthusiastically, and practically pull Barrett up the stairs with me.

My boyfriend (!) laughs and follows me to his room. Once inside, he locks the door and toes off his shoes.

"Remarkably unsubtle."

I laugh and sit down to take off my boots. "We can tell them all in the morning. Let them guess for now."

Barrett leans down and kisses me. I have one boot on, unzipped, the other discarded. I'm still wearing my coat.

Easily he lifts me into his arms and moves me further up the bed. He unbuttons my coat and pries it off my shoulders, then kisses his way down my clothed body to reach my boot. Pulling it off, he tosses it over his shoulder and presses a kiss between my legs, over my tights and the fabric of my dress.

"You're into this."

"I've been dreaming about this for a very long time," Barrett admits, hovering over me.

"Did you plan this out, too? Like you planned the perfect first date?"

He blushes. "Yeah. But it doesn't… we don't have to do it that way. We can improvise."

"I'm interested in finding out what you think would be perfect first sex."

"Any sex with you would be perfect," he says. "And it was. Some other night, we can live out my fantasy, but for now, I just want to love you. Is that okay?"

"Of course that's okay," I tell him. "Why wouldn't it be?"

"You might have wanted this to play out a certain way," he says. "Have you thought about it?"

"I've had dreams about it," I admit. "Of a certain nature."

Barrett's eyes go dark. "And did you come?"

I swallow at the hungry intensity on his face. "Yeah."

"Good. I would hate for your dream to pale in comparison to reality."

Twining my arms around his neck, I tug until he lowers himself onto me, his delicious weight pressing in on me on all sides, surrounding me. He's heavy, yeah, but it's a comforting weight that soothes the itch in my soul I didn't even know I've been trying to scratch. I wrap my leg around his waist, my socked foot pressing into the back of his thigh.

"You good?" HIs voice is rough, thick.

"Never better," I tell him, leaning up to kiss him. We take

our time, tasting each other, exploring each other. He tastes like honey and sweetness and a little bit like the wine we drank at dinner. I'm not drunk but I'm not entirely sober, high on the taste of him.

I break the kiss and pull back. "Actually, that's a lie," I say, and he frowns. "I could be better. We could be naked."

His face clears, and he grins. "We can make that happen."

Barrett removes himself from my body, and immediately I feel the loss. Slowly he unbuttons his shirt, tossing it aside to reveal the plain white t-shirt he's wearing underneath.

I nod to him. "Pants, too."

"Bossy, bossy," he says, though he looks pleased. He shucks his shirt and then his pants, leaving him in his plain plaid boxer shorts and socks.

Barrett rejoins me on the bed. I lean back against the pillows, my hair fanning out around my head. I could lose myself in the way he's looking at me right now. Now that I know how he feels about me, I'm not sure how I didn't know all along. I guess I was hoping so hard, I couldn't see what was right in front of my face.

His hands map my sides, caressing my ribs and hips. "Roll over," he says quietly, and I roll onto my side.

Carefully, gently, so gentle, he turns me onto my stomach. He pushes aside my mess of waves and presses a kiss to the back of my neck. Then another, an inch below, over the zipper of my dress. Then another, one more inch below. His thick fingers close around the zipper tab and slowly, *s l o w l y*, he pulls the tab down, kissing his way down my body. He helps the fabric fall away.

He moves back and then he rolls me onto my back again. Hovering over me, he pulls my arms from the dress and then works the fabric over my hips, tossing it away on the floor. He stares for a moment.

Propping myself up on my elbows gives the appearance

my chest is bigger than it is, something I've always been a little insecure about.

"Like what you see?"

Barrett meets my eye. "Yeah, I do. It's even better than I remembered."

"Have you thought about that night a lot?" Because I have. It's all I've been able to think about.

"All the fucking time," he says.

"Me, too."

He kisses me again, his hand cupping my cheek tenderly. I tug him down until his body covers mine again, his delicious bulk pressing into me on all sides. His hands thread through my hair as he devours me, holding me close.

It's so much better than the first time we did this. Now, there's no doubting how he feels about me. Now, I'm not trying to use him to take away my own pain. Now, we're on equal footing, secure in the way we feel about each other. We're doing this from a place of love and respect, not from pain and distraction. Barrett kisses his way down my neck, showing his devotion, as his hands roam over my skin. This won't be the last time we do this, but we can't get our first time back, as perfectly imperfect as it was.

That night, we fucked. Tonight, we'll make love.

He kisses me, learning my body, kissing my chest and my nipples over my bra, over my tensed stomach, over my panties. I'm wearing the same favorite pair I wore that first night; they're my lucky panties, and tonight, I'm getting lucky, damn it.

My legs spread, almost like they have a mind of their own. Barrett grins and, with a glance up at me, hooks his fingers in the waistband. I nod. He pulls the panties down, revealing my freshly waxed cunt to him. Even though I tell him pretty much everything, I've never seen a reason to disclose my personal grooming habits to him before, and now that he's getting up close and personal with my business, he's going to learn my waxing rotation whether he wants to know or not.

He takes a deep breath.

"What's wrong?" I prop myself up onto my elbow again.

"I love you," he says. "I might like your pussy more."

I laugh. "Show me, then."

He spreads my legs, hooking my thighs over his massive shoulders. And then he goes to town.

It's not hesitant. It's not gentle. He knows what he wants, and he goes for it, devouring my lower lips the same way he devoured my mouth, wholly and completely. I fall back against the pillows as pleasure courses through my veins, nearly overtaking my body.

And then his fingers get into the game, questing, exploring. Circling around my entrance, he slips a finger inside of me to the first knuckle, and I swallow and spread my legs further to help him.

"Barrett…" Need has me clenching around his finger.

"Yeah, baby?" He lifts his head, meeting my eye. His finger pushes deeper into me and back out, making me twitch.

"I need more."

Lowering his head, he draws the bud of my clit into his mouth, sucking firmly. My hips lift off of the mattress.

He sets his hand on my hip and holds me in place as his tongue does wickedly delicious things to me. Shifting, he sets his arm on my belly like a bar, keeping me from moving, as a second finger joins the first.

"Barrett, please."

"We gotta take our time, baby," he says.

"Why?"

"Because I don't want to hurt you."

"You can't."

"If you're not prepped, yeah, it would."

I pout. "I want you to fuck me."

"Oh, trust me, I will," he says, a little smug.

Threading my hands through his hair, I direct him back to my pussy, and he laughs as he lowers his head once more.

A questing third finger joins the first two. Barrett twists his wrist, finding that spot inside of me that makes stars burst behind my eyelids.

"B-Barrett. Please."

He doesn't let up until that tight, taut band inside of me snaps. I clench around him one last time as the tidal wave of pleasure blows me over. I'm helpless, along for the ride, as the sensations overtake me. His forearm on my belly grounds me through it.

Sinking back against the pillows, I work to get air into my lungs. Barrett withdraws his fingers from inside me and sucks them clean, and my eyes nearly roll back in my head.

"Holy shit, B."

"Yeah?" He looks smug. I want to kiss that cocky expression right off his face.

"Shut up. You already know you're good at that."

"Yeah, but it doesn't hurt to hear you say that."

I mash my hand into his face, and he laughs, collapsing on the bed beside me.

"Good?" He lets out a tired sigh.

I blow out a breath. "Good. So good."

Barrett rolls onto his back, and I curl into his side, my head on his furry chest. I'm naked from the waist down, wearing only my bra, and he's naked from the waist up, wearing only his boxer shorts. Maneuvering, I unclasp my bra and toss it aside, leaving me gloriously naked.

He makes a noise of interest. "Hm?" His big hand cups my breast.

"Yeah." Propping myself up onto one arm, I lean down and kiss him. He tastes like me. He threads his hand through my hair, cupping the back of my head. His other hand massages my breast, teasing the pebbled nipple.

My heart warms as my body clenches around emptiness. He's so focused on my pleasure; I've never experienced it to this degree with a partner before. This man is my whole world, my best friend. He's been there for me through thick and thin over the last fourteen years, and I believe him when he says he'll be there for me in the future. He is the best person I've ever had the pleasure of meeting.

My tongue meets his, and he lets out a ragged moan. I scratch my hand through the fuzzy hair on his chest, learning his skin, scraping my thumb over his nipple.

"Stop," he says, pulling away.

"Stop?" I edge backwards. What did I do?

His face falls. "No, no, everything is good," he assures me quickly. "It feels really good," he says.

Oh.

"Can I touch you?"

"Yes," he blurts immediately, and then flushes. He clears his throat. "Yes, please."

I cup him over his shorts, the length of him like steel wrapped in velvet enshrined in cotton. Working my hand inside the waistband of his shorts, I wrap my hand around his steely length and squeeze. He sighs and pushes his pelvis up. I learn the feel of him. I barely got my hands on him last time, more concerned with tasting him than touching him.

I don't regret our first time together. I was in pain, yes, and I needed a distraction, yes, and he delivered—fuck, did he deliver. There isn't anyone else in the world I trusted to take care of me in the way he did, without taking advantage or making the situation worse.

I care about him deeply. In time, I could grow to love him. We've only been dating for a hot minute, so I'm not quite there yet, but I can see it on the horizon once we know each other deeper in this way.

Barrett sighs and grabs my wrist. "Baby, if you want to get to the next act..."

Reluctantly I remove my hand from inside his shorts. Already I miss the feeling of him in my hand.

He rolls over, heading to his bedside table.

"I have an IUD," I tell him.

His eyes are wide as he looks back at me. "You want…"

"I got tested after our night together," I say. "I trust you. I want to feel you."

"I've never gone without a condom before," he says.

"Neither have I. It's a step I want to take with you, and only with you."

"An IUD isn't infallible."

"You wanted to marry me when you thought I was pregnant," I point out.

He blushes. "I want to marry you even if you're not pregnant. That doesn't mean I'm ready for it."

"I want forever with you," I tell him. "Whether we get married or not, whether we have babies or not, I want to be with you for the rest of my life. So if something happens, it happens. If it doesn't, that's fine, too."

Barrett swallows. "Diana…"

"Yeah?"

"I love you," he says, breathing out a laugh. "And not just because you don't want to use a condom. I just—I really fucking love you."

I'm not ready to say the words back, not yet. I have no doubt I will one day. Probably sooner rather than later. Any day now. Just not yet.

He works his shorts down his hips, kicking them away until he too is gloriously naked, his body on display for me. Barrett is a big guy in every sense of the word: thick belly, strong hips, broad chest, and a proud cock sticking straight up and slightly to the left.

His hand on my shoulder, he urges me onto my back against the mattress. He follows me, hovering over me.

"You're sure?"

I cup his cheek. "I've never been more sure of anything in my life."

He notches his tip against my entrance. My legs wrap around his hips. Slowly, slowly, he pushes inside.

It's like every nerve ending is on fire. I can't believe we're really doing this. Every time I kiss him, every time I touch him, I have to remind myself that this isn't a dream, that this is really happening.

Barrett leans down and ghosts his lips across mine in a whisper of a kiss. I wrap my arms around his neck, and he sighs, pressing against me more firmly.

I can't breathe, can't think, can't focus on anything other than the feel of him surrounding me, inside of me, the slow drag of his cock in me with nothing between us.

Perspiration dots his temples. He presses his forehead to mine, breathing hard.

"You good?" I ask quietly.

"Holy fuck," he breathes. "This is… it feels…"

Perfect. Fate. Kismet.

Barrett swallows and shifts, so his hands are propping him up over me. He withdraws and then lifts his hips, fucking into me slowly. Every slow drag of his length inside of me sends shockwaves through my body.

"Dee…" His voice is thick with emotion. Or maybe that's lust clouding his voice.

"Yeah?"

He shudders out a laugh. "I think I could come just from this."

I kiss him again, and when he lets me deepen the kiss, I dig my fingertips into his strong shoulders and lift my hips. I would never want to be accused of not being an active participant.

As much as I want to be wrapped up in his arms and loved forever, it's not getting me there. I work my hand between our bodies, and he grabs my hand, pushing it back to the mattress. He puts his weight into it, his delicious bulk pinning me down. My pussy throbs around his length.

"Barrett... I..."

"I'll get you there," he says. "Tell me what you need."

"Rub my clit. Firmly, not too quick," I direct. I slide my feet from his hips to the back of his strong calves, changing the angle of him inside of me. He's pressed up against that spot that never fails to drive me crazy. My eyes slide closed, and I have to work to keep them open.

He rises up onto his hands and knees, fucking into me now. His questing fingers slip between our bodies and over my clit, rubbing firmly, not too quickly.

"Harder."

His hips work faster, rougher, harder. He covers my breast with his massive hand, pinching and rolling my pebbled nipple between his thick fingers. When I moan, he wraps his hand around my knee, drawing it up until it's between us, changing the angle and getting deliciously deeper.

I have no doubts about how he feels about me. I have no doubts about how I feel about him. As we explore our relationship, as we explore each other, the time will come for dirty, sweaty, intense, mind-melting fucking.

For now, we'll indulge in sweet, sweaty, intense, mind-melting lovemaking.

As we climb that peak, as we work each other into a frenzy, I'm overcome with the realization that this could be the rest of my life. I have no doubt that there is nobody else in the world that could possibly hold a candle to how amazing Barrett is, and there is nobody else I could ever want to be with. He's my best friend, my favorite person in the world, the one I turn to when I'm happy and when I'm sad, when I'm angry and when I'm struggling. He's my person.

No matter what happens between us, whatever the future brings for us, I know we can make it through. Whether that's distance while I'm in grad school or my dad getting sicker and sicker, I know that we can make it through anything as long as we have each other.

Tension builds along my spine as I crest the peak that brings me higher and higher. Barrett kisses me, sweetly, chastely, even as his fingers touch me and his cock drives inside of me.

"I love you, Dee," he says quietly, breathing hard. His face is red and splotchy, his forehead damp with sweat. He has never looked more gorgeous.

I can't say the words, not yet.

Instead the orgasm hits me like a freight train. I dig my fingers into his back and throw my head back, riding the waves of pleasure like it's my job. He's gloriously thick inside of me, filling me in the best possible way. I'm surrounded by him, consumed by him.

He fucks me through it, and once I'm ready, he takes his pleasure. It's two, three, four, five strokes and then he's coming, his hot seed spilling inside of me, filling me.

Breathing hard, Barrett pulls out and collapses beside me onto his bed. I feel sweaty and sticky and so, so sated.

"You good?" He's breathing hard, his massive chest rising and falling as he works to get air into his lungs.

Even though we've just been as intimately close as physically possible, I want more of him, in any way I can get it. I curl into his side and rest my head on his chest, my arm thrown across his belly, my legs tangled with his.

I'm not ready to say those three little words. It's not the right time.

"I'm so good," I tell him instead, angling up for a kiss. "You?"

He delivers, bestowing upon me a sweet, gentle kiss.

"I've never been better," Barrett says.

epilogue

. . .

Barrett

MAY - Graduation weekend

Life isn't magically perfect now that Diana and I are a couple. The last seven months have been difficult, that's for sure. There are some growing pains there. We're learning how to be in a relationship, period, as well as how to be in a relationship with one another. For all that I knew Diana, for all that I loved her from afar, I don't think I really understood her until now.

She's bossy as fuck, both in bed and out of it, and I really like when she gives me instructions to follow. I like it more than I thought I would. She's a downright nightmare when she's sleep deprived—which I thought I knew. What I didn't realize is that she's like that even when we're up half the night with... amorous activities. No matter the cause of her lack of sleep, she's miserable to be around, a fact she's well aware of and has been successfully hiding all these years.

Diana got into her top choice program at Northeastern, so she's headed there for a masters in nutrition counseling this fall. That works out pretty well for me, too; we'll be only a few scant miles from my office in the financial district, so close I could walk in nice weather if I felt like it. I've already chosen an apartment for us with Quentin's help. Diana says she doesn't care where we live, so long as it's close to campus and she gets to decorate it, two conditions I was more than happy to concede.

The apartment is gorgeous, a two bedroom, two bath in an old brick building two blocks away from the building she's going to take most of her classes in. It's the perfect starter apartment. My parents were generous enough to gift me with a downpayment as an early graduation present, and with my new salary, I'll easily be able to afford the monthly payments, even without my trust fund. Diana will cover the utilities with her student loan, so she can contribute without needing to take out extra money unnecessarily. She doesn't know that the minute we get married, I'm paying off all her student loans. It's the least I can do for the woman I want to spend the rest of my life with.

My parents are coolly accepting. They don't approve, not exactly. I'm pretty sure they think this is just a phase, just a fling. What they don't realize is that Diana and I are in it for the long haul. Well, I am, at any rate, and I don't have reason to believe she isn't.

I plan to propose the summer we turn twenty-four, once she's done with grad school, and then shortly after my twenty-fifth birthday (and I receive access to the rest of my trust fund), we'll get married—to stave off any potential arguments, yes, and also because I think we need time to enjoy ourselves as an engaged couple without rushing into marriage. If babies happen before then, great, but Diana wants to establish herself in her career a bit before we start down that road, and I'm more than happy to wait for her.

Her dad is… well, he's not going to get better. His leg is healed, he can walk normally again, but his face is drawn and weary, and he always looks tired. He's on a new regimen of medication that's supposed to give him a better quality of life. I have yet to see if that's the case; it's a recent change, so only time will tell, and time is the one thing he doesn't have.

Now that we're both done with our respective athletic seasons, Diana and I make a point to visit her parents at least once a month, if not twice a month as schedules allow. We take the train or I call a car and we travel to Amherst on a Thursday night, since neither of us have Friday classes this semester, and come back Sunday evening in time for family dinner at my parents' house, getting some time in with all of the parents at basically the same time.

Sam made a joke last week about us spending so much time with our in-laws. Diana wasn't ashamed or embarrassed, and neither was I. It actually felt kind of nice. Stewart and Cecilia have welcomed me into their home, and now that we're officially together, that comes with extra perks like being able to sleep in Diana's bed with her and being able to hold her hand and kiss her whenever I want.

Family is important to both of us in different ways. She's close to her parents, to her family of origin. I'm more attached to the friends that have welcomed me into their lives over the last few years; they're my family now, whether they want to be or not. Dougie and I are talking more and more—he loves Diana, and he loves us together—and my cousin Nate has invited me to dinner with him and his boyfriend Quentin a few times. Twice they've come out to Newton, and one time we made the trek up to the city, so we're making an effort to see each other as adults and not only as cousins forced to spend time together at family events. Kira and Lyle have invited us to their house in Cambridge for dinner. Hannah and I chat online, and she promised to come up to Boston a few times this summer.

On her side of the family, Stewart is pleased as punch that we're together. He's gone out of his way to hug me or pat my back every time I've seen him. He exclusively calls me "son" now. It's like I finally have the father I've wanted all these years. I know he's rooting for us to get married while he's still with us, too, though he understands the reasons why we want to wait. At the end of the day, he only wants her to be happy.

We've been best friends since we were eight years old, and we've only been dating for almost eight months. We don't need to rush into forever and mess up the good thing we have going. We already know we're going to be together for the rest of our lives; the formalities can wait, at least for a little bit longer. I have no doubts that Diana Maire Whitehall is the woman for me, and she seems reasonably confident in her feelings for me.

As I stand on the graduation stage and accept my placebo diploma from the Dean of the Accounting and Business College, I stare out at the crowd of people assembled before us. My parents aren't in the audience, they had a trip to Barbados they simply couldn't reschedule, but my brother, Nate, and Quentin are in the crowd sitting with Diana, Stewart, and Cecilia. My football teammates are all in the student section, Sam and Mason and Mackenzie and Jill with them, and Mr. and Mrs. Cavanaugh are meeting us at the restaurant after the ceremony is officially over.

I have my own family now, built from scratch. I'm including the people who mean the most to me, the people who actively support me and help to raise me up instead of working to tear down my spirit. I'm surrounding myself with the people who enrich my life instead of focusing on wealth and riches, and in doing so, I'm actively choosing to pursue my own happiness instead of prioritizing my parents and their wishes.

The last year or so, I've had to zig and zag as life threw curveballs at me. Though it's come close at times, I haven't gotten sacked yet: I'm still standing on my own two feet, ready in the backfield. Ready for the rest of my life.

So many things have come to an end over the last several

months. My football career is over. I'm done with college, at least for now. I'm moving on and leaving the past in the dust.

I don't feel sad, not really. As much as I'm going to miss this time of my life, I'm more than ready for the next steps. Starting my career. Getting an MBA. Marriage. Babies. Forever.

Diana is sitting in the crowd in front of me, her heart in her eyes. Her eyes are on me as I cross the graduation stage, and as I pause for the photographer to take the classic photo, my eyes seek out hers again. I nearly stumble at the look of adoration and joy on her face.

She's happy for me and for my successes, as much as if they were her own. In a way, they are. We're individual people with our own lives and goals and interests, but we're a cohesive unit, a couple with shared ideals and hopes and dreams.

I don't have to play an evasive maneuver with my heart: it's all hers to do with as she wants. She's given me hers, and I play for keeps.

afterword

Thank you for reading *End Game*. This book is my baby and I absolutely love it to pieces.

You know what would make it even better? A review! Reviews are more important than readers realize. If you liked this book, please leave me a review!

Join my newsletter to stay in the loop! Lots of unfunny quips, unsuccessful attempts at wit, and general grouching about the writing process.

xoxo,

Allie

about the author

Allie is a queer and AuDHD writer with a hyper-fixation on inclusivity and representation. She loves the color purple, Michigan football, and the Boston Bruins. When she's not absorbed by a book, she likes to spend time with her nephews.

Born and raised in Southern California, she now calls South Carolina home. She is allergic to the cold, rain, snow, and mosquitos.

also by allie lasky

Want to see how it all started? Read THE GAME PLAN to meet sweet cinnamon roll football player Miles and the feisty sorority girl who stole his heart.

———

The story continues with FUMBLE, a best friend's sister secret relationship featuring a virgin and a celibate-by-choice bookworm.

———

Meet the Neurospicy Book Club in THE THOUGHT OF YOU: Falling for my Grumpy Roommate, where Johanna finds out she's autistic… because her happy-go-lucky new roomie (and reformed playboy ex-football player) has to tell her.